Praise for the Marco Fontana mysteries:

Murder on Camac

"All in all, this is a stellar effort that will leave readers eagerly awaiting the next book in what should prove to be a popular series."

—*SF GLBT Literary Examiner*

"The setting of Philadelphia suits the story well, with both a well-established gay community and an entrenched Catholic presence. If you're from the city of brotherly love, many landmarks were written into the tale, even including some gay establishments like the oldest gay bookstore in the country, Giovanni's Room. Don't be surprised if the gayborhood is far more exciting than in real life..."

—*Edge Philadelphia*

"So start clearing some room in your library, mystery and detective fiction aficionados, because Mr. DeMarco and his private dick hero Marco Fontana are going to warrant a space of their own on your shelves."

—*BookWenches*

A Body on Pine

"In his second book in this mystery series, DeMarco again provides a captivating and complex mystery that will delight purists of the gay mystery genre, for whom pickings have lately been sparse. The characters are colorful yet relatable, the Philadelphia setting perfectly nuanced, and the use of humor and personal emotions perfectly in the mix of a great read."

—*Echo Magazine*

Also by Joseph R.G. DeMarco

Murder on Camac

A Body on Pine

A Study in Lavender: Queering Sherlock Holmes
(editor)

Crimes On Latimer

From the Early Cases of Marco Fontana

Joseph R.G. DeMarco

Lethe Press
Maple Shade NJ

Published by:
Lethe Press, 118 Heritage Ave, Maple Shade, NJ 08052.
lethepressbooks.com   lethepress@aol.com

Cover by Niki Smith
Book design by Toby Johnson

ISBN 1-59021-374-2 / 978-1-59021-374-2

Library of Congress Cataloging-in-Publication Data

DeMarco, Joseph R. G.
Crimes on Latimer : from the early cases of Marco Fontana / Joseph R.G. DeMarco.
p. cm.
ISBN 978-1-59021-374-2 -- ISBN 1-59021-374-2
1. Gay private investigators--Fiction. 2. Gay men--Violence against--Fiction. 3. Philadelphia (Pa.)--Fiction. 4. Detective and mystery stories, American. I. Title.
PS3604.E449C75 2012
813'.6--dc23

2012004579

For Jason Li
And for my mother, Caroline

Acknowledgements

Thanks is a small word that encompasses a huge concept. I am very fortunate to owe a debt of thanks to some wonderful people. I have to thank Jason Li, my closest friend, who believes in me, gives me confidence and critique, is generous and kind, and is the best friend a person could ask for; my mom, Caroline, who has been an unfailing source of support and love; Michele Hyman who saw me through some dark times; Steve Berman whose friendship and guidance and whose sense about these stories has been invaluable; Richard R. Smith and Eric Mayes whose advice and critique have been so very helpful; Louise, Tom, Sal, Jody, Howard, Geneva, and a host of others who keep me grounded. There are some who I know are watching and guiding still, whose presence I miss: my father, Fred; my aunt Mary; Rusel; Harry L. and Harry M.; and most of all of these my late partner William Phillips. There are others. I am grateful and thankful and I'll never forget.

Table of Contents

The Kronos Elect

As he fell his nostrils flared, making his rough piggy nose seem even more porcine. The flabby pink cheeks of Patrick Bidding, the school disciplinarian, trembled each time he struck a step on the steep, deserted back staircase. The air in his lungs was forced out in grunts with every bounce. He hadn't had much time to think, once his foot engaged the thin wire drawn taut across the stairs. He had put out his hand but the banister was slick with oil causing him to fall even faster. Hitting the landing with a thud, the remaining air was knocked from his lungs. Bidding's last thoughts before the final blackout were very unchristian for the Head of Discipline in a very Catholic school for boys. He wheezed out his breath at the bottom of the stairs and was gone.

* * *

I'd gotten news of the murder the night before. The guys at St. T's have an informal network and when anything happens, news travels fast.

So I was surprised when I arrived at school the next day and didn't see total panic and chaos. Things were orderly, as orderly as they could be with more than one thousand boys trying to get into a school building all at the same time. I melded into the back of the crowd and watched faces. No one seemed sad or even ghoulishly thrilled. A murder had taken place right under their noses and no one seemed to care. Of course, it was Patrick Bidding, the disciplinarian, who'd been whacked. Not even his own son liked him.

Two older, pot-bellied cops were stationed outside St. T's huge, oak, front doors. No surprise there, I expected cops to be crawling all over the place. They peered at us as we streamed into the building. Cops didn't trust students any more than teachers did.

The whole scene reminded me of some movie about the end of the world. I glanced at the cops as I passed them and felt vaguely guilty for no reason at all.

Inside the building. That's where it was chaos. That's more like what I expected.

The foyer was alive with people wandering every which way, looking like they had no idea where they should be. Priests flew through the crowds flailing their arms. Faculty shouted orders that no one followed. Students walked quickly to nowhere in particular. The only ones not moving were the cops standing silently at the margins of the foyer, scrutinizing everyone.

Most of the students looked lost and meek, which was unusual since they were arrogant rich brats who generally acted like they owned the school. Which they sorta did since their families contributed so much money.

I was there on a scholarship, so most of them treated me like a poor relative feeding off table scraps. Me, I didn't care what they thought. I was in school for one reason and I'd get out with the same diploma they'd get.

A few teachers moved through the foyer looking even more like zombies than usual. I guess some of them could've been wondering who'd be next on the hit list and if it might be them.

The maintenance people hadn't even had a chance to take down the banner proclaiming: "Welcome Class of 1996." After three weeks of classes and now the murder, the banner drooped sadly. My senior year had started off with a bang, so to speak, and there were still more than nine months to go before June and graduation.

As I stared at the banner, a gang of freshmen whizzed by like a cloud of gnats. I wondered if I'd ever looked that small and geeky. I realized that I had, since I started high school before I was even thirteen. Thanks to the grammar school nuns who'd pushed me ahead a grade or two, I was graduating early and that felt both good and confusing. I glanced once more at the banner and blended myself into the flow of kids going nowhere.

Some adult shouted for people to keep moving and get to their lockers, which was like a splash of cold water and woke me up. A notice on the wall said the day would start with an assembly to "comfort" the school community. It wasn't bad enough somebody'd been murdered. Now we'd get treated to priests and counselors, and members of the religion department spilling platitudes like molasses over all of us. They'd say all kinds of things which wouldn't make anyone feel any better and might cause a few more murders.

Had me wondering what'd happen next. That's what I was thinking about as I walked to my locker on the second floor. I passed the conference room, which students were never permitted to enter, and was surprised by voices coming from the room. The door was partway open and I heard Mr. Sullivan gasp. It was a distinctive sound. Mr. Sullivan gasped a lot whenever something unexpected happened, which in his English Lit class was often. He was the nervous type and lots of kids enjoyed making him flinch. And gasp. The two always went together.

He was cute in his soft, gentle way. Not that I'd ever mention that fact to anybody except for my best friend Cullen. I wasn't exactly ready to tumble out of the closet to everybody. I think Sullivan must've guessed about me, though, because he never failed to praise my work and always gave me the best assignments on the school newspaper. My guess, Sullivan knew about me because Sullivan was also gay. Not that we could ever discuss that. Not in this school. Still I felt we had a kind of secret bond, even if we couldn't acknowledge it.

I'd gotten to know Sullivan pretty well from working on the school newspaper. He was the faculty moderator and was pretty serious about it. He'd worked on a real newspaper a few years before getting into teaching and knew his stuff.

If you know anything about newspapers, you know nothing ever happens on time and you've gotta plan for late nights especially around publication time. That meant Sullivan and the staff spent lots of time together, ate take out together, and had long talks on things we wanted to write about in the paper. As Editor, I probably spent the most time with him and he trusted me. Even better, I trusted him, which wasn't easy for me. I hardly trust anybody.

But Sullivan was cool. We worked lots of late nights together and he never even hinted around at anything sexual. Never made a move on me. That gave him a lotta points in my book.

When I passed the conference room and heard him gasp, I knew he was in some kind of trouble and I figured it was about the murder. Not that I could imagine Sullivan committing a murder. And I really couldn't believe he might've murdered Pat Bidding, the disciplinarian, who was a foot taller and a hundred pounds heavier than Sullivan.

Of course, I do remember Sullivan arguing with Bidding once or twice. It's hard to hide things like that in a school. Especially a place like St. T's. There's always somebody hidden around a corner or sitting in a room out of sight. I'd stumbled on plenty of things that people weren't happy about anyone else knowing.

When I thought about it, I realized that even if Sullivan was gentle and easily spooked, he did stand up for himself when he had to. In fact, he was one of the few who'd publicly called Bidding out on his habit of poking into the private lives of faculty and students. That's what I'd heard them arguing about.

Sullivan would argue, sure, but murder? No way. Sullivan didn't have it in him to do something like that. He wasn't weak. He was just too nice, which is why I liked him. Murder just wasn't in the mix of his personality. I refused to believe that. From what I knew of him, he was lots more moral than some of the faculty who liked dressing up as priests and pretending they had cornered the morality market.

I lingered outside the conference room and spied through a small opening in the doorway. I couldn't hear what they actually said. It all sounded like murmurs and rumbles and occasional gasps. I saw a tall, black guy in a rumpled suit standing over Sullivan. Had to be a cop. A ring of dark hair wrapped around his otherwise bald head, his back to me as I watched. When the cop turned and spotted me, I kinda coughed and got myself outta there. Whatever was going on, he didn't look happy. Neither did Mr. Sullivan.

* * *

I decided to hole up in the newspaper office after the assembly. Classes had been cancelled and students were allowed to leave or spend the day studying or working around campus. Most of the kids left the building like bats out of hell. Kids on sports teams or in activities hung around along with some who wanted to study or couldn't go home early. That didn't leave a whole lot of people in the building.

The third floor was deserted, which made sense. Most of the rooms on that floor were either school activity rooms, offices for counselors, or conference rooms. With everybody gone, the silence was almost creepy.

I unlocked the door, threw my backpack on the old couch, and went to the button fridge for a bottle of orange juice. For some reason, even after what I'd seen and heard, I felt at home and safe in the newspaper office. For all the time I spent there, it was like a second home. An old staff photo, stuck on the back of the door, caught my eye. We were all laughing and smiling in that picture. I was a freshman then and it was hard to believe it'd been almost four years. I looked so small compared to the others.

As I stared at the photo, I heard footsteps outside. Whoever it was stopped near the door. Then I heard him speak. It was Mr. Sullivan.

"You said it.... I can't believe any of this is happening.... It's all crap, Charlie. Total crap. They're looking for a scapegoat.... And I'm it," he said, sounding angry. I'd never heard Mr. Sullivan when he was really angry. "You've got to get me a lawyer, Charlie. Fast." He went silent for a moment.

I could hear him shuffling his feet as whoever it was on the phone must have been talking. Then Sullivan cleared his throat and started speaking.

"Of course, I'm angry. I should be angry. I'm innocent. I didn't kill anybody. Especially that creep. Figures that he'd be causing me problems even after he's dead. Of course, the administration is taking the cowardly way, as usual. I've just about had it with this place." He paused again. "Yeah, all right. I'll try to stay calm.... Won't be easy.... Okay. Find one fast, okay? Bye."

I heard him jangle his keys and knew he'd be coming into the office. I didn't want to get caught listening at the door so I dove onto the couch and tried looking bored. Just as I did, Mr. Sullivan opened the door, his arms loaded with papers and books.

"Hey," I said.

"Who's there?!" Sullivan gasped and dropped everything which went flying all over the floor. "Oh! It's you… I… didn't expect anyone to be here." There was a sad note in his voice. He bent down to pick up the papers and I knelt on one knee to help.

"Didn't feel like going home right away," I said. "And anyway, somebody's got to start writing the story…"

"The story?" Sullivan said, still picking up papers.

"Yeah, you know, Bidding's murder. The paper has to run something on it. Maybe we can even get our own suspect list together and talk about motives." I hoped this would give him an opening to tell me why the police had been questioning him that morning.

"Oh…" Sullivan sounded less than thrilled and occupied himself with straightening out his papers.

"I saw the police talking to you this morning." Might as well just plunge in rather than wait for him, I decided.

"They— they think I'm— not a suspect exactly. Well, yeah, I suppose they think I'm a suspect." Sullivan placed his stuff on one of the long tables and sat in the chair across from me. He let out a sigh so full of despair I was worried.

"Suspect!? You?" I said. "You couldn't murder anybody. Did you tell them?"

"They hear that from everybody they question. That's what they said. Nobody's ever guilty."

"But you're *not* guilty. You can't be…" I kinda thought this is what he'd say but it hit me like a hammer anyway. It felt personal. Sullivan was a friend.

"The administration seems to think the police have a point."

"What did they say?"

"They didn't come out and say anything exactly, you know how they can be."

"Yeah, I do," I said. The priests running the place could be cryptic whenever they said or did something on the record. Anything that could come back to bite them made them nervous, so they naturally weaseled their way around everything. After they were finished shading their views you could never tell exactly what they believed. So whatever position they took after the fact, they could claim that was their position all along. "What'd they tell you?"

"They suspended me. Without pay. Until this is all over. Of course, if it's all over and I'm in jail…" He paused and stared at the floor.

"How can they?" Not a lot shocks me but this did. I'd seen plenty even if I was only fifteen, but the way adults treated people they were supposed to care about, or at least stand behind, mystified me.

"I suppose I can understand their position—"

"*I* can't. It's not fair." I shouted. I was sure anyone in the hall outside could hear my voice. "You can't just sit there and take this."

"What choice do I have? They run the place. The faculty works at their pleasure. We don't have written contracts. Even if we did, they'd fill the contracts with clauses to allow them to do exactly what they've done." He sighed again. "That's the way it is. I'm a suspect and now I'm a suspended suspect. Without pay."

"What made the police target you?"

"Somebody told them about my arguments with Bidding. That, and they kinda have…" he went silent all of a sudden. As if somebody flipped his "Off" switch.

I looked at him hoping he'd come back to life. But he just stared at the floor.

"They kinda have what? What do they have, Mr. Sullivan?"

"A note. They've got a note from me to Bidding asking him to meet me. After school that day. The day he was—"

"That doesn't mean anything. Teachers were always having meetings with him. He was in charge of discipline, right?" But I knew that even if the note didn't mean anything it wouldn't look good and could be spun into something really bad. "Why'd you wanna meet him anyway?"

"Oh, just some problem…" Sullivan sounded evasive. "You know what Bidding was like. He annoyed students even more than faculty and he, he had…"

"What?"

"Nothing. Forget I said anything. This'll all blow over." His voice shook and I knew he was just trying to stop me asking questions. "I didn't do anything wrong. They'll see that. Don't worry about it, Marco."

"I got your back, Mr. Sullivan. If you need anything, just let me know."

"You're a good kid, Marco. I'll be sorry when you graduate… I mean I'm glad you're graduating. It's just… you're one of the best students I've worked with and I'll be sorry to see you go. If I'm not in jail, I mean. Then I won't even get to see you go."

"You'll be at graduation. Besides, I'm not planning on leaving the city for college. My parents can't afford much."

"Still, there aren't many students like you. You're a different breed than most of the kids here. Not so self absorbed."

"You gonna be all right, Mr. Sullivan?"

"I'll be fine," he said but didn't sound so sure. Then he stood, took a deep breath, and looked around as if he'd never see the place again. "You take care of the newspaper. You're the Editor. You'll get the issue out on time, no problem. I'm sorry I can't help you guys with it, but the Principal wants me off campus."

"They kicked you out?"

"Might've been worse. They could have had me escorted off the premises." He turned toward the door. "Got a lot of grading to do anyway. That'll keep my mind off things."

"I'll call to keep you posted. And… I may have some questions… about the paper." I probably knew enough to get the newspaper out, but I wanted to be sure it'd be okay to call him.

"Anytime. You've got my number, right?"

"Yep." Everybody on staff had everybody's numbers. A necessity when you ran a paper and a thousand things could go wrong.

He opened the door and glanced back at me as he moved out of the room. He had the saddest, sweetest look on his face. "Take care of yourself, Marco."

I nodded. I was at a loss for words. It was all unreal. But, I knew right then I had to do something. He wasn't a murderer and I intended to prove it. Even if I wasn't sure how or where to start. I'd never done anything like that before but I couldn't let that stop me.

* * *

I hung around the office a while longer, but I was too distracted to do any newspaper work. I'd call a staff meeting for the next day, to see what we could come up with. I was edgy and wanted to get moving. Mr. Sullivan's predicament had invaded my thoughts and wouldn't let go. I needed to get started on helping him.

Stepping out of the office I noticed how eerie the empty third floor was. The silence was like a blanket. Plenty of light streamed in through the old, leaded-glass windows, but that didn't help kill the strangeness. This was the oldest part of the old building which had been a Nineteenth Century mansion. The family who'd built it were bigwigs in Philly back then. They liked showing off their money, except these people hadn't had a whole lot of taste and ended up building a house creepy enough for a horror flick.

As I moved down the hall, I heard the distinctive pock-pock-pock of heels coming up from behind on the old wood floors. Turning around, I saw Ms. Hanford, white lab coat slung over her long red dress, a determined look on her face. She always seemed to be on a mission, even when she was just on her way to lunch. Her mass of frowsy blonde hair obviously couldn't be tamed, and the look in her eyes said she spent way too much time around kids.

"Hi Ms. Hanford. Not taking advantage of the early dismissal?" I asked, already knowing the answer. She was married to the job and usually stayed around well after most other teachers had gone home. She liked telling everyone how long she labored at her job. You'd think she was getting credit somewhere for all that.

One thing I did know about her was that she told the truth. I kinda have a knack for seeing through a liar and she wasn't one. Thing is, if Hanford didn't want to tell you something, she wouldn't lie. She just wouldn't talk.

"Got a lot of work to do, Marco. Setting up the labs, grading, you know how it is. A teacher's work is never done."

"Shame about Mr. Bidding."

She was silent. I wasn't quite sure how to take that.

"Were you here when it happened?" I asked.

"Of course I was here. I'm always here. Why?"

"Oh, no reason." I paused and started walking, then I turned back. "You didn't hear anything? That day, I mean."

"I wasn't in that part of the building, Marco. I was working in the science wing."

"Yeah, I was just thinking out loud," I said. Her domain was in the new building which was a huge glass and metal box by the side of the mansion. Even though that's where Bidding was murdered, it was still a distance from Hanford's science domain. "Seems strange that no one heard a thing. Kind of sad that he died that way. Nobody even hearing him."

"Sad maybe, but someone heard something that day. I remember one of the other teachers told me he'd heard noises or voices."

"You remember who it was?"

"Why're you so interested, Marco?"

I debated telling her about Sullivan but then nothing stays secret around here for long. She'd find out, so I figured I'd tell her and see how she reacted.

"I just found out that the police think Mr. Sullivan is a suspect—"

"You're kidding. They can't possibly think that."

"It's worse. The administration suspended him without pay until everything's resolved."

"The bast— Sorry, Marco. But they're wrong. Brendan isn't a murderer."

"Well, maybe the person who heard something can help. If they go to the police. You remember who it was?"

"Lemme think..." She placed a hand to her chin and closed her eyes. "So many people were talking, chattering, really. All nervous chatter. They were all upset, confused. It was an awful day. But one of them said— Who was it? Oh, right. It was Mr. Wheelan. That's who. He said he'd heard something in that same part of the building. Why don't you ask him?"

"Sure. I'll try and find him—"

"He's gone for the day. Couldn't wait to leave. Said the place gives him the creeps now."

"I'll catch him tomorrow. Thanks a lot, Ms. H."

She pock-pocked her way down the hall and over the skybridge to the new building.

My stomach growled, reminding me I hadn't eaten anything since breakfast, so I headed to the cafeteria before going home. A few students and teachers sat here and there in the massive room, but the usual noise was absent.

I picked up a Tastykake and a bottle of water from the counter. As I paid I noticed the cop who'd been questioning Mr. Sullivan. He sat alone at a table, flipping through a notebook. I needed to ask him a few questions.

"Hi," I said, taking a seat across from the man.

He looked up, his dark face growing a shade darker. He obviously didn't like being disturbed. He said nothing.

"You're a cop, right?"

"Detective. Detective Bynum What is—"

"Sure, detective, shoulda guessed. Nice to meet you." I stuck out my hand and we shook. It was cold and quick. He didn't want to be bothered. "So that's why you were questioning people."

"Just doin' my job. Now, if you—"

"I heard you're trying to nail Mr. Sullivan for this. Is he your top suspect? The police have a term for the one at the top of the list, right?" I thought if I played a little dumb, it might help. Aside from the fact that adults always think kids are dumb anyway.

"Listen, son, maybe you don't know how things work, but I can't comment on an investigation in progress."

"The way kids are talking, you're pretty sure it's Sullivan." I was stretching the truth but I thought it might get him to talk. "Sullivan is a guy who's afraid of his own shadow. Can't believe he'd whack somebody."

"I can tell you this, sometimes guys like that can do some pretty nasty things. And kids like you got no business sticking their nose in police affairs." He looked at me like I was a kitten who'd wandered out of it's box. Still, he had a kind face.

"Just trying to help," I said. I'm glad he thought I was just some kid. Maybe he'd slip and tell me something if he thought I was harmless. "There's a lot you probably don't know about a place like this. This school's funny."

"Tell me about it," the detective growled. "You better run along, kid. I got work to do."

"Well, if you need a guide, or somebody on the inside, lemme know," I said and smiled, trying to seem dumb and innocent.

"Yeah, sure. I'll give you a holler," he said more to his notebook than to me.

I turned around to leave then turned back again. "Uh, excuse me, detective?"

He looked up, his frown deeper, his eyes cutting into me. "What is it now?"

"Anybody tell you they might'a heard anything that day? You know, when Mr. Bidding was… killed."

"Listen, son, this is no kinda work for a kid. Let us handle it. We got it covered."

He wasn't about to crack. I had to admire his ability to keep things under his hat. I needed information, though, so I'd have to find a way to soften him up.

"Well, in case nobody else tells you, somebody did hear something that day. Don't let 'em tell you otherwise." I stood and looked him in the eye. "So long, Detective. If you need any help, my name's Marco. Ask anybody how to find me."

The look on his face told me he didn't have as much information as *I* had and he was curious. Maybe too proud to admit it yet. But he would.

I left the detective thinking about what I'd said and found another table where my friend Sam sat eating a greasy-looking egg and sausage sandwich. Healthy lunches for growing boys. That's what the school menu said.

* * *

When Sam and I ran out of jokes to tell and food to eat, he claimed he had to get home and left. It was late, and I figured I should do the same. A night with no homework was a good thing. St. T's policy was that, on an average day, every student went home with at least three or four hours of homework.

I shrugged into my backpack and ambled out of the cafeteria. Made sure I had a token for the bus and walked through the empty foyer.

Unlike the morning chaos, there was a deadly stillness now, until the door to the Principal's office opened and the police detective stomped out.

Shaking his head as if he was frustrated, he swiped a hand over his face. Looked like he could use a friend.

"Hey, Detective Bynum," I said as I walked toward him. "Looks like you just got a taste of the Principal's famous personality."

"Yeah, well, you gotta expect things on a case like this," he said, sounding like he wasn't expecting whatever the Principal had dished out.

"Anything I can—"

"I got a job to do and some people don't realize what that means," he said more to himself than to me. "Your Principal just read me the riot act. Says he's got a school to run and boys to protect. And I should get my investigation over quick. Like that's gonna be easy. He ain't gonna give me much space. How am I supposed to work like that?"

"You need somebody to smooth the way or find some short cuts."

"Like that's gonna happen. Budget cuts are mak—"

"I can help."

"You gonna go toe to toe with that man in there?" He pointed over his shoulder to the Principal's office.

"This is my fourth year at St. T's," I said. I was going to say 'St. Torture Chamber' but thought better of it. "I've learned a thing or two about getting around obstacles. Besides, I work on the school newspaper. I know my way around better than most."

"Well, maybe you can help, at that," he said, and a tentative smile broke out across his broad, dark face. "Nothin' official, though. Unnerstand? But if you hear anything or see anything, keep me in the loop." He pulled out a card with his name and number on it. "That's good day or night."

"Will do," I said, glad to have his cooperation. Now I could ask questions and feel like I had a right to do it.

"Keep this between us, uh, what'd you say your name was?"

"Marco. Marco Fontana," I said and stuck out my hand. "I'll keep it informal."

"You'll be my confidential informant. With the emphasis on confidential, got it?" The stern expression increased the lines on his face. "Don't go gettin' yourself hurt."

"Never crossed my mind, detective."

"Guess I'll see you around, then. As long as your Principal allows me to do what I've gotta do."

* * *

Nobody was at home when I got there, which was good. I had some thinking to do and I didn't need my family asking questions.

With four brothers and a sister, no house is big enough. You never get much space to yourself and privacy is just a word. I shared a room with my younger brother. My older brothers shared another room and my sister got her own room all to herself. Unless you counted the fact that mom used it as her sewing room and the place was stuffed with material and thread and whatever else you use when you make clothes.

It wasn't too bad, though. My older brothers were always out, either working or playing ball. My sister was in college and was hardly ever home and my younger brother was still in grammar school. Which meant he was a pain but easily intimidated. Still didn't make things easy.

I flopped onto the bed with the cordless phone and dialed Cullen, who was also a senior at St. T's. He lived on the Main Line but was never uppity like most of the other suburban kids. He definitely fit in with the rich set at St. T's, but he told me he never really felt a part of the world they lived in. He knew them all and they liked him. In fact they probably liked him lots more because he didn't really want to be part of their world and that intrigued them.

"I guess you left with the herd," I said when Cullen answered the phone. "I needed to talk, but you were gone."

"Hadda leave. They cancelled practice and that's rare. Besides, if I spent one more minute in that place, I would've exploded," Cullen said, his voice a mix of man and boy. "So, what's up? Got gossip?"

"Not really, but I've got a problem and you can help."

"A problem…? Hey, I like you and all but I'm not *like* you, if you know what I mean." Cullen laughed. He loved teasing me and I got the feeling there was a lot more beneath the surface of all that teasing. Cullen was a tall blond Nordic type with haunting ice-blue eyes. He also had the sweetest smile, which got him about anything he wanted.

"Don't worry, I wouldn't think of hitting on you." Not unless I had even a hint that you'd respond, I thought.

"Why not? I'm hot. All the girls say so…" Cullen almost sounded hurt.

"Because I've got other things on my mind."

"Like?"

"Like the fact that the police consider Mr. Sullivan a suspect in Bidding's murder, and the school placed him on unpaid leave until this is all over."

"Get out! That's fucking nuts. But how's that *your* problem?"

"I don't like seeing somebody railroaded. Just because the police suspect Sullivan, the school goes all red alert and kicks him to the curb."

"Yeah, well, St. T's has always been that kind of place. My father and my grandfather tell me stories all the time about when they were students. And you know what?"

"What?"

"Things don't change. That place has been the same for more than a hundred years."

"Doesn't mean I have to like it." I punched a pillow to make things more comfortable, then lay back again. "Besides, he's one of the good guys on the faculty, and St. T's doesn't have that many."

"So I guess that means we're goin' to help Sullivan, right?" he said.

That's what I liked about Cullen. He was willing to get involved. Not many of the rich kids at school were like that. They were more concerned with cars and clothes and what they were gonna do down the shore in the summer at the fancy homes their parents owned.

Cullen wasn't like that at all. His family had money, but they'd taught him something about being a decent human being, too.

"I'm gonna scout around and see if I can come up with anything. I'll have more of a plan once I think about the situation. Let's talk tomorrow at lunch."

* * *

I got to school earlier than usual the next morning. One long bus ride and I was there. The usual early birds scuttled through the halls to their favorite hangouts. Library assistants, the A-V kids, the crew team coming back in after early morning practice, and the rest. Anybody without a place to go usually congregated in the cafeteria which is where I headed. The smell of grease was too tempting, and I decided I was still hungry after breakfast at home. The caf is cavernous. It has to be to accommodate the number of students we have.

Before getting in line to order, I spotted Mr. Wheelan, sitting alone in a far corner, chowing down on something while reading a newspaper. I figured it'd be the best chance I'd get to question him.

Forgetting my hunger for a minute, I walked over to his table and sat down. Mesmerized by his food and the newspaper, Wheelan didn't look up until I'd been sitting across from him for a minute or two.

Bald, red-faced, and plump, Wheelan's chipmunk cheeks bulged as he smiled at me while turning a bright pink. He kinda reminded me of a leprechaun, a pudgy one.

"How ya doin' Mr. Wheelan?"

"Just fine, Marco. What can I do for you? Need a Latin refresher?"

"Nope, had all I can take. Just thought I'd say hi."

"Getting sentimental in your senior year? It happens. Hard to leave and St. T's has been your home, after all."

"Something like that," I said. "Did you hear that they suspended Mr. Sullivan?"

"Mr. Sullivan? Suspended? Why? When did this happen?"

"Yesterday. The police consider him a suspect in Mr. Bidding's murder and the administration kicked him to the curb like a devil worshipper." I let that sink in for a moment. "Anyway, I was hoping maybe you could help."

"Me? How can I help? I don't know anything about what's going on. Didn't even know Sulllivan was gone."

"Were you here the day Bidding was killed?"

"Yes, I was. So were a lot of people." He was growing a little uncomfortable, as if his seat were shrinking.

"It was a busy day, even after school. I remember."

"If you remember that, then you remember there were lots of people here"

"It's funny though…" I paused.

"What's funny?" he asked then placed a small chunk of pound cake into his mouth.

"Like you say, there were a lot of people here, but no one reported to the police that they heard or saw anything."

"Probably because they didn't. Don'cha think?"

"But you *did* hear something."

"Who told you that?"

"The same person you told. Ms. Hanford." I smiled and tried looking innocent.

He was silent and gingerly broke his pound cake into even smaller pieces. "What's it to you anyway? Let the police handle this."

"Maybe I took some of my lessons too seriously, like helping someone in trouble. Or helping the falsely accused. You know. I don't like seeing Mr. Sullivan getting a raw deal. I kinda thought you had the same moral compass."

He thought that over a minute. He always talked about doing the right thing. So I just stared and waited.

"I was there that day. Like a lot of people." He looked around guiltily.

"You were near the... um, the stairwell?"

"Ye—yes, I was walking by that stairwell. I heard kids running down from a couple of floors above. Sounded like a lot of them. Laughing, talking, foul language. Nothing unusual. After school, kids are all over this place like ants on candy. You know how it is." He looked at me as if for confirmation.

I nodded. "Sure."

"But, as I walked, I heard Bidding clomping down the steps. He's got a heavy walk. Had, I mean. I didn't think anything of it because he usually spent time chasing kids down. I figured he was on a mission." He shook his head. "The last thing I heard was Bidding saying something like, 'It's leaky. Stop it. It's leaky!' Which didn't make sense. By the time I stopped to give it another thought I was nowhere near the stairwell."

"No idea what he meant by that?" I watched his eyes. You can tell when they're lying. At least I usually could. He wasn't.

"No idea. But Bidding didn't always make sense." He looked down at his cake then popped another piece into his mouth.

"You're not the only one who says that." I implied that others had talked to me. He didn't have to know it was just other students complaining.

"He could be inconsistent sometimes, but he had a hard job. Which one of us isn't guilty of being inconsistent? Still, there are rules, and he didn't always apply them equally. Kids don't like that. Drives them crazy. Between you 'n me, I think he got a kick out of making some of them a little crazy." He looked at me as if he'd said something he shouldn't have, as if he'd just realized he was talking to one of the enemy, so to speak.

"Yeah, we can be crazy sometimes. But my aunt's a teacher, so I know how hard it is. Besides, I liked Bidding. He was always fair to me." So I was kinda stretching the truth, but I needed Wheelan to trust me.

"Bidding was all right. He had a tough life, but he was a good man." Wheelan said tacking away from his original thought.

"I've heard. I used to talk to Damian."

"His son? Poor kid. Can't even imagine what he must be going through." Wheelan seemed to have lost his appetite and pushed the remainder of his cake away. "You guys are gonna have to be nice to him when he gets back to school."

"Yeah, everybody's talking. I heard he's coming back tomorrow. I guess he needs to get back into things."

"He's got no other family. Maybe he feels safe here."

"I'll make sure to keep an eye out for him.

"That's what I like to hear, Marco. You're a cut above the others."

"Nah, I'm just like all the rest. I'm sure I gave Bidding as hard a time as most other kids."

"I don't think so. Your name never came up when we talked."

"Other kids gave him a tough time?"

"Got a couple of hours so I can read the list?" He pulled the cake back and munched on a few more pieces. "Would you believe that I actually heard one kid say he wanted to tack Bidding's skin to the wall and throw darts at it. What kind of world…"

"Wow! That's cold."

"That's what I mean, Marco. You're nothing like that."

"Kids are all talk. No one would actually ever do that. They're teenagers and underneath they're all scared little babies." I'd talked to enough of the kids in school to know. To me, it seemed like some of them were being cruel because they were covering up something deeper in themselves that they didn't much like. They didn't think anyone else would like them either, so they pushed everyone away with cruel behavior.

"If you think like that, Marco, don't become a teacher. They're not 'little babies' as you say. Some of the students here were born vicious. Can't really trust 'em."

"Can't be that bad. I don't know anybody that vicious, do you?" I watched him polish off the cake.

"I've had five of the worst ones in my classes in the past two or three years. Paul Lazar, Rodney Wilton, Teddy Nalan, Jim Colavecchia, Brian Donlon. All seniors, so you should know 'em. And they're grooming Damian Bidding to take over when they graduate. They've started poisoning the well. How's that for vicious?"

"Never really talked to that bunch. They always gave me the creeps. So I steered clear. You think they're vicious enough to hurt anybody?"

"Who knows what they're capable of? But if you're implying they could've hurt Bidding… No, I don't believe that. They're bad news but I can't implicate them in anything just because I don't like them."

I glanced down at my watch and realized I still had a few things to do before class.

"Gotta go, Mr. Wheelan. Thanks for talking." I stood and was about to turn away when I remembered something. "Why didn't you tell the police what you heard?"

"I…I didn't think it would be helpful. Meaningless really." He brushed off his shirt, then ruffled his newspaper and shut me out.

I still had to look at the scene of the crime, before the police and the school cleaned everything up. Now would be better since hardly anyone was in the building yet. Trekking over to the new building would give me a chance to think.

When I stepped over the threshold into the new building, it was like walking through a time portal. Behind me everything was old, creaky, and sinister. Before me the new building gleamed. It was like a bright smile and technologically it was miles ahead of the old place.

I had to pass Bidding's office to get to the stairwell and I couldn't avoid saying "Hi" to his secretary, Mrs. MacFee. She was the heart of his operation and knew all our names. MacFee was also a busybody and had access to everyone's record and more. She knew lots more than she let on.

She was usually ensconced at her desk in the outer office. No one was there, but the door to Bidding's inner office was open. I edged a little closer to see what I could see. I was getting to like the idea of skulking around and digging up information without anyone knowing.

"You gonna be okay, hon?" The voice belonged to her husband who worked around in the building on a part-time basis. I'd talked to him a few times.

"Yeah, doll, I'll be fine," MacFee's drawn out words and high pitched voice answered.

"Things don't look good around here," he said.

"Everybody's kinda glum, so I gotta at least look like I care a little that the big galoot is dead. But I don't."

"Hon." His tone was gently admonishing.

"The wicked witch is dead and I ain't sorry." She paused. "Don't look around. Nobody's gonna hear. This is… was his inner sanctum. Nobody comes near this place. That's how much they all hated him."

"How'd you do..."

"What? You think… ha! It was easier than you imagine. Fact is I thought it was gonna be hard, y'know?"

"What're you saying?"

"Once I decided, it was like one, two, three. Yep. Soon as I knew he was gone, I didn't waste time. He's gone and I'm sittin' in his chair. Where I should'a been all along. Since I do all the work anyway." She paused and I imagined her plumping her hair as she always did. "See? Your old lady ain't no slouch. She gets things done."

"But, hon, he's… dead."

"He always thought he was better 'n everybody. Just 'cause he taught Latin. Some shit that is. Latin. Who cares?"

"But, I can't imagine… You sure you're all right with all the extra work?"

"It's done. And I'm gonna push for this job. I know things inside out, I was the one who did all the work anyway. They need me."

Their voices got lower and I had a feeling they were ending their conversation, so I edged my way back toward the entrance. I couldn't believe what I'd heard. I'd always had the feeling she didn't like her boss, but she didn't strike me as the killer type. What did I know? I was new at all this. Now I had to decide what to do about what I'd heard.

Her husband, big and lumpy, left her office with a rolling gait. He saw me and his eyes turned beady. I'd never crossed him, but the times I'd seen him, it was clear he wasn't fond of kids.

"Hey Mr. MacFee. Is Mrs. MacFee in?"

"Shouldn't you be in class?"

"Not yet. How're you doing?"

He mumbled something and brushed by me as he left. I continued on toward the inner office.

"Hi, Mrs. MacFee." I said as I poked my head in the doorway.

An older woman with a face full of wrinkles, she looked up at me warily at first. Her trademark washed-out blond hair formed a stiff conch shell around her head. She wore glasses with corners rising into sharp points like alien goggles. When she saw it was me, she smiled.

"Marco, doll. How are you? Sad times. Are you takin' care of yourself?" Her voice was soothing. Another trademark feature.

"How are *you* holding up? Must be hard…" I looked as doleful as I could. She and Bidding had worked closely together, but she always seemed to resent him.

"I'm… I'm doin' okay, hon. This office is so busy I don't get much chance to think about other things anyway." She made a show of shuffling papers.

"Shame about Mr. Sullivan. Seems like everything is blowing up around here," I said and watched her.

"Yeah," the look on her face was noncommittal, as if she didn't want to appear to be taking sides. But I could tell she'd already done that.

"Poor guy really needs some help."

"Don't we all?" She turned back to her paperwork. "I got my hands full here now. That's for sure."

"I might need some information for the school newspaper. We're doin' a story on Mr. Bidding, and I know you probably have lots of memories." I thought this might be a good way to get her to talk.

Before she could answer, a student blew in from the hall like a runaway dustball. He carried a sheaf of papers and laid them on her desk. "Morning attendance reports for Mr. Bid…" The kid caught himself. "Sorry … I mean… who gets them now?"

"Don't worry, Andy, honey. We're all makin' that mistake. I'll take the reports."

The kid left, head down until he got to the door then he breezed out, happy again.

"Was I ever that small? Freshmen seem so young," I said.

"That's because you *were* young. You started earlier than most. And yeah, you were a peanut like him. Not anymore, though." She laughed and gave me a quick glance.

"Guess you see all kinds in this office. You gotta love kids to do this kind of work."

"They're all good kids. People just hafta take the time to see that. I used to tell Pat the same thing: take the time to look. Try and understand what they're goin' through. He never…" she stopped herself and looked guilty. "He had a difficult time, sometimes."

"You must feel awful right now. Can't be an easy time for you. You and Mr. Bidding were close, right?"

"Depends what you mean, Marco. We weren't close friends. But that doesn't mean I didn't respect him."

"Could'a fooled me. It always looked like the two of you were good friends. Always joking and laughing. Everybody thought this office ran so well because of that."

"Well…" She looked down at her desk piled with notes, papers, and rubber bands. The make-up was thick on her face and her perfume was beginning to overwhelm. "He was my boss, but he wasn't a person you could get close to. You won't find too many here who liked him." She gave me that look again, as if she'd slipped.

"You mean there were people here who hated him?"

"Hated? I don't know…" She paused. "You're not gonna put any of that in the school paper, are you?"

"Not me. Bidding and I got along and I'm not gonna do a hatchet job on him. But maybe it's good for me to know so I can avoid talking to people who hated him… I mean, didn't like him."

"Good point, Marco. You're smart, but I always knew that." She gave me one of her motherly looks. She was exactly that type, which is why so many people responded to her and opened up to her. She probably new plenty about a lot of things. Just a matter of getting her to talk.

"So who should I avoid? When I'm interviewing people."

"As far as students, Pat argued a lot with some of them. But that's normal. I mean, I've been around schools and kids all my life, hon, and arguing with kids is just the way of it. I've had some knock down sessions myself. Like Teddy Nalan. He and I don't get along. Hates me for no reason, the stupid lump of flesh." She made a face as if she had swallowed sour milk.

"Did Mr. Bidding ever argue with him?"

"Sure. The kid is malicious. He's like poison. The sooner he graduates, the better. He and Bidding had a real fight once."

"How do you mean real?"

"Oh, not fists or anything. Just yelling. If I was his mother I'd've slapped him silly. But when she comes in, all you hear is how sweet her son is and what a good Christian boy he is. Christian? He doesn't know how to spell it, let alone be it. The mother is just as bad. The fruit doesn't fall far from the tree, hon. Remember that."

"Did you hear any of their argument?"

"Of course I did. Everybody in the office and down the hall heard it. But there weren't any threats, if that's what you're drivin' at. They just yelled at each other. Things like, 'You'll do what you're told.' Or 'You can't tell me what to do. Nobody can.' Nothing you could use in court." She winked at me and I thought I saw her make-up crack.

"Yeah, kids are always sayin' things like that. It doesn't mean much, I guess."

"Well, there *was* something strange, now that you mention it."

I waited.

"Pat told Teddy to stay away from his son. You know Damian, right? He's a junior but I bet you know who he is. Poor kid, he must feel terrible."

Her eyes filled with tears and a few broke and fell, tumbling over her thick makeup. "Sorry, hon. Didn't mean to break down like that."

"It's understandable," I said, leaning on the counter, looking sympathetic.

"I feel so sorry for some of the kids. They don't have it easy. They may be rich and all, but they come from families like everyone, and some families are sick."

"Even Damian?" I coaxed.

"Damian, too. Mr. Bidding wasn't easy on his son. Pat used to teach classics here, before your time, and poor Damian never measures up in that subject. This is not an easy school, even for the best students. Damian is pretty bright, has a 3.8 average. But Classics is his weak point." She shook her head sadly. "Sometimes I think he didn't do well on purpose, just to get his father's goat. They had a few hiccups about that, I can tell you." She rolled her eyes extravagantly. "Bidding was never satisfied with Damian's grades, or his extracurricular activities, or his friends."

"Particularly Teddy Nalan?"

"Others, too. Ed Ryan, Jimmy Dale, and a couple others. I guess they all hung out because they're not exactly like the other kids. Not rich. Here because their parents work here and they get a scholarship. But Damian drove his father nuts."

"Hey, that's our job!" I said trying to lighten the mood but also get her to feel comfortable enough to keep talking. "We have to make our parents crazy. It's in the contract. And having weird friends is one of the best ways to do that."

MacFee laughed so much she began to cough.

"You're funny, Marco. You should visit more. I need a laugh."

"I'll bet. Dealing with discipline problems is bound to get to you."

"Oh, they're not *that* bad. I mean, every kid has something good in him. That's what I believe. I suppose even Teddy Nalan has something good somewhere deep down. He can't be as bad as he acts. He just can't," she sighed. "But Pat didn't like any of the students. Even the really good ones. That's the impression I got. And when Damian started to be more and more like his friends, Pat hated it. They had fi— I mean arguments all the time."

"Sounds like you get to see a lot."

"One time, I heard Bidding slap Damian. Now, it's his son, so I didn't say anything. But I don't believe in hitting kids." She punctuated this with a sharp nod.

She dropped a few more stories about Bidding and his son and some of the students but she became increasingly uncomfortable speaking ill of the dead. When I made as if to leave, she began to tell me what a wonderful job Bidding had done at the school and how the kids all respected him even if they didn't like him.

"And that's the way he should be remembered. When you write your article. Come back in and I'll have some thoughts written down so you can use 'em as quotes. Okay, hon?"

Backing out the door, I nodded. "I can use that kind of thing, Mrs. MacFee. Thanks. And thanks for talking."

Her eyes went all soft and she winked. "Anytime, hon."

I could tell she knew even more than she was telling and had her finger on the pulse of the underground at school.

* * *

I needed to get to my locker in the old building before first period class. But, since I was in the new building, I figured I might as well take a look at the scene of the crime. I didn't want to, I just felt I had to. I'm not ghoulish. I don't feed off things like that. But something told me I needed to see it and maybe there'd be something I could use to help Mr. Sullivan.

The door to the back stairwell wasn't far from Bidding's office. Opening the door, I stepped into an even quieter world. It'd be chaos once the bell rang. For now, I could explore without interruption. The "accident" happened two floors up so I started climbing. My footsteps echoed off the walls and made the hair at the back of my neck stand on end. It was dank and I felt clammy for no real reason.

The police had been here, doing whatever it is they do at a crime scene. So, I wasn't sure exactly what I'd see, but I kept climbing.

Finally I reached the landing where Bidding must have hit the floor. There was no chalk outline, I'd heard that police don't really do that. But

I felt surprised anyway. Still, there were signs that someone had been here, scraping things for evidence and whatever else they do.

I walked over the spot where he probably lay dead as a stone and stood at the bottom of the staircase he'd tumbled down. A shudder ran through me and I felt cold.

The silence around me became oppressive. I didn't particularly want to be alone but I had to do this.

Edging forward, I placed my hand on the cold, metal bannister. There was a slick residue, as if someone had sprayed oil over the length of it. It hit me then that whoever set this up wanted to make sure the disciplinarian had nothing to grab onto to break his fall.

In my mind's eye, I could see Bidding madly grasping for a hold on the bannister and slipping every time. I could almost feel his great bulk falling down the long flight from the top floor landing, hitting steps and finally breaking his neck on the landing.

I shuddered again. But I kept climbing.

As I neared the top of the flight, something caught my eye: a small hole in the wall at ankle level. I'd overheard some of the adults talking abut a tripwire. This must've been where it had been attached at one end.

Funny that Bidding, who noticed every hair out of place on students, didn't notice a set up like this.

Unless he'd been distracted by something unexpected. Or, someone.

There was nothing else to see, so I turned back around and began walking down the steps. Again, I imagined Bidding tumbling, smashing into the concrete steps. I put out a hand unconsciously and it slipped on the oily bannister. I nearly went head over heels and it was only luck that forced me to steady myself.

I stood absolutely still for a moment. The silence and the idea of what had gone on here and that someone was behind it all gave me the creeps.

One thing I knew, though, Mr. Sullivan couldn't have done this. This was a cold plan, a calculated plan. Mr. Sullivan wasn't like that. Visiting this place may have creeped me out, but it also made me sure Sullivan was innocent.

* * *

The bell sounded and I slammed my calculus book shut. My head was swimming. Nothing in the class ever made sense. If it wasn't a requirement, I wouldn't come near a math class.

Eighth period was my free period, and I'd agreed to meet Cullen in the newspaper office before the staff meeting I'd scheduled. At lunch I'd given him a list of the names Wheelan and MacFee had mentioned. He said he'd see what he could find out before the end of the day.

Cullen was resourceful and, because he was a Crew god, everyone looked up to him. Some of the kids would do just about anything he asked. I often wondered what it'd be like to have that kind of power over people. But it never seemed to faze Cullen. He never abused whatever influence he had. I admired that.

I trudged up the stairs, my backpack weighing me down, making me think again that June couldn't come fast enough. But I also wondered about Mr. Sullivan and how crappy he must feel being thrown out like that. If I was him I wasn't sure I'd want to come back. But I guess I didn't have to worry about paying the bills the way he did.

It was quiet. No one would be around until the last bell sounded, and that suited me fine. I needed quiet to get rid of all the math rumbling around in my head. I unlocked the door, threw my backpack on the floor and stretched out onto the couch. Before I drifted off, Cullen popped into the room and shut the door behind him.

"The Great Fontana is catnapping? Do I believe my eyes?" Cullen smirked, which drew his already handsome face into a particularly nice expression. His blond hair was longer than usual, which he blamed on crew practice and no time for a haircut. He leaned back on the door and waited for me to shake off the sleepiness.

I couldn't help but smile because it felt as he were protecting me from something, as he'd always done. He'd taken me under his wing when we were freshmen and I was younger than everybody else by a lot. He'd never let me down, so I knew I could count on him to help me now.

"Calculus is brutal. I could hardly keep my eyes open." I yawned and sat up.

"Good thing you don't need calculus to put a newspaper out. Of course..."

"Nooo! No math lectures. I've got a headache."

"Okay, okay." He laughed and sat in one of the threadbare soft chairs some newspaper staffer from years before had hauled into the office long ago. Flipping one leg over the arm of the chair, he sat spread-legged before me. He liked teasing, even if he wasn't conscious that's what he was doing. Of course he might be aware somewhere deep down inside. Could be it all really meant something and maybe I'd get to find out some day. If I was lucky.

"Listen to this!" he said breaking my thoughts.

"What? Did they arrest someone else?"

"No. But listen to what I heard. You might've heard it too if you weren't being a lazy ass and sleeping on the couch."

"I wasn't slee— oh, just tell me."

"I was on my way here and I passed Mr. Coyle's office," Cullen said. Coyle was the senior counselor and his office was down another corridor on this floor. "He was talking and... well... I kinda listened in for a minute."

"Anything interesting?"

"Maybe."

He smiled at me, and for a moment I almost forgot what he was talking about.

"Hello? Earth to Marco... you wanna hear what I heard?"

"Of course, I was just thinking."

"Sure you were. Well, Coyle was yakkin' on his phone and I heard him say some rotten things about Sullivan. Names and things you don't want me to repeat. Claimed that Bidding was blackmailing him, Coyle, just like Bidding must've been blackmailing Sullivan. Except Coyle said that he wasn't as stupid as Sullivan had been because he never put anything on paper like Sullivan had done. That make sense to you?"

"Yeah. Yeah it does. He say anything else?"

"Gets worse. Coyle said he was sure they wouldn't find out what Bidding held over his head. And that they'd never trace anything back to him or find out whatever it was that he did." Cullen nodded his head emphatically, his blond hair ruffled. "Sounds like Coyle has something to hide."

"No way. He said that?"

"Sure. But you know how it is, it sounds bad but it might not be."

"Point is that there's someone else the detective should be looking at." I ran a hand through my hair and stretched. "Bidding made a lot of people angry. The police probably stopped looking at anyone else once they had Sullivan."

"That's exactly what Coyle said on the phone. He thinks they'll stop looking now that they've got Sullivan."

"I won't stop looking. Coyle doesn't know that."

"Sullivan's lucky you're on his side."

"Did you manage to see any of the guys on the list I gave you?" I smiled, thinking how nice it would have been if Cullen had worn his running shorts instead of long pants.

"I talked to a few of them, and I managed to tail two of them at school. They never knew they had somebody on their ass. That was so cool. I might even be good at this private eye stuff."

"We'll both have to be good to get Mr. Sullivan off the hook. Did you see or hear anything that might help?"

"From what I already know about that bunch, Nalan is the ringleader."

"Nalan? He's dumb as a rock. He's the pack leader?"

"I didn't say he has brains, and neither do the other kids he hangs with. Somehow he gets them to do whatever he says."

"Figures. Dumb leads dumber."

"I followed Nalan for a while and listened in on him and his buds in the cafeteria. He's pretty vicious and controlling. I hated everything about him. He's like an ugly little mole on the face of life," Cullen said, his face twisted in an expression of distaste.

"Yeah and there's never a good dermatologist around when you need one."

"I followed him after he left the caf. Nalan swaggered around like he owned the school. I stayed close enough to see what he did. Which was mostly nothing. Except for one thing…" Cullen paused. I even thought he sorta winked, knowing I'd explode if he didn't finish telling me what he'd seen.

"And… and?"

"I saw him go to where Bidding took his fall. I tried staying hidden but for a minute I thought he knew I was there and that's why he went into the stairwell. I figured he wanted to trap me in a secluded place."

"What'd you do?"

"I realized I was wrong. He's too stupid to notice me tailing him."

"He actually went to the crime scene?" That was odd. I needed more information. "So what was he doing in the stairwell?"

"At first I couldn't figure it out. I crept as close as I could so I could see in through the window in the door. Looked to me like he was reading something on the wall. But while I watched, Mr. Crejewski came up the stairs, saw Nalan, and yelled for him to stop whatever it was he was doing. Nalan said, 'Fuck you, baldy.' and ran down the steps laughing. After everything was clear, I went to see what Nalan had done."

"Which was…?" I tried not to snap at Cullen.

"Okay, okay. Nalan had scrawled something on the wall. Maybe Crejewski chased him off before he finished or maybe not. It said, '*In Nomine Pat…*' All in caps. I know what it means, but it seems meaningless in that spot." He stared at me.

"That's all? '*In Nomine Pat…*'? That's the whole thing?"

"That's all I saw. I was six inches away from the wall. Couldn't have been clearer. He used a permanent marker. My mother hates stuff like that. Says it's nearly impossible to clean. If I ever did anything like that, she'd put my ass in a sling for a month. Nalan's a menace."

"Why would he be writing a blessing on the wall?" I said.

"I don't think Nalan was marking a prayer on the wall. Especially since he didn't get along with Bidding from what I hear."

"*In Nomine Pat…* Maybe it's complete the way it is? Think that's possible?"

"What are you talking about?"

"Well it sounds like the beginning of 'In nomine patris et filli' and so on. But what if instead of meaning 'In the name of the father and of the son…' Nalan was just writing 'In the name of Pat"? Bidding's first name was Patrick."

"Makes sense in a sick kind of way, but do you think Nalan is smart enough to use Latin like that?"

"It's something we all know from grammar school. It doesn't take much of a mind to change the phrase in such a simple way."

"You could be right," Cullen said.

"Maybe I should have a talk with Nalan. Find out what's going on."

"You sure that's safe? You don't know what to expect from him. I'm coming with you."

"I can handle myself," I said flexing my arm like a comic book character. I didn't work out like the Crew team, but I spent time in the school's weight room a few days a week. And my cousin Tony had taught me a few things about protecting myself and being street smart. Of course, I didn't carry a gun, like Tony recommended. But I learned plenty of other useful things from him.

"Nalan is pretty vicious. I should be there."

"I may not be a Crew god like some people I know." I gave him as sidelong glance. "But I do live in South Philly and you learn a thing or two."

"If you say so. But I'd feel better if I came with you."

"People like Nalan are cowards. But if you wanna come along, I can't stop you." Actually I thought it'd be good to have a witness in case anything did happen.

"And maybe after we can go to your house for dinner?"

Now things became clear. Cullen loved my mother's cooking and he used any excuse to wangle an invitation.

"Sure. Mom loves company, and she especially swoons over you. You're so blond. You're like from another planet. She loves that."

"Cool! Let's go get Nalan's address from the office."

"Better idea, let's get it from Mrs. MacFee. That'd be easier."

When we neared Bidding's old office, I spotted Detective Bynum talking with Mrs. MacFee. She was sitting behind her desk like a queen bee in a hive. Student runners stood waiting for her to give them something to do, but her attention was on the detective. As we got closer I heard her plaintive tone.

"I don't know what things are coming to, Detective." she said as we entered the office. "Things are terrible here."

"I know what you mean, ma'am. This generation, what do they call it? Generation X, right? This generation is plain ornery. Do anything. Just as long as they get what they want."

"Hey, Mrs. MacFee," I said when she turned and noticed me. "What's wrong?"

"Marco," she said. "This is Marco Fontana, detective. And that's Cullen Haldane. These two are not like the others. Good boys is what they are. Never a hiccup. Always on the level." She smiled at us and I noticed Cullen blushing.

"I've had the pleasure of meeting Mr. Fontana," the detective said. Only it didn't sound like he'd been pleased to meet me.

"They wouldn't do things like that," she waved her hand toward the door to Bidding's inner office.

"What's goin' on?" Cullen asked.

"Lookit. Look what some kid did to my – uh – Mr. Bidding's door."

Cullen and I moved closer to the door. Scrawled in black under the nameplate was: "The Kronos Elect" And there was a deep slash through Bidding's name.

"What do you make of that? You kids have any idea what it means?" MacFee stood and walked over to the door. She rubbed at the letters with her finger but they didn't even smear. "Can't get it off. They must'a used permanent marker. These kids are rotten."

"Any ideas, Cullen?" I asked as I thought about what it meant.

He stared, a look of concentration twisting his face into a squinty-eyed look.

"Nope. Doesn't mean a thing to me," he said finally.

"Sounds like a club, doesn't it?" I said.

"Yeah, but there's no club like that here."

"Just destructive nonsense," the detective said. "Not worth the bother, in light of other things." The detective leaned against the door jamb and gave us all a knowing look.

"It just makes me crazy, is all," MacFee said.

"The detective's right, Mrs. M," I said, though I continued staring at the words. Something about them nagged at me. The reference was classical and I had a feeling it wasn't as pointless as the detective thought. But I couldn't figure it out.

Besides, I'd promised myself that I'd get to the bottom of Bidding's murder so I could help Mr. Sullivan. The graffiti wasn't putting me any closer to doing that.

"Why'd they put it on Bidd— sorry, Mr. Bidding's door?" Cullen asked. "I mean, why not the outer door?"

Easier to get away with it," MacFee said. "I took a coffee break earlier. Now, when Mr. Bidding was still here, I'd just walk out and take my break. Never locked up because he was there, y'know? Never had to worry about things. I guess I forgot he wasn't there anymore."

We got Nalan's address after making up some excuse about an assignment for having to see him.

"Sorry about the door," I said as we left.

"Don't give it another thought. Maintenance will have to clean it. I'm not gonna let it bother me. It's not gonna get me down," she said and went back to directing the office like she owned the place.

On the way out, the detective walked along with us.

"Why do I get the feeling you two aren't going to see this Nalan kid because you need to finish an assignment like you told the nice lady in there?"

"Busted!" Cullen said. "That's why you're a detective. I guess the excuse *was* pretty lame."

"Lame's not the word," I said. "Doesn't matter. We've gotta talk to him."

"Tell me you're not gonna do somethin' foolish," the detective said. "You know somethin' you gotta let me know. Wasn't that the deal?"

"Don't remember, exactly. Anyway, we don't have anything. Not yet."

"But you think you have enough to go and talk to somebody?" The detective grumbled something under his breath. "Bad enough your Principal makes it hard to investigate, now you're gonna go and get yourselves hurt."

"You told me you could use some help. Right? That's all we're doing. Nobody's gonna get hurt."

"You were only supposed to nose around on school property. Off the grounds, that's my territory."

"He's telling the truth, detective," Cullen said. "We really don't know much. All we're gonna do is ask some questions."

"Yeah, and if you're lucky you'll be able to close the case if we find out anything." I said.

"I'll be lucky if the both'a you are still in one piece tomorrow."

* * *

"Where're you headed?" I said to Cullen. We've gotta get goin' on Sullivan's case."

"Crew practice, remember? I miss one more and I don't go to Henley if we make it this year. Short practice today. I'll be back in plenty of time."

"Okay. We'll head to South Philly when you get back."

I watched Cullen leave and imagined what it might be like to watch him change into his singlet. For some reason, the crew team looked even better in singlets than the wrestlers. I put those thoughts aside for the moment, and once Cullen was out of sight, I headed for the newspaper office.

The office was empty. Papers were scattered everywhere from our recent meeting and no one had straightened up. The hand-done mock-up for the front page stared me in the face with its headline: Disciplinarian Murdered, English Teacher A Suspect. I didn't like it. All it did was add to my edgy feeling. I needed to do something, not sit around doing nothing until Cullen got back.

Physical activity was usually my answer for edginess. I knew the weight room would be empty, since it was mostly the crew team that used it this time of year and they'd all be down at the river. I went to my locker, pulled out some gym clothes, and went down to the weight room in the basement of the old building.

The rambling, run-down basement wasn't my favorite part of the building. Dim lighting from bare bulbs made lots of sinister shadows appear on the walls. A musty odor floated on the air and a small drip-drip-drip sound seemed to come from everywhere all at once.

The old locker room was located in the basement and, from the smell, it hadn't been given a good cleaning in about a hundred years. A series of winding corridors and unused offices in the basement would have made a great location for one of those Halloween horror tours. Except it was all real. The weight room was the nicest part of the area, and it wasn't all that good. At least it was sort of clean and orderly because people used it regularly.

I'd made the mistake of seeing all the Halloween movies, so of course, that was all I could think about as I moved through the grungy halls toward the weight room door. Every shadow made my skin crawl and when I thought I saw something move, the hair at the back of my neck stood on end. When I saw the dim emergency light over the door of the weight room, I felt relieved. Almost.

The door was almost always locked, but since I maintained a nominal membership on the wrestling team, I still had access to the weight room. Unlocking the door, I flicked on the lights. More bare blubs and even more shadows. None of it did much to dispel the creepy feeling I had being there alone.

I shook off the chill, placed my gym bag to the side, and went over to one of the weight machines. The dumb repetitive action of the machine would let me focus on Sullivan's case and my next steps.

Setting the machine for the levels I wanted, I settled into the seat and picked up the crossbar. As I lifted the bar, the weights made tiny bell-like sounds when they struck against one another. It always seemed strange how so much weight could make such a small clear sound.

I tried clearing my thoughts and concentrating as I lifted. I felt my muscles work against the weight, felt the flow of my breath in and out. Each time I lifted the weight to a certain height, I paused. And that's when I heard it. A small sound that was out of place in the weight room. It wasn't the sound of equipment. Or of anything else in the room. I listened again.

Nothing. I figured it must have been the building groaning. The old structure and made strange sounds as it settled, especially deep in the basement.

When I started to lift the crossbar again, that out-of-place sound came again. This time it was more distinct, more clear. I slowly moved the crossbar down, and the weights it controlled clunked metallically into place. Turning to look around, I saw that I was still alone.

I moved back around, settled myself in the machine's seat. I placed my hands on the crossbar and was about to lift when the lights went out. Without windows, the room was pitch black.

I fought the sudden, powerful sensation that the walls were collapsing in around me.

"Hey!" I shouted. "Who is it? What's going on?"

No response.

There was no choice but to move. I'd have to feel my way back to the door.

In the total darkness, I turned and lifted my leg over the seat in an attempt to get out of the machine.

As I turned again, I felt someone at my back. Felt hot breath on my shoulder. The heat of another body.

One powerful arm went around my neck in a lightning quick move. Then my assailant locked his arm in place with his other hand and squeezed.

I twisted and resisted. But he never loosened his grip for a second.

My breathing was slowly being cut off. He knew just how to apply pressure. The vise grip grew tighter and I felt myself dropping to the floor.

"Listen, you fuck up," the voice was a ragged whisper. I didn't recognize it.

"I—" was all I could gasp out.

"Don't talk. Listen." He squeezed again and I saw tiny fireworks displays. "Keep outta this case. Sullivan's guilty. Leave it that way. Keep outta this or you won't make it to graduation."

I could only make a guttural choking sound.

"Got it, Fontana? Nod, so I know," he ordered.

I nodded as best I could, trapped in his muscular arm.

When he was satisfied that I understood, I felt the pressure on my neck increase and then nothing.

Next thing I knew, I was on the floor of the weight room looking up at Cullen and Simon peering at me as if they were worried. Cullen knelt on my right. Simon on my left. Both of them dripping sweat and dressed only in their singlets. If I was hallucinating, I liked it.

"Marco?" Cullen gently tapped my cheek. "You all right?"

"What happened, dude?" Simon asked. "You pass out from the exercise?"

I shook my head but decided I didn't want to tell them the truth. Not right then.

"You're lucky Simon and I got back early. Coach sees you layin' here, you'll never be allowed in the weight room again." Cullen said. "Why'd you press yourself so hard?"

"I'm o-okay," I struggled to sit up. The dizziness wasn't as bad as I'd feared and I was able to get to a sitting position. My throat wasn't even sore. My assailant had known just what to do to knock me out. "S-should get goin' though, right, Cullen? You were gonna come to South Philly with me?"

"Dinner at Mama Fontana's?" Simon laughed. "How come I don't get an invitation?"

"Next time. Promise," I said. Looking at Simon, I realized that I certainly wouldn't mind having him across the table from me. "This time Cullen's helping me with some work. Dinner is payment."

"I'll get changed and meet you in the foyer," Cullen said as he and Simon took off for their lockers. "You sure you're all right?" Cullen called over his shoulder.

* * *

"You're shittin' me! Right?" Cullen's expression registered shock and amazement. "Somebody strangled you into a blackout?"

"You got it." I said as we walked through South Philly on the way to Nalan's house.

"You didn't pass out from too much exercise?" Cullen laughed. "You're still a runt, even if you're a senior."

"Waitin' for the growth spurt. It'll come. But I thought this guy would finish me. Except he knew just what he was doing."

"And he warned you off the case?"

"Right again. I must've touched a nerve."

"And you're not giving up." Cullen stood still a moment and looked admiringly at me. "You got balls, dude. Big balls."

"I've got a headache is what I've got. Let's talk to Nalan and get to my house where I can get some food and some Advil."

Nalan lived in a part of South Philly only a few blocks from my house. But it might as well have been another town. It was a different parish and that made it another world. Even in the same parish different neighborhoods meant different territories. You had to know where you were and whose lines you might be crossing. According to my grandfather, things were way worse when he was a kid. There were gangs trying to control the neighborhoods, and if you crossed invisible lines, you'd end up with a beat down.

This neighborhood was shabbier than mine. Quite a few houses were for sale and some others didn't look well cared for. It was a sign of the times. South Philly was losing its Italian character fast.

The Nalan home was ratty. The brick front was badly in need of pointing. The rickety storm door had a screen that bulged making the door look pregnant. The building had an air of despair.

I could sense Cullen's nervousness. He didn't get to slum it often and was used to well-mannered Main Line districts. We stood together outside the house, and I knew Cullen had probably never in his life seen a neighborhood quite so run down. It was almost funny. Tall and muscular, Cullen sort of hid behind me for protection. I kinda liked the feel of his body brushing up against mine.

I opened the screen door and the faint aroma of something cooking wafted toward us. The family was getting ready for dinner, like everyone else in the neighborhood. Teddy would probably be there waiting to be fed.

I pressed the doorbell and heard muffled voices inside the house. The door opened halfway and sullen, dark-haired Teddy peered out at me with dull, vacant eyes. His droopy face and slack lower lip were as unappealing as the rest of him.

"Teddy! Got a minute?" I tried being upbeat. But I could tell that he knew we weren't here to ask him to come out and play

"Whaddayou want? I'm busy." It was a challenge.

"Hey, Teddy," Cullen said. I was impressed with his cheerful tone. "We gotta ask you something. Won't take long. You're probably getting' ready for dinner. Smells great!"

"You guys are fuckin' nuts. You never even say 'Boo' to me at school and now youse wanna talk?" Teddy wasn't part of the in group at school. In fact, word was he was one of St. T's charity admissions, placed on the rolls to make it look like the school was diverse, accepting, and open to a variety of students.

"Yeah, I know. And I'm not gonna shit you, either. Things are complicated." I said, trying to sound apologetic. "Doesn't mean we can't change stuff. And right now we could use some help. Can you spare a minute?"

I knew that even if he was as tough as a box of nails, he still wanted to be liked by kids like Cullen and maybe even me. Nalan didn't get much attention from anybody at school. Probably not even at home. So, bad ass as he might sound, I knew he'd talk to us.

Teddy turned back to look into the house, then peered at us again. He looked unsure, like maybe this was some kind of joke. I was sure he'd been the butt of practical jokes all his life, which is why he turned so sour once he got to St. T's. Sour and bitter and ready to tear down anything he didn't like because he knew it didn't like him. He wouldn't be easy to crack.

"Listen," Cullen said, leaning in as if to take him into his confidence. "We got a line on something fishy goin' on at school and I figured you might be the guy to go to for information."

"Get the fuck out! Whadda you think I am, stupid? Gonna implimate myself in something' I don't know nothin' about?" Teddy glared at us, one hand twitching at his side.

"Nah, Teddy. Cullen didn't mean anything like that," I stepped in closer to Teddy. "What Cullen meant was that you get around at school like other kids don't. You've got friends all over the place there. You know things because you keep your eyes open. You probably see more and know more about what's goin' on than almost anybody else. Am I right?"

Teddy maintained his suspicious stance, but a small self-satisfied smile worked its way onto his face. His dull piggy eyes almost gleamed with this new attention he was being paid.

"Yeah?" he said as if he didn't care what I'd just said. "So, what if I do?" He tried sounding like he was above us, better than us, but he moved in closer, which said to me he wanted to be in with us. Maybe *be* us.

"Somebody tagged the wall where Bidding was killed. You hear about that?" I asked.

"Course I heard," Teddy bragged. "What's the big deal?"

"Just cool that somebody had the balls to do something like that," Cullen said. He knew what I needed and we hadn't even rehearsed.

"But that detective... You know who I mean, right? That black guy who's been nosin' around school?" I asked.

"Seen him. Looks lost most'a the time."

"Well I overheard him talking to somebody. And he says whoever tagged the wall is probably also a suspect in the murder."

"Big fuckin' deal," Teddy spat out the words. "Sounds like they got a lotta nothin' if you ask me. How's taggin' a wall put you down for a murder?"

"Don't know," I said. "All I know is what I heard. Sounds like the detective had some other evidence." Okay, so I didn't really overhear anything and the detective was stuck on this case worse than a Great Dane in a Chihuahua-sized doggie door. But if I was gonna help Sullivan, I needed something to go on.

"Anything in the wind about who might'a tagged the wall?" Cullen asked. "I mean, maybe we should warn whoever it is. Personally I think he's cool doin' something like that."

"Yeah… it was kinda cool," Teddy said and a look of surprise crossed his face quickly replaced by his usual scowl. "Like when I saw it, I thought it was cool, y'know? I figured whoever did it deserved a medal." He smirked.

I guess he thought he'd made a good save by trying to change his facial expression. Just like Cullen had told me, Nalan didn't know that Cullen had actually seen him mark the wall. The fleeting expression on his face confirmed what we knew.

"So? Is 'at all youse wanted?"

"Just thought you could pass along that warning… in case you know whoever did it," Cullen said. "Personally I'm not gonna miss Bidding. He was a pain in my ass."

"Tell me about it," Teddy said, an evil glint in his eye. "Fat pig deserved what he got."

"I heard you didn't get along with him either." I said making him think I belonged to the same club. "Somebody said you argued a lot with him."

"I bet that bitch in his office blabbed, didn't she?" Teddy's right hand formed a meaty fist at his side. He began pounding his leg. "She's got a big mouth. Wants'a get me in trouble. She hates me."

"Same person told me that you argued with Bidding on the day he died."

"What if I did?"

"Fine by me," I said. "But if she tells the police, who knows?"

"She's the one who argued with Bidding. All the time. And she's the one who told us we should stand up for ourselves." He jutted out his chin.

"She's right," I said. "We gotta stand up for ourselves. Guys like Bidding take advantage—"

"Damn right!" Teddy said. "She said we shouldn't let him, and she was right. She's a bitch but she was right about that."

"Who else did she tell that to?" Cullen asked. "She told me I hadda be careful around him but I thought it was only me."

"Nah, she told that to all of us. She thinks she's like everybody's mother."

"Well, somebody said they saw you writing on the wall at the crime scene. I heard that when I was in her office and she said they'd call your father."

"They better not..." Teddy glanced around, fear in his eyes. And for the first time I saw the scared little kid under all that tough talk.

"Your father won't believe them, I bet," Cullen said.

"I... I don't know." Teddy said. His voice shook, all the bravado gone. "Last time they called he nearly punched my eye out. And my mom's too."

"If you know anything about who tagged the wall, maybe you'd better tell the school before the police call your father." I said.

"I ain't a rat."

"Witnesses placed you in the stairwell, Teddy. Maybe they're lying, maybe they just want you to take the fall. Must be a really good friend, if you're gonna take this all on yourself."

"Fuck off and get out," Teddy growled. But there was a note of uncertainty in his voice, and he didn't move like he really wanted us to leave.

"Look, Teddy, we just came to warn you and maybe see if you knew anything. Don't blame us." Cullen said. "But if I knew something, I'd tell. Rat or no rat, I'm not spendin' time in jail for anybody."

"I guess we should go, Cullen." I said and stretched.

Cullen threw me a puzzled look. "Huh?"

"We did what we came to do, right? We warned Teddy. So, I got a lot of homework and—"

"S-sure." Cullen agreed reluctantly.

"Hey, Teddy," I turned back to him. "You belong to the Kronos Elect, right?"

Teddy flashed a sinister smile, "Yeah – wait! How'd you know about that?" The look he gave me was pure evil anger.

"I didn't. Not exactly, but you just told me."

"Fuck you, Fontana!" Teddy glared. Get the fuck away from me."

"So, is it a group at school?" Cullen was wide eyed. "Teddy, you gotta tell me, man. What kind of group is it?"

"Somebody in that group told you to tag the wall, right?" I said.

"I told you, I ain't a rat. I got friends and they depend on me. I ain't rattin' anybody out." Teddy concentrated on whatever was at his feet on the pavement. The pain in his voice was pitiful, and if there were even something tiny that I liked about him I would've felt some compassion.

"I'm just trying to save you trouble. They'll find evidence that it was you who tagged the wall. Fingerprints, fabric, something. That and MacFee telling them about you arguin' with Bidding… that's gonna put it away for the police. You'll take the blame and do the time."

"Not to mention you'll probably get expelled," Cullen said.

"That kinda sorta happens when you go to jail," I said.

"My friends won't let that happen. You don't know about friends like that, do you, Fontana?"

"Your friends trust you so much, they're willing to bet you'll stay silent. So they can get away with murder. And you get a record, a big time record, while they go free. It's not worth it, Teddy. You're eighteen. You'll do time in a real jail, not some juvie facility."

Teddy was silent. But he was thinking so hard, I could almost hear his head working overtime.

"Don't do this to yourself, Teddy." Cullen sounded totally sincere. Knowing him like I do, what he'd said was genuine. He hated seeing anybody in trouble for no good reason.

The silence went on a few beats longer. Then Teddy shifted position. It was a small move, relatively speaking but it was huge for him, I think.

"Squeaky." Teddy said the word so low I thought it was just the sound of a shoe scraping the cement sidewalk. "It was Squeaky," Teddy repeated, louder this time. "He told me what to write and where to write it."

"Who's Squeaky?" I asked.

"Damian. That's what we call him. Squeaky. That's what everybody calls him, even his father." Teddy shut down completely then and didn't say another word.

It didn't matter. I knew who'd killed Bidding and it wasn't Mr. Sullivan. Now all I had to do was convince Detective Bynum to ask the right questions.

* * *

The next morning I got to school extra early. Hardly anyone was in the halls and the building was quiet, which gave me a chance to think. If the detective was already in, I figured he'd probably go to the cafeteria to try and corner people he needed to interview. So, that's where I headed.

Deliverymen filed in ahead of me. One trundled cases of Coke to the counter, another struggled with a load of something labeled "Grade D but edible" and others pushed or pulled cases of snacks and candy.

I stood just inside the doorway, scanning the place and saw the detective talking with one of the cafeteria staff. I didn't want to interrupt so I approached and waited at just the right distance for him to notice me.

Which he did. He shook the staffer's hand and thanked her.

"Mr. Fontana. Got good news for me?" He looked tired and frustrated.

"I don't know if it's good, but it's a lead and I think it's solid."

"Let's move to that corner so we won't be bothered."

I followed him to a table and we both sat down.

"Did you talk to Mr. Wheelan like I told you?"

"Sure did, chief," he said and straightened his back, an amused look in his eyes. "And he told me what he heard. Makes no sense though."

"He told you that Mr. Bidding was yelling about something being leaky, right?"

"Right. Just like you said he would."

"And what about Mrs. MacFee? Did she tell you about how Bidding treated the kids here?"

"She was only too happy to tell me everything. Got herself a promotion, did you know that?"

"Promotion?"

"She's takin' Bidding's place till the end of the year." He gave me a knowing look.

"Sounds like motive, I guess. But I think you might like to hear what I found out. You saw the writing in the stairwell, over the spot where Bidding fell?"

"Yep, somebody told me they thought maybe whoever did it was kind of writing a memorial, 'In the name of Pat' or something."

"That's what I thought at first."

"All rightie then, we're on the same wavelength."

"Not exactly anymore. I've been thinking and now I believe it means something else."

"Okay, shoot," Detective Bynum said.

"The tag was an unfinished sentence. That's what I think. It's how we begin and end prayers while making the sign of the cross. 'In nomine patris' is just the beginning of a longer sentence."

"Let's say I buy what you're selling. How's that help?"

"It's kinda complicated and it means you have to put together a few things before it makes any sense."

"I don't like complicated. Murders are simple. Somebody's got a motive and acts on it. Simple."

"Sure. You're right."

"Why, thank you. Glad to know you approve." His smile was warm.

"I'm not saying you're off about motive and things. But in order to get to the motive—"

"If you think MacFee's got motive. I don't buy it. Or, that other teacher you told me to look into. He's not worth lookin' at either." The detective ran his hand over the tabletop as if smoothing down an invisible cloth, then looked at me. "I know it's not what you wanna hear, but I think we got the person who has the real motive. All I have to do is nail it down."

"I'm telling you, you're wrong. You don't have the right guy, so you can't have the right motive. This is more complicated." I think I really got under his skin by telling him he was wrong. On the other hand, he wasn't walking away.

"I'm willin' to listen," he said with forced patience and leveled his eyes on me. "But not for much longer. Got it?"

"You saw that other piece of graffiti in Bidding's office, right?"

"What? That 'Crony Select' thing?"

"Yeah, except it was 'Kronos Elect' that was written on the door. I gave that a lot of thought, but when I put those words together with the other piece of graffiti, things began to fall into place."

"You lost me."

"Listen, 'In nomine patris' means 'in the name of the father' okay?"

"Still cloudy."

"Things'll get clear in a minute. 'Kronos Elect' is apparently some kind of secret group here at school. I'd never heard of it, but it's real. You know the old Kronos myth?"

"Can't say I do," the detective glanced toward the door, either bored or looking to escape, or both.

"Kronos was the father of the Greek gods. Zeus was his son and he led a revolution against Kronos. Zeus killed his father and set up a new order on Olympus."

"Nice story but what's that got to do with—"

"The other piece of graffiti said 'in the name of the father' but it was unfinished. The next part of the blessing says 'and the son.' They were really saying 'in the name of the son'! What they left unsaid, was what they were really saying. See?"

"No. I don't, young man." He made as if to stand.

"Wait! Don't you get it? The one who killed Bidding made sure we all saw the graffiti. He was tempting us to figure it out."

"And you did?"

"I think so. It's all about fathers and sons. Bidding abused his son Damian. Some of the kids Damian hung with decided to form a group, The Kronos Elect. They identified with one another because they were all abused in some way by their fathers or even father figures."

"And they all killed their fathers?"

"No. Not yet. So far, just Bidding. But I'll bet they have plans to do more."

"So you're sayin' what?"

"That it was Damian who killed his father. Remember what Wheelan told you he heard?"

"Yeah about Bidding yelling that something was leaky, or somethin' like that."

"Bidding was yelling something but it wasn't the word leaky. He was calling out to his son, Damian. Damian's nickname is 'Squeaky.' And he did something to lead his father to the top of those steps where he tripped on the wire and fell to his death."

"The hell you say!" The detective looked at me in disbelief. "That's another good story, son. But—"

"Question Damian and Teddy Nalan, and Jimmy, and whoever else is in the group. I got some of this from Nalan already. His father abuses him and his mom. Same with the other kids in that group. And they had plans. Big plans. Bidding was just the first."

* * *

It didn't exactly feel good to see Detective Bynum leading Damian Bidding out of the building in handcuffs. Damian didn't look particularly sad or frightened, though. As I watched him marched out, I kept telling myself that he must've been stunned by everything that happened. That and he'd taken plenty of abuse from his father. But if I was really honest about it, I'd have to admit that Damian was cold and calculating. He didn't show any remorse, because he had none.

The only thing that felt even halfway good was the fact that I'd helped uncover the truth. That was sweet. And Mr. Sullivan was really grateful, even if he did tell me that he'd be looking for another job as soon as the school year ended. He didn't feel comfortable at St. T's anymore, and I could understand that. In any case, seeing him so happy at being exonerated felt good.

Somehow, I knew we'd remain friends.

Now, all I had to do was figure out what I'd do with my life after graduation.

The DaVinci Theft

If Luke hadn't been a one man charm factory and if the case hadn't included a stolen DaVinci, I might've turned down the deal and missed a great opportunity. A whole lot of great opportunities.

I'd known Luke Guan a little over a week. His housecleaning service, Clean Living, came highly recommended by one of my clients who'd had a big mess to straighten up after a certain event he'd rather no one ever mention. He told me because people tell private eyes lots of things they wouldn't tell their priests.

Knowing that my mother had scheduled one of her occasional forays into Philly's downtown, which always included a visit to my house, or more accurately, an inspection tour, I'd decided to hire professionals to clean. They'd make sure every surface was clear and without a speck for mom to find during her white glove treatment. Every dish washed, every cabinet organized, every floor vacuumed. It'd be spotless and sparkling. That's what Luke promised, and that's what I got.

Two days after Luke's guys had cleaned house, my mother crossed my threshold and I could see in her eyes that she was taken aback by the state of things in the place. It was clean. Not a trace of dust, not a filament out of place, not a streak on any glass surface. She'd been taken by surprise and that was no mean feat. I whispered a silent "Thank You" to Luke.

The visit had been a success, the only fumble coming as she left the house.

With my sister in tow, Mrs. Fontana strode through the dining room and into the parlor, marveling at the sparkle and shine. She'd gazed around slowly as she moved toward the foyer. Her sharp, brown, Italian eyes which never, ever had missed a dirty detail anywhere, homed in again on every possible trouble spot. Looking for something I'd missed, some slip up. Some way to bend my ear with a lecture.

She found nothing to complain about.

Her smile indicated she was both pleased and disappointed. After all, a son who could take care of his home, could clean, cook, even make the bed, that was something to smile about. But missing an opportunity for a good motherly dressing down, that couldn't be. Italian mothers lived for those occasions. I'd purloined that moment. From the look in her eye, I knew she realized I'd discovered the secret to cleanliness and she might never get to lecture me on that point again.

"So?" She'd stared at me accusingly as she waited by the door. "Who is he?"

"Who's who?" I asked innocently, knowing she meant who had *really* cleaned the place. She was too smart to be fooled.

"The man who did this. That's who. Who cleans like this?"

I suppose I figured she'd guess. She's too good at scoping things out, at calling a liar a liar, at finding the culprit in every situation. I get lots of those qualities from her.

"What?"

"No. Who? 'Ats what I said. Who? You having trouble hearing me?" She stared, defying me to lie.

"Who what?" I knew I couldn't make her believe I'd cleaned the place.

"You don't fool me, Marco." She puffed herself up a bit and I noticed my sister looking uncomfortable.

"I don't know… I mean…" I lost all sense and reverted to being a Third grader whenever her withering glare focused on me. "All right, all right," I relented.

"So, who is it?"

"His name's Luke and he owns a house cleaning agency. I should've known I couldn't fool you. But I hadda try."

"This Luke," she paused significantly, then swiped a finger over a bookshelf and peered at the lack of dust. "This man, he's good-looking?"

"He's… yes, he—"

"And he owns his own company? Makes good money?"

"I suppose. I don't know him that well."

"Marry him." She'd said it without a hint of humor. There was nothing light in the way she spoke. It was an order. An order she knew very well I wouldn't obey, one which she would add to the catalog of my offenses when the next opportunity to lecture me came along. And it would.

My sister rolled her eyes in sympathy. She'd had her own clashes with our mother and always silently supported me. Silently, because open rebellion wouldn't be tolerated. Would be crushed and ground to dust.

They left, and I stood looking at my shiny clean house feeling that it had been a pyrrhic victory at best.

A couple of days after that visit, Luke called to ask for an appointment.

* * *

Luke walked into my office, all five foot eight of him, looking serious. His resolute expression did nothing to obscure his classic, handsome face. His manner was equally striking. There was a determination about him which I thought must account, in part, for his business success. Chinese, a little younger than me, and possessed of an elegance and an enviable inner peace, he closed the inner office door and strode over to my desk.

"You did a bang-up job at my place, Luke," I said after we'd shaken hands. He had the smoothest hands for a person who ran a housecleaning business. Even if he was the boss and never touched a scrub brush anymore, a callous or two would be a little more earthy. But Luke wasn't about doing things for show or about deception of any kind, as I was learning.

"Glad to hear it. My crew did a good job, then?"

"It was so clean, my mother said I should marry you. She thought you did the job yourself."

"Marry you?" Luke smiled. "And she knows I'm a man?"

"Not everybody makes a good impression on Mrs. Fontana," I said. "If you can clean a house and keep it that way, she doesn't care if you're a man or a woman."

Luke laughed. "Well, maybe I should meet your mother before she pushes you down the aisle with me."

"That can be arranged." I looked into his eyes and Luke stared back. I got the feeling that he hadn't considered this possibility before and was giving it some thought.

"I'm up for a challenge," Luke said.

"But you didn't come here for a marriage proposal." I smiled. "When you called, you said you had a problem. Something you thought I could help with."

"Not me exactly, Mr. Fontana."

"Marco. Call me Marco."

"Mikey's the one with the problem. He's one of my workers, so his problem is mine," he said.

"One of your crew?"

Luke nodded. "He's been accused of something he didn't do. I'm hoping you can help to clear him."

"Something he did on the job?"

"That's the way it looks," Luke said.

"Bad for business, huh?"

"I'm not worried about my business, Mr. Fon—Marco. The company will weather it, whatever the case."

"Then what's…"

"Mikey's a good kid. He's been working for me quite a while now. I know him, and he'd never do anything illegal."

"What's he accused of?"

"Stealing. From a client's place during a cleaning job." Luke said, shifting in his seat, as if even the thought this could happen made him uncomfortable.

I nodded. Maybe I'm less trusting than other people. Scratch that. I *am* less trusting than other people. It's my Italian nature to be distrustful. When the cleaning crew came into my apartment, I made sure I was there. Nobody gets the opportunity to search every corner of my place without me supervising. Of course, Luke's staff was nice to look at, so it wasn't difficult carving out the time to watch them work.

"What's he accused of stealing and from whom?"

"A piece of art. A sketch by DaVinci. At least that's what the client says it is."

"I suppose he's got documentation and a photo of the missing piece?"

"He's got everything. One of his sons is an art expert and knows everything about everything, so he claims." Luke gave me a look that told me he wasn't too thrilled about the art expert son. "I took a tour of the place before my crew went in. Standard procedure. I look over a place and give a price for the job. At the same time I'm checking out the client. I'm used to dealing with the public, and I can tell pretty quickly if someone's gonna be trouble. This client didn't seem the troublesome kind."

"Did you see the DaVinci?"

"I must've. There was so much art on the walls that I don't remember one piece in particular. The client's not the type to brag about what he has. Which is another reason I liked the guy."

"Where was the sketch?"

"He says it was hanging in the den. A room they don't use much. I was in that room, and the walls were covered with framed pieces maybe more than in the other rooms. I can't remember anything in particular. Not even a DaVinci."

"I guess a sketch might not look like much, even if it was a DaVinci," I said. Sketches I'd seen in museums were a mixed bag. Some were impressive but a lot of them faded into the background.

"DaVinci or not, I don't believe Mikey stole it." Luke turned and gazed out the window which faced Latimer. His calm resolve and determination was like armor.

"Who's the client?" Might as well know who I'd be going up against, if I decided to take the case. I had to take that into account. Even though Luke's belief in his worker was compelling, I didn't know Luke well enough yet to make a decision based on that.

"Client is a Mr. Haldane. Lives with some of his family in a ginormous Skye Tower condo. Getting the Haldane account opened a lot of doors for me. With a relatively new business, accounts like his are better than any advertising I could do." He gestured elegantly with his hands as he spoke.

The name Haldane was familiar to me and one I hadn't thought about in a long time. But the Haldane I remembered lived out on the Main Line and ten years in the past. There were some nice memories associated with the name Haldane.

"I guess the art theft might close some of those doors, if word gets around. You could lose some rich clients."

"That's not important. I can always find clients. Keeping an innocent kid from being prosecuted for something he didn't do – that's what's important." Luke looked me in the eye when he said that.

"You and Mikey close?"

"Mikey's a friend, a good one. He's thrown himself into his work, and he helps me out when things get tough." Luke brushed a hand through his thick black hair. "Thing is Mikey's got no one else. No family and few friends. He doesn't know where else to turn, and he's kind of panicked. I don't want to see him railroaded." Luke's eyes were bright with indignation. Didn't sound to me like he was trying to blow smoke. That's the kind of thing I can tell a mile off.

"Why do you think Mikey's being railroaded?"

"I know Mikey. He's not the kind of person who'd do this." Luke paused. "I've got a the feeling he's being set up. Somebody's framing Mikey but I can't figure out why."

"You're gonna need more than feelings, Luke. The police aren't gonna take anybody's feelings into account. If there's evidence, circumstantial or not, they'll run with it."

"So, Mikey's as good as arrested, right?"

"Has Haldane pressed charges?"

"Not yet. For a guy who owns half the property from here to Cape May and a few major companies thrown into the mix, Haldane seems pretty fair minded. He says he doesn't want to see an injustice done." Luke smiled weakly.

"Sounds good. At least he's not chompin' at the bit to get his insurance claim in. What else did he say?"

"He'll wait a little while to see if we can clear Mikey. At some point, though, he'll call in the police. What he wants more than anything is to have the piece returned."

"All right, tell me everything you know." I was falling for more than the case, and I knew I had to be careful.

"Then, you'll take the case?" Luke asked, his voice filled with more energy. It was easy to see he cared about something other than his financial situation. I liked that.

"I'm not promising anything."

"I can pay your fee, it that makes a difference. You don't have to worry about the money." He brandished a checkbook. Luke was good-looking and his willingness to pay to keep a kid from being railroaded was an appealing quality.

"I'll need all the details to make a decision. Whatever you can tell me."

"I've had the Haldane account a few months. Once we got the account, I put Chip in charge of the Haldane place. He can tell you more about the whole thing."

"Chip's the guy who wears a red bandanna on his head? He was at my place, am I right? You trust him?"

"Good memory. That's him. Chip's been with me almost since the company started. I was still doing jobs myself when I hired Chip and took him along with me on bigger jobs. I trust him implicitly, and he's never let me down." Luke paused and resettled himself again. "Chip took a crew of three on the Haldane job. Took them the better part of a day to finish the first time. Getting used to the place, finding out what Haldane wanted and didn't want. Takes a couple of visits to establish a routine."

"That makes sense," I said. Then I stood. "Need something to drink? I've got coffee and water and, uh, that's about it." I stood to pour myself some coffee. "How about it? I need coffee."

"No. I'm already edgy enough. Thanks."

I needed the edge. Caffeine and I were old friends. I poured a cup and sat back down.

"So, how long, on average, do they spend at Haldane's place?"

"The Haldane job usually lasts three hours or more. It's a huge place. Lots of bathrooms, lots of dustcatchers. But Chip's good and Haldane was happy."

"And Mikey was part of the crew."

"Not at first," he said resettling himself in his seat. "Chip also trains my new hires. I couldn't let him stay on the Haldane place forever. Once things had become routine, I put one of the others in charge and added Mikey to the team."

"How long ago was that?"

"Two, two and a half months."

"When did the theft take place?"

"Haldane discovered the sketch missing less than a week ago. Less than a day after the cleaning crew left. He claims it was there before they arrived."

"You believe him?"

"I guess I have to. There's no reason not to."

"No. You don't have to. You hardly know the guy. He could be playing insurance fraud for fun and profit."

"Didn't seem like that type, y'know? He's got a bank account bigger than some small countries."

"What about his kids?"

"They've all got trust funds. None of them needs money."

"But were any of them at home when Mikey and the crew were there?"

"Good question." Luke placed a hand to his chin as if he were thinking. "I don't recall Mikey saying anything. Can't remember if I even asked."

"What evidence do they have that Mikey stole the sketch."

"One big thing. Video from their security system. They've got cameras covering halls and entrances. They showed me the video. You can see Mikey going into the Den alone and coming out again after a while. He's got his backpack with him. That's a violation of our policy. The bag is big enough to conceal something like the sketch."

"That's all? No odd shaped lumps in that backpack? No video of him stuffing the frame into his bag? Just him goin' in and comin' out?"

"Right, just him going in and out of the room. Nothing else." Luke had an expression that said he hadn't considered the video not being quite as damning as he'd thought.

"They have anything else?"

"I don't know. That's all the son would let Haldane tell me. The son wants the police in on this."

"I think it's time I talked to Haldane and your workers."

"Then you'll take the case?"

"Don't ask me why, but yeah…" I trailed off. I didn't exactly know what my motivation was. There was money. That's usually enough of a starter for me. There were other considerations. Luke was hot but it was more than that. I didn't want to let him down and watch those bright eyes of his turn sad and disappointed. And then there was the issue of the Haldanes. The name Haldane brought some memories to the surface that had been submerged for a good long time. A tall, good-looking blond came along with those memories. And a high school crush I had on that blond. Cullen Haldane lived on the Main Line in the family mansion. This couldn't be his family but I didn't want to pass up the chance to find out for certain. Funny things memories. They get you to do something stupid now and then.

It wasn't like I risked a lot by taking this case. Luke would be paying for whatever I turned up, good or bad. Thing is I believed him. I didn't think Luke was lying. I could tell he wasn't. Of course, all that could mean was that he believed what Mikey had told him.

It'd be an adventure, I convinced myself. I needed something like that.

* * *

Mikey was waiting for me when I got to Luke's offices in one of the Penn Center buildings on Market Street. The employee break room was small with a window that faced West toward Drexel and Penn. A long way to look for a kid with not much education and even less luck. Mikey sat at a long narrow table running down the center of the room. A coffeemaker chugged and wheezed on a cart next to a small refrigerator.

"Mikey?" I said as I stepped toward him.

"Mr. F-Fontana?" Mikey stood up and extended a hand. Short and dark-haired, his sad eyes were a deep brown, flecked with gold. A tentative smile flickered across his swarthy face and disappeared even more quickly. His rough-hewn handsome features couldn't manage a smile for very long.

He was young. Maybe it was the worry creasing his forehead that made him appear older. His hard knock life had undoubtedly also contributed to his mature demeanor.

"Nice to meet you," I said and took a seat at the table across from him.

"I didn't do it, Mr. Fontana. I didn't." He looked at me with such pleading and his voice was strained. I noticed the circles under his eyes now and the tired slump of his shoulders.

"That's what we're going to try and prove, Mikey. I'll need your help."

"Anything," he said. He straightened up in his seat. "I'll give you whatever help you need. I didn't steal anything."

"I've done my homework, Mikey. You've got a sealed record."

"Juvie offenses. I did some things when I was younger…" his voice trailed off as he peered at the surface of the table. His shoulders slumped again. "But that don't mean I did this. Right?"

"Of course not, but it's better if I know more about your background. Just in case. What's in that sealed record?"

"Kid shi—stuff. You know."

"No, but you're gonna tell me."

"I was arrested a few times when I was a kid. Mostly small stuff." He paused and took a deep breath. "I ran the streets like a lot of kids. My family didn't give a shit. Nobody came looking for me when I didn't come home. I hung out with other kids and sometimes we got into trouble."

"Like…"

"Misdemeanors mostly. Once I got caught with some weed. There was one charge of petty theft and a couple'a shoplifting charges. But I only took small stuff. Nothing big. Sometimes it was stuff I needed to stay alive on the street." He kept his head down as he spoke.

"That's it?"

"I never stole anything… big. I never hurt anybody. Not like…" He stopped in midsentence.

"Not like who?" I watched him but he didn't raise his head.

"R-Rick and Cass." His voice was a whisper. "They… they hurt people. They forced me to steal a couple things. Nickel and dime stuff just to prove myself. Show them I could be trusted to do what they asked."

"How long did you know these guys?"

"Couple'a years. You gotta understand, I was totally livin' on the streets then. My family threw me out because I… I'm gay, y'know?"

"This Rick and Cass, they took you in?"

"No. Nothin' like that. They gave me odd jobs. First it was just taking care of their place. Cleanin' up and fixin' shit."

"And then…"

"Then they wanted me to run errands. Take packages to people they knew."

"No idea what was in the packages?"

"I was homeless but I wasn't dumb. Y'know? I had an idea what they were doin' but they gave me clothes and food and sometimes they found me a safe place to sleep. I wasn't gonna say no when they asked me to do them a favor."

"So you were a mule?"

"Yeah. But it wasn't drugs they had me carrying. They fenced stolen stuff."

"Fences?" This didn't sound good. Innocent as he might look, Mikey had exactly the sort of underworld connections he'd need for dealing with stolen art. "You ever see what kinds of stuff they handled?"

"They never told me anything except where to take the packages. Nothing else. Like you said, I was just a mule. But the…" his voice became less than a whisper.

"What's that? Mikey?"

"But they wanted me to do a bigger job for them. Said they'd cut me in for a lotta cash. They said I needed to prove myself."

"Why'd they all of a sudden want you to steal something major for them?"

"I don't know. That's the truth. Maybe somethin' else fell through. I don't know. But I never did. Do that job, I mean."

"You just refused? How'd they take that?"

"I would'a refused but I didn't have to."

"How's that?"

"I was arrested for shopliftin' and put in the Youth Study Center. I was in there a while. A long while. Things happened to me in that place, things

I still have nightmares about. When I got out, I decided I needed to make some changes."

I'd heard about overnight conversions before, but being me, I had a hard time believing them. One thing helped me think Mikey might be telling the truth. Or something close to the truth. And that's the fact that he spent time at the Youth Study Center. The Center's kind of a cross between a prison for kids and a colony of Hell on Earth. I'm looking forward to the day they tear it down.

"You still have contact with Rick and Cass?"

"N-no… not really."

"What's that supposed to mean? Listen, Mikey, you've gotta be straight with me. You're lookin' at felony charges here. Grand theft. Who knows what else the law will think up to tag you with? So, no lies. Not even half lies. Or I'm outta here."

Mikey stared at me, his big brown innocent eyes, glassy. He was like a puppy. Trouble is he probably knew it. He might be innocent of art theft, but he wasn't all that innocent otherwise. Looked to me like he knew how to wrap a guy around his little finger and do whatever he wanted with him.

"*They* called *me*. I don't know how they found me but they did. I told them not to call anymore. That I had a job and I didn't need anything else. They called a couple more times before they stopped."

"Never lie to me, Mikey. You're not good at it. These people call you again, I wanna know about it. Hear?"

"Sur—yes. I hear you."

"Tell me about why you went into the den at the Haldane place. You're on video goin' in and comin' out. All by yourself. With your backpack. Time enough to steal the sketch, and you had a bag big enough to hide it."

"But I didn't steal—"

"What were you doing in the den? Admiring the view?"

"I—my blood sugar was low. I hadda check it and I hadda eat something or I'd collapse. So, I ate one'a those special bars. I hadda wait until I felt better before I walked out."

"And you couldn't do this in front of the others?"

"Naw, I couldn't. I…" he let his voice trail off.

"You're diabetic. That's nothing to be ashamed about."

"Makes me weak. Everybody else holds their own. I gotta take shots, check my blood, worry about passin' out. Like some old fart who can't take care of himself." His voice was very low, filled with self-recrimination.

"So you're not like everybody else? You think your friends care about that?" I waited for a response. There was none. "You got proof of your condition?"

"Yeah," he murmured. "And I cleaned up after myself in that room. No wrappers. No nothing."

"Anything else? Tell me now. If this goes to the police, they'll search your place and they'll search you like you've never been searched before. So, you got anything else to tell me, now's the time."

Mikey slowly reached into his pocket and reluctantly placed a folded piece of paper on the table between us.

"What's this?" I reached for the paper.

"I f-found it…" He hesitated. "I-in… in my backpack when I got home."

I slid the paper over and gently unfolded it. It seemed to be the provenance of the sketch. Who'd had it, how much they'd sold it for, and on and on. It started sometime in the Eighteenth Century and ended with the sale to Haldane some years ago. The paper looked old. I was certain they had a copy in their files. I'd never heard about anyone doing something like this. But it made sense to keep a copy of the provenance with the work itself.

"How'd you get this?"

"I told you, it was in my backpack. I noticed it when I got home." He looked at me pleading with his eyes for me to believe him. "I don't always look in my bag when I get home, but I needed the test kit. And when I put my hand in, this was on top."

"You leave your bag anywhere after you tested your blood?"

"Sure, I left it with all the other stuff the guys bring in. They all got backpacks, bags, equipment."

"Nobody was keepin' an eye on the stuff?"

"Who's gonna steal from us in a place like that?"

Good point, I thought.

"You've got a lot goin' against you, Mikey. I'll be honest."

"I didn't do it, Mr. Fontana. That's all I can tell you, 'cause it's the truth."

He hung his head down and his shoulders slumped even more. This was a kid in despair and I wasn't going to add to that. If I could help him I would.

Did I believe him? The little jury I carried around with me was still out on that. But I believed Luke. Even though I'd only known Luke a little while, I felt I might be able to trust him. Mikey, not so much. Not on everything and not yet. Maybe he'd grow on me.

I squeezed his shoulder. He felt small and bony. The kid had had it tough and even if I couldn't trust him completely, he deserved to be treated fairly.

"You…" he started then hesitated. "You gonna take the case? Luke said he heard you were good."

"Did he?"

Mikey nodded warily.

"I'll take the case. But one lie and you'll have to get yourself out of this mess on your own."

* * *

"What'd I tell you? He's innocent, right?" Luke said as I entered his office after interviewing Mikey.

"Let's say I'm not convinced he did it, but it's a long way from your opinion and mine to clearing Mikey of the crime. Right now, all I've got is your opinion and Mikey's claims of innocence."

"Can I help? I can't say I've done any detective work. But cleaning houses, you learn a lot about people and you see things you probably aren't supposed to."

"Good point. Maybe you *can* help. Who else was on the crew with Mikey?"

"You're thinking one of my other guys might be responsible?" Luke paused. "I suppose everybody's a suspect."

"Somebody did this. If it wasn't Mikey, it was somebody else. Your crew has got to be on my list." I swiped a hand through my hair. "I'm not saying any of your guys did this. But, they were there, maybe they saw something. Maybe one of them noticed something and doesn't realize it."

"That's true. They're good workers and they've got sharp eyes. I don't hire just anybody. They're all bonded."

"Then you knew about Mikey's record when you hired him? The insurance company didn't balk?"

"It's a sealed juvie record. Sure, I knew about it. In fact, he told me about it himself. I thought that was pretty brave. But the record was sealed. It's not public. He was just a kid when all that happened."

"Still, it doesn't make him look good. Any prosecutor will squeeze blood outta that stone."

"Prosecutor?" Luke looked genuinely shocked.

"If it gets that far. But we're not gonna let that happen." I smiled. "Get me the files for the other guys on the crew with Mikey. And if you can set up interviews for me here at your office, that'd be great."

"You got it." He scribbled something on a pad in front of him, then looked up at me, his eyes gleaming. "What's next?"

"Now I go back to my office and set up a meeting with Mr. Haldane."

"You need me to come along? Smooth the way?"

"Probably better if I do this myself, Luke."

* * *

It was a good walk from Luke's building on Market, around City Hall and down to Twelfth Street. From there it was a straight shot to my office on Latimer. The walk gave me time to think about my next steps. More than anything about the case, I was puzzled over why anyone might want to frame Mikey. He was either a convenient pigeon, or there was more to his past than he was letting on.

As decrepit as the old, three-story walk-up was, I was happy to see the building. A quiet structure on a quiet street, I felt blissfully alone as I took the stairs. I entered my office and walked through the darkened reception area. I was still short one secretary, the empty desk forcing me to think about Josh and how I'd been unable to stop any of what'd happened. Which led me to thinking about Galen and if he was all right, wherever it was he'd disappeared to. The memories were all still raw and painful. There was nothing I could do for Josh, but someday I'd find Galen. I had to.

A new secretary would keep some of those memories at bay and bring some life back to the office. Not that I'd ever forget Josh or Galen, but I had to put everything in perspective, if I expected to move on. Maybe getting a new office wasn't such a bad idea, either. To do that, I'd need more money.

For now, I had to help Mikey and Luke. That was enough for the moment.

I made a note to call another private investigator who I knew had been in on a number of cases involving stolen art. He wasn't a big-time expert but he'd give me a quick lesson on the glorious world of art theft. A little older than me, he'd been a P.I. for a lot longer and talking with him was always an education.

First, though, I had to meet Haldane and see the crime scene. A quick call got me an appointment later in the afternoon, which meant I could have lunch and pull together some questions.

After locking up, I took the stairs to the street and walked to More Than Just Ice Cream. The restaurant was one of my favorite places for a calming break in the day. Even when it was crammed with people, you could still hear yourself think. The giant wall of windows and potted plants often made it seem like you were sitting in a peaceful solarium. The scenery wasn't bad either, cute waiters and lots of guys walking back and forth outside.

Taking a table at the back, I sat and pored over the menu, which I'd just about memorized long before. Reviewing the familiar items was just another way of letting my subconscious do some thinking about the case while I did other things.

While reading the menu, I sensed someone standing at the table staring down at me. I looked up and saw Luis Cartagena, all smiles, looking at me expectantly.

"I was walkin' by and saw you," he said, pulling out the chair to sit across from me. "Did you give it some thought?"

"Luis, hey," I said and nodded, glad for the interruption. "Thought? About what?"

"The dancers, man, you know." His dark eyes were a liquid brown and bright. He reached out a stubby hand for the menu. "You order yet?"

"Not yet. Staying for lunch?"

"If you're gonna talk dancers with me, I'll stay." He rustled the menu. "Anything good here?"

"Pretty much everything."

"I heard about Mikey," Luis said nonchalantly, as if the whole thing had been on the morning news.

"How'd you hear? No one knows about this." There's not much that shocks me, but the speed of the grapevine, especially in the gayborhood, can be staggering.

"Promise that you're gonna talk with me about startin' that group, and I'll tell you what I know."

"Deal." I said. Luis had been badgering me about starting a male strip troupe. Said he had all kinds of things lined up. He claimed having a group of male dancers would make me a lot of money. That'd gotten my attention. Who can't use more money? Of course, I had to consider whether or not I was ready to add this to my already loaded plate. My bank account said yes. "I promise, Luis. It's been on my mind, anyway. Soon as this case is in the bag, we'll talk."

"I know you don't break promises, Marco. That's what they say. But you break this promise, and I promise I'll be sittin' in your office butt naked every day until we *do* talk."

I smiled. Seeing portly little Luis sitting naked on my couch was not something I'd need first thing in the morning.

"We'll talk. No need to take off your clothes," I said.

"I thought you was gonna jump at the chance to see me naked."

"So whaddayou know about Mikey and the case?"

"My cousin Ramon, he works for the cleaning agency with Mikey. They're good friends, and they was on that job together. Ramon says Mikey wouldn't steal nothin' but that Mikey was actin' all strange from the first time they got the job at that condo." He nodded brusquely as if he'd just given me the solution to everything. "Big place that apartment, from what I hear. Lotta stuff. Rich people…" He went back to reading the menu.

Maybe Ramon would be more forthcoming.

* * *

Skye Towers was a whole lotta building. Fifty-five stories, brilliant design, and seated right in the middle of Center City, which brought a lot of rich hoo-hahs to live in Philly. Some from the burbs and some from New York who decided that Philly's cost of living was low enough for them to commute. The ten year property tax abatement didn't hurt either. The rich get richer.

Haldane's apartment was split between the fiftieth and fifty-first floors. My homework told me there weren't too many apartments like that in the building and those few were especially large.

The front desk had been notified, maybe warned was more like it, that I'd be arriving. I stepped into the glittering lobby, filled with brass and creamy-colored granite, and oozing the words class and money. The windows lining the place let in plenty of light, almost as if you hadn't stepped indoors. A tall tiered fountain in the middle of the lobby spilled water into its base, filling the air with soothing sounds.

I ambled over to the front desk where two people sat behind the counter and three or four security guards paced back and forth near the banks of elevators. The desk staff looked me over like I was an errand boy who needed watchful eyes on him. I told them I was expected, gave them my name, and, after checking their list, they let me through.

A plush but understated wood paneled elevator drew me up to the fiftieth floor more quickly than I expected. Before I knew it, the doors slid open and I was in a bright hall, lined with sleek décor. There were only three apartments on the floor and a sign indicated that 50A was to the left.

At the end of a long hall, I came to a simple, unassuming beige door. No name. Just the number 50A. Knocking, I realized it was a metal, security door. In case the squad of guards at the desk failed to stop an intruder.

I heard tiny feet scurrying inside and a short, blonde, older woman opened the door. Her blue, flower print dress was partly covered by a large white apron.

"Mr. Fontana." She said it knowing full well I was expected and swung the door open more widely. "Mr. Haldane is waiting for you."

"Thank you, " I said as I stepped into the wide, modern oval-shaped foyer. A staircase led to the second level on the fifty-first floor, and there were doorways into other rooms or halls off the foyer. Something familiar about the furniture dotting the area dredged up feelings from the past that momentarily disoriented me.

"Follow me," she said and quickly turned to lead me down a hall.

The condo was elegant and spotless. My mother would be thrilled. American antiques studded the place, contrasting nicely with the slick modernity of the condo's architectural design. Lots of paintings graced the walls as Luke had described. Again, some of the furnishings we passed looked vaguely familiar. I was either experiencing déjà vu or this was the Haldane family I'd known and visited on the Main Line when I was in high school.

When I was shown into the living room, I saw Haldane standing in the middle of the enormous space. It was the same man I'd known years before. Father of my best friend in high school. Rich property baron. Older now, he stood soldier straight and in control. Tall, tanned, and silver-haired, Haldane held out his hand.

"Mr. Fontana?" He looked into my eyes as if remembering something. "My son Cullen's best friend in high school? The same Marco Fontana my son talked nonstop about back then? You're – you're all grown now."

I took his hand and we shook. His grip was strong, but instead of the macho tug of war some men engage in, there was friendliness and warmth in his handshake.

"One and the same. I couldn't have changed all that much in nine or ten years."

"You've changed enough for me to have to think twice. Same piercing eyes, though. And your smile's still the same. Cullen will kill me for not telling him to be here. But then, I wasn't sure you'd be – well – you!" He laughed, and it was the same throaty sound I remembered.

"How is Cullen? I'd love to see him." And that was no lie. I'd had a serious crush on him in high school. Unrequited love is a bitch. Even when the object of your affection is straight. Still, seeing him again would be fun. Maybe the years had lost him some hair and gained him some weight, and I'd be over him once and for all.

"Cullen's doing well, for the most part. I'm sure he'll be here at some point. Especially after I let him know it's you who's on this case."

“Speaking about the case, sir,” I said. “Luke is grateful that you’re giving me the chance to see what actually happened.”

“Please, not so formal,” Haldane said. “As for the case, I feel compelled to make sure things go right for that boy – what’s his name? Michael?”

“Mikey.”

“Yes, Mikey. I understand he’s had a hard life. I don’t want to make things more difficult for him. So I want to be certain he’s guilty before I call in the authorities. Plenty of time for that. I’m afraid they pounded the idea of social justice into me at St. T’s and I haven’t forgotten. I expect it’s the same for you. Am I right?”

“St. T’s won’t let you out the door unless you’ve learned at least that much. It hasn’t changed since you were a student.”

“That’s what Cullen always says,” Haldane walked over to a corner of the living room with three stuffed chairs and a loveseat placed cozily together. The soft pastel colors of the chairs made them appear to float over the surface of the hardwood floor. He indicated I should sit, then took one of the chairs for himself

“Great view you have.” From fifty floors up you could see across the Schuylkill River into New Jersey and the misty horizon beyond. The cityscape under the cloudless blue sky was stunning.

“I should hope so from this height. Everything is laid out at your feet. Sometimes it scares me, though.” Haldane looked uncomfortable, almost haunted.

“Tell me about the DaVinci.”

That seemed to rouse him. “Well, Marco, between you and me, there are some that say it isn’t really a DaVinci. Candidly, I don’t care. The sketch means more to me than whether or not DaVinci touched it.”

“Why is that?”

“The sketch has been authenticated to a point. The provenance is all in order, at least as far as it goes. We’ve got all that documentation. It’s from DaVinci’s era and if it isn’t his, it’s certainly from a follower or student of his, but— ”

“But nothing.” Someone approached from behind us and I turned to see who it was. “It’s a DaVinci and it’s valuable. Very valuable. Don’t let Tom or anyone else tell you otherwise.”

"Seamus, this is Marco Fontana. You've heard your brother talk about him, haven't you?"

Seamus was a darker version of Cullen but with glasses. Like Cullen, he was tall and athletic, but he lacked a certain spark that his brother had plenty of. Seamus had dark hair, while I remembered Cullen's being a lighter blond color. It was easy to see they were brothers, even if they were several years apart in age. I could see Cullen in that face.

"Mr. Fontana," Seamus extended a hand and we shook.

"I don't think we ever met. But Cullen told me plenty when we were in high school."

"I remember him mentioning you."

"Seamus is an art history professor, now. Can you believe it? And he's a consultant on art restoration projects here and in Europe."

"Maybe you'll believe me when I say the sketch is a DaVinci, I know what I'm talking about." He pulled out a glossy photograph and handed it to me. "That's a picture. Doesn't do it justice but it'll give you an idea. I've printed the actual dimensions on the back."

I studied the photograph for a few minutes. The sketch had been done in sepia- toned ink or whatever they used for sketching five hundred years ago. It all appeared yellowed, but the drawing was distinct and clear. Three horse heads. One a ghostly sketch with traces of slightly different poses one atop the other, as if the artist had changed his mind. A second horse, full on from the front, broad muscular chest, proud head with its mane tossing behind. The third was just the beginnings of a drawing not really completed. Toward the bottom of the sketch, three small horses complete with riders cavorted from left to right. Mere outlines, they were not at all complete but the artist's skill in representing the figures with a few simple lines was so great, they didn't need to be complete to give you the feeling of horses and riders, prancing off the page.

"Impressive," I said. "Do you have a copy for me?"

"Keep it," he said and tapped the picture with a long delicate finger. "So, what do you think? That sketch could be worth – who knows? The sky's the limit."

"I think it's a beauty of a sketch, but it doesn't matter if it's a DaVinci or if it was done by one of his students. It's stolen goods and your father hired me to find out who stole it."

"But if it's worth—"

"Seamus, it doesn't matter what it's worth. I'm not placing it on the auction block. I'm more interested in getting a possibly innocent boy off the hook for this theft."

Seamus was silent.

"Your father hired me to get to the truth of the matter. A lot depends on that."

"He's right, Seamus," Haldane said. "Anyway, if we don't find the real thief, we may never find the sketch. Then it won't matter if it's a real DaVinci or what it's worth. It'll be gone. Just another piece of stolen art."

"Matters to the insurance company," Seamus mumbled. I couldn't decide whether he was being petulant or protective of his father's interests.

"That sketch represents something more than insurance money," Haldane said and stared out at the city in silence for a moment. "I bought that for your mother a long time ago, when we'd been married only a few years. Something about it touched her. I never knew exactly what, but she would stare at it for hours."

"How—" I started.

"She passed away some years ago," he said quickly, tonelessly, as if it hurt to say more. "Now, when I look at that sketch – when I can make myself look at it – I think of her. I still wonder what mysteries she saw in it. Sometimes I sit in the den and it's as if she's sitting there, too, staring at the sketch."

"My mother loved history," Seamus took off his glasses and tumbled them in his hands as he spoke. He moved in place, edgy and impatient. "The Renaissance and art of that period were her favorites. The DaVinci sketch was more than just a drawing for her. It was like a doorway into another world. We've got to report this to the police, dad. We wait too long and it'll be gone for good"

"I'll make the police report when Marco is finished. Let's give him a chance, at least."

I nodded my thanks to him and turned to look at Seamus. Dark and brooding, he wouldn't meet my eyes.

"Why don't you sit in with us, Seamus? I can use all the information I can get."

He finally looked at me. Anger, hurt, resentment all flashed across his face. The resemblance to his brother faded more and more as he talked and moved. Cullen, at least the Cullen I remembered, was far more adept at handling people and problems. His movements were also more graceful. Or they had been back in school. I shook off thoughts of Cullen and what I'd hoped for when I was a teenager. That was all in the past.

Seamus moved with reluctance and sat inelegantly on the loveseat.

"Tell me what you remember about the day the piece was found missing." I addressed my remark to Haldane.

"Truthfully, I don't remember much. It was a day like any other. Luke's crew arrived in the morning as they always do and Helen, that's our housekeeper and cook, let them in. I was here, probably in my office upstairs."

"Anything out of the ordinary about that day?"

"You mean other than having a piece of art worth millions being stolen from under our noses by some kid?" Seamus said.

"Seamus!" Haldane snapped.

I noticed Seamus wince. He glanced at the floor, then stole a look at me.

"No, Marco, there wasn't anything different about that day." Haldane blushed. "Other than the theft, of course."

"So you don't remember seeing anyone who didn't belong here? Or, seeing anything that didn't make sense?"

Out of the corner of my eye, I saw Seamus squirming, ready with a sharp answer. To his credit he restrained himself and stared at his father.

"I don't really know Luke's crew. I don't pay attention…" Haldane stopped, embarrassed. "I suppose that sounds callous or—"

"No. Sounds like you're a busy man who doesn't concern himself with things he doesn't have to."

Haldane gave a curt nod. "Nevertheless, I should have been paying some attention. If I had, maybe this wouldn't have happened."

"How long was it before you discovered the sketch missing"

"A couple of days," Seamus said. "Dad doesn't use the den much. Nobody does. I went in there a day or so after they'd cleaned the place. I didn't notice it at first. Notice it missing, I mean. But I was reading something and looked up to where the sketch was supposed to be and it was gone."

"Then…?"

"Then I found dad and asked him if he was aware the sketch was not on the wall. I thought maybe he'd taken it down for some reason."

"That's how it happened, Marco," Haldane said. "We both went back to the den and had a look around."

"It was just gone." Seamus leaned on an arm of the loveseat and stared at me. When I looked into his eyes, he turned away.

"What did you do next?" I asked.

"I didn't know what to do," Haldane said. "Nothing like this has ever happened before. I couldn't exactly believe that someone had stolen the piece."

"I told him to call the police, but he refused—"

"Just until we were sure that something had actually happened." Haldane said, defending his action.

"Is that when you decided to look at the security video?"

"We tried to figure out who'd been in the apartment over the past few days. Other than family and Helen, only the cleaning crew had been here. That's when I thought to review the video for that day."

"Makes sense. Of course, since none of you use the room much, it could have happened some time before or after the crew was here."

"The recorder doesn't keep material too long. Maybe a few days. I'm not entirely sure," Haldane chipped in. "We don't have someone watching twenty-four hours a day, and we don't want a system that needs a lot of attention. Having the system was necessary to placate the insurance companies, since there's so much art in this place."

"So, what you're saying is that there may be no record of the time before Mikey was in the den. I'm guessing that after you spotted Mikey, you didn't look any further at the video?"

Seamus sat, one leg bouncing up and down nervously. "Y-yes. I guess that's true. We didn't think we needed to."

"You see, Seamus. Marco's already pointed out something neither of us considered."

I could also point out that Haldane didn't sound all that confident in his son's judgment. But I kept my mouth shut.

"All right," Seamus admitted. "But without anything else to go on, that kid, Mikey, seems like the culprit."

"Any chance I could borrow the recording device and hard drive from the security system?"

"Why would you want that?" Seamus snapped.

"Just to satisfy my curiosity. Maybe there's something on disk that didn't get wiped. We all know that nothing ever gets completely erased from drives."

"Of course," Haldane said. "Seamus, can you handle disconnecting the box?"

"I think so. I'm not at all happy about doing, this but I'll get it for you." Seamus stood and walked out of the room.

"He's a good man, Marco. Still thinks he has to protect my interests." Haldane laughed but not so heartily this time. "He gets around, though and knows his stuff. But I'm afraid that he's a bit emotional about the DaVinci sketch."

"Has anyone ever expressed interest in buying it from you?"

"Many times. I always turn them down. As I said, the sketch is special. Wrapped up in memories of my wife. I could never sell it. But offers come in frequently."

"You said that it had been authenticated by others but that there are still open questions about it?"

"Yes, we've had it tested and examined more times than I wanted. Nothing is ever conclusive. That suits me. I don't care who produced it. I just care that Chloe loved it. It's as if her spirit still lives in it. That's why I want it back. Not for the money, not because anyone in particular made that piece."

"I understand, sir."

Haldane shook his head and stared out the window.

"Who's Tom?"

"Pardon me?" Haldane said still distracted, dreamily staring at the city below.

"Seamus mentioned someone named Tom."

"Oh, Tom. Yes. Tom is my daughter's fiancé. She has Seamus to thank for him."

"How so?"

"Tom works at Cleary & Daley, the auction house. You've heard of them?"

"Who hasn't. Didn't they sell that Cezanne recently for more than a million?"

"That's the house. Tom works there as a restorer and a dealer. Seamus got to know Tom and brought him around. He and Megan fell in love soon after."

"What's he think about the DaVinci?"

"He's not convinced it's the real thing. In fact, he's adamant that it isn't. Of course, he and Seamus never get along on these kinds of things."

"Strange they should become friends, then."

"Well, who doesn't love a good argument? They may be at loggerheads most of the time, but it keeps them both on their toes. Each of them having to prove his point."

"What did Tom have to say about the DaVinci?"

"Only that it isn't really a DaVinci. It's a period piece, he says that's certain. But he points to several things, tiny details, that I can't make out even with my glasses and a magnifying glass."

"What's the significance of the elements he brought to your attention?"

"He says those details prove it's not a DaVinci, that they are not techniques DaVinci used. Seamus, of course, disagrees."

"So Tom feels it's worthless?"

"Not at all. He says it's still worth a great deal of money, but since it can't definitively be proven to be a DaVinci, it's worth drastically less than it would be otherwise."

"Well, I've taken up enough of your time, Mr. Haldane." I stood and put my notebook away. "I'll probably need to bother you again, if that's all right?"

"You've got my full cooperation, Marco." Haldane said as he stood to see me out. "But hold on a second while I see what's keeping Seamus. He should have had that recorder disconnected by now."

Haldane left, walking in that odd military fashion I remembered. I remained standing in the wide expanse of the living room. All muted yellows and oranges gave it a pleasant Tuscan feel. The homey scent of bread baking wafted into the room and I guessed that Helen was getting a jump on dinner.

Voices in the hall brought my attention back to where I was and I turned to see a woman and a man enter together, arguing quietly. They only stopped when the woman noticed me standing there.

"Who're you?" she asked with a hauteur not even her father pretended to.

I extended a hand to her. "Marco Fontana."

"Should I know you? Are you here about the leak in the upstairs bedroom? I called over a week ago but—"

"Your father hired me to investigate the stolen DaVinci," I said.

At that, she blinked a few times then frowned.

"I'm Tom," said her companion. "And this is Megan."

Tom and I shook hands while Megan continued to stare at me.

"I don't believe he actually went through with this. We know who stole the thing. What's he hope to gain?" Megan finally found her voice again.

"I guess he's looking for justice," I said. "From what I remember about him, your father's a fair man. Doesn't jump into things before he checks them out. And he's not the kind who calls in the cops before he's sure."

"Well, *I'm* sure…" Megan mumbled.

"You know Mr. Haldane?" Tom asked.

"I went to school with Cullen, and I've met Mr. Haldane a few times. I know enough about him to respect him."

"You went to school with Cullen?" Megan asked. "High school? St. T's? You went there?" She sounded surprised that the hired help actually attended a private school. One more illusion shattered.

"Class of '96, same as Cullen."

"So can we help you with anything? Have you spoken to Mr. Haldane yet?" Tom was either being hospitable or wanted to get me out of his way and get on with his day.

"We've just finished, but now that the two of you are here, I have a few questions."

"I've got a lot to do this afternoon," Megan said but didn't make a move to leave.

"We're pretty busy. Wedding plans, you know?" Tom winked at me and I smiled.

"Won't take a minute," I said. "Maybe we can sit over there." I pointed to where I'd just been with Haldane.

Tom took Megan's arm and they reluctantly moved to the loveseat. I followed them and sat back in the soft green chair again.

"I don't know why he's making a fuss about that worthless piece of paper," Megan fumed.

"It's not worth what your brother thinks, Meg. But it's not exactly worthless, either."

"How much would you say it'd go for at auction?"

"At auction, it's always hard to say, but without proof that it's a DaVinci, it'd be worth thousands. Just how many thousands is up to the buyers and collectors. Some collectors just have to have these things. And they'll pay whatever it takes."

"You have some experience, I was told."

"Sure do." He smiled that smile again. I was sure he was good at his job. "I work for a big auction house. I've learned that it's not always the piece of art in itself that fetches a big price. Sometimes there are collectors who want everything and anything to do with the area they collect in. I think they're unbalanced. But I guess any obsessive collector isn't exactly totally sane. They'd pay almost anything to have what they want. Assuming they have the money to throw away."

"Are there a lot of people like that? You've actually met some?"

"There aren't a lot who have enough money to get everything they want. I've rubbed elbows with some of them. Can't say I know any of them personally."

"What about dad's sketch? You think it can be recovered from that kid, or did he sell it already?" Megan asked, obviously not wanting to hear more about her fiancé's work.

"The kid may not have stolen the sketch," I said. "I was hired to find out who *did* steal it. If we can recover it, that'll be a bonus. Your father's attached to that piece, no matter what it's worth."

"We don't really know much of anything, Mr. Fontana," Megan insisted. "I don't see how we can help."

"Were either of you in the den before or after the theft occurred?"

"The den? I never go in there. It's daddy's preserve. More like a 'males only' kind of room. I don't feel comfortable there."

Tom shot a look at Megan which said she wasn't being entirely forthcoming. He let it drop, though, and his eyes snapped back to looking at me.

"What about you, Tom. May I call you Tom?"

"Sure," he said and stared directly into my eyes. "I've been in the den now and again. Some wonderful art on those walls. I don't remember being in there around the time of the theft."

"But you've both been in and out of the condo over the past couple of weeks?"

"Well, of course," Megan snapped. "I live here, and Tom may as well live here, he's in and out of the place so often."

"And neither of you saw anyone who might not belong here? Or, who may have been here for some other ostensible reason?"

Tom shook his head.

"Maybe the security cameras picked something up." I said just to see if there was any reaction. Neither of them blinked.

"I wouldn't bet on it," Tom said. "The system doesn't hold its recording very long. We were lucky that boy was caught on video going in and out of the den. If we'd waited another few days, that recording might've been lost. I don't remember seeing anyone else on the video."

"They say computers never really erase everything. Who knows? There may be something left. I know some people who can find whatever might be lurking on the drive." I didn't know if this was strictly true, but it'd get the pot boiling.

The moment I said this Haldane and Seamus entered the living room. Haldane smiled when he saw us sitting together. Seamus, carrying what looked like a small DVR box under his arm, didn't look happy.

"That the security system?" I asked and stood to greet them.

"This is it, for all the good it'll do you," Seamus said. "You can't possibly think they'll find anything."

"Let Mr. Fontana do his job, Seamus," Haldane said without a bit of condescension in his tone. Turning to me, he smiled. "The sooner you can get to the bottom of this, the better for everyone, especially that young man."

Seamus handed the box to me and I made a show of accepting it. As I did I glanced around at all of them. No one seemed especially ruffled, but none of them, except Haldane himself, seemed happy.

"I'll take this to my office and get the tech people I know to give it a going over."

"How long will this take," Seamus asked. "The sooner we get the police involved, the better the chances of getting the sketch back."

"I'll get the guys working on it right away." All I had to do was find the "guys" I kept mentioning.

* * *

Walking back to my office, I hefted the recorder box and thought how light it felt and how much weight it could have in determining Mikey's fate. Whether or not it contained exculpatory evidence, I had no idea. I wasn't even sure my tech friends would actually find anything. But just having the box was part of a plan I'd devised. Getting the word around as to the whereabouts of the box was next. The news that I had the box in my office might just lure the real thief to try and get it before the techs had a chance to find anything.

I walked away from the condo tower and headed for Twelfth and Latimer. I decided to head over on Pine since it was classy and sedate, particularly in the older part of town. Things were still quiet in early April before the really good weather arrived bringing with it tourists, joggers, and strollers. One red brick structure after another gave the area a mellow symmetry. Street lights, made to look like old gas lamps, lined the sidewalks and windows sporting shutters gave each home a stately feel. It was easy to imagine walking the same street more than a century before.

There was still a good bit of the afternoon left, and I had more than enough work to fill it. I reached my building and climbed to the third floor. The creaky steps announced my movements but the few people in other offices paid little attention.

I unlocked my door, swearing once more to find a new location, one that wasn't forlorn and dismal. Moving to my inner office, I placed the security device on a table then got the coffeemaker going. I sat at my desk to map out my next moves and make some calls.

I reached Luke at his office.

"Make any progress?"

"Not yet," I said and that was true. "I spoke to Haldane and his family."

"How'd that go? Was he still willing to let you investigate before he calls in the police?"

"He is, but his family..." I allowed the comment to hang. "Anyway, we've got a little time, which means we've gotta use it well. I'll need to talk to the guys on the crew for Haldane's place, especially someone named Ramon."

"You can talk to them all. Why Ramon in particular?"

"Something one of my contacts told me."

"Is he, I mean, do you think he's involved?"

"He may know something. I don't know any more than that, Luke. But I'll keep you in the loop."

"I'll have them in your office first thing tomorrow."

"And let them know I've got Haldane's security video recorder."

"He let you have it? But what can that tell you? As far as I know the video only makes Mikey look worse."

"My tech friends tell me that computers remember lots more than we'd like to think. Maybe there's something on that drive that'll point us in another direction."

"As long as it's not one of my guys," Luke said.

"Still interested in doing some work on the case?"

"How can I help?" Luke asked.

"Think you can do a little background research on Haldane, his sons, his daughter and her fiancé Tom Brooks? Anything you can get that tells me more than the basics."

"Piece of cake. I'll give you the results when you come in to interview my guys."

After giving him the details on the family, including Tom, I told Luke I'd call him in the morning.

Finding someone to help run through and possibly restore the contents of the security recorder was a high priority item on my list. Several calls later, I'd found someone to deal with the system's contents and arranged for him to pick up the recorder's hard drive. According to the tech, the job might take longer than Haldane was willing to wait, so I hoped other things would pan out first. Like somebody, knowing the security video was sitting in my office, a glittering gem waiting to be plucked, coming in to pluck it. Maybe somebody would take the bait.

I stood and stretched then poured some coffee. Though the aroma was perfect, I'd never learned the secret to making coffee that tasted halfway good. The sludge I swirled in my cup would have to do until I found someone who could do better.

At first I wasn't sure if it was the caffeine tweaking my senses or if I'd really heard the stairs creaking with the weight of someone trudging up to the third floor. Just in case, I sat back down behind my desk and faced the door to my office. My gun was in the top drawer and easily accessible. Unannounced visitors sometimes came with lucrative cases, sometimes with more trouble than I needed.

The complaining squeaks from the stairs got louder as whoever it was reached the third floor. The door to the reception area was closed and all I could see through the frosted glass was a blurry figure moving in the hall.

I expected the knock at the door, but when it came I still felt a tingle at the back of my neck. A second later, whoever it was knocked again.

"C'mon in. Door's unlocked." Just in case, I slid open the drawer and placed my hand on the gun.

The door opened slowly and when I saw him, I realized I'd been holding my breath.

"Cullen." I breathed his name and all the memories of my high school years came galloping back. All the feelings of that adolescent crush I'd had on this man gripped me again, and I knew I hadn't gotten over it. Might never get over it.

Cullen stood in the doorway staring at me. Tall, blond, and wearing the same fresh-faced look I remembered so well from our St. T days. He hadn't changed at all, at least not to my eyes. He was as beautiful as I remembered him.

"Marco? It's really you! Dad said you'd been to his place but I didn't believe him. I thought it had to be someone with the same name." He moved into the room, like a boat on smooth water. Not a hair out of place, not a blemish on his skin, not a thing wrong. The smile spreading across his face was at first uncertain, as if unsure of the reception he'd get. "But it *is* you. It's really you. It's been too long, Marco."

"You can say that again." I stood and moved from behind my desk to greet him. We grasped each other's hands with the force of shared memories. I knew I was smiling like a kid, but I didn't care. I was glad to see him and more than glad.

"You're a private eye. I can't say I'm surprised. I knew you'd get into something like this." He looked around the office, and I knew he was appraising everything. Not that money meant much to Cullen. He had plenty of it and never acted as if he did, but when you're used to finer things, you look at everything with a certain critical discernment.

I didn't feel as if he were judging me, but I knew that my shabby office was not what he expected.

"I'm good at it and, even better, I'm happy," I said, holding onto his hand, soaking up the warmth and the memories he'd brought back to life. "What about you, Cullen?"

"A long story which I'm sure you don't want to hear," he said with an almost shy tone in his deep voice.

"The hell I don't." I let go his hand and gestured for him to sit. "I want to hear everything. Like you said, it's been too long."

"Once you put this case away, I promise, we'll have drinks and catch up." Cullen made it sound sincere, but I could tell he was here for other reasons. A reunion wasn't on his schedule.

"So, what can I tell you?"

"Dad's more upset about this theft than he lets on," Cullen said as he got comfortable in the chair, crossed one leg over the other, and kept both arms on the armrests.

"Believe it or not, I could tell. I like your father, Cullen. I want to help him on this. But I also believe him when he says he doesn't want to see an injustice done."

"Neither do I. You know me, Marco." His startlingly blue eyes held a depth and a passion that I remembered well. I'd often thought that he could have anything or anyone he wanted, with just one look.

"I do, and I know you wouldn't want an innocent kid to get put away for this," I said. "Besides, if the police go after the wrong person, then whoever really stole that sketch will have even more time to unload it. Your father might never see it again."

"It's not the sketch so much as it is my mother. His memories of her are partly wrapped up in that piece. He may not show it, but he's broken hearted about it being gone. I've come into his place and found him in the den staring at the wall where the sketch had been." Cullen's voice choked and he looked away.

"I understand."

"Dad tells me you've taken the security video. You really think you'll find anything on that?" His voice had taken on a different tone. Curiosity? Or was it something else?

"I can't say. But I have somebody who's gonna work on it, and then maybe we'll have some different information."

"You actually suspect someone in the apartment took the sketch?" Cullen stared at me.

"Truthfully, I don't know what to think." I shifted uncomfortably. I had to ask questions the implications of which he might not like. I didn't want to chance aborting this reunion before it even got started. But I had an obligation to my client and to Mikey to see this thing through. If it meant I'd miss an opportunity to reconnect with Cullen, then that's what it would mean.

"Who'd have a motive? Everyone in that house or who comes through has money and plenty of it."

"No one ever has enough. At least that's the way I see things," I said. "I've gotta ask you something, Cullen."

"Shoot." He seemed to relax into an old familiar mode. He looked more and more like the boy I'd known in high school.

"Well, the thing is, I don't wanna ask but…" I paused and thought about what I wanted to say. "In the interests of being complete. Purely so that I can say no stone went unturned—"

"You wanna know if I had anything to do with this?"

I nodded. "Were you in the den around the time of the theft? Did you have any—"

"You bastard!" Cullen smiled as he said this then broke into laughter. "You haven't changed a bit. You'd suspect your own mother if you had to. You never trusted anyone at St. T's. "

"True. Things haven't changed all that much. So, you gonna tell me? Were you in the den around the time of the theft?"

"I get to dad's condo just about every day. I like looking in on him and since that whole mess with…" he stopped and swiped a hand over his face. "Let's just say that things haven't been going well in other parts of my life and I spend lots more time at dad's. Probably lots more than is healthy for my social life." He laughed, embarrassed.

"You haven't changed much either. When we were at St. T's, you could never answer a question straight out. Still can't, I guess."

"Point is, I don't remember if I was in the den or not. I might've been. I'm always at the apartment. It's impossible to remember if I was in the den, much less when."

"Think about it and get back to me. You might've seen something that can help." I wanted to believe Cullen, but something about his evasive answers warned me not to allow an old crush to keep me from seeing the truth.

"How long is your guy gonna take to look at that security video?" Cullen's gaze swept the room as if he were looking for something.

"He didn't say. But I told him I needed results quick. I know you father needs this as soon as possible. He's willing to wait, but I'm not willing to make him wait long."

"You always were a nice guy," Cullen said, pinning me to my chair with his ice-blue eyes. "I have access to a tech lab that could crank this out in a few hours. I could take the box and have it back tomorrow."

"Cullen, I'm surprised."

"Why? Didn't I always watch out for you in high school? When you were a runt of a freshman, I was there. Just because you're big and built now doesn't mean I can't still help."

"I'm surprised because I thought you went to law school."

"You're right. Yale. What're you getting at?"

"You take that box and it suddenly becomes contaminated evidence. You're not exactly a disinterested bystander. Who'd trust the results of work done by friends of yours?"

"I'm not a thief, either. I resent your implication, Marco. You've become a real hard-ass since we were in school."

"You understand my position, right?" I'd probably just ruined any chance I might've had to renew our friendship. Maybe that was for the best. I couldn't go through life pining after a straight man. "I know you're smart, Cullen, and I hope you don't think I'm stupid or naïve."

"I never thought you were stupid, Marco. Just the opposite. In fact, I've always admired you."

"Nice to know, Cullen." I smiled, even though I knew he only half meant what he'd said. We'd been good friends at St. T's, but that all ended when we graduated. There was no fight or big blow up. We just went our separate ways, and since Cullen belongs to a wealthier tribe than I'm from, the ways we went were different enough to keep us from even bumping into one another on occasion.

"Yeah, I know that didn't sound sincere, but I meant it. And I really was just trying to help."

"I know, Cullen," I said. "It's been a long day. I want to do the right thing by your father and for Mikey, too. The kid's had a rough life and I don't want to slip up and make it worse for him."

Before he could say anything, the phone rang. Without a secretary to run interference, I had to answer. I shrugged and held up a finger indicating Cullen should wait a moment.

"Fontana," I said into the phone.

"Marco. Marco, I think I may need your help," Luke said, not sounding at all like his usual balanced self.

"What's happening? What do you need, Luke?" I glanced at Cullen.

"It's Ramon. He came into the office for something and when I told him you needed to interview him, he threw a fit. He ran around the office shouting incomprehensibly. Then he locked himself in the bathroom. He won't come out."

"You think I can talk him out?"

"I don't know, but he won't even speak to me now."

"Does he have, I mean, will you be safe until I get there?"

"He's not dangerous. At least I don't think so. But I'll lock the door and wait outside the office just in case."

I hung up and turned to Cullen.

"Gotta go, Cullen."

"Need some help?"

"I think I've got this. But when the case is closed, I'll be expecting a call so we can catch up."

"You've got a deal. Unless you put me behind bars." Cullen winked. "I'll let you get to work."

He stood and gave me a look which was a blend of sad and happy. I didn't understand, and it tugged at me. I had this feeling that he wanted to say more. I felt I needed to keep him close and talk with him, but I didn't know what to say or how to say it. Instead, I was rushing out the door, leaving behind the best chance I had of getting close to Cullen again.

"Be seein' you, Cullen. Behind bars or not." I laughed, but he didn't.

Instead he, gave me a small, almost shy, wave of the hand and left.

* * *

For the second time that day I found myself in an elevator in Luke's office building. There were a fair number of people in the halls after normal business hours.

Luke stood leaning back against the door of his office, arms folded across his chest, a stern expression on his face. The light from his office filtered through the frosted glass of the door to combine with the soft, warm incandescent light bouncing off the marble walls of the hall.

When he saw me, his face lit up.

"I'm glad you're here," he said. "Sorry I had to bother you, but I thought you might be able to calm Ramon down. Now that I think about it, I'm not sure, since it was your name that made him panic."

"Let me see what I can do. I know Ramon's cousin Luis. I can always call him in, if necessary."

Luke unlocked the office door and swung it open. Once in, he pointed to the bathroom door.

Even though Luke had said Ramon wasn't dangerous, I approached cautiously and from the side. Being a target in a doorway wasn't what I had in mind for the evening.

Standing next to the door, I took a moment to think.

"Ramon," I said keeping my voice low and calm.

No answer.

"Ramon, it's Marco Fontana. What's goin' on, Ramon? Luke says you don't wanna talk to me. Is that right?" I paused and waited to see if he'd respond. "Ramon? Everything all right in there? Can you hear me?" I looked over at Luke and he shrugged.

"He must be scared out of his mind."

"You sure he's all right? I mean, he isn't…" I allowed the thought to float on the air. For all I knew the kid might've hurt himself and needed help.

"Ramon isn't like that," Luke said and closed his eyes. "He can be sensitive and high strung, but he's pretty solid. He wouldn't hurt himself…. At least, I don't think so."

"Well, if he isn't hurt, something's up in that bathroom. Maybe he passed out or hyperventilated?"

"Could be. He was hysterical. Ranting about breaking rules and not wanting to lose his job. He didn't threaten to hurt himself." Luke shot me a worried look. "Although, he did say he'd never leave the bathroom again, if I forced him to talk to you. You don't think he… did… anything, do you?"

"Is there another way out of that room?" It was either find another way in or break down the door.

"No windows and no other way out, or in, that I can think of."

"Ramon?" I shouted. I figured I wouldn't be frightening him any more than he already was. Assuming he was conscious.

There was no answer.

I placed an ear to the door and listened for a moment. Other than a sound like flowing air, there was nothing to hear. No whimpering, no sniffling, no nothing.

"I hate to have to do this, Luke, but I'm gonna have to force my way in. That okay with you?"

"Sure. He could be hurt or passed out," Luke said. "Need help?"

"Lemme give it a try first."

I put my shoulder to the door and shoved. The door balked and bounced me backward. I shoved against it again with increasing force. And again with little result. In the event Ramon was splayed out on the floor, I didn't want the door to whack him when it opened.

Eventually there was a little give, but the relatively gentle force I'd been applying wasn't enough. I had to hit harder.

"Here goes nothing," I said to Luke. Then I brought my foot up and placed a good kick just below the knob.

Wood cracked and rattled, but something held the door in place.

"Ramon! Get your ass out here." I was through coddling him.

No response.

I positioned myself for another kick and just as I was about to haul off, the door eased open.

Ramon, short, slender with dark hair and wide brown eyes, stood a moment, framed in the doorway.

"I didn't do nothing wrong," he gurgled, then collapsed in a heap.

"He fainted," Luke said. "It's not the first time. Ramon is a drama queen. Big time."

"You think?" I couldn't suppress a smile.

Luke and I knelt to help him.

I patted his cheek and brushed his hair out of his face.

"Help me get him to the sofa," Luke said, grabbing Ramon under one arm and waiting for me to mirror his action.

We maneuvered him to the leather sofa and I made him comfortable.

"I'll get some water," Luke said as he walked into another room.

"Ramon." I gave his cheek a gentle pat.

"No, no. Not now *papi*," he murmured. He squirmed a little before becoming still and quiet.

"Any better?" Luke asked as he returned with a bottle of water and a wet towel. He bent over Ramon and placed the towel on his forehead.

Ramon's eyes fluttered open and he brought one hand up to his face. When he saw me, his eyes widened and he tried sitting up. "No, please. I didn't—"

"Don't' try to sit up, Ramon," Luke said. "Take it easy for a minute.

"But... h-he's *here*. He's gonna get me in trouble."

"I'm not here to make trouble for you, Ramon," I said. "I only wanna talk. You want to help Mikey, don't you"

"S-sure, but I didn't do nothin' wrong."

"Nobody claims you did," Luke said. "We need your help, though. If you know anything, or if you saw anything..." He let the suggestion drift in the air.

"I didn't see nothin' at all." Ramon, lifted his head again but obviously felt dizzy and lay back down.

"Luis seems to think you know something." I said. "So it's kinda funny that you say you know nothing."

"It's true," Ramon pleaded. "You gotta believe me."

"No, I don't *'gotta believe'* you, Ramon. But I do believe Luis. He's always been straight up with me. He says you know something, you know something."

"You might be helping Mikey," Luke said.

"You gonna fire my ass. I know it." Ramon's voice quavered. "I'm in between one'a them rocky hard places, you know." Ramon shrugged.

"No, but you're gonna tell us, right?" Luke said, his nice-guy veneer wearing thin.

"It's not my fault. You told us never to do things like this. But I couldn't help it. He wanted me to do it. How was I gonna say no? You tell me."

"Who wanted you to do what?" Luke asked.

"Did someone force you to help him steal that sketch?"

"No!" Ramon's eyes widened, making him look like a goldfish flopping around on the couch. "No, nothin' like that. I would never steal nothin' from nobody."

"Then what?" Luke didn't disguise the annoyance in his voice.

"It was that guy. It was his fault. He made me do this," Ramon said. "I told him it was against the rules. But he told me it was all right. He said his rules were more important."

"Who are we talking about here, Ramon?" I said.

"One'a the guys that lives in the apartment. The young one."

"Seamus?" I asked. That had to be who Ramon meant. Only Haldane, Seamus, and Megan actually lived in the apartment. But Ramon could've meant Tom. "What's this guy look like?"

"He's young. Got blue eyes, like the sky. Dark hair. Not as dark as mine but dark. And tall. He's tall." Ramon closed his eyes as he spoke. Forgetting himself, he smiled and moved his shoulders as if getting comfortable against someone.

"Has to be Seamus," I said to Luke. Then I turned to Ramon, "What exactly did he want you to do?"

Ramon opened his eyes and the panic was back. He edged backward as if trying to melt into the couch and disappear. "Y-you gonna fire my ass, I know it."

"Ramon, I promise I won't fire you. Okay? Unless you committed a crime, I'm not gonna kick you out. Tell us what Seamus wanted."

"What they all want," Ramon snapped. "They want it and then they never call you again after they get it. That's what he wanted. Sex."

"And you…" I led.

"I went with him in that room. The one with the stolen picture. The pen."

"The den," Luke corrected.

"Then he tells me to look around at all the art on the walls. Lotta old pictures. I don't like them much but he says they all worth a fortune."

"That's when he asked you to help him steal one?"

"No, that's when he says he's gonna sell some and then he's gonna be rich enough to take me away to some place nice. Forever. Just him and me." Ramon grunted. "Yeah. Someplace nice. The only place nice he went was to my ass."

"So he didn't ask you to steal—"

"*Pendejo*! All he wants is my ass. He's never gonna sell that art. It don't even belong to him." Ramon folded his arms across his chest. "And I'm tellin' you, my ass don't belong to him neither."

"But just that once, you and Seamus…" I hesitated, trying to lead him back to the point.

"We did it, yeah. Okay, so I'm guilty."

"You and Seamus – uh, you did it? In the den?"

"At least I didn't steal no picture."

"So, you're afraid that we might see you and Seamus on that security video, am I right?" I asked. "Is that why you panicked?"

"I knew you was gonna think I stole that picture. If you see me on that video, you're not gonna think Seamus stole it. You're gonna think the Puerto Rican kid has fingers that stick."

"I know you didn't take it, Ramon. I want to know what else you may have seen or heard. Something that might help Mikey?"

"I gotta think. Now I'm all flushed. I can't think."

"Try, Ramon," I said. "Your cousin Luis said something about Mikey actin' all strange. At least that's what he remembers you saying."

"Mikey? Actin' strange?" Ramon closed his eyes again, placed both hands against his head as if he were trying to keep it from splitting apart. "Yeah. Now, I'm rememberin' things. You got me all combusted. I can't think straight no more. But, yeah, Mikey was working with us like usual. When he saw Seamus talkin' to me, he got kinda weird, you know? Like he was afraid or I don't know."

"Did you ask him about it?"

"Did –? No, I didn't have no time to ask. The guy, he takes me in the den, and by the time we get out, nobody's around."

"Did you see Mikey again?"

"Yeah. On the second floor with the crew. He was still actin' funny. Like he didn't wanna be there or like he hadda do something but wasn't happy about it." Ramon paused to take a breath. "Don't ask me what. 'Cause I don't know."

* * *

We pulled as much as we could from Ramon, which wasn't much at all. Seems he had sex with Seamus and felt guilty and angry about it. Guilty because he'd broken the rules and angry because Seamus hadn't called him for a rerun. Turns out Ramon hadn't seen Mikey enter the den. The only people he saw in the condo were the cleaning crew, Seamus, Mr. Haldane, and Tom, who arrived just before the cleaning crew had finished for the day.

No mention of Cullen or Megan. Not at the time the cleaning crew was present.

Luke agreed to get the rest of the cleaning crew to speak with me the next day. By the time we'd finished with Ramon, it was past dinner time.

The office building was quieter when I left. A security guard on the front desk was the only sign of life in the lobby. My footsteps echoed off the marble walls as I walked to the revolving doors.

I decided to take Market street back toward my office. There wasn't much foot traffic and I felt like a dot on the pavement as I moved down the street between the rows of tall buildings.

City Hall was up ahead, looking gray and surrounded with scaffolding for the restoration project, which looked like it might take a century to finish. I was anxious to see what it would look like once they unwrapped it.

When I reached Fifteenth Street, I stopped to take a look at the giant clothespin sculpture sticking out of the ground, as high as a three story building. It was a whimsical touch in a city overloaded with grim reality and politicians who only knew how to line their own pockets. As I stared at the clothespin, my cell phone began to ring. I flipped it open without looking at who was calling.

"Fontana."

"Mr. F-Fontana?" Mikey sounded frightened.

"Mikey? What's wrong?"

"I gottta talk to you. Somethin' happened."

"I'm listening."

"Not on the phone. Can we meet someplace? The Westbury, maybe?"

"Be there in ten." I knew I could be there in three minutes. Being able to get to a location first was sometimes the difference between living to tell the story and not. I'd found out the hard way when I started. The P.I. business came with a steep learning curve no matter what other experience I'd had.

He'd named the meeting place almost too quickly. There could be a lot of reasons for that, one of which was that this was some kind of set-up. Though I couldn't dismiss that entirely, I didn't think Mikey would try anything with me. I was practically the only chance he had at staying out of jail. I had to trust my instincts. Another thing I'd learned about the business.

The Westbury on Thirteenth and Spruce was almost six blocks away. I started walking over as the last of the late afternoon sun swept over the city. Stragglers from office buildings headed into parking lots or down subway entrances. Restaurants were filling up. Bars waited patiently for their late night crowds. Philly's Center City was on the upswing. It wasn't exactly boom time, but things were humming along nicely and the city was looking good.

On the way to the Westbury, I felt adrift and isolated. Something was missing and I wasn't sure what. The events of the past couple of years had turned my life inside out. I was in a rebuilding phase but lacked the materials for the job.

Galen always said the right things come along when you need them. He was a lot more in tune with that kind of thinking than I had ever been. He'd mentored me and I'd learned a lot from him. When he disappeared without a trace, it proved to be the first of a mind boggling series of events which led me down some dark and dangerous paths. I wanted to think the worst was over and that I'd figure things out eventually.

Having to meet at the Westbury was what caused these thoughts to bubble up. The bar had been one of Galen's favorite haunts. He liked the low key nature of the place and the fact that he could sit undisturbed for as long as he liked. I laughed when I remembered the look Galen's face took on when he didn't want to be disturbed. Truthfully, he could probably sit in any bar and not be bothered if he didn't want the attention. That's just how fierce he could appear to be. But I knew better.

I pushed open the Westbury's door and found myself in the cool dark space I remembered well. It was too early for the bar to be even a quarter filled, especially on a week night. I didn't recognize the bartender, an older man who obviously kept himself fit and wore a t-shirt like a second skin. His grizzled beard was dark and streaked with silver like his hair.

He smiled and placed a napkin in front of me as I sat on the barstool.

"What'll it be?"

"Molson's."

I'd taken a seat at the other side of the bar, so I could face the door and keep an eye on the rest of the place. My uncle always said I should never sit with my back to a door, and with the connections he'd had when he was alive, he should know. I believed almost everything he ever told me. Once or twice, his advice had even saved my ass.

The bartender brought my beer. I lifted the bottle and took a long swallow. A heady rush overtook me for a moment, and I felt the day's events fade. It was nice to forget for a while, even if it was only temporary. It was always easy enough to reconnect with trouble.

I heard the door open and looked up. It wasn't Mikey. But the man looked familiar. When he smiled and nodded, I remembered he was one of the attendants at my gym. We'd never actually spoken more than a few words. Never pegged him for a Westbury guy.

Five minutes later, Mikey walked in. Shy and unassuming, he looked around and spotted me. A ghost of a smile passed across his face so quickly, you'd miss it if you blinked. Taking the seat next to mine, he leaned one arm on the bar and turned to face me.

Before he could say anything, the bartender asked for his order.

"Beer. Whatever's on tap is fine," Mikey said sounding anything but sure of himself.

"Let's see some ID first," the bartender said without a smile.

Mikey took a wallet out of his back pocket and plucked out his driver's license.

The bartender scrutinized it, then smiled and winked before turning around to get Mikey's beer.

"What's goin' on, Mikey?"

"I'm, uh, I need your help. Please." He sounded down and frightened and lost.

"What's happened? Tell me."

"I didn't do anything, Mr. Fontana. That's the truth. These people, they think they can say anything. They think — You gotta know I was bein' honest with you."

"Who're we talkin' about, Mikey? And what's got you so scared?"

"Rick and C-Cass. They been callin' and botherin' me. They want—" he stopped as the bartender returned with his beer.

"I thought you ditched them? Why're they bothering you now?"

"They think I stole that painting."

"How'd they even know about it?" Word gets around. If Luis knew about the theft, I shouldn't have been surprised that people who actually dealt in stolen art would know. "Don't answer. It doesn't matter."

"What am I gonna do? They threatened me. They said they know I have the painting and if I don't give it to them, they'll make me regret it. And they will. They'll hurt me."

"Shit." These buffoons weren't likely to believe Mikey no matter what. I'd have to get involved. "Can you set up a meeting?"

"Do I have to? I don't wanna see these guys anymore." The pleading tone in his voice told me plenty. He was desperate to leave his old life behind.

"You won't have to see them. I'll meet with them myself. Tell them you hooked up with somebody new, and that I'm handling things now. Tell them they'll have to deal with me." I didn't exactly have a plan, but I'd come up with something before the meet.

"When? They expect me to deliver the piece tonight. I don't have it, Mr. Fontana. I can't deliver it."

I thought quickly about the best place to meet, somewhere that'd give me an advantage. Then it came to me. The empty office on the first floor of my building could work. It was seedy enough to be believable. There was a back exit, which might come in handy, and room enough for me to maneuver if they tried anything. I'd just need a little time to get things ready.

"Set up a meeting with them for midnight tonight." I gave Mikey the address and told him to stay away, which he was only too happy to do. Then I asked him to tell me everything about Rick and Cass. I especially wanted to know their soft spots.

* * *

As I left the Westbury my stomach growled, the beer had worked up an appetite. I headed to the Venture Inn knowing I could have a quiet dinner while I thought about how to handle Rick and Cass.

The VI still had a loyal following and was more than half full when I entered. The lights were dim and the conversation was low. As I peered around, Bobby, a waiter who knew me from before I'd started the private investigation business, came up to me and asked if I wanted a table. I nodded, and he found me a seat at the back where I could think and make a few calls and not bother anyone who was trying to have a quiet night.

Without being asked, Bobby brought me a glass of Merlot and gave me some time with the menu. I didn't mind eating alone, especially when I had a problem to work through or a case to work on. When Bobby returned for my order, he looked down at me mournfully.

"Alone again, doll?"

"By choice, Bobby. Got a case to work on."

"You always got a case. What you need is a man. You've heard'a them, right? They come in nice packaging, but they're even better unwrapped. You need some help findin' one?"

"I think I've got it covered, but if you have a suggestion…"

"Oh, I've got suggestions. Boy do I have suggestions," Bobby said as he walked away.

Mikey had seemed sincere and I was certain he was telling the truth about not wanting to get involved with Rick and Cass again. Even though I'm pretty good at catching out a liar, sometimes I get thrown off the track. Was Mikey the kind who could lie so convincingly, it'd throw me off my game? If he'd been involved in stealing the art and had already gotten rid of it, that would be a good reason he'd want Rick and Cass off his back. I was a convenient sap to use as cover for him.

But I didn't feel that Mikey was using me. I had to go with my instincts. Mikey might have been lying about something, but it wasn't the DaVinci.

I made a few calls while I waited for Bobby to bring my food. First to the building super. He happily let me use the mostly empty first floor storefront. It had been abandoned by its last tenant, some fledgling company that claimed to be able to do everything anybody wanted. Of course, that kind of business takes a dive real quick, and that's what had happened. They'd had to leave everything behind. For tonight, it'd look like the place was mine. Shabby and seedy but all mine. Besides, if Rick and Cass were smart, they wouldn't be expecting a respectable art dealer in a fancy set of offices. They'd be expecting a guy in a place like that first floor dump.

Next I called Kevin, a bouncer at a new bar in town called Bubbles. I'd been there a number of times and had gotten to know him. A big bruiser with a baby face, which allowed him to carry on his drag "career" when he wasn't breaking the necks of troublemakers at Bubbles.

Kevin had helped me out on a few cases, including one in which he got to use his drag identity, and he liked the work. When I told him I needed him to be my muscle and all around sidekick for the evening's meeting, he agreed immediately. He also agreed to bring along another of the bigger bouncers.

I ended the call and was about to tap in another number, but Bobby set my plate down on the table and stood back staring at me. The stern expression on his face said he wasn't happy.

"Well, you gonna eat that?" he asked, one hand planted firmly on his hip.

"Yes, mom, I'll eat all my food, even the vegetables," I said and peered up at him. "Then can I have dessert?

"You're working too hard and you're skipping meals. I know it," Bobby said. "When was the last time you were in here for dinner?"

* * *

The first floor storefront was a dismal piece of real estate. I'd picked up the key from the building super and had started rummaging around. Cracks and holes in the plaster walls, dirty windows, and the only light came from a couple of tired, dull-looking wall sconces. Just enough lighting so Rick and Cass would see me but only just. I was glad the place looked filthy and decrepit. Perfect for an impromptu meeting. Rick and Cass dealt with the underbelly of society every day. They shouldn't expect fancy offices. All I wanted to do was throw a scare into them, get them to forget about Mikey. Which is why I needed Kevin and his friend, types who looked like they had no conscience and could take care of any dirty work I might have in mind.

Kevin arrived with a guy, even taller and more bulky than Kevin himself. He was introduced to me as Den and when we shook hands, I felt the power in his grip.

I explained what I wanted them to do. Essentially they were to stand their ground by my side, stare at Rick and Cass without let up, ball their fists menacingly, and generally look like they chewed nails for snacks and drank battery acid for fun. They nodded enthusiastically and immediately got into character.

I'd brought my gun along, even though Mikey said his fence friends never carried. I hadn't known a thug yet who wasn't armed. Rick and Cass would be no different.

With fifteen minutes to go, I leaned back against the dilapidated desk at the back of the room. I could see the front door and anyone who came through. Kevin and Den took positions one on each side of me, a step or two back.

The heavy silence which gripped the room was broken by the sound of footsteps outside. I could see backlit figures approaching the door. A raised hand. A knock.

Den lumbered to the door and opened it.

I had to assume it was Rick and Cass standing in the doorway, peering into the darkness.

"C'mon in." I said, my voice low.

I wasn't sure which was which, but one of them was about six feet tall and the other barely came up to his chest. One was neat and well groomed, had a flawed face, and a mean expression. The shorter one was stocky, edgy, and unkempt. His face was bland, which could be more menacing.

Den shut the door and stood beside them. Kevin walked over and flanked them on the other side.

"Hold it, boys," I snapped. "Let's see what they've got." I waved my hand nonchalantly.

"Against the wall," Kevin ordered

The duo dragged their feet but complied, casting wary glances over their shoulders at Kevin and Den.

Once against the wall, Kevin kicked their feet apart, forcing them to place their hands on the wall for balance and support.

"What the fuck is this?" the taller one said.

"Just making sure you two are clean. I don't like surprises." I said.

"Look what I found," Den growled. He slid a gun out from under the shorter guy's jacket. He continued the pat down and found a knife, a large one.

Kevin did the same to the taller thug and came up with another gun, a knife, and brass knuckles.

"They're clean," Kevin announced. Then he and Den moved back to flank me and stare at Rick and Cass.

The pair was allowed to stand again. Facing me they looked like intimidated whelps. Not at all the tough thugs Mikey had described.

I said nothing but stared at them. I allowed the silence to grow until it forced one of the pair to speak.

"W-We're here about—"

"I know why you're here. Reason *I'm* here is to tell you to forget it. There's no deal, because there's no art to deal with. It's gone. Long gone. Your friend Mikey didn't snatch it. He's not that good."

"Don't shit me. I know the painting's been stolen. Mikey had an agreement with us. He never came through. Now he's got a chance to make good."

"He didn't come through, 'cause he didn't steal no painting. Got it?"

"Not what I heard. Word is Mikey did this. And he owes us."

"You heard wrong, then. The art is gone. It ain't gonna be found for a long time." I yawned. "I'm gettin' tired of this."

"Why'd you set up the meeting, then?"

"Two reasons." I flicked my fingers. And as we'd planned it, Kevin and Den moved forward, so they could be seen. They balled their hands into fists and looked like they were barely able to hold themselves back from pounding Rick and Cass into dust.

"Yeah? What reasons?" said the shorter thug, his voice unable to conceal his fear.

"Reason one is to tell you to forget about the art. Don't ask questions about it. Don't even think about it. I got ears everywhere." I said. Kevin brought his hands together and cracked his knuckles. I saw the taller man wince. "It gets back to me that you been asking questions again, I'll make sure you don't ask no more."

"Yeah, sure, sure," the shorter one mumbled.

"What else?" The taller thug still needed convincing.

"Reason two is to tell you to lay off Mikey. He owes you nothing. You're outta his life as of now. Touch him and you deal with me. Clear?" At this Den stepped forward and moved in on them. They both backed up without even realizing. "I get even a whiff you been talking to him, you're both goin' on a long trip. My guys'll punch your tickets. Got that?"

"Why should we? Who the fuck are you?" The taller one moved forward again, though tentatively, as if he were stepping on hot coals. "Mikey's *our* boy. He owes us. You think you scare us? You're outta your mind."

The shorter guy looked over at him as if he were crazy, but shorty had no choice but to chime in. "Y-yeah, you got no right…" His voice faded as quickly as his courage.

"I guess you didn't hear me," I said to them. "Whaddayou think?" I turned to Kevin. "You think they heard me? Maybe they need their ears cleaned?"

Kevin walked over to the taller guy, obviously knowing he was the key to the smaller thug. Crush him, they both fold.

"So, tell me again," I said. "Who is Mikey?"

"Mikey's mine. I fed him. I trained him. I gave him money and whatever he wanted. He owes us."

"And here I thought you were smart. That's the wrong answer."

Taking his cue from me, Kevin throttled the tall guy and shoved him up against the wall.

"One more try?" I said.

He refused to answer.

Kevin hit him in the stomach so hard I felt the blow. The guy doubled over and retched a couple of times. On all fours, he took deep breaths.

"You," I said to the shorter guy. "You got hearing problems, too?"

"Y-yeah… I m-mean, uh, n-no. Got no prob-problems." The shorter guy whimpered.

"Lemme hear what you heard. What're you gonna do once you step out that door?"

"G-gonna – gonna forget that… you know, uh, what we, uh, talked about."

"And?"

"A-and, Mik-Mikey's off base. Startin' now. We don't know the kid. Never heard of him, right Cass?" Short and chubby addressed his friend who was still on all fours.

"Y-yeah." Cass drew in a breath so he could speak again. "Who's Mikey?" He looked up at me, tried a weak smile but was too frightened to maintain it.

"Right. You got it. Now get out, before I let my friends here have some more fun."

Rick helped Cass up off the floor. Half scrambling, half looking over their shoulders at us, they got themselves out the door. When the sound of them running faded into silence, Kevin and Den and I all laughed until we cried.

"How'd that kid get mixed up with those jerks?" Kevin asked, when he stopped laughing.

"Guys like that can only deal with kids like Mikey. They prey on poor kids who don't have anyplace else to turn and take advantage of them. They get kids to steal then they pocket the profits."

"Slimeballs," Den said. His voice was so deep it sounded like it came straight out of Hell.

"I owe you guys."

"You don't owe anything, Marco. This was fun."

"Yeah," Den growled. "More fun than sittin' at the bar waitin' for something to happen. This was real shit."

"Still, I'm taking you both to dinner, at the very least."

"Gotta get my beauty sleep," Kevin said. "Gonna host a thing tomorrow at Twelfth Air. You oughta come by."

"Maybe I will." I said. "Right now I've gotta go back to my office and then get some beauty rest of my own."

"You must'a got plenty of that already, cutie." Kevin quipped. "See you around."

"Thanks again," Den said, as they moved out the door.

I locked up the storefront and walked into the building's general entrance. I didn't feel like hauling my ass up the stairs, but I'd left some things in my office in case the meet with Rick and Cass didn't go well.

Creaking and moaning, the wooden stairs accompanied my every move as I walked to the third floor. When I reached the top of the stairs, I heard sounds coming from my office. I stopped and listened.

Someone was creeping around inside, trying not to make much noise. The state of the wooden floors made silent moves impossible.

I pulled my gun and moved as smoothly as possible to the door of my place.

The sounds inside stopped, as if whoever it was had paused to listen. I didn't move. It was a long while before that person moved again.

There was nothing I could do but rush the room and hope the intruder didn't have a gun.

When I heard movement inside the room again, I stepped to the door. In one swift move turned the knob and pushed it open.

The darkness nearly concealed the person but ambient light filtered in through the window and I could make out a man standing in the middle of the room.

I reached back with one hand and flicked on the lights. He stood there, black ski mask over his head. His hands went up when he saw the gun.

"Don't move."

"Don't shoot. Please." The voice was familiar. He was tall and well built.

"Get that mask off," I ordered, gesturing with the gun. "Slowly."

With one hand, he picked at the edge of the mask and lifted it over his head. When it came off, he blinked and then smiled nervously.

Tom. Megan's fiancé.

"Should'a called first, Tom. The office is closed."

"Door was open when I got here." He tried sounding nonchalant but it didn't work.

"Tell me you're here because you missed me," I said. "We hardly had any time together this afternoon."

"I—"

"Aw. You're not here because you wanted to see me again, are you? I'm disappointed." I held the gun on him and watched his expression change along with the emotions that must have been running through him. "I'll bet I know why you're here, though."

"Why's that, smart guy?" he said, a haughty arrogance filling his voice, making it ugly.

"You're here to get that video recorder, am I right?"

"Video recorder?"

"C'mon, Tom. You might be able to fool Megan and her brother, but I'm not them."

"I still—"

"I think you're on that video. In fact, you've probably got a starring role, am I right? There's footage of you going in and out of the den after Mikey had been there. Long enough after that nobody bothered to look at more of the video after they saw Mikey. You knew the security system would catch you, but you were counting on them finding Mikey first and running with that. Which—"

"Doesn't prove a thing," Tom regained some of his composure. "Other than the fact that I was in that room. Not exactly an uncommon event, as I'm almost part of the family."

"For now. But not for long. I'm betting you've gotten what you wanted and you'll be making some excuse to back out of the wedding. Or, maybe you'll just disappear. You've done that before. Right, Tom?"

He was silent.

"Sources tell me you're not as clean cut as you look. You're a little slippery, aren't you? You've managed to leave a small trail of disappointed women, or have I got that wrong? Are you an equal opportunity thief? Were there some rich men, too?"

"You have no idea what you're talking about"

"So, what did you do with the DaVinci? Oh, wait! You said it isn't really a DaVinci, didn't you?

"It's not. It's a Renaissance piece but not a DaVinci."

"Tom, Tom, Tom. You can fool some people with your authoritative way of strangling the truth. But I know better. Seamus is actually right. Isn't he?"

"Seamus is an academic geek who wouldn't know a DaVinci from a van Dyck."

"So you assume. But even somebody like Seamus gets a chance to be right now and then. Turns out he's right about the DaVinci. And what's more, you know he's right."

"You're crazy."

"You lifted that piece because its potential worth is staggering. At least for a poor kid from South Philly like me, several million dollars is a stunning amount for a bunch of scribbles on parchment."

Tom glanced around like a trapped animal looking for another way out. I could've saved him the trouble. There was no other way out. Much as I'd've liked that at times.

"You're holding me here against my will. That's false imprisonment."

"Let's call the police, then. Shall we?" I moved toward him, still pointing the gun at his chest. If I fired now he'd go down and stay down. "You wanna get the phone or should I do the honors?"

"L-look, I was just – you're right," he said and his shoulders slumped. I could see sweat beading on his forehead. "You're right. There's something on that video. But, it's not what you think."

"Okay, then tell me what it is."

"I—it's.. the den is the only place I can get any privacy in that home. That family is intrusive. And Megan, she can be a shrew. I retreated to the den for privacy and just to get away from them all. You have no idea what it's like."

"Why not simply leave the condo and go home when it gets too much?"

He was silent.

"And if that's the case, what's the big deal about anyone seeing you on the video? If you're part of the family, then there's no problem you going in and out of that room."

"What if I wasn't alone? That's not going to go down well, especially not with Megan."

"Who are you claiming was with you?" This was a development I half expected. It didn't let him off the hook. He could have met someone in the den and still taken the sketch after whatever it was, was over and done."

"Seamus. Surprised?"

"Not really. Seamus apparently has a thing for doing it in the den. You're not the only one he's been there with. Surprised?"

"He—he uses the… You're lying. Trying to bait me into saying something that you can use." Tom was silent for a moment. "I can see right through you."

"Your boy Seamus has already had a starring moment or two on that system and with different costars." So I stretched the truth. If Ramon had been with Seamus in the den, I was sure there'd been others. "Besides, you being in the room with Seamus doesn't prove anything. You snatched the DaVinci after you and Seamus were through."

"Not true. None of it. You've got it all wrong."

"Was Seamus in on it with you? Sleep together, steal together?"

"I don't know what you're talking about."

"How about I get Seamus up here? Must be what? One in the morning? He's probably still up. Waiting for you. Right?"

That got a small reaction. His eyes narrowed but he said nothing.

"Yeah, I think that'll help. Seamus didn't look too happy when I took that video recorder. I'll get him up here and the three of us can have a nice conversation about what we do next." I moved toward him, all the while keeping the gun trained on him. "Face the wall."

Silently, he moved until he was flat against the wall. His hands still raised above his head, palms against the wall. I placed my hand against his back and kicked his feet apart.

"I'll make that call now."

I glanced down at my desk and with one hand scattered the papers there until I found the one where I'd scribbled phone numbers. I refused to drop my guard even with him facing the wall, and kept the gun stuck in Tom's back so he could feel it.

Tapping in a few numbers, I saw Tom flinch.

"Don't," he said. "Don't call him."

"Why not?" I paused. "If he's a party to this theft, I want to hear it from him. Then, he'll have to answer for it, same as you."

"He—he's not. He doesn't know anything about this…" he trailed off.

"Then he wasn't in the room with you?"

"He was, just not the way I said. We were in there arguing."

"About…"

"About the sketch. He's certain it's genuine. I was trying to convince him it wasn't and wouldn't be worth much."

"But you know better, right?"

"It's a real DaVinci."

"You know this how?"

"A c-collector. A client. He's a fanatic. I convinced Haldane to let me take the piece for testing. This client insisted on it. He had to see it for himself."

"This the guy you stole it for?"

"Once he knew it was real. Once he knew..." Tom's voice was low, weak. "H-he forced me to steal it."

"C'mon, you're a big boy. You don't have to do anything you don't want to. How could he force you?"

"He-he'd have me k-killed." Tom slumped against the wall. "He's rich. Powerful. He gets what he wants. Nobody ever says no to him. Nobody." Tom paused. "I'd just disappear one day if I didn't do what he asked. Who'd care? Nobody would even look for me." Tom stopped talking then and became still and silent.

"No way you're gonna get that sketch back, am I right?"

"No. There's no way. He'd never let it out of his sight. I don't even know where he's got it. Out of the country is my guess."

"You realize I've gotta tell Haldane. I'm not letting an innocent kid take the rap for this."

"Can't we work something out?" Tom spoke, still facing the wall. "I mean he hasn't gone to the police, and even if he does, he's not getting it back. That client would rather kill than let it go. He's a fanatic in the worst sense of the word."

"Look, I was hired to make sure that Mikey didn't do this crime. I wasn't hired to track down the DaVinci. Haldane doesn't care whether it's real or just another piece of work by some DaVinci student. He doesn't care if it's authentic in any way."

"He doesn't? Then why..."

"He cares because it was his wife's favorite. Something she loved. She was all wrapped up in that sketch. It was like a part of her. And he doesn't want to lose that, too. His memories of her are part of that sketch. He just wants it back. I'll bet he won't ask questions."

"What're you saying?"

"Me? I'm not saying anything. All I know is that if the sketch turns up, whether it's authentic or not, Haldane will be happy to have it and his memories back again."

"I can't... my client will k-kill... he'll torture me f-first..."

"A guy like you has lots of contacts. Good ones, shady ones. Am I right?"

"It's the nature of the business. There are all sorts of people who – wait, you aren't suggesting—" He didn't finish his thought. Or, rather he began thinking on overdrive. I could almost hear the gears grinding."

"Yeah, not even the art world is above it all. Plenty of you slimeballs hanging in galleries along with the art."

Tom said nothing. I imagined he was still devising a plan around what I'd planted in his mind.

"You've got a chance to do something good, Tom. You set a kid free and let him have his life back. And you make an old man happy. You give back something that's precious to him."

"I'm still gonna have to tell him I took the sketch."

"I don't care what story you make up as long as you get Mikey off the hook and get something like that sketch back to Haldane."

"But, Seamus will know, won't he?"

"If you're at all cozy with Seamus, maybe you can make him forget about the sketch. On the other hand, I doubt it, considering he's convinced it's the real deal. But I'll leave that up to you, too. You made this mess, you clean it up. All I care about is getting Mikey off the hook and maybe seeing Haldane happy again."

* * *

"You did it," Luke said.

I wasn't sure whether to feel complimented or mildly insulted by the amazement in his voice.

"Thought I couldn't handle this, huh?"

"N-no, it's just… well, all right, I wasn't sure. I'd heard you were good but there's nothing like seeing for yourself." Luke raised one eyebrow.

"I'm sure Mikey is relieved."

"You have no idea. He's ready to become your indentured servant for the next few years." Luke laughed. It was a hearty laugh and sexy. "How about dinner on me? I feel like celebrating."

"You got it." I smiled at him and Luke made it clear that dinner wasn't all he wanted which was all right with me.

The G-String Thief

I should've seen it coming but I can't have eyes everywhere.

The slender guy in the black jacket had been staring at Kyle with more than passing interest, but I thought he was just another love-struck patron who couldn't get enough of one of my strippers. I'd let it go and turned my back on them to take care of other things. That was my first mistake. I'd only formed the stripper troupe a little while ago and I was still learning the ropes.

As soon as I turned away, I heard Kyle shouting, "Hey! Ow! Get the fuck away!"

When I turned back around to figure out what was happening, all I saw was a crowd growing around the bar. The only thing visible was Kyle's head and shoulders and his jerky movements trying to fend someone off. The slender patron who'd been paying Kyle too much attention was hidden in the mass of people. But I assumed he was causing the trouble.

All I knew was that Kyle kept shouting and I had to get to him quick.

Patrons had formed a dense wall around Kyle, forcing me to push and shove my way through. It almost didn't matter, because no matter how fast I moved, everything else moved faster and I couldn't stop it.

Kyle shouted sharply enough to cut through the crowd noise. "Get the fuck off me," he yelled.

As I pushed my way closer, I spied the tall, dark-haired customer, hands outstretched, pawing Kyle's legs, reaching for his g-string. Jacket sleeves pushed to his elbows, he yanked roughly on Kyle's g-string. Kyle held on with one hand and slapped at him with the other. The guy's expression said he took pleasure in Kyle's discomfort.

Alone on top of the bar, Kyle was vulnerable. No one from the staff could get to him quickly enough. The bartender tried to help, but he couldn't reach over the bar enough to push the customer away. Two bouncers waded through the crowd but they were farther away than I was.

Kyle did his best fending off the attack. Pushing at the guy's hands was useless. I knew he didn't dare try kicking the guy. That would throw Kyle off balance and off the bar top onto the glasses and bottles.

Kyle was trapped until I could get to him.

Just before I reached them, the dark-haired guy succeeded in ripping off Kyle's white satin g-string. He grinned maliciously, then broke roughly through the crowd heading away from me and toward the door.

I wanted to chase after him, but Kyle needed me more. Kevin, tall and burly, dashed out the door even before I signaled him to do it. But I knew it was already too late.

Finally at the bar, I reached out my arms to Kyle, indicating he should jump down. He seemed caught between anger and embarrassment and for a moment wasn't able to move. Sleek and tan, Kyle covered his crotch with his hands and stared at me.

"Hop down, Kyle. I'll catch you." I gestured with my arms as I shouted.

Kyle stared angrily at the patrons gawping at him. He wanted to jump but didn't want to reveal any more than he had already.

"C'mon, Kyle. Let's get you out of here." I signaled again for him to hop down.

The spell finally broken, he looked down as if seeing me for the first time. Keeping one hand over his crotch, he reached out his other for me to grab. I helped him slip off the bar and into my arms with as much dignity as possible under the circumstances. Once he was down, I immediately wrapped my jacket around his waist and walked him back through the crowd.

Kyle was a favorite with the patrons. Thick, dark blond hair, masculine jaw line, deep-set eyes. He moved as gracefully as possible, his lightly muscled body taut. Flushed with embarrassment, he leaned into me, holding me tight and huddling close as if he wanted to disappear. He felt warm and he trembled slightly as we moved through the staring patrons.

I felt everyone's eyes on us, all wanting a look, and I knew Kyle felt it even more acutely. Though they'd seen him nearly naked on any number of nights, this was different. This exposure made him vulnerable, made everything more real. It felt as if they fed off the pain and the novelty.

"You all right, Kyle?" I asked.

"Just shaken up… and totally bare," he said, his voice elevated. "I hope they all got a good look." He was angry and bitter. "Fuck! This is the second time in three nights that guy bothered me. None of the other dancers, just me." He huddled closer to me as if I could protect him. I should have. It was my responsibility. "Can't you do something, Marco?"

I'd started StripGuyz a year or so ago, and there was still a lot to get used to. It all felt new in so many ways, especially since we'd moved our operation into Bubbles and had begun an even bigger program than we'd started with. The rules were generally the same as when the troupe floated from bar to bar, but being in one location most of the time came with new challenges. Protecting the dancers came first. I'd hired staff to watch for trouble and deal with it, but sometimes it was not enough. Bubbles had several of their own bouncers who happily took care of troublemakers. But the bar staff was new to the idea of having a nightly strip show, and we were all working things out as we went along.

Of course, in a strip club customers get close to the performers. That's the draw and the drawback. You don't want things getting out of hand, but there are too many variables and not enough ways to control the human animal. Dancers were especially vulnerable when performing on the bar or working the floor. I'd have to talk to Stan, the bar owner, about taking on more security.

"I'll hire more bouncers. For now, let's get you dressed."

"It wasn't just that he took the g-string," Kyle said as we headed up to the dressing room.

"He did something else?"

"He kinda threatened me. It wasn't specific, though," Kyle said.

"What'd he say? Can you remember his exact words?"

"He told me I'd better stop stripping. Or else." He shuddered.

"We should find you a place to stay for a few nights."

"Thanks, Marco. But when I think about it, I can guess what this is all about. At least I think so. I hate that it's happening, and I don't want everybody to know about it."

"You know who's behind it?" I was not entirely surprised. Kyle came to the group with a lot of secrets. He'd told me some, but he was still largely a mystery. "Tell me, Kyle. Maybe I can do something."

"My family. That's what I suspect, Marco. I told you a little about them, didn't I? I'd bet anything they're behind this."

"You don't really know for sure, though."

"Who else is gonna want me outta the business? I don't play around outside of work. I don't do drugs. I'm duller than dull, Marco. You know that."

"I wouldn't say dull, Kyle. Not the way you dance."

"It's all an act. You know that, too. Guys might wanna rip off the g-string and see what's under there. But who's gonna do that and then tell me to quit stripping?"

"You have a point," I said.

We'd arrived at the dressing room and Kyle seemed more relaxed. With all the noise and edginess downstairs, the second floor was quiet and peaceful.

"T-thanks, Marco." Kyle held my jacket around his waist and leaned over to kiss me on the cheek. "Thanks for getting me outta there."

"Go ahead and get dressed. Then tell me all the details. We'll put a stop to this."

"I'll tell you," Kyle said as we pushed open the dressing room door. "But you won't like it, and you won't be able to do much."

The bright dressing room lights made me squint until I adjusted. Some of the dancers sat staring into lightbulb-lined mirrors primping. Some stood at full-length mirrors inspecting themselves for blemishes or a few extra micro ounces of fat. All of them were beautiful. None of them was secure about it. I felt a pang of responsibility for all of them.

Heads turned to see who entered the room. Eyes went wide when they saw Kyle, bare to the bone, handing my jacket back to me.

"Can't get enough tips with your g-string on, Kyle?" Dane quipped, then turned back to flexing in the mirror.

From the back of the room, Caleb rushed over to us.

"Oh no, Kyle. Not again." Caleb looked Kyle up and down as if checking him for wounds. At nineteen, Caleb was one of my youngest dancers. Kyle brought him in one rainy night, Caleb looking like a drowned cat. A very cute, very sexy drowned cat. We all fell for him, especially Anton, who has a soft spot for strays. Caleb quickly became Kyle's "project." He trained Caleb and taught him routines with Anton's help. They bought him thongs, g-strings, costumes, and whatever else he needed. But it was Kyle who really took Caleb under his wing.

They were tight, but they weren't a couple. Kyle was more like the kid's mother hen. He'd told me once that Caleb was on the run from an abusive situation. Kyle wasn't generous with information about Caleb.

"This time he got my g-string and took off, the bastard."

"Do you remember what he looked like, Kyle? Could it have been—"

"No. He was tall, dark haired, dressed really well, and looked like he was comfortable in a gay bar." Kyle said.

"You sure?" Caleb was frightened, but it wasn't all for Kyle. I could see that.

"I'm sure, Caleb," Kyle said, as if there was to be no more discussion.

"C'mon, Kyle, let me take you home. I'm through for the night, and you need to get some rest." Caleb looked at him with a mixture of concern and adoration.

Kyle gently moved from my arms, turned to look at me gratefully with those amber eyes of his, then put his arm around Caleb's shoulders. Together, they moved toward the lockers. Kyle's usually upbeat personality was flawed by something taut and bitter at his center, something he never talked about with anyone. That quality gave him an air of mystery, but it also made him difficult to know.

As I turned to leave the dressing room, Anton barged in, nostrils flaring, crystal blue eyes gleaming with anger. Wearing a tank top, Anton's tension showed in his muscled arms. Sleek and like a puma ready to spring, Anton gazed around the room, taking in everything and everyone.

"What happened down there? I stepped out for five minutes to get some air. I come back and there's chaos. Everyone's babbling, and I can't get a straight answer from anybody. Did one of our guys get hurt? Did someone grab a dancer's…?"

"Don't worry, Anton," Dane said. "Marco took care of things."

"Don't he always?" A deep voice from the back of the room rumbled.

"We've got things under control, Anton. Nobody's—"

"Who was it? Is he hurt?" Anton peered around searching for the injured dancer. "Why didn't anyone come and get me?"

"It was like a lightning strike. All I could think about was getting Kyle out of there quick."

"He okay now?" Anton said, beginning to relax. The look in his eyes softened.

I put my arm around his shoulders, feeling the heat rising off his body and the tension still zinging through his muscles.

"Some guy pulled off Kyle's g-string. He's shaken, but he's okay," I said. "And before you ask, I'll be telling Stan to hire more bouncers."

"How about if I train our guys to kick pervs in the teeth when they get out of hand. That'll get their attention." Anton faced me, and I saw he was serious.

Anton was the first dancer I hired when I started StripGuyz. After a while he began assisting with scheduling and hiring. He was good, and I relied on him more and more. Tall, lightly muscular, with dusky blond hair and blue eyes, Anton was imposing and he knew it. The scar that transected his left eyebrow was sexy. It added to his sultry good looks and was a testament to his Czech-Hungarian temper. Despite that, Anton could be kind and gentle, especially with the guys in the troupe. He was also a hopeless romantic, which was a source of tension for us.

He and I had an undeniable mutual attraction but Anton refused to settle for anything less than total commitment, monogamy, and everything that went with it. That explained his no hanky-panky policy. He was not about to give away the milk unless I bought the cow. I wasn't ready to settle down on the farm just yet.

"I wouldn't mind seeing a creep like that get what's coming to him. But as satisfying as kicking him in the teeth might be, it won't help business. Not for Bubbles and not for StripGuyz."

The telephone rang and heads snapped in its direction. It wasn't often that the dressing room received calls. Dane picked up the receiver, said hello and listened.

"It's for you, Kyle." Dane held the phone languidly, his pouty pink lips forming a little rosebud as he waited.

"Don't answer it," Caleb said, gently pulling Kyle back.

Kyle shook his head, reluctantly moved toward Dane, and took the receiver.

"He—hello?" His voice shook. As he listened, his expression morphed from perplexed to frightened to angry.

"Fuck off, and don't call again!" Kyle slammed down the receiver so hard it cracked.

"Kyle? Wh—who *was* that?" Caleb asked.

"Nothing. Just some creep." He pulled on his shirt and smoothed out the wrinkles.

"Don't you think we ought to talk about this?" I said as he shut his locker and slipped one arm into the strap of his back pack. He remained silent for a long while. I sensed a huge struggle going on inside him as he desperately tried to contain the emotions he must've been feeling.

I placed a hand on his shoulder and gently squeezed. "Whatever it is, Kyle, I'm here for you. Anton's here, too. We can figure this out. You don't have to go it alone."

He said nothing but leaned into me as if he wanted to let go and let someone else take charge. He felt like a tightly wound spring ready to uncoil.

Before I could say more, Caleb stepped up. "C'mon, Kyle, let's get you home so you can relax." Caleb gently pulled him away from me.

Kyle took a deep breath and looked me in the face. His eyes were glassy and filled with a sadness, the source of which I could only guess at. Kyle turned toward Caleb and a weak smile played across his lips. He slipped an arm around the younger dancer, and they moved out the door, clinging to one another like orphans.

After that night, Kyle reported that he'd been bothered a few more times, but only by telephone both at work and at home. He eventually told me about his problems with what was left of his family. Their parents having been killed in a yachting accident, Kyle, his brother, and a cousin had all been taken in by their paternal grandfather. Life was easy and pleasant for a while. Kyle's father's family was wealthy, but his mother was from old money and plenty of it. She left it in trust for her children to be shared by them when Kyle turned thirty. The paternal grandfather had a huge bundle of his own, most of which he'd placed in trust for Kyle's cousin, as he'd had no other family money. The three kids were his only living relatives.

That was the good part. But there was a darker side to Kyle's family situation, and it had to do with his personal life.

The grandfather and relatives on his mother's side objected when Kyle came out, wanting to live his own life. Even Kyle admitted that he could be headstrong and provocative and that sometimes he lashed out. But never without justification, according to the way he saw things. Stung by his family's reaction to his personal life, Kyle, secure in the knowledge that he would be financially independent once he turned thirty, decided to do whatever would upset his family most in order to get even with them for rejecting him. Coming across an ad for StripGuyz, Kyle decided that becoming a stripper was the perfect way to embarrass his family.

Ten months after he started dancing for StripGuyz, things began to blow up in his face. He felt it was his family, though he admitted they'd never physically attacked him before. Still, he said he knew how angry they were, and he also knew they wouldn't be satisfied until he submitted. Family dynamics are a funny thing at the best of times. Throw some money into the mix and all hell breaks loose.

* * *

A few days after the latest incident, I was posting dancer schedules on the board in the dressing room at Bubbles when Anton shouldered through the door supporting Kyle, who looked disheveled and shaken. Kyle was bleeding from his nose. His upper lip was cut and bleeding as well. His clothes were ripped, torn, and smudged with dirt.

"What the hell happened?" I said.

"He was assaulted a block away. I don't know how he got here, " Anton said, "He said this guy came out of nowhere, knocked him down, and started kicking him."

"This is related to the other night. There's no way around that." I said, kneeling on one knee in front of him. It had to be connected. There aren't any coincidences, as far as I'm concerned.

Kyle was too shaken up to speak at first. He looked stunned.

Out of the corner of my eye, I saw Anton reaching into the cabinet on the wall for the First Aid kit. That kit had come in handy more times than I could count. Strippers ran into plenty of mishaps on the job, small and large. But other than falling on broken glass and slipping off the bar while dancing, being attacked by out of control patrons was one of their worst fears.

"Y-yeah…" he murmured. "You're right…" Kyle's voice trailed off.

"Can you tell me what happened, Kyle?" I knew he was hurting, but it'd be better to get the details fresh.

"Let him rest, Marco," Anton said, deciding what he'd need from the First Aid kit, and clearing a place on the table.

Anton placed a pillow behind Kyle's back, so he'd be more comfortable. Then he chose cotton swabs, hydrogen peroxide, and other items from the kit. Placing them all on a table, he got to work. Anton could only do so much with what he had. It would take time to heal Kyle's body. But I was more worried about his spirit. If incidents like this kept happening, Kyle would eventually be worn down to a nub. I had to do something and fast.

"You should probably be at home," Anton said. "How about I call Caleb and tell him I'm driving you to your place?"

"N-no. Ow! Don't bother Caleb. He'll just worry."

"Okay, we won't call." I shot a glance at Anton, then turned back to Kyle. "The last thing you feel like doing is talking, but the only way we're gonna make this stop is if you help me." I hated pushing him, but I needed some starting point, some handle on the situation, if I had any hope of stopping it.

Kyle lay back his head and closed his eyes as Anton worked on him.

"Did you see who did this to you?" I tried being gentle. But there was no choice, I had to keep the questions coming until he remembered something.

"I don— ow!" He looked at me and winced. "I don't know. I didn't see his face."

"Was it the same creep who bothered you at Bubbles?" Anton asked and stepped back to lean against the wall.

"Coul—sssst. That hurts," Kyle said when he moved his arm. "Could'a been the guy. They were both tall and dark-haired. But I didn't get a look at this guy's face."

"Do you remember anything else?"

"Like?" He closed his eyes and sank back into the chair.

"His clothes, things he said, the sound of his voice, the way—"

"Yes… yes. His voice. That was familiar. And what he said." Eyes still closed, he tried remembering. "The guy who stole my g-string said the same things. So did the guy on the phone. That I'd better stop stripping. Stop embarrassing myself. Take responsibility for my actions. He said I'd ruined lives. Lives I had no business touching."

"What did he mean by that?" Anton asked.

"I don't know." Kyle looked at each of us and seemed uncomfortable. "Like I told Marco, I think this has something to do with my family. I guess I've ruined their lives."

"Got it. Because you're a stripper." Anton said.

"And… and he said something but…" A strange look came over Kyle. He closed his eyes tightly, but a tear squeezed out and rolled down his cheek.

"What is it, Kyle? What else did he say?" Anton hovered over him.

"He sa—" Kyle's voice caught in his throat and he couldn't get the words out. He tried sitting up but winced with pain.

Kyle's physical pain and fragile emotional state put all of us on edge. Anton, tense and angry, looked around the room as if he had no idea what to do next. He hated sitting around waiting. He needed to be able to fix things, make things better. He was like me in that respect. But there wasn't much either of us could do about this.

"How about some of your famous coffee? I could use some," I said, hoping to keep Anton busy. He'd still be tense but he'd be occupied.

He reluctantly moved to the coffeemaker, rattled mugs and utensils, then left to get some water. I watched him walk out of the room, one hand holding the pot, the other clenched into a tight fist at his side. Senseless violence, especially when a friend was involved, bothered Anton more than most other things. I'd never yet discovered why.

Looking at Kyle and the state he was in, I wanted to punch someone out, too. But while that might feel good, Kyle needed someone to keep calm and to make him feel safe again. That was my job. I held Kyle's hand and rubbed his neck. I got him to take a few deep breaths, which seemed to relax him. He eventually settled back into the chair again.

"If you're feeling up to it, we should go over this again. I know everything must hurt right now. But while things are fresh in your mind, you may remember details better." I couldn't let it go, and he knew it. I was also sure he didn't want me to drop the matter. He wanted this behind him.

Kyle sat up, cleared his throat, then drew in a deep breath. He looked at me and his eyes were filled with fear. "He told me that this was the last warning I'd get. That the next time, someone would finish it. That's what he said. 'finish it.' I'm scared, Marco."

* * *

Three weeks after Kyle's beating, things at Bubbles had almost returned to normal. For a while, my dancers had been afraid for their safety and had gotten overly cautious while performing, but eventually they relaxed into old patterns and behaviors. Two new bouncers constantly patrolling the floor during shows didn't hurt, either. The crowds kept filling the place, and Stan was happy with his overflowing cash box.

Once Kyle had been patched up at University Hospital and took a few days to heal, he found himself settling into his old routines at Bubbles. More wary, less trusting of anyone, and always making sure he was never alone, he tried to cope with his newfound insecurity until we found a way to figure out who was behind things.

I wasn't crazy about Kyle's return to work. Mostly I feared for his safety. But I also worried about my other dancers and what his return would mean for their safety and their peace of mind. If all my guys went into panic mode, there'd be chaos.

Kyle was relentless in badgering me to reschedule him, though. I eventually relented, but only because he'd been hanging around Bubbles every waking minute anyway. Besides, I thought it'd be better to have him where we could all keep an eye on him. Still, once Kyle started performing again, I kept my fingers crossed. I was sure his attacker would be back to keep his promise to finish things.

Even though Kyle's situation was always front and center, I couldn't keep all my attention on him. I'd reeled in quite a few paying cases, and I needed the money. Paying customers grease the wheels. So, I'd left StripGuyz mostly in Anton's hands, though I was still in and out every day. He'd been wanting a chance to show me he could take charge when necessary. He also wanted to hang up his g-string and go back to school. Managing StripGuyz would fit his plans perfectly. It suited me fine. Anton was a good manager, the guys loved him, and I needed to spend more time on investigations.

Still ensconced in my office on Latimer, I hadn't yet hired a new secretary. I went through all the hiring motions. But after two or three interviews, no one had clicked, and I dropped the idea. Maybe I was still feeling the pain and guilt that came with what had happened to Josh. Whatever it was, my front office remained empty with no one to act as a buffer when someone came calling.

I was thinking just that when I heard someone open the door and walk through to my inner office without hesitation. Anton, exuding confidence and grace, strode in and stood in front of my desk.

"I thought you were letting me handle things at Bubbles?" Anton said. Not whiny, not hostile, just matter of fact. He never whined or played the wounded party. He just got what he wanted in a no nonsense way.

"Anything give you the impression you aren't?" I said. I wanted to get up and plant a kiss on his lips, but this wouldn't have been the right time.

"For starters, Kyle is performing again tonight which makes almost two weeks in a row. Nobody else's schedule has them on stage that many times."

"I was surprised the kid wanted to come back to work. It was his choice. Having him onstage more frequently was something he and I decided on. He needs the money. Poor kid missed a lot of work after the beating."

"There's nothing poor about him. I wish I had the trust fund he'll be getting."

"Not till he's thirty. He can't live on air until then. And I didn't mean 'poor' in that way," I said. "He's been through a lot. Maybe working distracts him from his problems."

"Seems to me that working as a stripper is what causes all his problems. We all know this. We all heard him tell us what that guy said. I can't understand why he'd come back. Or why you'd let him."

"There's more to your anger, right?" I said and watched Anton pacing like a tiger in front of my desk. He seemed on edge, ready to pounce.

"Damned right, Marco. All the guys are complaining. Kyle is getting more time on stage than anyone else and they need the money even more. That goes for me, too."

"It's just that—"

"If I didn't know better, I'd think you and Kyle had something going. Are the two of you…?" His voice trailed off into a disappointed sigh. I felt a pang of guilt for no reason. We hadn't made any promises to one another, and I wasn't fooling around with Kyle. But my Catholic upbringing had instilled a guilt factor that just wouldn't go away.

"There's nothing going on between us, Anton. Kyle wouldn't want that even if I did, which I don't."

"Well why favor him so much?" He sat in a soft chair in the corner looking like a lost kid. A tall, muscular lost kid. I wanted to hug him.

"I'm not exactly favoring him."

"Things were okay before. But this new schedule has made things worse. The other guys are talking about him… and you. They resent him now. They didn't before."

"How serious are we talkin' here? Do I need to get involved?" I closed a folder on my desk and leaned forward to stare at Anton.

"I don't think so. But keep me in the loop. Let me know what the hell is going on. I can handle the guys, if I know what the story is. And you haven't told me the truth yet."

"Okay. But what I'm telling you stays here. Got it?"

"When did I ever reveal secrets?"

"Don't let me get started." I smiled as innocently as I could. "I'm letting Kyle dance as often as he wants for a reason. Two reasons, actually. One, I get to keep an eye on him without having to babysit him or hire a bodyguard. Keeping him at Bubbles makes things easier all around."

"Makes sense. What's the other reason?"

"Kyle wants to smoke the guy out. He intends to bring on whatever that guy wants to do next. Maybe we can stop him in the act and settle everything."

"Sounds crazy. Not to mention dangerous. The guy could really hurt Kyle."

"It was Kyle's idea. He's willing to risk it."

"But you aren't with him around the clock. He goes home sometimes. He's got a life outside Bubbles. Besides, he didn't get beaten while he was on the job."

"All true. I got Kevin to agree to walk Kyle home and then pick him up again when he leaves his place. That's as much as he'll let us do. Kyle wouldn't stand for a bodyguard round the clock. But he's happy with Kevin and the arrangement we made."

"Okay," Anton said, a hint of doubt in his voice.

"Kyle can be pretty stubborn. Reminds me of another blond dancer I know. He refuses to stop dancing because of the threats. Kyle claims that if he quits, they win. And, he never finds out the truth about who exactly is behind the attacks."

"Like he told us, it's probably his family. It makes sense. You don't have to be a P.I. to figure that out."

"That's what he thought at first. But now he feels more confused. His family doesn't like what he's doing, but he just can't imagine them going this far to stop him. If the plan works and it turns out his family's behind this, he'll have the goods on them. He's talking about a lawsuit."

"A lawsuit, huh?" Anton said, with more than a little distaste. "I like Kyle, but sometimes it feels like he's all about the money. How could you be interested in a guy like that?"

"Who said I was interes— Anton, you're—" I stood up and took him in my arms. "I'm not interested in Kyle. I don't have space in my life for a relationship right now." He felt good in my arms, and I wanted to hold him and keep him close. But we both knew this wouldn't work. At least not for the time being.

"I know you aren't fooling around with Kyle. But your dancers think you're playing favorites. As far as they're concerned, there's only one reason you'd do that."

* * *

That night at Bubbles, Kyle didn't show. Kevin told me he'd walked Kyle back home the night before but had never received a call from Kyle to meet before coming in for his set.

"Have you heard from Kyle?" I asked Caleb, who was scrutinizing himself in a full length mirror. Caleb may have been new at this work, but it never took long for the new ones to learn what they had to do to maintain themselves to be successful strippers.

"I spoke to Kyle this morning. He said he needed some time alone. He does that once in a while. He spends a lot of time thinking. And he takes off at the strangest times. Sometimes I don't see him for a day or two."

"It's not like him to blow off work, though. He's never done that before," I said. I took out my cell phone and called his apartment. There was no answer. "I think I should get over to his place just to make sure."

"You think something's wrong, don't you?" He stopped primping and stared at me, his baby face a mass of worry.

"I don't know, Caleb." I moved toward the door and placed a hand on Anton's shoulder as he got ready for his set. "Put your clothes on, Anton. We're going out."

"But my second set—"

"I'll make it up to you." I pulled my jacket on.

"Promise?"

"Promise. Let's get going."

"I'm coming, too." Caleb said.

"No, somebody's got to stay and work. The customers will get testy if there's nobody dancing on the stage." I shot him a look over my shoulder as we left. The worried expression on his face said it all.

We hoofed it over to Kyle's apartment on Walnut Street not far from Bubbles. The cool night air caused Anton to shiver and he drew closer to me as we walked. It wasn't even midnight, the streets should have been lively but things were way too quiet. Even on an off night, a lot of guys pounded the pavement going from one bar to another searching for the elusive. Things hardly ever slowed down until after three or four in the morning.

"You couldn't get him on the phone?" Anton asked. "That doesn't necessarily mean anything, does it?"

"Ordinarily that wouldn't mean much." This was anything but ordinary. I had a feeling things wouldn't be good. "Now, I'm not so sure."

Anton gave one look at the apartment building Kyle called home and groaned. "This is a dive. I had no idea he lived here."

The smeary glass doors of the front entrance were unlocked. There was no front desk and no security of any sort. The lobby smelled like old socks and stale beer. I reflexively held my breath. After punching the elevator button, we both watched the number display slowly mark the progress of the elevator as it slipped down to the lobby.

The battered elevator took even longer going back up to Kyle's floor. Once we reached the floor, we stopped in front of his door and we looked at one another as if to say "Now what?"

I pressed the buzzer, then knocked. No answer. We waited again.

Placing my ear to the door, I heard nothing inside the place. I knocked again, harder this time. I didn't understand why, but I knew that Kyle was there and needed our help.

"Kyle!" I pounded on the door causing someone's dog to start barking and howling. "Kyle, open the door!"

"Give it a—"

I didn't wait for Anton to finish. I brought my foot up and smashed the door open. The lock was only meant to keep out the casual burglar, not to withstand even a mild assault. Wood splintered and clattered to the floor. The door swung open with a creak. Everything went silent. Even the dog stopped barking. No one popped their head out of their door to see what the racket was. Great neighbors.

Signaling Anton to stay back, I moved cautiously into the room. I felt the wall for a switch and flicked it up. The yellow glow of a lamp filled the room. I couldn't quite believe Kyle lived in the shabby little apartment. A lumpy couch with stuffing flooding out of a tear on its side, a wooden chair with so many cracks it looked ready to collapse, and milk crate shelving filled with paperbacks comprised the bulk of the furniture. A threadbare oriental rug was bunched up near the wall. A lamp had been toppled and lay on the floor near an overturned glass, its clear contents puddled out in front of it.

I indicated with my hand that Anton should follow, but I put a finger to my lips to keep him from saying anything.

We moved toward the bedroom, passing the microscopic kitchen along the way. The sink, piled with dishes, gave a delighted cockroach plenty to inspect.

The stillness made my flesh crawl, but I kept moving, dreading what I might find. Anton stayed close behind.

The bedroom door was closed. I put out a hand to turn the knob.

"What if he's—?" Anton whispered hoarsely. He gripped my shoulder.

"We don't have much choice." I said as gently as I could. I knew this wouldn't end well, but we'd come this far. "Kyle might need our help."

We both heard the moan at the same time. It was faint but clear. Anton looked at me, fear and hope in his eyes.

I pushed and the door flew open. Anton moved in just behind me and together we saw Kyle tied spread-eagle to the bed.

Nude and bloody, his chest moved only slightly as he attempted to breathe. His head was turned toward the wall and his face wasn't visible. But he moaned faintly again and we rushed to the bed. I thought we'd had everything covered. That we'd kept an eye on him at work, that Kevin saw him home each night. I assumed once he'd reached home, he'd be safe. I was wrong. I wouldn't let that happen again. If I got another chance.

Anton leaned over Kyle, hesitant to touch him. I moved around to the other side of the bed so I could see Kyle's face. He needed to know we were there and we'd help.

He'd been bleeding for a while. Blood stained the bed and dripped to the floor. His body was cut and bloody, his hands marked with defensive wounds. He must've put up a fight in the living room, been knocked out and dragged to the bed, then tied down. He couldn't have struggled much after that.

I stared for only a second, then began to move as if by rote.

"Call 911 and get an ambulance, Anton." I tossed him a look which got him moving. Then I turned my attention to Kyle. "Kyle," I whispered. "Kyle, we're here now." He didn't respond, though he took a ragged breath.

His face had taken a major beating. It took all I had to look at him closely. His beautiful face was battered and bruised. One eye was swollen shut, with a slash oozing blood just below it. His nose appeared broken and his lips were split, distended, and bleeding. There were other contusions and cuts which looked raw and painful. Kyle was in there somewhere, but this was not his face. His raspy breathing was so faint I was afraid he was slipping away.

I began undoing the restraints, speaking softly to him as I did.

"Kyle, open your eyes. Don't sleep now." I wanted to touch him, to caress his face just to let him know we were there. But it looked as if touching him would only increase his pain. "The ambulance is on its way, Kyle. Stay with me."

I undid the last of the restraints and tried making him comfortable. He moved, but it was a weak tremor.

Anton slipped up next to me, touched my shoulder, and said, "How is he?"

"I undid the restraints. I don't think it'd be smart to do anything more," I said. "Might do more damage. And the police are gonna want to see this as it is."

Anton nodded in agreement then dropped to one knee by the side of the bed, peering at Kyle. Standing behind Anton, I knew there was nothing much we could do until the EMTs arrived. That made me feel helpless and frustrated. Two things I couldn't afford.

I glanced around, thinking about my next steps. Kyle's bedroom was strangely comforting. The soft yellow color of the walls magnified the glow from the bedside lamp, making the whole place seem like a gentle sigh. It had a calming effect on me, and I began noticing things. An oak wood frame on the bedside table held a photograph of Kyle and another young guy. Their arms around one another, they wore smiles of such genuine happiness that it almost hurt to look at them in light of the situation. In the photo Kyle looked at the other guy as if nothing else existed. I wondered who he was and if he were still in Kyle's life. I'd never heard anything about boyfriends from Kyle, not that he told me everything. If this guy was still involved with Kyle, I hoped I could reach him to tell him what'd happened before he heard it some other way.

Still taking note of things in the room, I almost didn't notice it. When Kyle moaned again, my attention was drawn to him and I saw it. The white satin g-string that had been stolen from him was tucked under the pillow where his head had lain before I released the restraints and moved him. I hadn't seen it as I rushed to untie him. But there it was. Had his would-be killer had left it as a sign or a warning or was it placed there as a mocking gesture? Whatever it was, it was cruel. When I found the bastard who did it, I'd ask him and not so gently.

Anton tapped me on the shoulder. "I'll stay with him. When the ambulance gets here, it might be better if you spoke with them." He was angry and I knew he didn't trust himself when he was emotionally invested in something like this.

"I'll take care of it."

As I walked back into the living room, there was a knock at the door. I opened it expecting to see the EMTs. Instead, Caleb stood there looking lost and scared.

"Something's wrong, isn't it? When you didn't come back right away, I was afraid. Where's Kyle? What's happened?" He tried pushing past me, but, small as he was, it was easy to keep him back.

"Hold on. You've got to calm down before anything else." I felt the tension in his body as I continued holding him. Gradually he relaxed and when I sensed he was calm enough, I explained what we'd found, which set him off again. He struggled trying to get out of my grasp.

"Promise me you won't make a scene, Caleb. Kyle doesn't need that." I gripped him tighter and he looked at me, his eyes wild as he twisted to get away. "I'll let you see him, just remember it's not pretty in there. Kyle is unresponsive, and I'm not sure what all of his injuries are." That seemed to sober Caleb in a hurry. He stopped struggling and stared at me.

"Is he— will he live?"

"Just let him know you're there. Don't touch him, don't make a fuss. Just be with him." I called for Anton to come and help. He was fond of Caleb and the kid responded well to him.

Anton took him aside and whispered something to him. Then, an arm around his shoulder, he walked Caleb into the bedroom. Caleb gasped and I could hear Anton murmuring something to him.

I turned back to waiting for the EMTs. Something had caught my eye in the living room just before Caleb arrived, and I wanted to check it out. A tiny red light blinked in the center of an answering device designed to hold a cordless phone. The phone was missing. I decided listening to the messages was worth the risk of spoiling the crime scene. I pushed the button.

The machine announced each message and the time of the call. The first message was Caleb's, asking when he could see Kyle. The poor kid sounded so alone it hurt to hear his voice. The second message was from someone who didn't identify himself. He asked if they were still meeting that evening. I wondered if it was the kid in the picture and if he was still waiting for Kyle to show up. Another guy, who also failed to identify himself, said he'd be early and that Kyle should have what they'd agreed on. There was no explicit threat but the message didn't sound good.

One more message announcement appeared, dated the previous morning. "Kyle. If you're there, Kyle, pick up right now. It's Emily, and we need your answer. We've got a lawyer all set to go. Trent has agreed to manage the trust, so all we need is your agreement. You promised you'd think about it. Grandfather is getting old, Kyle, and he makes more mistakes every day. Do you really want him managing all that money? Call me, Kyle. Don't let us down."

Kyle said his family was unhappy with him, but the caller seemed more frustrated than unhappy or hateful. Of course, she was trying to get Kyle to do something, so she'd make sure she didn't sound like a raving homophobe. Looking into Kyle's family wouldn't be easy or pleasant, if Kyle had told the truth about them. This call gave me something to start with.

I wanted to listen to the messages again, but just then the EMTs arrived.

* * *

The drive out to Gladwyne to meet Kyle's family, the next morning, took me through most of Philadelphia's Main Line – old money enclaves. There are some mansions in those burbs that look the part: forbidding stone structures defending their owners and their secrets from the world. If you're not part of the charmed circle of money and breeding, you'd know, just by looking at the façades, that you don't belong. It's another world, a foreign place where you would be adrift and unable to decipher language or meaning. Breeding counted even more than filthy lucre in some places. You could have your stone pile and not much else, but you were a member of the club by birth and breeding. The ones with money might despise you, might talk about you behind your penniless back, but they'd never turn against you. In public.

I drove past rows of trees strategically placed so you could only see the dim outlines of an imposing structure situated somewhere far from the road and nestled among even more trees. None of the important homes could be seen from the road. Even the less important ones, the ones of which only a partial view was possible, were impressive in design and size.

Finding a sidewalk in this part of the world was difficult. No one out here was eager to have the hoi polloi able to walk freely around the community, much less have easy access to a front door. Everyone here desired lives of privacy and privilege, free from prying, sometimes critical, eyes.

Kyle's paternal grandfather lived in a Tudor-style mansion which had its own name and a nearly one hundred year history. It took a while to locate, since suburban signage is not made for the Sunday driver. You have to know where you're going, and knowing places by sight helps even more. I stumbled onto the estate eventually and started up the long driveway. After driving past a sizeable gatehouse, the mansion seemed to rise up out of the greenery. Grand was the first word that came to mind, after I shoved my working class resentment back down my gullet. The home was palatial. Eventually the driveway took me to what I supposed was the front entrance. It was hard to tell with digs like this. There were lots of ways in and out. I pulled my car onto the beige pebble apron in front of a set of stone steps leading to a wide grassy expanse and a set of massive doors. There were no other cars, and I was certain I'd committed sacrilege leaving my oil-dripping, dented, mess of a vehicle sitting on the pristine pebbles.

According to what Kyle had told me, dealing with this family wouldn't be a picnic. But I had to start somewhere, and since Emily had made that call, the family seemed like a good place to start. Families are such fertile ground for secrets, hostilities, rivalries, betrayals, and general discord. It'd be a hell of a start.

I approached the door, reviewing what I'd say first. I'd called ahead to set up the appointment, but that didn't make things easier. I was asking to discuss something they obviously didn't want to talk about. None of them had been to the hospital to see Kyle. No one had called asking after him. I could at least start with the good news that Kyle was holding his own.

Reaching the tall wooden doors, I was disappointed that there was no huge, lion's head knocker. Instead, a neat, clean doorbell was all there was. I pushed the bell but couldn't hear the bell from outside the door. The house was so large that sounds were lost inside, and people's lives were swallowed along with them.

Before long, a young woman opened the door with some effort. She was clearly of the horsy set but not the horsy type. Coppery red hair, sky-blue eyes, and a body that wore clothes like it was all high fashion, she had a graceful manner. She was no hired help, that was certain. She peered at me as if I were applying for a job, and she didn't even want my application form.

"I'm Marco Fontana. I called about—"

"Oh. Yes, grandfather said you'd be coming. Go on in." Her stiff-jawed manner of speech was soft, not exaggerated, and very familiar. "Beck will take care of you." She indicated the tall, darkly handsome butler who stood at attention in the middle of the piazza-sized foyer. Leaded windows shed an eerie, church-like glow on Beck, and he almost seemed like a cleric who'd lost his way.

I nodded to her then Beck. He stared at me, his eyes burning with some inner turmoil that was eating him alive. But he smiled officiously and bowed curtly in my direction. His was a flawed beauty, as if clumsily assembled, then rejected. His face wasn't quite right. There was something too big or too lopsided, I couldn't quite figure what it was. But it made me uneasy.

"Mr. Detwiler is waiting for you in the library." Beck's voice was reedy, not what I expected to come out of that tall, stern façade. He didn't wait for me to respond. Instead he pivoted around and moved quickly down the center hall.

Beck led me down an elegant hall lined with mirrors, old portraits, and windows. He stopped at a door that looked two stories high. After knocking, he waited and when the signal came, we entered.

Detwiler sat at a cherry-wood desk, polished so highly that the light reflected from the windows hurt the eyes. A stiff-backed older man in a blue suit, Detwiler was in his seventies but looked a lot younger. His eyes sparkled and his hair was the kind of white you couldn't believe was real. He didn't smile or stand as Beck introduced me. He extended a hand and we shook. Then he gestured toward a chair, indicating I should sit.

The room wasn't at all what I expected, like the man in it. It was modern. The books lining the floor to ceiling shelves all looked relatively new. Computer monitors sat on a long glass table against one wall, along with a printer, a scanner, and other equipment I didn't recognize. The flat screen monitors had stock market tickers running across their screens as well as other financial figures moving and glowing. Detwiler was high tech and looked as sharp as his technology. Kyle had never mentioned his grandfather's business or how he'd made the family fortune, and I'd never asked.

"Mr. Fontana, is it?" Detwiler looked at me questioningly but without a trace of hostility. Surely he knew I was more than just a P.I., that I employed his grandson as a stripper. He was rich enough to know anything.

"That's right." I didn't smile. "I want to say how sorry I am, sir. Your grandson is a friend and a good person. He—"

"Don't be coy, Mr. Fontana. I know who you are and I know that Kyle may be your friend but he is also your employee. What can I do for you?"

"I don't do coy, Mr. Detwiler. It's my nature as well as my professional policy to be discreet. But I'm glad you know what's what, because that will make things easier."

"How so, Mr. Fontana? What 'things' are there to make easy? Kyle is lying unconscious in a hospital. He chose to lead his life by his own lights, and this is what it's come to. There's nothing easy about any of it." There was genuine emotion in his voice which made his words quiver and his voice tighten.

"I'd like to investigate this situation on Kyle's behalf and with your cooperation. I want to find out who did this."

"Don't the police do this kind of thing in Philadelphia? Or, are they too busy with more serious crimes like parking violations?"

"In a way, you could say they don't care about cases like this one. But I do."

"They don't care about attempted murder? Come now, Mr. Fontana."

"Mr. Detwiler, you said you knew that Kyle works for me. Then you must know all the implications of that work."

"I'm well aware that my grandson is gay, if that's what you mean. I still see no reason the police shouldn't want a full investigation of this incident."

"The reality is, sir, that the police want closure as quickly as possible on any case. Or, failing that, they're satisfied to kick some cases under the rug if they think they don't merit their time and that no one will raise a stink. They leave them open and—"

"Ignore it? Because he's gay?"

"Not just gay, but a stripper." I saw Detwiler wince, it was slight, restrained, but it was there. "Not one of the jobs that gets a lot of respect in any circle, let alone among the police."

"I see." He lowered his head a moment, and seemed to be thinking. Looking up as if he'd made a decision, he said, "How much?"

"How—?"

"Only a fool works for free. How much are you asking?"

"Kyle is a friend. I want to get to the bottom of this because I care about him. All I'm asking is your cooperation. Money—"

"Is the grease that makes the machine of life work better than it could otherwise. I and my family will cooperate, but only on the condition that you charge your standard fee for a case such as this."

"I wouldn't—" I hesitated. I wanted to do this for Kyle, not for the cash, no matter how much I needed it.

As if he'd heard my thoughts, Detwiler said, "You took Kyle in and gave him a job. And, if what you say is true, you also gave him your friendship. Quite possibly, if it hadn't been for you, Kyle might have been dead long ago from his own intemperate actions. I think he might want you to have something in return."

I objected.

"Not in payment for your friendship but as a way of returning the favor you did him, a gesture of friendship. Kyle is like that. If you're truly his friend, you'll know that. Even if he doesn't care much for his family, he loves his friends, as I recall."

"I don't feel comfortable with this."

"I'm not asking you to. I want you to find out who did this. For Kyle and for me." He drew a checkbook out of the top drawer of the desk and picked up a silver pen. "How much is your retainer?"

Asking for money in a case like this felt sleazy. But the old man was obstinate. I gave Detwiler a figure and his right eyebrow, as white as the rest of his hair, arched slightly. I didn't know if he thought it was too low or too high. I didn't ask.

"When can I question the family?"

"I can have them available any time you wish."

"Since I'm here, how about if I start with anyone who's at home?"

"That would be me and my grandson, Hayes, Kyle's cousin. I'm afraid that my grandson Trent is working on a project and won't be back for a few days. His wife Emily is here, or rather, she will be as soon as she gets back from the city."

"I'll start with Hayes, then. You and I can speak afterward?"

"Certainly. I'll have Beck take you to Hayes."

Detwiler pushed a button somewhere under his desk and Beck appeared at the library door. Dour but graceful, Beck led me back down the hall and through to the foyer. I wanted to ask Beck a few questions. He might have something to contribute as an objective observer. He looked disgruntled and might be inclined to give away secrets the others wanted buried. I'd do that after I had more information to work with.

I was led up a grand, polished wood stairway. A rich oak affair with curved bannisters and deep crimson carpeting, it felt like Hollywood. We stopped in front of a door on the second floor. Beck opened the door, let me into the room with no introductions, and left, closing the door behind him.

A young man I figured to be Hayes stood looking at me or through me. I'd seen that face before and it threw me for a moment. I searched his face, trying to remember where I'd seen him, but I don't think he noticed the stare.

He turned to the side as if he'd heard someone call to him and I realized where I'd seen him. He was the other guy in the photo on the table next to Kyle's bed. There was more to their connection than family blood. Hayes seemed about the same age as Kyle and just as good-looking. He was swarthy where Kyle was blond, thin where Kyle was shapely, sad-eyed while Kyle's eyes sparkled. Hayes had the posture of an underpaid accountant. He needed more meat on his bones and a crash course in good posture.

He looked over at me, and it appeared he'd been crying. His sad brown eyes seemed to scream out for something. When he managed a smile, it was forced and weak.

"Hayes, I'm Marco Fontana." I extended my hand.

His handshake had little conviction in it.

"I know why you're here." He gathered himself and looked me in the eye. "Why would anyone do this to Kyle? Do you know? Is that why you're here?"

"I want to know, too, Hayes. That's one reason I took on the job. I'll find out. I can promise you that."

"Because grandfather is paying you?" There was no anger in his voice, just sadness.

"Because Kyle is a friend. That's the reason. But I won't lie to you, I'm acting on your family's behalf, too. Your grandfather insisted on paying. But I'd investigate pay, or no pay, I want the bastard who did this."

Hayes kept his eyes locked onto mine and nodded his head.

"Who could possibly want to do this?" He glanced away and I noticed a tear fall to the polished wood floor.

"What can you tell me about Kyle's friends?"

"I don't know any of his friends." The answer came too quickly.

"Then you haven't had contact with Kyle in a while?"

"That's… right." He was lying, sometimes you can just tell, but the photograph I'd seen told me what I had to know.

"No contact? Weren't you two close after all those years living here?"

"Not—not really," Hayes said, refusing to meet my gaze.

"Could have sworn Kyle mentioned you a few times," I lied. I wanted to get some reaction out of him.

"He'd never have mentioned me. Kyle wouldn't—"

"You two are about the same age, am I right?"

Hayes nodded, wary of where this was going.

"I guess I thought the two of you would have lots in common. Especially after living under this roof all these years."

"You don't understand Kyle, then. He had little regard for family. His family of blood was a bunch of strangers he happened to be born into. He always said that it was the people he chose as his friends who were his real family."

"But you were in both Kyle's families. You're blood relatives, but you're also good friends. Close friends. That's right, isn't it?"

"Kyle and I—"

"Are involved. Am I right? You're lovers." I watched his face as his carefully-constructed, serious expression melted into sadness and grief.

Tears tumbled over his cheeks as he wept. "No one in the family knows. And I don't want them to know. It's none of their business. They hate Kyle. They all hate him." He drew a breath and straightened up. He swiped at his face with one hand and looked me in the eye again. "I love Kyle, and he loves me. They'd never understand."

"Did any of them hate him enough to...?" I let the question finish itself. I disliked reminding him of the violence and the danger to Kyle, but I had little choice.

"Maybe," he said, his voice quavering. "We were planning to get away someday. Just the two of us. I almost had him convinced to do it now. But he didn't think it was a good idea."

"Why not? Why didn't you both get away from all this. Together."

"They wouldn't understand. That's what Kyle said. We had to wait so they couldn't hurt us."

"Who?"

"The family. Kyle said they'd have cut me off without anything if I left. Kyle didn't want that." Hayes paused and wiped at his eyes again. "Kyle wanted to be sure I'd be secure. He was afraid the family would try to interfere with his inheritance and then we'd both be left with nothing. So he said we should be cautious and protect ourselves. He wanted to wait and now..." Detwiler couldn't finish his thought.

"From what Kyle told me, his inheritance would have been enough for the both of you forever."

"You don't understand. They've got lawyers. They can try to take everything away from us."

"That's not all, though, is it?"

"No. He—he was looking out for me. He didn't want the family to hate me the way they hate him." He drew in a shuddering breath, shook his head sadly. "Can I see him? Is he—"

"Of course you can see him." I stepped to his side and gripped his shoulders. "He's not in good shape. He slipped into a coma last night and he— Just prepare yourself before you see him."

"D-do you think he'll make it?" The despair in his voice was heartrending. "I didn't get a chance to say anything to him before… And I wanted to tell him that everything's all—" It was as if he lost steam and came to a stop, unable to say more. I put an arm around his shoulder.

"It'll be good for you to be with him, Hayes. It'll be good for him, too."

"You think so?" He asked. The pain in his eyes was difficult to take, and I looked away for a moment.

"He loves you and he'll know you're there. He'll feel it."

"I can go this afternoon. Would—would you come with me?"

"I'll meet you there. Some of his friends will probably be there, and it'll be good for you to get to know them."

We agreed to meet later. Then I traced my steps back to the grand staircase and went down to have a talk with the patriarch. Beck was nowhere in sight.

Detwiler was still in the Library and told me he was preparing to have lunch.

"Will this take very long? Brigitte hates it when I don't have lunch on time and good help is not very easy to find, so I don't displease her more than I have to."

"Just a few questions this time."

"There'll be another time?"

"Probably." I didn't give him an opportunity to object. "Are there any problems between Kyle and other family members that you're aware of? Aside from the fact that none of you approve of his life."

"No. No problems that I'm aware of." His rheumy blue eyes avoided my gaze. He was trying to hide the truth, keep family business private.

"Nothing concerning Kyle's trust fund?"

"The financial concerns of this family are not public business."

"Not normally, but under the circumstances…" I paused to let him think. The message on Kyle's answering machine indicated something was brewing over the fact that Emily and her husband didn't trust the old man to handle the money. "I understand there was some disagreement about the administration of the trust fund?"

"Not as far as I'm concerned. Some people are never satisfied." His anger was barely controlled.

"Kyle, you mean?"

"Not at all. The boy never said a word about that. I must say I admire him."

"You ad—admire him?" I was taken aback, and that's not something that happens often. "Pardon me, Mr. Detwiler, but I've only ever heard that Kyle's family hates him with enthusiasm."

"We may not like his life choices," he pushed away from his desk, ready to leave the instant the interview was over. "But we've never hated him. Never. He's family."

"Some things are not a matter of choice. Kyle may have chosen his line of work, but he didn't choose who and what he is."

"Perhaps. But I do admire him for going it alone. He didn't want a cent from me, even though the trust allowed me to distribute some of the money to him, if necessary."

"You're the administrator, then?" I knew this, but they don't have to know just how much you know. It helps them open up without realizing it.

"Yes, and I intend to keep it that way. Those were Marjorie's wishes. Kyle's mother. She wanted me to administer the trust. Not her older son."

The last he said almost as a throw away. Maybe he was talking to himself, maybe he wanted me to hear. I took his lead. "Does Kyle's brother want to administer trust?"

"Trent? I don't believe he cares. He seems quite content with his job and his life. He always agrees with Emily, of course. Backs her to the hilt."

"He and his wife wouldn't mind replacing you, then?"

"Emily has some idea that she and Trent together should administer the trust. What right she has to make any suggestions about family finances is beyond me. But Trent never argues with her about her ideas."

"Could they gain anything by removing you as administrator?"

"There's always a financial element, of course. Trust administrators are entitled to some small benefits. They can invest the money as they see fit to keep the trust healthy. The administrators can also take a modest fee for the service. I don't, of course. Take a fee, that is. I don't need the money, and Kyle will need every cent he can get." Detwiler was silent a moment or two, as if he were trying to work something out for himself. "Maybe now, now that Kyle's been hurt. Maybe they'll stop haranguing me about the trust fund."

"You can always hope."

"They're not as clever as they imagine. And I still have a few things working for me." He stared at me and his eyes revealed a cunning nature that lay beneath the white-haired, gentlemanly surface.

* * *

The drive to Philly was quick. It felt as if I were reentering a whole different reality after my visit with Detwiler.

Once back, I headed for my office. The light on the answering machine was blinking non-stop, making me wish I hadn't been so picky about choosing a secretary.

I sat down, pen in hand, and started listening to the messages.

There were calls from Luke wanting to get together, from Jimmy probably wanting to get out of work at Bubbles, from Cal no doubt needing an advance on his pay. There was one from Rose requesting me to do some investigating for a case she was prosecuting. That would bring in some cash for sure. A number of other calls were from prospective clients, making me happy I'd placed print and internet ads. The last message was from Anton asking me to meet him at the Village Brew and saying he "had information." Anton enjoyed helping me on cases and loved it even more if there were a sense of intrigue or danger. Scheduling meetings in cafés to pass information created just the dramatic flair he needed. Since he almost always came up with good leads, I decided to meet him. And, to be honest, I enjoyed being with him. We'd grown closer working together on StripGuyz.

Heads turned with momentary interest when I entered the café. I was just a new distraction and, after a second or two, they'd turn back to their laptops and coffees. Anton had taken a seat near the window. He looked edgy and distracted.

I leaned over to give him a kiss. His fresh soapy scent was arousing. He turned his face to me and our lips met briefly.

"I've got news," Anton whispered.

"Can it wait until I get some coffee?"

"If you have to…" He frowned but then immediately smiled. "Go ahead."

"Okay, spill it." I was back in moments setting my coffee down on the table.

"I decided to do a little digging to see if I could find anything on the guy who stole the g-string." He smiled knowingly. He purposely made me wait as he doled out the information bit by bit. He was an expert in the art of the tease.

"And?"

"I had a talk with some of our more shady customers. People I wouldn't sit next to on a bus."

"You get anything for your trouble?"

"I got a name. I'm good at worming information out of guys."

"Okay Natasha, what's the name?" I enjoyed playing along when Anton toyed with me. His eyes sparkled with a mischievous quality I found attractive. At times like this, I wondered whether I should take a chance with him and let things play out.

"It isn't *the* guy, actually. I mean, it's not the guy who snatched Kyle's g-string."

"So what's his connection to this?"

"Seems this guy, the one I'm telling you about not the one who stole the g-string, this guy has a best friend." He looked at me as if I should have gotten it by now.

"And?"

"And, his best friend is the one." Anton beamed at me.

"I guess I'm not getting it, Anton. He's the one? The one what?"

"The one who stole the g-string. You can be really dense."

"How do we know this information is good? I've seen you twist guys around your little finger. Once you get going, they'll tell you anything just to keep you near them."

"It's good information. Dane met a guy who knows the guy in question. They got to talking. Dane confirmed what that customer told me. So it's good."

"Okay." I was still trying to tell one guy from another. "What do we do with this, assuming it's true?"

"I have a plan." His eyes sparkled but I was wary. Anton came up with great plans. Sometimes. When they worked they were good. When they didn't they were spectacular failures. The time we tried rescuing Anton's friend, an escort who'd been trapped by a client, was a stunning disaster. Some of what had happened couldn't be avoided, that's true, but the rest… I'd just as soon not get into that kind of situation again.

"Okay, shoot." I said. I could at least listen.

"Dane's friend will bring the guy, the g-string thief, into Bubbles."

"You think he'll come back in after what he did?"

"The guy is nuts. He told Dane's friend that he actually wants to go back to Bubbles to see if anyone recognizes him. He wants to be noticed. He thinks he's untouchable."

"So, what happens once Dane's friend gets him there?"

"I'll get him to tell me what he did and why. People like him enjoy bragging. They love thinking they got away with something. Makes them feel they've got big balls. Even if he's not that type, I can be pretty persuasive."

"You're pretty good at profiling your marks. I've watched you work the room at Bubbles. But this is different. What if things get out of hand? If you seem too interested in getting information out of the guy, he'll get suspicious. Right?" I worried that Anton might get himself into something over his head. "This guy wasn't just some bozo out to steal a g-string and hang it on his trophy wall. There was more to it than that. What he said to Kyle proves it. He's dangerous. You've got to think this through with me before you do anything."

"I'm willing to take the risk. I don't think it's as dangerous as you imagine. But I'll clear every detail with you, I promise. And I'll be careful."

"He's unpredictable, Anton."

"I'll make sure he's off guard. I'll get a couple of drinks into him. On the house. I'll make him think he'll be getting more than a drink if he plays his cards right."

"And if it all goes sideways?"

"You'll be there. Like you always are. And the bouncers and the other customers."

"I don't like it."

"All I'm doing is asking questions in a bar. Out in the open. The most he can do is refuse to answer and move on."

"He can do a lot more than that, Anton. He might be armed."

"We can have Kevin standing close by. Right?" He looked at me, still excited about his plan, but more subdued.

"We'll do whatever we have to. I don't want you getting hurt. Ever." I put out a hand and stroked his face. "When's this supposed to happen?"

"Tonight. Dane said his friend would bring the guy in tonight."

* * *

I got to Bubbles early, loaded with trepidation. I tried keeping busy with schedules and with setting up for the show. I stationed bouncers strategically and made sure every escape route was covered. Then I mixed in with the patrons, glad-handing regulars and greeting newbies, all the while keeping an eye on everyone and everything.

"All set, boss?" Kevin, the tallest, toughest bouncer we had, was a mountain of a man. His clothing couldn't conceal his bulging muscles or his broad chest. At the same time, Kevin was one of the best drag queens I'd seen. Tonight, though, he was all bouncer. Two-hundred-fifty pounds and six-feet-four inches of muscle and meanness.

"As set as we're gonna be," I said. "When Dane comes in, you know what to do."

"I'll be on him and his friend like lipstick on lips."

I smiled and hoped it looked sincere.

A few moments later, Dane walked in with two men at his side. One was a friend of his I'd seen before. The other, taller man, trailed slightly behind and appeared somewhat uncomfortable. I peered at him. He certainly looked like the one who'd stolen the g-string. Things had happened so fast that night and he'd gotten away clean, so it was difficult to be sure. This guy's hair was a different color and he wore more casual clothes than when Kyle was assaulted. But his face and his build were what I recalled from that night a few weeks before.

It was him, or at least close enough to the memory I had of him from the night he snatched Kyle's g-string. Dane had the night off and usually hung out at Bubbles. Even off stage, strippers command an audience and get treated like minor celebs. Dane was an audience pleaser with a following and quickly drew a crowd. His friend, the g-string thief, basked in the glow of Dane's popularity and didn't seem at all self-conscious or worried about being in the spotlight. That meant he'd be off guard and relaxed.

At some point, after Dane had been presented with a drink from a fan and his friend had ordered his own drink, they settled in to watch Bruno, as he neared the end of his first set. He made a point of cozying up to Dane. They were friendly competitors, and Bruno liked to show how good he was. Dane smiled and placed a tip in his g-string.

As Bruno moved away, the MC introduced Anton.

He'd decided to open with a decade-old song, "That Boy is Mine," making me wonder what had happened to Brandy and Monica. Anton moved luxuriously to the dreamy sound of the harp which opened the piece. The patrons grew silent. Though Anton kept talking abut retiring, he could command attention like none of my other dancers. His body had a golden glow, enhanced by the spotlight. The delicate blond body hair, covering his legs and torso, added an almost eerie shimmer.

As the music beat its way gently through the onlookers, Anton tempted them to think he was theirs and theirs alone. I was just as enchanted as I'd been when I auditioned him.

Slowly the music segued into something with deep beats and a heart-thumping refrain that caused bodies to vibrate and rhythmically move. The chords and beats reached deep into the crowd, and Anton's movements brought it all home. Jaws dropped, eyes widened, attention was paid.

Though he appeared the hardened sensual performer, Anton was really gentle, sweet, and vulnerable. For the patrons he was their fantasy for the night. Like all the other dancers they ogled.

Moving around on the bar top, Anton passed the g-string thief a couple of times, acknowledging him only as another of the many fans who'd come to see him dance. As the music heated up, so did Anton's moves and the crowd responded. His muscular form and nearly bare ass elicited more than a few cheers and whistles.

His performance was deliberate and sensual. He moved as if he what he really wanted was to take everything off and revel in naked abandon. Giving his attention to everyone, he concentrated on those waving money to tip him. And there were lots of tips, bushels of them.

Anton had sprouted so many dollar bills in the band of his g-string, he had to remove them to continue. Gyrating gracefully, he pulled out the money and in a swift movement that did not break his routine, he handed them to the bartender. As he did this, the music melted into something slower, more sexy. Anton's moves flowed naturally to the new rhythms and like a rippling sea creature, he moved to stand before the thief. Undulating his hips in the man's face, he caressed the thief's cheek with his hand.

The thief was mesmerized. Dane glanced at the guy with a smug expression on his face. He knew that Anton had hooked the man and was about to reel him in.

Anton turned his bare, glistening back to the thief, and ground his hips slowly as he lowered his ass to within inches of the man's face. I almost felt sorry for him as I watched the man dissolve into a mass of helpless jelly. He seemed to have lost all sense of where he was as he focused intently on Anton's body. Unhurried and remaining level with the man's head, Anton twisted slowly around on his powerful legs until the full pouch of his g-string came tantalizingly close to the thief's face.

The guy never took his eyes off Anton, content to live, even for a moment, as if he and Anton were the center of everything and all there was. He weakly stretched out his hand clutching a few dollar bills, indicating he wanted to tip Anton. Slowly Anton brought his crotch closer and closer to receive the dollar bills, all the while bumping his hips so that the pouch bounced up and down threatening to slip and reveal everything.

Anton extended a hand and stroked the thief's face and I noticed the guy react with pleasant surprise. Even from a distance I could see light reflected off the beads of sweat forming on his forehead. He smiled, looking up expectantly. Anton gradually rose to a standing position, taking his crotch out of the guy's face. The thief seemed confused until Anton made a slow and sexy turn allowing him to present his smooth ass with a slow tempting wiggle giving the guy a good look. Anton slid his hands temptingly over his ass cheeks as if to say, "See it. Feel it. It's yours, if you know what to do."

I pitied the guy. He had no hope of resisting as Anton worked his magic. When the man lifted his hand to offer another dollar bill, Anton took that hand and slapped it full onto his bare butt, allowing the guy one brief moment to feel the smooth, golden-pink flesh. The thief smiled so broadly I thought his face would crack. Suddenly he plastered his other hand on Anton's other cheek and tried drawing Anton closer to his face.

Just as Anton's butt was about to dock with the thief's face, Anton made another gentle revolve. The thief's hands left the surface of Anton's ass as if they were parting with life itself. This time Anton bent at the waist to bring his face close to the thief's. At this point, Anton could ask for anything. He knew it and I watched as he whispered something in the man's ear. For emphasis, he brushed his lips with the thief's.

The guy's face lit up with the hopeful expression of a man long ignored or always disappointed. What Anton would eventually do with him wouldn't change much for the poor sucker.

Anton did one more circuit around the bar, paying some attention to his regulars until his set ended.

I met Anton back in the dressing room.

"He's going to talk with me. The bastard fell for it. I could barely keep from punching him in the face. But I wanted to do this for Kyle. I've gotta get dressed and meet the creep in a few minutes." Anton was exhilarated by his success and filled with anger. This could be bad. Anton was good, but he was too close to this. I knew this would be the case, but I couldn't stop him.

"Be careful." I held him by his shoulders and looked into his eyes. I'm not sure what I saw there but it made me want to hold him and never let go. "Don't take chances. If he's the guy, there's no telling—"

I was interrupted by a falsetto shriek and turned to see Caleb in the dressing room doorway, white as porcelain, holding a piece of paper.

"Caleb? What's wrong?" Anton and I moved closer to him.

"Th-this note was— how did anybody get in? Who could have done it?"

"Slow down, Caleb and show me the paper." I held out my hand and he passed the note to me.

It seemed hastily written and said, "You're next, butt boy. Stop hurting people." This threw a whole new light on things. The note used the term "hurting people" which was what had been said to Kyle. If this was the same perpetrator, then either Kyle's family was after both of them for some reason, or they weren't in this fight at all.

"Did you see anyone in here earlier?" I handed the note to Anton as I spoke. There wasn't a full complement of dancers, this being Tuesday. It would have been easy for someone to slip in and out of the dressing room unnoticed.

"Could it have been the same creep?" Anton asked. "Did he leave Dane's side before my set? Dane would know. If it's him, we've really got the goods on him."

"We all had eyes on the guy from the minute they stepped up to the bar. Hard to see how he did this. I can ask Dane if his friend was out of his sight before they came over to the bar." I stared at the paper again. "Anything's possible."

"I've got to get out there to meet him."

"Remember, stick to the script. Don't take risks, Anton."

Anton pecked me on the cheek and left. I knew Kevin would be keeping an eye on him but I wanted to be down there, too. Except I needed to calm Caleb, who was still a wreck over the note. I placed an arm around his shoulder, and he held onto me. We both stared at the floor in silence.

* * *

"The guy's name is James and he says he's never heard of you, Caleb." Anton toyed with a French fry, swirling it in ketchup on his plate. At three in the morning the only thing I could stomach was hot tea.

The Midcity Diner was a late night haven for every character prowling the city at that hour. The so-so food was cheap, and the waitresses were tough, competent, and fun. The fragrance of greasy hamburgers and strong coffee was strangely comforting.

"He could be lying." Caleb brought his Coke shakily to his lips.

"I don't think so," Anton said. "He answered every question I asked."

"What did you have to give in return?" I asked, wiggling my eyebrows but feeling uncomfortable. Watching Anton being pawed when he danced at Bubbles was one thing. It was something else thinking about him in a private liaison with a customer. I never allowed my dancers to do anything remotely close to a lap dance or anything like it.

"I didn't have to give anything like your dirty mind is imagining, Marco." Anton winked. "And why do you care? You haven't put a ring on my finger. Unless you've got one hidden in your pocket ready to propose?"

"What exactly did you get for whatever it is you gave?" I ignored his "ring" jab.

"James is the g-string thief. He admitted it. Said he took it." Anton smirked.

Caleb gasped, his eyes trained on Anton.

"Lone operator or was he paid to do it?" I asked.

"Hired hand. But he swears he had nothing to do with hurting Kyle. Didn't even know about it until I told him. That's why I don't think James knows anything about the note Caleb received." Anton popped a fry into his mouth and munched. "James is kind of a sweet guy, in a way. Really sorry about bothering Kyle. He said he liked watching Kyle dance and almost didn't want to steal the g-string. But he was afraid the thug'd kill him."

"Anton! Your new best friend James harassed Kyle two or three times and may have beaten him nearly to death. Even if he claims he didn't. How's that add up to sweet?" I liked Anton. And probably his ability to see the good side of everyone was one reason I did. But this time he went a little too far.

"Well…" He looked down guiltily at his ketchup-smeared plate.

"Well, nothing. You've gotta be careful." I was more worried that some time or other, in the middle of something potentially dangerous, he'd let down his guard and get hurt because he wanted to give someone the benefit of the doubt.

"I know."

"Did he say who hired him?"

"Hey! You guys got a light?" A haggard-looking man in a tattered suit, had stumbled over to our table and saw no problem interrupting us.

"Nobody here smokes, pal."

"Too good for smokin'? You fags are ruinin' a good thing." He burped loudly, turned around and, trailing a scent like three day old fish, staggered away.

"Did your new friend James say who hired him?" I asked again.

"Some thug. James doesn't know him really. The thug gave James his orders," Anton said. "James overheard this thug speaking to somebody on the phone. Whoever that was is the one behind it all."

"Did you get the thug's name?"

"James didn't say and I didn't wanna push. He was being pretty open. I was afraid if I pushed, he'd close down."

"You did the right thing. If he'd given you just a little more, though..."

"He promises to come back in tomorrow night. I can get him to talk again."

"But you're not scheduled to dance."

Anton squinted at me and the set of his jaw was firm. I knew that look. It meant he wouldn't budge. "I've got to be scheduled. James wants me to dance just for him. Says he has big bucks and wants to shower some of it on me. Not gonna miss that kind of money."

"If you believe him. What makes you so sure, Anton."

"Just something about him. I'm not a bad judge of character," he said. I knew he was right.

"If you think so…" I let my voice trail off. Was I worried about what the guy might do or did it bother me that Anton would be alone with him for another night?

"You're such a nut, Marco. You really think it's all about the money?"

I stared at him. "You're interested in this guy?" I couldn't hide my surprise.

"No! What're you thinking?" Anton's eyes narrowed. "I made him promise to get me the name of the thug who hired him. I told him that'd be the only way I'd dance for him again. Well, that and the money." Anton smiled mischievously. I'd memorized that smile and everything else about his face.

"You really sure he's not the one who left that note for me?" Caleb asked interrupting my thoughts. His voice was shaky. Without Kyle here protecting him, he must've felt lost. "If he got into our dressing room, maybe he could get to me at home? Maybe he knows where—"

"You can stay at my place tonight," I offered. "That way you won't have to worry about anything."

"He won't?" Anton shot me a glance.

"He can't stay at his place all alone. Not after that note." I looked at Anton and tried appearing as innocent as possible, which, for me, is not that easy.

"I can take him in for the night." Anton said. "He's comfortable with me."

I didn't like talking about the kid as if he were some wall hanging.

"Caleb, it's up to you. You want to stay with Anton or me?"

"I'd feel better if you both stayed with me. You never know if that guy will have someone with him if he tries to… you know."

"That's a great idea!" Anton beamed.

The kid was brilliant. I'd have to reevaluate him. He managed to ensure that neither of us would have him all to ourselves and neither of us could complain. I had to hand it to him.

Anton led him out the door while I gave the cashier some money and the check. I followed and told them where I'd parked way down on Chestnut. There were still a few spots the valet-parking vultures hadn't claimed.

We took my car, intending to make a few stops before ending up at my house. First to Anton's apartment to pick up what he'd need, then to Caleb's place which was also Kyle's, in order to get his stuff.

We hadn't gone two blocks when I noticed the other car. A dark old-model Chevy. He was a sloppy tail, which meant he wasn't a professional. If he was this bad, I might be able to lose him. Except that there was no traffic at this hour and it wouldn't be easy.

"Listen up, guys. I have to make some detours. We won't be stopping anywhere just yet. Hold on." I headed over Twelfth and, when I turned onto Sansom, it was a little faster than I'd intended and we nearly hit a post. I knew the neighborhood well enough to lose the guy, if I could stay in one piece.

"What's going on, Marco?" Anton didn't sound happy.

"We've got company. I need to lose him." I swerved around another corner and was on 13th Street. Looking back, I spotted the Chevy rolling cautiously onto the street, too. In the middle of town it'd be difficult losing the joker. I turned back to Chestnut then onto Twelfth again and zipped down to Pine Street. I couldn't see the other car but without much traffic, he'd catch up sooner or later. I headed toward the Old City section of town where there were back streets and tight turns and I might be able to do a better job of evading him. In the mirror, I saw the car way in the distance. A car or two had jumped between us and that helped. But he was there, and I didn't like that.

"Who is it?" Caleb's voice shook. "Who's following us? Is it him?"

"Don't know, Caleb." I sped through a yellow light. "You have any ideas?"

"Me? Why would I?" he said and there was something curious in the way he responded.

"Why would Caleb know this guy?" Anton said. "Just get us out of here."

As if I wasn't trying to do just that.

Turning onto Third Street, I looked back and didn't see our tail. I turned quickly onto Delancey, hoping that we'd lost the guy for good. From Delancey, I turned onto Fourth, nipped into a quiet street called Gaskill and cut the car's lights. I pressed a finger to my lips and whispered, "We'll wait here. Keep calm."

Damned if I didn't look down the street to see the old car zip past Gaskill and miss us completely. That was nice but it also meant that he'd kept up better than I liked. He'd realize soon he'd lost us. I had to act quickly.

With the lights still off, I started up and rolled the car out and back onto Third.

"Where're we going?" Anton asked.

"Odds are he doesn't know where you or I live."

"Right."

"He could know," came a weak voice from the back seat. "He might know where you live Anton. He might know a lot," Caleb said, his little kid voice hesitant, quavering.

I was headed toward for my place anyway, so I turned on the lights and hit the gas. We practically flew to Spring Garden and up to Nineteenth. My house was situated inside a new complex on the lower level of a set of piggy-back homes.

I doused the lights before I got to the gate leading to the courtyard. Pulling into a parking spot at the other end of the lot, away from my house, I got Anton and Caleb out of the car and onto the shadowed sidewalk. At four in the morning only the nosiest neighbors might be up and snooping. We moved quickly to the back door of my house.

As soon as we were inside, the telephone rang.

"We're not home," I said to Anton and Caleb. The phone kept ringing.

"Who'd call you at this time of night?" Anton said.

"I told you," Caleb's voice was softer than it had been. "He knows."

"How could he know, Caleb? You're not making sense." I knew that one more ring would get the answering machine going. "Even if it is the guy, I don't want him knowing we're here."

"Should I turn out that light?" Anton indicated a small lamp in the living room.

"No. I always leave that on. If he's got an eye on the place, he'll see it go out."

The answering machine picked up on the next ring. After my outgoing announcement, there was no message left. Whoever called said nothing. The silence went on and on.

"He'll get into the house. I know it." Caleb said, sounding completely unnerved.

"Caleb, calm down." Anton said a little too harshly.

"I can't. He was after Kyle, and now he's after me."

"Who, Caleb? Did you see the guy who tried to kill Kyle?" I asked gently.

"N-no." Caleb's voice shook.

"But you know something, don't you?"

"Not about who beat Kyle. No. It's—" The telephone rang again, and Caleb froze for a moment. Then he turned to me, the fear so clear on his face, it was painful. "He knows we're here. He knows."

After only two rings, the phone went silent.

"Who knows we're here? Who is it, Caleb?" I said. "If you know, tell us. We can do something if we know." I sat him down on the couch and sat next to him. The house was in semi-darkness. The only lamp I'd left on didn't provide much light. Caleb's eyes were big as wagon wheels and dilated to catch every bit of light. Placing a hand on his shoulder, I turned him toward me. "Who's out there, Caleb?"

"M-my father. I… I t-think. It's *gotta* be my father. He said he'd g-get me. Or maybe my brother." Caleb's voice grew smaller with each word.

"Why're you so sure it's them? What do they want?"

"Me. They want me. They think I'll go home with them. Back to Lancaster."

"Did they threaten you?"

"And Kyle. Because I was staying with him."

"How long have they been bothering you?" I asked.

"A few weeks. Ever since they found out I was in Philly. Somebody saw me in the city and told them. So my family tracked me down. They're crazy people."

"How'd they find out where you live?"

"I don't know how. I don't. Maybe it was somebody in the bar. I don't know. I just want them to stop. I don't wanna go back." Caleb seemed on the edge of panic. I motioned Anton over to help. I knew he trusted Anton.

I went to phone the police.

Before I could even tap in the numbers, the door buzzer sounded. And didn't stop. It was as if somebody pressed the button and wouldn't let go. At the same time, someone pounded on the tall wooden gate leading to my front yard. The gate wasn't meant to hold out a determined maniac. Moments later, wood splintered. I heard footsteps and someone began pounding on the front door. Unlike the gate, the metal door would hold.

But we had to think fast. I called the police, slammed down the phone, and pulled my gun.

"What do we do?" Anton said as he and Caleb came to stand with me.

Before I could answer, a heavy planter crashed through the big front window. Glass went everywhere. The metal frame of the window twisted inward.

A large men barreled through the wreckage of the window, followed by a second, just as large but older man, who got caught on the twisted metal and jagged remnants of glass.

Caleb screamed and clutched my arm.

Anton crouched into a fighting stance, ready to protect Caleb.

I centered my feet and pointed my gun at the intruders. "Hold it!"

"Caleb! You son of a bitch!" The larger of the two men, tall, blond, and puffy-fat from too much beer, looked around as if trying to decide who to kill first. Letting out a guttural cry, he lunged at Caleb, glass shards dropping like confetti from his clothes.

To reach Caleb he barreled through me, knocking my gun out of my hand.

Caleb leaped to my left, tripped and went down. Instantly the tall man jumped on the kid, slapping and punching at him. The boy's body shook with each blow, but he struggled fiercely against the much stronger man.

I turned on the guy and tried pulling him off Caleb. He rose up to slam Caleb's head into the floor and I connected with his jaw. I swung my foot up and struck a blow to his chest. The young blond reeled back, falling flat on his ass, dazed.

The older man, just as big and no less wild, had extricated himself from the window and turned his attention on us. Ignoring his bleeding arm and leg, he charged. Out of the corner of my eye, I saw Anton raise one of my teakwood dining room chairs.

Before the guy knew what hit him, Anton smashed the chair down onto his head. That took care of him and my chair. He didn't look as if he'd get up any time soon.

The younger guy groaned and jumped up before we could stop him. He shook his head, ducked like he was playing touch football and rushed me.

This time I was ready. With a small maneuver, I managed to flip him onto his face, twisting his arm behind him. Helpless, he resisted but never cried out in pain.

"This your brother, Caleb?" I huffed as I held the struggling man.

"Y-yeah. Seth."

"I'll kill you, you little faggot. You'll end up like the other fag." He struggled against the pressure I exerted on his arm, then hissed in pain. "You hurt Mom and Dad, even Sis. You nearly killed them, turnin' out the way you did."

"You tried to kill my friend? You hurt Kyle?" Caleb shouted.

"I wanted to. Because of what he did to you. Teachin' you all that stuff. Makin' you a fag. You're a disgrace. Takin' your clothes off for other men! I wanted to kill him."

"You're sayin' you didn't kill Kyle?" I twisted his arm again forcing him to answer.

"Ow! I didn't kill nobody. He was already dead," he said, his voice gruff, filled with pain. "I would'a though. He—"

"What're you saying?"

"I'm sayin' the fag was already dead when I got there. I wanted to kill him, but somebody beat me to it. It wasn't me, but I wish it was," he growled. "I left and closed the door behind me."

"Didn't even bother to call the police?" I couldn't help myself, I had to twist that arm again.

"Why should I? He was dead. If he wasn't I would'a finished him." He hissed from the pain.

"Bastard," I said and tugged on his arm.

"Then it was you?" Caleb asked. "You left that note in the dressing room?"

Seth was quiet, other than the groans of pain, every time I got a better grip on his arm.

"Answer the man," I ordered.

"I w-wrote the note, yeah." He twisted in my grip. "Oww!"

"How'd you get it up to the dressing room?"'

"I p-paid some fag kid to take it up. I wasn't gonna go up there."

"The police are gonna be real interested in your story." I was more interested in who'd actually beaten Kyle.

Squad car sirens wailed, brakes screeched, and I heard car doors thump shut outside. Anton had already opened the door and was waiting for them.

I looked around at the wreckage which had once been my house. For good measure, and a little revenge, I twisted Seth's arm once more. He screamed, but that wouldn't pay for all the repairs I'd have do.

* * *

The second time out to Gladwyne seemed quick, but then I had a lot to do and my mind raced as I drove. The mansion still impressed when it came into view and my car was still the only one spoiling the beige pebbles. This time a pert maid in a dowdy outfit opened the door and let me in.

Detwiler said he'd assemble his family as I'd asked when I called. I was ushered into a room off the grand foyer. It was lavishly furnished with sedate Federal style pieces. The cream-colored walls and blue fabric on the furniture gave the room a peaceful air. I felt anything but peace as I waited for them to arrive.

Detwiler entered shortly after I did.

"Mr. Fontana. You have some information for me?" He extended a hand. His eyes were a brilliant blue and spoke of a highly intelligent man.

"I have information. You may or may not like it."

"The others will be here in a moment. Can you tell—"

"I'd rather wait, if it's all the same to you."

"We'll do it your way, Mr. Fontana. Ah, here's Hayes."

Hayes walked into the room, and when he saw me his eyes spoke volumes.

"Mr. Fontana." Hayes nodded. "You know something about Kyle's attacker?"

"I do, but where's—"

Trent and Emily entered the room before I could finish asking.

"We're all here, Mr. Fontana," Detwiler said. "What have you found?"

"It took a little digging and a lot of legwork but I've got a name for you," I said holding out a folder. "James Korn is the man who harassed Kyle at his place of work."

I told them about Korn's meetings with Anton, without saying exactly how Anton had gotten the information. They only needed what they needed.

Korn was as good as his word and had given Anton the name of the thug who'd hired him.

"My associate said the name was Paul Rand." I looked around at them to see if this elicited a reaction, and I was satisfied when I saw how one of them took the news.

"This Rand is the person who hurt Kyle?" Detwiler asked.

"Did you find him?" Hayes asked.

"Didn't take long. I found Rand and the police have him."

"Then it's finished," Emily said. Her voice steady, her face drawn into a mask of seriousness. She stared at me, then looked toward her husband. "Trent, you should call your friends in the Philadelphia District Attorney's office."

Trent said nothing.

"It's finished as far as Rand is concerned," I continued. "But he wasn't the big fish, if you catch my drift."

"There was someone else?" Detwiler asked, his eyes a hard steely color now.

"Rand didn't know Kyle," I said. "Didn't have a motive to hurt him. Except for the cash he was paid to do the job."

"Someone paid this guy to hurt Kyle?" Hayes asked. His whole body tensed and, skinny as he was, I saw him clench one hand into a fist ready to strike. I casually moved toward him, to fend off any reaction to what I would say next.

"Rand was pretty quick to give up the name of the person who paid him. Said he met this person in downtown Philly at some dive bar." I stood next to Hayes, placed a hand on his shoulder. "You happen to remember the name of that bar, Emily? It was you he met there, am I right?"

"You're insane. That man lied because you pressured him. You probably told him what to say."

"Do I look like a ventriloquist? Rand speaks pretty well for himself and he's probably doing plenty of talking right now at police headquarters."

"Emily?" Trent spoke for the first time and I couldn't help but hear Kyle's voice in his. "Emily did you do this?"

Emily was stone silent.

"She did it, Trent. And then some. She paid Rand to harass Kyle. He had no desire to go into a gay bar so he hired Korn to do that. When Korn failed to have the desired effect, Rand was told to step it up a notch. Right Emily? That *is* what you told Rand."

Emily refused to meet my stare. She looked at the floor as if something very important were written there.

"We know what happened next. And Rand isn't willing to take the fall all by his lonesome," I said. "I think when the police check bank records they'll have an even more clear connection between Emily and Rand."

"How could you?" Detwiler said. His eyes were trained on Trent's wife. "I gave you and Trent everything you could ask for. You'd be inheriting a trust the size of which will last you both a long time. A very long time. But you wanted more? Is that it? You'd like everything, I suppose. Is that what you want?"

Emily's head snapped up and she stared at Detwiler with a hateful, vicious look on her face. But she said nothing. She'd be spending whatever money she and Trent had to defend herself in court. She must've been pondering that and wondering how all her schemes had gone so wrong.

"Grandfather, this is outrageous!" Trent shouted.

"For once you're right, Trent. Your behavior—"

"But you can't think I…" Trent stood, mouth open and working, but his voice was less than a whisper.

"It's all very clear to me, Trent."

"But I didn't… I wouldn't…" Trent found his voice again but it was weak and he sounded defeated. "I had no idea, grandfather. None."

"She's your *wife*, Trent. How could you have no idea?"

"We haven't been husband and wife for some time. No one notices those details around here as long as nothing appears different on the surface. You don't even notice me. None of you. I'm gone for weeks at a time, and when I get back it's as if I'm still gone. I might as well be a portrait on the wall."

"I should have guessed it was you, Emily," Hayes spoke, his voice controlled. "You hated Kyle. You hated all of us. But hurting Kyle, how could you?" Hayes made a move toward Emily but I still had my hand on his shoulder. I pressed against his forward motion keeping him in place.

"She's not worth it, Hayes. You and Kyle. Just think about that. That's all that matters for you. She'll get what's coming to her."

His body was taut but he looked at me and nodded. I felt him begin to relax.

"I'll call the police." I flipped out my cell phone.

"No." Detwiler said. "I'll handle that." He strode over an picked up the phone. "I should have handled much more. This is my responsibility."

* * *

"I'm glad playing footsie with James got results. Catching Emily made it all worth it. That and the money he gave me." Anton sipped his iced tea.

"You got results. That's what counts."

"When James told me he'd given Kyle's g-string to that thug Rand, I almost slugged him."

"So that's how the g-string made it to Kyle's bedroom when he was beaten. One more piece of the puzzle. Rand is a hard person. Not a human emotion in the guy."

"At least James wasn't that bad." Anton drank more of his tea.

I'd never been to Anton's apartment before and I was surprised he'd invited me up. Not that I had any expectations. He had his rules. But just being here was progress. His kitchen was spotless and the window looked down onto a courtyard filled with flowers beginning to bloom and trees greening up. It almost made the past few weeks seem like a bad dream instead of grim reality.

I watched Anton as he sat at his kitchen table drinking iced tea. His masculine demeanor and deep voice made him appear tough and untouchable but there was a vulnerability underneath. We'd known each other almost two years and there was still a lot I didn't know about him. Like what made him so vulnerable at times. I knew he was masking something, keeping some part of his past from clouding his present. Maybe we'd get to sharing that some time.

"You made a difference in the case, Anton. I'm glad you did what you did. I mean, I'm not glad you had to play up to James Korn, but it helped. I wouldn't have connected Emily to this without you."

"Thank you. Nothing I couldn't handle, though, and I kinda had fun." He stared at me with those crystal blue eyes and I saw tiny cracks in his tough façade. "Weren't you the least bit jealous while I tangled with that guy? Or was I just another tool in your detective kit?"

"Jealous?" I squeezed the lemon wedge so hard, it snapped and splashed into my iced tea. I knew what Anton was getting at and he'd nicely backed me into a corner. If I said yes, he'd take it as more meaningful than it was. If I said no, it would hurt him more than I cared to think about. I took a swallow of tea buying myself some time. "I was jealous. Maybe. A little," I said. Then quickly added, "But I was really concerned for your safety. That's what I was thinking about more than anything. Even the case."

"You're bullshitting me again, Marco." Anton touched my hand.

"No. I was worried." That was no lie, I *was* concerned. "But I knew you could handle yourself. And you did."

"I did. Didn't I?" He perked up and drained his glass in one long swallow. "How's Kyle? Last time I was there he was still half out of it."

"Saw him this morning. He's up and talking. He's still not strong. But the doctor said he was through the worst of it." I sipped some tea. "The real surprise came as I was leaving."

"What was that?"

"Detwiler walked into the room."

"Bet Kyle didn't expect him."

"Trent and Hayes were with him. I think that's gonna help Kyle a lot. They were even nice to Caleb which gave Kyle more of a boost."

"You think Kyle's gonna want to come back to work at Bubbles?"

"My guess is yes. When he's ready."

"I'll have to tell him I'm keeping an eye on Caleb until he gets back into things."

"Yeah, I've noticed an improvement in Caleb's routine. Your doing?"

"I think it's just because Caleb's happier now. He feels safer with his father and brother behind bars."

"Bars!" I said, remembering an appointment. "Bars on my front window. I've got to get to my place. I promised to meet the repairmen."

"Gonna cost a lot?"

"I've got insurance. But I've decided to move. I'll get the place in shape and find a condo closer to my office and Bubbles."

Anton nodded.

"I owe you, Anton. So does Kyle. I haven't forgotten."

I moved to his side, and he turned to face me. His eyes searched my face. They were deep and blue, and I felt as if I were falling into them. I leaned over, took his face in my hands, and kissed him on the mouth. It felt good, *he* felt good. The closeness and the warmth. I found myself feeling that I could get used to this.

Too Many Boyfriends

There was no one at the Dilworth's front desk which meant anyone could have access to the building. Not a good thing. Sassy, head of security and chief desk attendant, must've been on break without anyone on back-up duty. Since Sammy had asked me to meet him as soon as I could, I decided it was more important to get up to his place than to wait for Sassy.

The Dilworth Arms was a great spot to call home if you didn't mind the holes in security. Right in the middle of downtown Philly and the gayborhood, the Dilworth had rental fees that were almost a steal. Lots of people I knew who lived there said lax security was their only complaint.

Sassy, the drag queen who occupied the front desk most of the time, wasn't exactly a Border Patrol Agent. She'd stop you, especially if you were good-looking and she wanted a good look at you, otherwise she'd let you slip into the building pretty easily. If she did happen to stop you, all you needed to do was to appeal to her flirtatious side and she'd let you pass. Sassy was fun. No doubt about it. But she was no defense against intruders.

The lobby was eerily still and empty which was unusual. People were always bustling through the airy entrance. I ignored my sense that something wasn't right and headed for the elevators. Sammy lived on the third floor. He'd insisted on a low floor when he moved in. "Fire rescue ladders can't get past the tenth floor," he'd said. I wasn't so sure about that, but who am I to argue with people's fears? I'd known Sammy a long time and had seen him through good times and bad, but after years of friendship, I learned that the most constant thing about him was the fluidity of his life and his ways. That made him both fun and frustrating.

When the elevator opened on the third floor, I took a right and padded down the long, carpeted hall to Sammy's place.

I rang the bell a couple of times, then pushed open the door. Sammy often left his door unlocked when he expected company. Now that he was temporarily disabled, he left the door unlocked all the time to keep from having to maneuver his wheelchair around to answer the door. This was not the wisest move, but Sammy was Sammy and no one was going to change him. I couldn't blame him, though. With two broken legs and three surgeries to correct the breaks, he was not in great shape. The unwieldy leg casts made everything difficult. The only time he locked his door was when he wouldn't be at home.

"Sammy?" I called softly in case he was napping. After the third surgery and lots of rehab, his struggle to recover was exhausting. So, he napped often and the nurse who looked in on him had told me that plenty of sleep was a good thing. I half expected him to be snoozing every time I got to his place.

This time, though, something didn't feel right. There was a stillness that didn't say "nap" to me.

I called out, a bit louder, "Sammy?"

There was no answer.

"Hello?" Shutting the door behind me, I moved cautiously into the apartment. The faint fragrance of chili hung in the air and I knew that Bart, Sammy's ex had recently been there making his famous party chili and looking after Sammy. Bart had never gotten over the breakup and took any opportunity to make Sammy like him again. He was desperate to get Sammy to forget the things he'd done that made Sammy throw him out in the first place. Bart's efforts worked to a point. They'd become friendly enough for Bart to get an invitation to Sammy's holiday parties, but Sammy would never forget the betrayal or the hurt he'd felt. No matter how much chili Bart cooked up.

I moved past the kitchen and into the hall leading to Sammy's bedroom.

"Sammy? You decent? I'm coming in, ready or not." I called. There was no answer. Moving silently over the carpeted floors, I went past the bathroom and the tiny room he used for TV and video games. The next door was his bedroom, and I dreaded what I might find.

"Hey!" I tried once more and knocked at the door. Nothing.

When I pushed in the bedroom door, I saw him.

It looked as if he were asleep, but blood was spattered everywhere and soaked everything. The wheelchair he used was pushed into a corner where he could never reach it. He wouldn't have been able to get out of the bed on his own without it.

The closer I got, the more blood I saw. Blood drenched the bed and cast-off blood made an ugly pattern on the wall and ceiling. Head wounds gush lots of blood, but this one looked like more than a simple bump on the head. This was bad.

Placing two fingers to his neck, I felt for a pulse. It was faint but still there. His breathing was shallow. I flipped out my cell phone, called 911, explained the situation, and described the scene. I told them I'd wait for them.

In the meantime, I looked over the scene without touching anything.

It didn't appear Sammy had put up much of a fight. He couldn't have in any event, with both legs in casts. His attacker must've found Sammy lying in bed and battered him before he had a chance to react. I didn't see a weapon or anything that looked like it might've been used as a weapon. Maybe it'd turn up when the police searched.

Looking around, I realized the room had already been thoroughly searched. With Sammy lying there, I hadn't noticed the disorder. The closet door was open, and everything in it had been thrown out onto the floor. The dresser drawers were emptied, and piles of clothing littered the floor around it. Sammy's desk was a wreck. Drawers pulled out and emptied, papers scattered, everything in disarray. It appeared that his computer was missing. I had to assume Sammy's TV room and maybe even the living room had also been tossed by whoever had done this.

I turned, ready to check out the other rooms, and came face to face with Dan standing in the bedroom doorway. Eyes wide, a hand to his mouth, he stared at Sammy then at me.

"What've you done!" A little strangled scream escaped him. He rushed over to the bed, where he knelt by Sammy's side and wailed.

Instead of answering his question, which would've been useless anyway, I kept quiet and wondered if Dan had been in the apartment all along. Maybe he'd hidden when he heard me enter. Could be that he was the one who knocked Sammy senseless. I looked over at him, still crying up a storm, and figured his tears seemed real enough. So I stood back and gauged his actions while waiting for him to get the drama out of his system and maybe give me a hand. That didn't look like it'd happen any time soon.

Dan was a once-cute, now pudgy, former boyfriend of Sammy's. His high-pitched, gravelly voice was incongruous in his paunchy body, but it was his mark of distinction and he never failed to make an impression with it. If Dan's screeching didn't bring Sammy to his senses, my old friend was in real trouble.

Eventually, Dan's caterwauling wound down, and he got to his feet as if struggling under the great weight of grief. Finally standing again, he pressed his hands to the sides of his head, closed his eyes, and took deep breaths. It was hard to keep from laughing.

"Who did this?" Dan demanded as he emerged from his trance and struck a pose in front of me. His blond hair looked tarnished, and his blue eyes had not seen enough sleep. "Why would anyone do this to Sammy? He's a sweet guy and totally harmless."

"Harmless maybe, but Sammy likes playing with fire and sometimes a person gets burned doing that." I paced as I spoke. "Look at him. Two broken legs and those other injuries. All because of some crazy stunt."

Sammy had been staying at his brother's Ocean City house and trying to relive his glory days as a college frat boy. He'd gotten it into his head that he wanted to repeat a water skiing stunt that had gone over well when he was nineteen. Nearing fifty now, Sammy had tried balancing two hunks on his shoulders while flying over the waves on water skis. There were other details but that was the main act. It wasn't a hit.

It took his brother a long while and a lot of nursing care to get Sammy well enough to travel back to Philly. Sammy still needed major help after his return and remained largely housebound. The only plus was that he'd survived.

"So, it's true, then, about the stunt?"

"All true. Sammy's no kid anymore, but he thinks he is."

Dan screwed up his face, peered over at Sammy then glared at me. "All right, so he's too stupid to know he's old, but what's that stunt got to do with this beating?"

"Probably nothing. But I've known the guy a lot longer than you and finding him this way is not entirely a surprise." What happened to Sammy made all kinds of sense when you thought more deeply about the kinds of things Sammy got himself into. Even Dan should have known that much after having lived with the man for two years. But Dan wasn't thinking. Of course, that was Dan's major problem and that was why he was no longer Sammy's live-in partner.

"How can you be so cold?"

"Stop and think, Dan. Think about the things Sammy got himself into when you lived with him."

Dan stood looking from side to side, wavering like a flame as he thought. His face displayed a range of emotions and feelings.

"Who could've done this, Marco?"

"Right now that's wide open. I was supposed to meet him to discuss some article he wants to write for some gay scandal blog or a newspaper or something. He wasn't clear about that part. When I got here, the door was open. I found him this way."

"What article? He never told me about any article. He usually likes to get my advice." Dan scowled at Sammy, as if he'd been betrayed. If Sammy ever consulted Dan about anything, it certainly wasn't about his work. Sammy had stopped communicating with Dan in that way a long time ago.

"It was some piece about the secrets and scandals of powerful players in the community. Sammy mentioned something about having lots of dirt on certain people. He said the article was sort of a trial balloon for the book he wants to write exposing the inner workings of the city's movers and shakers."

"Oh." Dan looked confused. "Sure, the power—uh—brokers. Yeah, I knew about that." His tone suggested he knew nothing of the sort. "Somebody'd do this over some article?"

"Can't say for sure, Dan. But it's hard to imagine somebody would get this crazy over some kiss and tell article." I glanced at Sammy, wondering when the damned EMTs would get to the apartment. "This looks more like the result of pure rage. Whoever did this was ferocious. Really wanted to make Sammy pay. This is not blowback from some stupid article hardly anyone knows about and that he hasn't even written yet."

"Maybe… maybe it was his job? He came in contact with a lotta strange people at city hall. Maybe one of them…" Dan trailed off, lost in his thoughts.

"Could be," I said. "He always had mysterious things going on at his job. He knew plenty of shady types. And he made all of them angry one time or another."

"He had enemies? Not Sammy. He didn't have enemies." Dan seemed surprised. "When I lived here all kinds of people came in and out of the apartment. But none of them looked dangerous."

"Well, Sammy had a lot more going on outside of work," I said.

"Tell me about it," Dan spat out the words. "Like all those telephone hook-up lines he used or the online sex sites. He let them all into this place. People he didn't know. He did whoever he wanted, whenever he wanted. Even when I was livin' with him. This could've been done by some stranger that Sammy let in and— this is so horrible."

"This might have been done by someone he knew, too. Could've been anyone. Even old boyfriends…" I let that hang in the air to see if Dan reacted. He was as good a suspect as anyone else as far as I was concerned.

"Old boyfriends! Are you… are you sayin' that…" Dan's train of thought got derailed as something else popped into his head. "That reminds me, did you see Bart? Wasn't he here? Didn't you see him? Where is that creep? When you said old boyfriends, you reminded me that I…" Dan didn't continue. Instead he cast a sideways glance at Sammy. Dan either didn't take the hint that I might've meant him when I'd said "old boyfriends" or he was trying to throw the blame on someone else.

"I reminded you of what, Dan?" I asked. He was maddening at times. Leaving things half said or not said at all. "And what do you mean about Bart?"

"Nothing." He licked his lips, shifted from one foot to the other as if he had to use the bathroom. "When you said 'old boyfriends' you reminded me that Bart is one of Sammy's old flames. Not that I think Bart did this, but he and Sammy lived together after I was outta the picture."

"A moment ago, you asked did I see him. How could I see him? What're you not telling me?"

"Well… I was just—"

"Spit it out, Dan."

"I don't want to get anybody in trouble, y'know?" Dan shifted his weight again. "Bart could've had a good reason. For bein' here, I mean." He paused and looked at his feet. "Bart was right behind me when I came in here." Dan moved tentatively toward the bedroom door and peeked out into the hall as if expecting Bart to jump him for ratting on him. "I don't know where he went. He's not here now. He's gone. But he was behind me when I came in just now. I saw him clear as I see you." Dan turned back to face me.

"You came here together?" That was strange. Dan and Bart hated each other with a passion only my relatives could understand. Bart was Dan's successor in Sammy's bed. Once Bart took up residence, he'd never allowed Dan any privileges in the apartment. Even if Sammy didn't agree, he always let Bart have his way. Dan never forgot the treatment he'd received from Bart, and he could never forgive his young replacement. I was sure Dan even resented Sammy for agreeing with Bart.

"Together? Us? Together? Are you smoking inferior product? I wouldn't walk with Bart to his execution, if that was his last wish." Dan fumed. He glared at me. "That turd snuck up behind me when I was waiting for an elevator. He whined about needing to see Sammy. I couldn't stop him from getting on the elevator. It's a free country. So, we rode up together." He made a sound of disgust. "Of course, he never looked at me. Not once the whole way up. He followed me off the elevator and was right behind me when I saw Sammy's door was open. I walked in and saw you and poor Sammy. And all I remember is screaming."

"Bart, huh?" Though he worked hard at keeping Sammy's friendship, I knew that he hardly ever stopped by on a whim. He always called ahead for Sammy's permission. "Bart never said what he wanted with Sammy?"

"Nothing. He said nada. Not one word, the little Irish shit." Dan rolled his eyes.

"He was standing behind you. On the surface, it looks like you and he arrived together, after Sammy was beaten. Make sense to you?"

"I… I guess," Dan reluctantly agreed.

"Any number of people could have done this," I said. Sammy let so many guys into his place it'd be a job just finding out their names. I knew Sammy's habits would catch up with him one day. I was sorry to see it happen, though.

"So, you're gonna do nothing about this?" Dan confronted me, hands on hips.

"Not much I *can* do until the police get here," I said. It had only been a couple of minutes since I'd called, but Dan made it seem like hours. I wanted him gone so I could talk to the police without him nosing around.

"The police? Why do we need—"

"You're smarter than that, Dan. Look at this place. It's a crime scene. The police are gonna be all over this. Anyway, first thing is to make sure Sammy's all right."

"There's a— oh! You think he may not be? It's that bad?" He spoke as if he'd never considered the possibility that Sammy was in serious condition.

"It doesn't look good from where I stand."

As I said that someone pounded at the door.

"Philly PD! Open up," the voice boomed.

I opened the door and a young officer stepped, in brushing by me. He glanced around suspiciously as he moved through the room.

"EMTs are on their way up. What've we got here?"

I explained as I led him into Sammy's bedroom. The officer subtly recoiled at the sight of all the blood.

"I'll call my sergeant. He'll get a detective down here." He turned to leave the room, then pivoted back. "You two better step out of the room. Crime scene. The EMTs will take care of your friend." He was almost apologetic.

"Oh, shit," Dan said looking over at Sammy on the bed. "Shit. Shit. Shit. How'd you get yourself into this, Sammy?"

* * *

There was something familiar about the detective who came through the apartment door as the EMTs worked on Sammy in the bedroom. He glanced at me and Dan then disappeared into the bedroom. Muffled voices floated out of the room as he spoke with the EMTs. Then I heard the sound of the gurney being readied. Moments later, the techs rolled Sammy out toward the door.

Dan asked to accompany Sammy to the hospital and the detective assigned a police officer to stay with them both.

"I'll need to question you later. Don't go anywhere," he said after taking Dan's name.

The detective turned toward me and I realized who he was. A tall black man with snowy white hair rimming his bald pate, the detective had the same determined look as he'd had the first time we'd met. I was in high school and he was assigned to investigate the death of the school disciplinarian. He'd changed quite a bit in the years since we met, but not in the way he approached a crime scene.

Turning, he reentered the bedroom and I stood in the doorway to watch him work.

He gazed intently around the room and I knew he was memorizing every detail. Not noticing me at first, he concentrated on the blood spatter and the ransacked desk. As he finished his mental inventory of the room and allowed one of the CSIs to take some photographs, he turned in my direction.

"And who're you?" He peered at me as if he thought he should remember who I was but couldn't.

"Detective Bynum. It's good to see you again," I said and stuck out my hand. "Mar—"

"Marco Fontana! I'll be damned."

"Maybe you will be, but not because you have a bad memory."

"Been a long time, young man. Never thought I'd meet up with you again, Fontana. Leastways not mixed up in something like this." He glanced around the room, then landed his gaze back on me.

I explained how I'd come to be there and that I'd called in the police.

Bynum smiled broadly and shook his head. "Still got your nose where it don't belong."

"Not this time, Detective. I'm a P.I. now, and my nose usually leads me into a mess like this."

"Well, Mr. P.I. Fontana, with you bein' a friend of the victim, whaddayou think?"

"Truthfully, Detective, I don't know what to think. Sammy was a nice guy, but he probably had some acquaintances who wouldn't mind bashing in his head. Ex boyfriends, hook-ups, people he worked with at City Hall. Lots of other things he got himself into which he never told me much about. Except, me being me, I kinda knew when something shady was happening."

"The guy had a lot goin' on. You mentioned hook-ups?"

"Sure, but a lot of people—"

"Not judgin' your friend, Fontana. I just wanna know did he let a lotta strangers into his home?"

"Yeah, you could say that."

"Makes this harder, you know what I mean? Can't go find some stranger we don't even know about."

"I'm thinking there's plenty of possibilities for who did this that won't be so hard to find. People in his life that we know about or could easily find out about. My guess: that's the best place to start."

"Like…?" Bynum stared at me, friendly but serious.

"It'll still be a long list of choices. Sammy could drive people crazy, even his friends. Sometimes a guy can get under your skin without even knowing it. And sometimes…" I paused and looked at the blood-soaked bed.

"Yeah? Sometimes what?"

"I was gonna say that sometimes a guy like Sammy ticks people off by doing what he does, by just being who he is."

"So you're tellin' me the guy had enemies he didn't even know about?"

"Not enemies exactly." I hedged. "Like at work. Sammy was— is good at his job. Steps on toes if he has to. And that can piss people off. He's an accountant. A numbers guy. He knows more about some people than they know about themselves. That sets people on edge. You know any accountants who don't make people nervous?"

Bynum chuckled.

"You say the apartment was unlocked when you arrived?"

I explained how Sammy operated and Bynum just shook his head.

"People do some dumb things, if you ask me. No offense to your friend, but he's livin' in downtown Philly, anything can happen."

I agreed with him. We batted around some theories and Bynum allowed me to hang around while he searched the place. When the CSI team began going over the apartment bit by bit, I took a hint and left. There wasn't any more that I could do at that point anyway.

As I left, Bynum told me he'd keep me in the loop. He didn't tell me not to leave town, but I knew he was thinking it.

Back on the street, I took a moment to gather my thoughts. I told myself I should just leave it to the police but I knew I couldn't do that. I headed back to my office. Passing the Village Brew, I spied Sean, the barista, behind the counter, his taut sexy body and rakish smile mesmerizing yet another customer waiting in line for coffee but wanting so much more.

My office, on Latimer Street, was in an old building that housed a few other small businesses needing cheap quarters. I'd been wanting to move to a better location but rents in downtown Philly kept me using the old dump. The worst feature of the location was an industrial-looking fortress of a building that some family had built so they could live in the city and not *be* in the city all at the same time. Nothing about that house faced out onto the neighborhood. The nuts and bolts exterior, faced with metal plates, seemed hostile at best. Never mind that everything else around was red brick, this old steel bucket of a building refused to be neighborly. The window in my office looked out over the Fortress of Hostility which was never a nice view.

The stairs squeaked and creaked as I moved up to the third floor. It was a homey sound, comforting. One of the few things I liked about the building.

"You are here!" Olga, my secretary, greeted me as I entered. "People are calling from early morning. I cannot say to them where you are, because you are not telling me." She stared at me. "Poor boss. You are looking like raining for ten days."

After having worked for me a little while, Olga got the idea I needed nurturing. Her Russian mothering skills were comforting, even all-knowing. She often sensed something was wrong before I said anything.

Olga also liked making a fuss. Maybe it was her Russian capacity for drama. Whatever it was, she made me glad I'd finally hired a secretary. Someone I know would say that the universe was just waiting for me to meet Olga, who had exactly the talent and temperament I needed for the job.

We met when Olga was on trial for the murder of her fourth husband. Her lawyer hired me to do some investigative work. While I'm usually inclined to believe the spouse did it, especially when the fourth one in a row dies under suspicious circumstances, once I'd actually met Olga, I knew she was innocent. There were plenty of other suspects, but the police zeroed in on Olga. It took a while and a lot of legwork, but we found what we needed to get them to drop the charges.

After that, Olga kind of followed me back to my office and started doing chores without being asked. I figured she needed something to do now that her fourth husband was gone. Besides, truth be told, I'd warmed up to her motherly fussing. When I told her I could use some help around the office, she jumped at the chance. She didn't need the money, since her four marriages had left her more than well off, so the pittance I could afford to pay her didn't matter.

"Sammy Denning has been taken to the hospital. Somebody tried to put a new hole in his head. The hard way."

"Sammy? Sammy is dead?" Eyes wide with astonishment, she half stood then sat back down. "Is possible? Yesterday he is talking on phone." She looked balefully at her telephone. "He is saying broken legs making him crazy. He is wanting to be out. And now is dead." She sighed, a weary Russian sigh, and shook her head.

"Sammy's not dead, Olga. He's unconscious, maybe in a coma. They took him to the hospital. Keep your fingers crossed."

"I will do better," she said. "In church I am lighting candle."

I nodded my thanks, entered the inner office, and shut the door behind me. I needed the silence. But, no sooner had I sat down than the phone rang.

"Is it true?" He didn't identify himself but he didn't need to. I knew his voice, and it was like a delicate finger tracing a line up my back. Luke's booming housecleaning business got him into lots of places, and he often used that ability when he helped me on cases. He also knew a lot of people and came across loads of gossip, rumors, and news through his business. I wasn't surprised he'd already heard about Sammy.

"Tell me what you think you know." I had to assume news about Sammy had made it onto the Drama Queen Network and was spreading fast.

"Sammy Denning was killed. That's what I heard. And you discovered the body."

"Only half right, Luke. Sammy was unconscious and in bad shape when I found him. But he wasn't dead," I said. "Where'd you hear this anyway?"

"People are talking. But I got most of what I heard from one of my guys doing a job at the Dilworth. He saw the ambulance. Said he saw Sammy being taken away and that they'd drawn a sheet over his face."

"Your guy is kinda dramatic, isn't he? They did take Sammy, but he was still breathing when they left."

"Well, Reese can be overwrought sometimes. You know what he's like. That's why I called for confirmation. I guess you're on the case? Anything I can do?"

"I'm not officially investigating, but I'm not gonna sit around and wait for the police to figure this out."

"Any ideas what might've happened?"

"All I can say for sure is that it wasn't an accident. Looks like somebody surprised him while he was napping."

"Why would anybody do that to him? I know he wasn't a real sweetheart, but he wasn't so bad. Who'd hate him that much?" Luke asked.

"I'm not sure it was somebody who hated Sammy. The way the place looked, it was more like somebody who wanted something Sammy had. Whoever did it turned over his apartment looking for something."

"Or, maybe somebody just turned the place inside out to make it look like there was a search. Maybe it wasn't about that at all. Sammy made a lot of people angry. All kinds of people. It could be anybody. Exes, co-workers, anybody he ticked off. And he managed to tick off people by the boatload."

"Could be. Off the top of my head, I can think of a couple dozen people who had some serious problem with Sammy. That doesn't count people he worked with or whoever he dealt with through the new consulting firm he started. It's not gonna be easy figuring out where to begin. Friends, co-workers, tricks. I can probably eliminate lots of them, but that still leaves quite a pile."

"I'll be at your office in ten."

"Uh, maybe—" But I didn't get the words out fast enough. He'd hung up.

Before I got down to work, I put in a call to the hospital. The duty nurse said there was no change in Sammy's condition. But, she wouldn't give more than that, no matter how I asked. That information was reserved for the family. Sammy had some but I didn't know them. I hung up the phone and looked at a half empty mug of coffee on my desk. Couldn't have been too old or Olga would've swept it away and cleaned it. I took a slug. Cold and bitter. But caffeine is caffeine.

I pulled out a pad and began making a list. I like lists. They're solid things. I can hold them, look at them, rearrange items, shape them to help me and make sense of things. Not like the rest of the world. Lists and my old tack board came in handy, especially on a case where information is hard to connect and patterns don't come easy.

After a few minutes, I had quite a list of names. People I knew he'd been involved with one way or another, except for his mostly-anonymous flings. His casual internet and telephone contacts probably wanted to stay in the shadows. It was no use worrying about them anyway, since the crime didn't seem random. His place had been tossed. Somebody was looking for something, meaning they knew Sammy and what they were looking for. Or, whoever did it was sent by someone Sammy knew. Of course, that opened the door to someone not necessarily on my list, someone who was just an errand boy.

I'd put Bart on the list. Sammy's latest ex was a boy with more guts than sense and with, as far as I remembered, a healthy appetite for revenge. An aspiring musician, Bart was cute but lethal. Sammy had fallen in love with the angelic face, the light blond hair, and the winning smile. What Sammy didn't bargain for was the emptiness behind that smile, an emptiness that often made Bart sullen and caustic. Bart also had a roving eye. Always looking for a better deal, more pleasure, more anything than whatever it was he had. He was never satisfied, and because of that never knew when he had it good. So, he did plenty behind Sammy's back and when Sammy couldn't take it any more, he dumped Bart and sent him packing. Bart never forgave Sammy and had creepy ways of showing it. For several Christmases, Bart sent Sammy his old Christmas cards, ripped to shreds, and spattered with something resembling blood.

So, yeah, Bart was near the top of my list.

After Bart, there were two other exes who could qualify, such as Cal, also of the sweet but poisonous variety, and Mack, who'd been unceremoniously dumped and left with his belongings on the sidewalk after selling one too many of Sammy's possessions to support his habit. Most of the time, Sammy and his boyfriends parted amicably, and one of them had even dumped Sammy. Still, I'd have to look into all of them.

I wasn't forgetting Dan, though. He might've put on a good show at the apartment, but that didn't totally disqualify him. He didn't have as great a motive and wasn't as deranged but he'd been there. Some people who commit crimes get off on coming back to look at their handiwork.

Then there were co-workers. He'd told me about some rocky times with a few of them. I remembered Sammy talking about one of his supervisors and some others. Of course, I wouldn't keep them off my list. One of them might have as good a reason as any of Sammy's exes. I'd put that list together next. For now, all I could do was add possible motives to the names and try to prioritize the list so I could get started.

When Luke arrived, I realized it was almost dinnertime.

"How about dinner at More Than Just Ice Cream? We can talk there," I said as he pecked me on the cheek.

"As long as I get to pick dessert," Luke winked.

* * *

I found myself dragging as I entered the office early the next morning. Luke had kept me up late, not exactly against my will. It took sheer force of will to roll out of bed, shower, and gulp some coffee. Walking down Broad Street, allowing the fresh air to slap me awake, had only marginally helped. I needed more coffee to be able to tackle Sammy's case.

Olga wasn't in yet and I had the place to myself. Before anything else I made a pot of coffee. Knowing my late-night habits, Anton had gotten me a blend called "All Nighter" and it had opened my eyes on more than one occasion. I filled the coffeemaker and allowed it to do its stuff.

As the machine wheezed and bubbled in the background, I tried tracking Bart down. The old number I had for him dated from the time he'd left Sammy's apartment and moved in with a friend. That turned out to be a dead end. Other contacts I had for Bart didn't pan out either. There were a couple of numbers from old friends of Bart who'd wanted to date me. If they didn't pan out, I'd have to hoof it over to his last known address.

I picked up the receiver and was about to tap in a number when I heard the outer office door slam shut. I placed the receiver back without making a sound and listened again. I stood and cautiously stepped to the door leading to the outer office. Through the frosted glass I could make out a man standing at Olga's desk. Anyone well behaved enough to wait at an empty desk for service, didn't seem like much of a threat. I opened the door.

"Fontana! Just the man I want to see," said Martin Van, acid-tongued, sleazy, gossip columnist for a local rag. Tall and angular, with dark blond hair which fell in luxurious waves around his head, he sat back on Olga's desk to look at me. His face was long and not unattractive but marred by cruel, almost sadistic features. He had a certain animal magnetism, as they say, which seemed to get him into almost any bed he wanted. And he wanted a lot.

"Marty!" I said cheerfully, knowing he hated the nickname. "What brings you here? Certainly not because you need me?" Unless, he wanted me to be his bodyguard and that would happen the day after never. Martin Van was universally despised. All right, maybe his mother liked him, but I wouldn't bet money on it. Everybody else, though, wanted to see his heart roasting on a spit. And that might happen but for one thing. All those people who hated him also feared him. His column in City Underground and his blog *PhillyShh!* had a way of releasing little tidbits of really nasty information. He never used names though the threat was always there, of course, and sometimes the details were enough to make some people very uncomfortable. He spotlighted lots of sensationally kinky peccadillos in his column and did it so that the guilty parties and anyone who knew them would know exactly who he was talking about. It also wasn't difficult for smart observers to guess at who his victims were. Thing is he never wanted anything for his revelations. Never asked for quid pro quo. He just basked in the power and status it got him.

There were probably lots of guys whose boyfriends he'd stolen, or wives whose husbands he'd snatched that would also have loved to get the goods on Martin but none of them dared. He'd dropped his pants in more bedrooms than a male hooker anytime he liked and with almost anyone who caught his fancy. So far, he'd done it all with impunity. No one complained because they didn't want to see information, that Marty could dig up, printed in his column or his blog.

Maybe he needed my help because someone finally found a way of getting even. I hoped so. It'd be proof that there was justice in the cosmos.

"You bet your ass I'm here because I want your services." Peering at me, indignation twisting his features, he held out a ragged accordion folder.

"What's this?"

"That's what I want *you* to find out. I came into work this morning, and some skinny-assed, filthy messenger flew right in behind me. Made me sign for this and dropped the package on my desk. Then he buzzed out without even waiting for a tip. Not that I'd have given the bastard one." He drew a breath. "May I sit?"

"Make yourself comfortable." I backed into my own soft swivel chair. It was both strange and fascinating to watch Martin. He moved into the chair like a panther: compelling and lethal.

"Someone either thinks this is a wonderfully funny practical joke or they have the nerve to think they can actually blackmail me."

"Blackmail?" I pulled the material from the folder. Photographs. Martin and a companion were the subjects. Actually Martin and several different companions. Good old Marty performed acts you only see in gay porn films. His companions, all considerably younger and lots hotter than Marty ever was, seemed vaguely familiar. One set of photos, again with Marty and a younger guy, had a frame in red permanent marker drawn around them. I couldn't make out the face of the young guy in any of the photos but something about this set was obviously important to the blackmailer.

"Doesn't look like your shutterbug pal is joking around, Marty. Did this come with a note? If it's blackmail, you usually get asked for something. But I don't see a note, so what makes you think this is blackmail?"

"Could be the phone call I got after the messenger left." He said this as if I should have known it.

"What did the caller say?"

"It was a male voice but I couldn't place it. The first thing he said was, 'Got 'em yet?' Of course, I knew what he meant. So I told him the folder was on my desk."

"Did he make you an offer, ask for anything?"

"He said that there were more where these came from. And that they were even better. Whatever that meant."

I could guess what that meant, especially looking at the red framed photos.

"Did he ask for anything? In exchange—"

"He wants me to quit my job. Leave town. Forget my column and my blog."

"That's all he wants? You get outta town and he lets you go?"

"He also wants money, of course. A lot." Marty sat up straighter, his dignity returning along with his anger. "Don't they always want money? As if he'll get anything. I'd like to see him try to do something with those... that trash. Anything!" He looked at me and his eyes were glassy bright. I wasn't sure if it was arrogance or the fear that had to have been eating away at him.

"He give you a deadline?"

"No. He said I should think about it. Said he had more and he'd send that soon. Once I get the new stuff, he wants an answer. Fast."

"And you want me to do what?"

"Find him. Stop him." Marty said, his voice raw and angry. "I can't let some unknown little shit ruin my life. I can't afford the money he's asking, and I'm certainly not quitting my work. These pictures—"

"May not hurt you as much as you think. Could even make you famous."

"But he said he has more. What if he has something really bad?"

"Is there something? Really bad, I mean?"

"N-not that I can think of. I sleep around. I take pictures for investigative pieces I'm doing. There's nothing illegal. I swear, Fontana."

"So what's to fear if he releases the pictures?"

"My sources would dry up. They'd be afraid their pictures would be taken. That I might hold pictures and materials over their heads for personal gain. I'd never do that. I want this little turd stopped."

"That begs the question, Marty. How'd this guy get those pictures?" I looked at him for a few seconds. "Do you have camera equipment installed in your place? You photographing yourself for posterity?"

Marty was silent. I could see the answer on his face. He didn't need to speak.

"You're even kinkier than I suspected. Not to mention sleazier and more unscrupulous."

"I still deserve my privacy. No matter how sleazy anyone thinks I am."

"Any idea who could have stolen this stuff from your place?"

"None. I bring lots of guys home with me. Then there's the housekeeping staff, the building staff gets in on occasion, maybe others. I don't know."

"It'll cost you, Marty. My fees for this kind of thing aren't cheap. It's dangerous work."

"I can pay. And you won't regret it, Fontana.

* * *

"What is all this, Marco?" Luke said, picking up a pile of papers then sitting down in the best chair in the office. He looked sexy even in his wire-frame glasses.

"Material for Martin Van's case. These," I pointed to a stack of news clippings, "are his most recent columns. I've got to generate a list of names. People who might want to blackmail him."

"Blackmail?" Luke said.

"This goes no further, Luke." I peered at him. "Understand?"

Luke nodded. He looked so sad when he was being serious.

"Marty's sure his whole life will topple if the blackmailer releases the pictures," I said and then explained but without showing the photos. "I'm not so sure it'd be that bad if the photos came out. Marty's already got a bad reputation. Stuff like this can't really hurt."

"What if the blackmailer has a way of carrying out his threat? I mean, maybe he's got more."

"You sure you weren't listening in when I talked to Marty?"

Luke smiled. "Why?"

"The blackmailer said he had more to show Marty. Stuff that would convince him. So, he's got Marty running scared."

"Wow," Luke said. "How'd he get himself into this situation? I thought he was cagier than that."

"He likes what he likes and it ain't always free, y'know? But even Marty doesn't deserve to be blackmailed."

"Yeah," Luke said.

"I've gotta jump on this and make some progress fast. Photos like those don't stay buried long. The guy wants Marty to leave town and never come back. All I can figure is that Marty burned this guy bad and now he wants to get even."

"Sounds like Marty needs your help a lot more than Sammy."

"At least the police will be workin' Sammy's case. Marty goes to the police, he's finished."

"I thought you said the police probably won't work all that fast on Sammy's problem considering what else they've got to do."

"They probably won't. But they won't be working Marty's case at all."

"I've known Sammy quite a while, not as long as you. He's a strange guy but he's a friend and I hate seeing his case ignored."

"They won't ignore it. And neither will I, Luke."

"But what about Marty's—"

"This wouldn't be the first time I worked two cases at the same time. With you helping, it'll all work out."

"I'll do what I can," Luke said. "Where do I start?"

"Go through Marty's columns, make a list of names. Almost anybody Marty mentions in his column would love to see him gone. But one of them will probably have a bigger motive than the rest. We've got to see which one that might be."

"Sure, boss. And…?"

"And get Olga to suss out some information on the names you find."

"Where will you be while we're working off our asses for you?"

"Trying to get some information out of Sassy."

"Good luck with that," Luke said and chuckled.

"I'll need it." I took his face in my hands and planted a kiss on his very kissable lips. "For luck."

"Get going," Luke said. "I promised I'd check in with Chip to see if he needs anything."

"Treat you to dinner later," I said as I left the room.

* * *

There were too many possibilities in Sammy's case. They had to be narrowed down. Thinking about my next moves as I exited the building, I walked to Locust Street headed for The Dilworth. I needed to start with Sassy. She'd been on duty the day Sammy got his head bashed in so maybe she'd recall something significant. Sassy was usually pretty good at remembering who belonged in the building and who didn't, especially the male tenants and guests. As long as she was paying attention, she'd have something to tell me.

Locust Street had become a mixed bag lately, drawing an assorted variety of underbelly types who did nothing for the ambiance. Drug dealers dodging the police, prostitutes and johns, and lots of other action had become routine. Passing by Uncle's, I noticed the early crowd gathering for their first drinks of the day. Laughter spilled out of the huge open window fronting the place, a reminder the scene kept going no matter what else happened.

A couple of blocks later I entered The Dilworth, and Sassy flashed a big, bright smile. Her platinum-blonde wig was all curls and crimson ribbons. The lavender dress she wore stretched tightly around her generous form and did nothing for her image. For a change, her make-up was subtle.

"Hey, Marco!" Sassy greeted me like I was saving her from something awful. I figured she was bored.

"How's my favorite front desk diva? They keepin' you on your toes?"

"Nah, this job's a cinch, nothin' to do, doll, and that's a fact. Sometimes I wanna curl up and go to sleep under the desk, it's so boring." She tossed a fashion magazine aside and peered at me. I was probably the most entertaining thing she'd seen all day.

"Got a question for you, Sassy."

"Shoot, dollface." She smiled, and her nut brown face brightened.

"You were on duty the day Sammy got hit, am I right?" I knew I was right, but it helps to let them think they're telling you something.

"Damn right, I was. And there was nothin' I could do about it. 'Case somebody told you otherwise. Lotta busybody types here think I can wave my gorgeous hands and make everything all right. Well I can't and that's a fact." She glared.

"Whoa! Don't get excited, Sassy."

"They don't think I was to blame, do they?" Her angry expression melted into one of fear and, I was guessing, guilt. Guilt that she might've let Sammy's assailant into the building. The job might bore her out of her mind but she loved being in charge. Anything that called her competence into question was an affront.

"Nobody thinks you're at fault for anything, Sassy. Has anyone said anything like that to you?"

She shook her head, eyes sad.

"You let me know if they do, got it?'

"You got it, doll. So, what's in it for you? Why're you askin' about all this? Besides bein' Sammy's friend, I mean?"

"You know I was the one that found Sammy. I guess, I kinda feel I should help find out who did this to him. The police are working but not fast enough for me. I'm in the dark right now. Sammy had a lotta friends."

"Had a lotta people who didn't like him, too.

"That's my point, Sassy. Too many avenues to follow. I'm trying to figure out where to start." Hinting that you might need a little help made some people open up. Of course, sometimes they'd lead you in the wrong direction, if they had something to hide.

"How can I help? I can't remember much from that day. Not a whole lot went on." She stopped, looked embarrassed. "Uh, I mean, except for Sammy. Poor bastard. Is he gonna…?" She let the question linger.

"Think, Sassy. There must've been a lot of people in and out that day. Any of 'em stand out? Anybody connected to Sammy?"

"Lemme… well, wait a minute. No. It's not easy to remember in a building like this. Lots'a people in and out all day long."

"Maybe there was somebody you hadn't seen in a long time? Old friends of Sammy? Or, guys that Sammy… you know." I winked and Sassy smiled.

"Sammy's not the only guy's got friends in the building. Or, that other kind of friend, either. I could tell you some shit." She paused. "But you don't want none of that other gossip. Lemme think on it." She placed a hand to her chin and stared off as if floating back in time. "Friends, huh? That who you think did it?"

"I don't know what to think, Sassy. I'm looking down every alley right now."

"Was a boatload of people in and out that day. None of 'em signed in but most of 'em said hello."

"Anybody stand out in your mind?" Questioning her was like scratching labels off bottles.

"Lemme think a minute, just wait. Seems to me that day there was some new faces in with the same old tired bunch that traipses in and out."

"Can you describe any of them?"

"One cute blond. He was a pretty-boy. I gave him all I got but it wasn't nothin' excitin' for him. Then this girl came bouncin' in, too. All sunny and sweet, I wanted to throw up." Sassy gagged then looked up and smiled. "One little short guy came marchin' in that day. All dark curly hair, you just wanna run your fingers through it. But I remember him most because of his eyes. Deep, brown eyes. Hard eyes that look right through you. Gave me the chills. Didn't say 'Boo' to me and I didn't care. He walked past and got on the elevators. Everybody else that came by waved to me or smiled. Not that little man. He was intense."

The description she gave could fit a lot of guys and there was no reason to think he went anywhere near Sammy's floor. "Anything else about him?" I hoped she'd remember something that connected him to Sammy.

"Nah. He was just a cold, short guy in a long coat. Looked familiar, but he's like a lotta Italian types I got the hots for."

"Anybody else you remember? Somebody you see all the time or somebody you haven't seen in a long while?"

"One other guy. Looked real familiar but different. He's just like a guy who came in and out with Sammy some time back. I'm talkin' a ways back. Maybe they was living together back then, for all I know. I keep myself to myself, you know?"

"I do, Sassy." Of course, I knew Sassy was a gossip sponge, and if there was something to know, she'd try her best to know it.

"But I ain't seen that one in a while. I heard Sammy kicked him out. But that's just rumors, and I don't pay them no mind. Maybe you know who I'm talkin' about? You and Sammy are friends, you'd know the one I'm talkin' about. Looks like a kid. Innocent. And sweet except, he ain't."

"That's one of Sammy's types," I said. "You saw him the other day here?"

"The one I saw the other day was different. He had curly red hair and blue eyes. Looked real sweet. The guy that used to be with Sammy had blond hair and he had a smile that said 'dirty dirty dirty' all over his face. The guy I saw the other day could'a been his twin. Well, 'cept he had a more innocent smile, and red hair and, yeah, a little more of a tummy. Still, I wouldn't mind being in a sandwich with 'em both."

Except for the red hair and the tummy, it sounded like Bart. Innocence was an act he had down pat. He could've dyed his hair. Sammy had a thing for redheads. Maybe he was using that to worm his way back in since he and Sammy had broken up. As for his tummy, well, he might have let himself go after the breakup.

"Thanks. That gives me something to go on, Sassy." I smiled. This was another witness who'd seen Bart in the building that day. I could confront Bart with it, if I managed to find him. "Did you catch the redhead's name?"

"Can't say I did. You know how it is. Busy in and out."

"Did he check in with you about who he was seeing in the building?" Strangers in The Dilworth were supposed to check in at the front desk allowing the person on duty call the intended apartment. Obviously Sassy only followed procedure when it suited her.

Sassy's face darkened. She looked up at me, her eyes half closed in a defensive-threatening stare. "I was busy. Like I said. I can't catch everyone goin' in and out."

"You got a good look at him, though."

"I always get a good look. Don't mean I get a chance to ask 'em all where they goin' when they come in. Shit happens. Got a lot to do here."

"So you don't know where the redhead went?"

"Didn't I just say that, Fontana? You beginnin' to get on my nerves. He didn't tell me, and I was too busy with other things to ask."

Not too busy to get a good look at him. Not to busy to watch him go to the elevators.

"So that's it?"

"Yeah— No! Wait," Sassy said, eyes brightening, smile returning to her face. "I seen him again. On his way out. They was arguin' then."

"Arguing? 'They?' The redhead was with someone and they were arguing? Who was he with?"

"That short mean little guy I told you about. The elevator door opened and they was there yellin' and carryin' on like old housewives. 'Course, soon as they spotted me, they shut up. But when they passed by my counter, that redhead was hissin' under his breath and pointin' a finger at the short guy's chest."

* * *

Sounded to me like Bart had been there a lot earlier than I suspected. Even before Dan spotted him. That zoomed Bart to the top of my list. Bart and the unidentified short guy. At least, I had more ammo to confront Bart with, when I found him. All I had was the address he'd moved to after he and Sammy split. I had to hope he was still living at that address.

Bart hadn't gone far after the breakup, in hopes that he might change Sammy's mind and move back in. So, he'd chosen The Chestnut Arms, a rundown apartment building a short hop from The Dilworth. The buildings might have been only blocks apart, but the Dilworth was light years away in design, upkeep, and clientele. The Chestnut Arms was a tired old place on a deteriorating section of Chestnut Street. The building looked like it wanted nothing more than to be imploded so it could rest. But that would never happen. It was an historic old hotel, now in the hands of apartment moguls. Over the years The Chestnut Arms had housed a herd of rough tenants and had long ago given up trying to seem like a nice place to live. That Bart had been reduced to such quarters must have offended his royal sensibilities. But he was stuck, from what I'd heard. One boyfriend after another came his way, but none of them had money.

The lobby of the Chestnut Arms had a faded grandeur about it, but it had been badly handled over time and now looked haggard and cavernous without any of its former beauty shining through. Finding the elevators wasn't hard, but riding in one took an iron stomach. The smell in the small box of an elevator was like decomp. Fortunately, Bart lived on a low floor and the ride wasn't long.

I reached his apartment after climbing over a drunk sprawled in the hall and found Bart had left his door open. I watched from the hall and saw him scuttling to a back room after dropping something into a suitcase, then returning with more. I guessed he'd endured these living conditions as long as he could. He was ready to leave the rat hole. I wondered how he could afford anything better on his waiter's salary.

I walked in and Bart turned to me, a startled look on his face.

"Marco! H-how'd you get in?" He dropped the underwear he'd been carrying. His carrot red hair was strikingly different from his formerly blond curls.

The living room was threadbare and dull. Walls with plaster that had been white long ago were now grey and dusty. He'd placed a couple of suitcases on chairs and had just about filled them up.

"You left the door open, Bart."

"Why're you here?" Bart picked up the underwear and placed it into one of the suitcases. "What do you want from me?"

"Glad to see you, too. Looks like you're about to blow town."

"I'm just blowing this pig sty and moving into better quarters. I'll still be here in town." He tossed me a look and a wink. Then he turned his back and bent over to pick something up from the floor, thereby showing me his glutes. He was a looker and though he had a bit of a tummy, he'd kept his buns in perfect condition. Still had a slutty streak a mile wide, too. Bart never stopped trying to bed anyone he was the least bit interested in, which is why he had a list of bed partners larger than the Manhattan voter rolls. "Things have changed and I'm glad."

"Good for you, Bart. New job with better pay?"

"New boyfriend. One with money. I won't have to lift a finger or live like a mudpuppy anymore."

"Do I know the lucky guy?" I wondered who he'd managed to snag. Who in town wasn't aware of Bart's reputation and would fall for him?

"Possibly. But I'm not getting into all that. I've got to get out of here today. Right now."

"Need some help?" I picked up a couple of folded shirts and looked at him.

"Sure, toss them in there." He pointed to a battered, old leather suitcase.

As I placed the shirts gently on top of other things he'd carelessly thrown in, I looked up at him. "You were seen at Sammy's building the other day."

"What are you talking about?" He was good, but not that good, and was unable to keep a tremor of fear out of his voice.

"I'm talking about the day Sammy was bashed and left for dead." I stood up again and looked down at him as he dropped some clothing into another suitcase.

"I was…" He hesitated.

"No use denying it, Bart. There were witnesses. What were you doing there?"

He exhaled as if a burden had been lifted, and he fell back to sit on the couch.

"When I heard what had happened… to Sammy, I didn't know what to do. I mean, I didn't go into the apartment. I didn't know they—" He stopped as if he didn't want to say more.

"They who? Who else was there?"

"You have to leave now. I've got things to do." He scrambled to his feet and stared at me as if he were trying to explode my skull by sheer force of will.

"Bart…" I warned. "I'll find out everything eventually. Why not make it easy on yourself?"

"There's nothing else, Marco. I was there. But I had nothing to do with whatever happened. That's all. That should be enough."

"It won't be enough for the police. This is gonna end up in their hands one way or another."

"I'll get my lawyer to handle it, then.

"Your lawy—" I was taken aback. Here was a boy who could hardly afford an apartment – no, could *not* afford an apartment on his own – and he had a lawyer. "The new boyfriend is a lawyer. I get it. I hope he's a good one."

"How did you— well, it's really none of your business."

* * *

I rode the reeking elevator down to the lobby of The Chestnut Arms and was ready to upchuck by the time the doors opened. Once outside, I gulped air to get rid of the odor.

As I enjoyed the fresh breeze, I noticed Preston Flaherty sitting in his Lexus outside the front entrance of The Chestnut Arms, as if he were waiting for someone. Anyone who knows Preston, knows that he is definitely not the type of lawyer who has clients living at a dump. Preston's more comfortable in tony Society Hill or Chestnut Hill or on the quietly wealthy Main Line, but not here.

Then it dawned on me. I moved toward the car.

"Press! Waiting for Bart? He won't be long. Just about finished packing now." I leaned in at the passenger side window and watched the blood drain from his face.

"How did you know…?" He sputtered for a moment then regained his composure. You have to give it to these WASP-types, they can pull it all together at a moment's notice. Members of my family would spout blood and scream until they were exhausted before they realized they'd given away what they were trying to hide.

Not Press. He threw a cold stare my way and snapped, "What is it you want, Marco?"

I'd occasionally done some investigative work for Preston when he didn't want to get his hands dirty. He knew I always got the job done. So he knew me enough not to try and bullshit his way out of something. Confronting him on the street might end my lucrative association with his firm but that wasn't important. Getting at the truth was.

"I'd like a little honesty for starters, Press. Bart won't give and I figure, being an officer of the court and all, maybe you see honesty as more important."

"Bart is none of your business, Marco. For all you know he could be a client of mine."

"In a pig's eye, Press. Bart can't afford a drink at the Westbury let alone be able to afford your fees. And you're wrong about the other thing, too."

"What thing?"

"Bart is my business if he had anything to do with Sammy's bashing. Between you and me, it's looking more and more like he did."

"He didn't… he said he—" Preston shut himself up and stared ahead.

"We don't have to finish here, Press. You can tell me later this afternoon. But you're gonna tell me. Know how I know?"

"Beat it, Marco"

"I know because you don't want a splash in the papers and the blogs about this business with Sammy and Bart. You being involved with the kid and all. I think maybe your high priced clients might not like to be associated with that mess either. They definitely won't like their retainers going to a guy who hangs—"

"That's enough, Marco!"

"That's what you think, Press. Why not just get it over with? Tell me now."

"There's nothing to get over, Marco. I haven't done anything wrong and neither has Bart. As far as anyone is concerned I'm driving a client home or maybe he's the son of a client. It's just a good deed, Marco. Something you wouldn't know much about."

"Is that what Bart was doing when he tried to kill Sammy? A good deed? Because I've got an eyewitness that puts Bart in Sammy's building. And now I've got you connected to Bart. Bart is no client, Press. He even said as much." I didn't like stretching the truth, especially as I wanted to get at a bigger truth that Press was trying hard to bury.

"He said—?"

"Said he was moving into better quarters. Said he had a boyfriend now who'd be paying the bills. Hush money, Press? Because Bart knows more than you'd like?"

Press turned the key in the ignition and started the car. I must've hit a very sensitive nerve. He didn't want to stay and couldn't go. He wasn't going to pull away, not without Bart.

I stood there, riveted on his face, watching as he squirmed on his own hook, though exactly what the hook was, I needed to figure fast. There had to be more to this situation. Bart couldn't be the whole story. Then I remembered the other guy Sassy had seen in the building, the short guy in the long coat. The one Sassy saw arguing with Bart.

"Press," I said sharply.

"Huh?" His head snapped around and he looked at me with fear in his eyes.

"Press, maybe I had this figured all wrong. Couldn't have been you involved. It had to be the other guy."

"What other guy? There's no other guy. There's nothing else to tell, Marco."

"The short guy. You know his name. Short, steamy looks, dark hair, youngish, partial to wearing long coats." Except for the long coat, the description could fit any number of Preston's many boyfriends. He was partial to smoldering Mediterranean types.

I didn't think Press had any blood left to drain from his face but I'd swear he got whiter by the second.

"You're good, Marco. Good at fabrication and deception. You've got nothing but a few tattered shreds of something you'd like to weave into whole cloth. It's not possible, Marco. Didn't they ever tell you there's a time to forge ahead and a time to hang back?"

"No, never heard that one. I'll keep it in mind."

He threw me a poisonous look but said nothing.

"Didn't you date someone who fit that description? Cute Italian guy, am I right? A hot little number everyone had their eye on. But you were the lucky one. You got him. Everybody was envious. I remember how they talked behind your back. They wanted you dead. They wanted to be you, have what you had. But they hated you. Not to your face. No one does that. Everyone's better at sucking up. But you left a sour taste in their mouths. A rich lawyer like you always skimming the cream of the crop of hot young men because you had money and power. You have any idea how they coveted what you had? How lucky everyone thought you were?"

"Lucky, Marco? Luck was not in my corner. Then or now for that matter. Whatever I had slipped through my fingers like mercury and was just as poisonous. Even Car—" He stopped himself and looked away. I didn't see his expression but I could guess.

"Carl! That was the steamy little guy's name. Whatever happened to him?" I tucked the name away. Carl could be the one Sassy had seen. Or, he could be another dead end.

I was concentrating so intently on Press that I didn't sense someone come up from behind. I was already off balance, leaning into the passenger window. Whoever it was easily pushed me off the car and onto the ground. I went down hard, heard a car door slam, and got a face full of exhaust as tires squealed when Press peeled out of there. The car snagged my jacket as it sped off, tearing a long ribbon of material which trailed away with the car.

* * *

Things were more scrambled than ever. I'd made an inch worth of progress on Sammy's case but was nowhere with Marty's problem. Both cases were more tangled than a bucket of eels. As I trudged back to the office my thoughts were a jumble but not as bad as my clothes. It was Bart that'd pushed me to the ground. Had to be, or Preston wouldn't have pulled away. That didn't make either of them look innocent.

Luke was sitting in my office waiting for me when I got back. His broad smile faded when he saw the look on my face, my dirty clothes and ruined jacket.

Olga followed me into the inner office.

"Boss is hurt?" Olga asked. When I shook my head, she looked me up and down. "You are needing tea and dry cleaner. Maybe seamstress." She tugged at my torn jacket.

"Olga's right. You look… battered. What happened?" Luke moved to my side and ran a hand over my face. For a guy who ran a housecleaning agency, Luke didn't have a callous or a cut on those hands.

"Settle down. I'm fine. It's nothing. A little fall, a snag or two. I've looked worse."

"Yes. I am seeing worse. I will make tea." Olga waddled out of the room.

"You find anything on Marty's case while I was prowling the gutters?"

"I did," Luke said. "Here's the list of people Marty eviscerated in his column and his blog. It isn't short. You've got your work cut out for you." Luke held up a sheaf of papers, his silky black hair spilling into his eyes.

"I didn't figure it'd be a short list. Marty's got a big mouth and spews a lot of acid. Bound to be a long list."

"What about you?" Luke asked. "The way you look, you must've come up with something."

"I have a couple of leads. All it took was legwork. And a little slumming."

"Leads on Martin's case?"

"On Sammy's bashing." I shrugged out of my jacket and threw it onto a chair. "From Sassy."

"That must've been fun."

"She described a couple of people who sound a lot like Bart and a guy named Carl. Do you remember somebody named Carl?" I asked. Luke and I hadn't known each other all that long but we knew a lot of people in common. Luke through his housecleaning business and other connections and me through the different jobs I'd been involved with. It made our friendship seem older and deeper than it could be in the time we'd known one another.

"Can't say that I— wait a minute. Is he the cross-dresser who kept thirty-five cats in his studio apartment at the Locust Towers? He was a funny guy. Bad taste in clothes but funny."

"No, *his* name was Chaz. Not him. Carl was a short guy, serious-looking, hot but no nonsense. He was kind of stuck on Preston Flaherty for a while."

"I vaguely remember someone like that having a crush on Press. Or, maybe it was the other way around. But that was before I knew you, so it's been a while."

"If Sassy was right, it could be Carl who was at Sammy's building around the time Sammy was beaten. She remembers faces really well. Especially when those faces are attached to hot young men."

"I guess that means we've gotta find this guy. Any ideas?" Luke was an enthusiastic person and when he worked a case with me, he brought an energy to things that made a difference. But things weren't always as easy as he assumed.

"Sure. We'll find him. Just like that," I teased. "Neither of us even remembers his last name."

"Okay. True, But you've got a plan, right? You've always got a plan. We can start with Press." Luke said.

"Preston's not gonna tell us a thing. He's a lawyer. He knows when to keep his mouth shut. We've gotta come at this sideways."

"How's that?"

"We look into Preston's friends. Some of them must remember Carl. Press and Carl weren't together long but it was a splashy affair and all Preston's friends were riveted on Carl. They lusted after the kid, were all envious of Press. They'll remember. Maybe they'll even tell us something we can use."

"You still in contact with any of his friends from back then?" Luke asked.

"I know a few. Can't say we keep in touch but they'll remember me."

"Two of his friends use my cleaning service. Press is pretty cozy with some of them, from what I could tell. I've been invited to some of their parties and Press was always there, too. Maybe one of them remembers Carl."

"Parties? You're on the Preston Flaherty circuit?"

"Not exactly his circuit. Just parties he's also been invited to. I've never gotten an invitation from him just from his friends. It's not like you ever missed anything, though. Plenty of booze and lots of gossip. Always tons of great food. But mostly a bore."

"Maybe talking to your clients is worth a shot, Luke. And if they don't pan out, I'll try the guys I know."

* * *

After a brief visit to Luke's office to get the information on his clients, we were on our way.

First up was a Mr. Clyde who lived in the Society Hill section of the city. According to Luke, the guy was retired and spent his time day-trading. So, Luke was reasonably sure we'd find him at home.

Walking down Pine was a treat now that tourist season was past. It was quiet, less trafficked, and peaceful. The red brick buildings all around gave a sense of stability, history without overwhelming grandeur. Clyde's home was an impressive three-story, red-brick townhouse near Second Street. It had obviously been cared for over the years and that took money. A lot of it.

Luke decided it was better if he stayed out of the picture so as not to have to explain that he gave out confidential client information. I stepped up to the deep-maroon door, prepared to tell Clyde that I was a friend of Preston and knew him to be one also, having been at some parties together. That was a small stretch. But I was sure we'd each been to some party or other that Preston had given even if it wasn't the same party or at the same time. Jesuitical thinking, sure, but it came in handy at times like this.

I used the brass knocker which made a satisfying thud. After only a moment, a natty older man opened the door.

"Mr. Clyde?"

"Yes? How may I help you?" He looked at me with a mix of mild sexual interest and not so mild suspicion. He had to be eighty or older, but the weight of years did not slow him down one whit. Though Mr. Clyde came to the door himself, Luke had assured me that the man had money enough for servants, a chauffeur, and then some. Clyde's eyes were bright and clear and his movements sharp.

I introduced myself and explained the case I was investigating. I mentioned Preston, and Mr. Clyde smiled.

"We think he had a boyfriend a while back who might be a witness in this case," I said, without naming Carl, so as not to affect what he might remember. "We'd very much like to contact him. Unfortunately, though people recall seeing him, no one remembers his name or where he might live now."

Clyde opened the door wider, indicating that I should enter. I stepped into the cool interior and felt a little overwhelmed by the lush surroundings, the subdued lighting, and the music filling the air like a fine mist. The house was deeper than it was wide but it was filled with so much furniture, books, and bric-a-brac that it didn't seem as large as it was.

"You play the market, Mr. Fontana?" He said, as he walked toward a room at the back of the first floor.

"No, I haven't tried my hand at that." Hell, I hardly had money enough to look at the stock market pages of a newspaper, let alone buy a share.

"You should. You're young but you should be thinking about the time when you'll be my age. Which is, what would you guess, Mr. Fontana?"

"Please, call me Marco." I smiled. "Guessing someone's age is the quickest way to lose a friend or never make a new one."

"Go on, take a guess. I won't be offended. Haven't got anything to be offended by. I can buy whatever I need or want. Age doesn't matter when you have money, Mr. Fontana. Remember that. Another reason to start dabbling in the market now."

"I'd say, maybe seventy." I took at least ten years off whatever I was thinking and that usually worked with some men.

"Ha! You aren't serious." He laughed. "Seventy! Ha! I'd like to see that year again, Mr. Fon— Marco." He laughed again and opened a door into what looked like his study. "Thanks for the laugh. But the real number is hovering around eighty. I won't tell you which side of that number."

So, there *was* a bit of vanity involved in his game. You can never be too careful.

"I'd've never guessed."

"Guessing is only good for parlor games, Marco, remember that. With the market you need to analyze things, study the companies, look at the external climate. Of course, it doesn't hurt to be a bit of a magician. But I've come up with a system that, if you follow it, can make you a small fortune and you wouldn't have to gumshoe it around all your life. Know anything at all about the market?" He sat down at his desk and stared at the large flat screen of his computer monitor. Vibrantly colored stock charts flipped and changed constantly. A stock ticker ran across the bottom of the screen. "And pay attention to the Vix, that's one of the keys. The Vix can tell you what to do, if you know how to read it."

"I only know what I've seen on TV or read in the paper. Nothing close up like owning a stock. What I'm really concerned about is settling this case. Maybe then I can spend a little time studying the market."

"I'll see what I can tell you, but promise me that when the case is settled you'll come back and take a lesson or two? I might just make your portfolio fatter than you can imagine." He pointed a bony finger at the screen. "It's all there, if you know what to look for. And I do."

"Deal." I smiled. The guy wasn't wacky, just lonely. His money could buy him whatever he wanted except someone who really cared about him. It was a deal I'd keep, not for the money because I had none to invest.

"You say this man was a boyfriend of Preston Flaherty? Tell me again what the young man looked like." Clyde idly kept his hand on the mouse of his computer, sending the arrow skidding around the screen.

I explained again and watched as he closed his eyes in an effort to recall his memories.

"What did you say his first name is?"

"I didn't. I was hoping you'd remember without my telling you. Makes it a bit more certain for me if you remember." I smiled apologetically.

"Well, better tell me because I can see Preston in my mind's eye but…"

"We think the boyfriend's name might be Carl."

"Carl! Why yes. That's a name I remember in association with Preston. Slick boy, that Preston. Always snatching the pretty ones for himself. Made lots of people angry."

"I've heard that people were envious of Preston," I said. "And that there were a lot of bad feelings even after Preston dumped Carl for someone else."

"Press is a crazy one, that's for sure. He never minded making anyone angry." Clyde shook his head as if Preston was the bad boy who everyone loved to hate. "Had a lot of boyfriends. Still does from what I know. He changes them with regularity. You'd think word would get around and there'd be no one left for him to hurt." Clyde went silent for a moment or two. Then, "Carl. That's the one you're looking for. Carl. Yes, that was his name."

"You remember his last name by any chance?"

"Can't say that I do. But if you have a card, I might be able to check around and see what I can find." He looked a bit down at not being able to remember or maybe it was because I'd leave and he'd be alone with his computer, his money, and his memories.

"Here's my card." I said handing him one of the new ones I'd had made. "And as soon as I crack this case, I'll be by for that lesson in stocks 101. That's a promise."

"You will?" He brightened considerably. "I'll do my best to track down a name for you, Mr., uh, Marco. You can be sure of that."

Luke sat waiting in a sunny patch on someone's front stoop, his head resting on one hand. Earbuds firmly in place, I knew he was listening to a book. That was his usual recipe for relaxation. As I got closer, I saw that his eyes were closed and there was a smile on his face.

"Hey!" I said, touching his shoulder and rousing him from his book. He looked up and stared at me.

"How'd it go? You were in there so long I thought you'd…" A lascivious grin broke out on his face.

"Information has its price," I said and hoped I could keep from laughing.

"You didn't!" He gawked at me. "Did you?!"

"I had to get the information. Didn't I?"

"Now I know you're kidding." He yawned and stretched. "Did Mr. Clyde remember Carl?" He smoothed out his clothes, then sat back waiting for an answer.

"He sorta remembered him but not exactly his last name. But he said he'd check around. So, we've got to find another source. Who's next on the list?"

The next guy lived near the Art Museum and Luke thought it'd be faster if we took my car.

Traffic was light for a change and once we zipped onto to the Parkway, it didn't take long to get to The Philadelphian, a sprawling condo complex where Luke's client, Mr. Stein, had an apartment.

I parked the car on Pennsylvania Avenue, a wide, tree-lined boulevard running parallel to the Parkway. It was kind of a grand entrance into the city, at least until you reached the part of the avenue that ended in a rundown motel. But the huge apartment buildings located on Pennsylvania Avenue had great views of the city's skyline. We dodged traffic as we crossed the boulevard to get to the layer-cake of a building.

Luke decided he'd wait for me in the huge, gaudy lobby, lined with shops and a restaurant or two.

"Be nice," Luke said. "Stein was one of my first clients. He gave me a break and helped my business get off the ground. Needed someone to clean his place after his partner died and he couldn't handle it all alone. He's a good guy."

"I'll do my best. But I need this information, so just in case, I brought my blackjack."

Luke stared at me for a moment as if assessing whether or not I was kidding.

Before I started toward the elevators, my cell phone rang.

"Fontana." I said. "Mr. Clyde, how nice. You work fast." I listened for a moment. "Spell that again for me? Thanks. Thank you very much. As soon as this is over, I'll give you a call for that lesson."

"What? What'd he say?" Luke's dark eyes sparkled with excitement.

"Mr. Clyde came up with a name. According to him, Carl's name is Sonnino. Carl Sonnino. Ring a bell?"

"Sonnino. Carl Sonnino? Not familiar. At least not Carl and Sonnino together." Luke shrugged. "I don't recall hearing about Preston being with anybody by that name. But I do remember that your client Marty had a boyfriend with a name something like Sonnino or maybe it was Sorrentino. I don't remember a first name, though."

"I didn't realize that you knew Marty."

"My company did some work for him occasionally. My client list is a Who's Who of Philadelphia queens who don't like to clean."

"I resent the implication," I said and laughed. "But tell me more about Marty."

"What I know is mostly second hand. Through my workers. Marty was with a guy by the name of Sonnino or Sorrentino. But just until Marty found somebody else and dumped Sonnino like three week old fish. Marty even put his things out on the sidewalk. Changed the locks at his place and everything. From what I heard, Sonnino or Sorrentino, never forgave Marty."

"Now that you mention it, I remember something about Marty having a big, flashy argument with one of his boyfriends. But he had so many boyfriends and even more arguments, I didn't pay attention at the time. Besides, all that drama drives me nuts."

"By that time Marty had found a regular houseboy to do his work. But the houseboy was the cousin of one of my workers, so the gossip kept coming."

"You ever hear anything that might be relevant to the case?"

"Not directly. That houseboy was working the day Marty and the guy had a big blow-up," Luke said. "But this is all through my worker's cousin. I never witnessed a thing."

"Something is better than nothing. I can always try and get corroboration, if it sounds good enough."

"According to the houseboy, Sonnino came in and started throwing things around, breaking vases and objects, screaming at Marty, ripping up photos, tearing clothes. Marty gave as good as he got according to my guy's cousin. This Sonnino or Sorrentino left a lot of damage in his wake. Supposedly, he threatened to get even. That was more than a year ago. And it doesn't sound like the guy Sammy used to know. I don't remember Sammy ever having a knock down drag out fight with anybody."

"So, either Sonnino really gets around or we're on the wrong track. Might be worth looking into him. But I'm not sure it's gonna lead anywhere. It makes sense that a thug like Sonnino would want to get even with Marty. But I don't see why he'd hurt Sammy."

"It doesn't seem to make sense." Luke said.

"This Sonnino may not even be the same guy that Sassy saw in the building. Besides, I don't remember Sammy saying that he'd ever hooked up with one of Marty's flings. Odds are that Marty had an entirely different boyfriend."

"That's what I think. But I don't run a social registry. My business is housecleaning. I can't keep track of every queen and their boyfriends, too." Luke winked at me and smiled. "Does this mean you don't have to talk with Stein?"

"No. I'd still like to talk and see if I can get him to remember a Carl or a Sonnino. If he confirms the name, that'll give me something more to go on."

"Okay, I'll window shop." He glanced around at the lobby which was like a miniature mall.

"Then maybe we can have lunch."

"You're on." Luke winked as I walked toward the elevators.

Stein lived on the twenty-fifth floor and when he let me into the apartment after I'd given him the same explanation I'd given to Clyde, I saw that he had a place the size of downtown Los Angeles.

"It's really three apartments made into one," he said when he noticed the look on my face as I gazed around at the room.

"This is huge, Mr. Stein, and beautiful. Just my kind of apartment except I couldn't afford a place this size."

"This is rare in most any building. My late partner had the money to do it. He loved lots of space, rooms for guests and the help, all that. He also had plenty of friends with crazy ideas for decorating." He looked around as if remembering everything that went on in the condo over the years. "Of course, I didn't really care about all that. I was happy. Everything looked good no matter what we had or did." He stared at me a moment. "Those where the days, Mr. Fontana."

"Call me Marco."

"Yep, I was a happy bugger. Now I rattle around in this old barn of a place."

"How long were the two of you together?"

"Thirty-five years. Not always easy years. Lotsa fights, lots of… well, you don't wanna hear all that. I'll just say that sometimes it was worth the heartache."

"I—"

"You came to ask me a question about someone we know mutually. Isn't that what you said?" He looked me straight in the eye and didn't blink.

"Preston Flaherty and a friend of his you might know."

"I know Preston well. Had dinner with him last week, in fact. Who's the friend?"

I described Carl without naming him. "Do you happen to remember his name?"

"Of course. That's Carl. Heartbreaker, he was. Hottest little Italian I ever saw. And a package that looked like two Thanksgiving dinners rolled into one, if you know what I mean."

"Do you happen to remember Carl's last name?" I asked. Stein was as sharp as Luke had said. I was certain he was snappy enough to remember.

"Last name? It was Italian, of course. What was it? Wait a minute." He zipped out of the room leaving me standing there.

Turning toward the wall of windows which looked out over North Philadelphia, I stepped closer to take in the whole view. North Philly isn't pretty, not even from the twenty-fifth floor. Unless you like the bleak and decrepit nature of the landscape. Too many abandoned buildings and empty stretches of land. It was a sunny day and even that didn't make North Philly look good.

Stein returned, moving with a military, choppy, quick-step. He stood by my side holding a photograph.

"Look here. Is this the guy you're looking for?" He pointed a pale finger at a dark-haired young man. This was the Carl I remembered but the last name that Clyde gave me just didn't ring true, even Luke hadn't recognized it and he knew Preston as well or better than I did.

"He fits the description," I answered.

"That guy's name was Sorriso. Carl Sorriso. I remember because it means smile in Italian and I thought that was funny because the kid never smiled." He raised an eyebrow and looked at me as if cautioning me. "Never even cracked a smile the night I had them over here to watch All About Eve, the funniest, classiest movie ever made. Ever see it?"

"Sure. It's the best." I'd seen it a couple of times but that was with a certain someone and the memory still hurt.

"You bet your ass it is. The guy you're looking for is Carl Sorriso, dry and serious. He's what Margo Channing means in the movie when she says, 'Everybody has a heart – except some people.' The some people is him."

"That bad?"

"Person who never smiles can't be all good." Stein said and tossed the photo onto his coffee table where it landed next to a candy dish.

* * *

Back in the lobby, I found Luke in a shop that sold expensive knick-knacks and rescued him before he made a purchase. The shop was dense with a heavy perfume which reminded me of one of my aunts who's better left unnamed. Whenever she hugged me, my clothes would hold the smell for days and the memory of my aunt would hang around with it.

"Ready, Luke?" I touched him on the shoulder.

"Did Stein confirm the name?" Luke asked as we left.

"He claims Carl's name is Sorriso. Says he remembers it because it means smile and Carl never did."

"That's it!" Luke said. "I remember now. Carl Sorriso. Hot but sour. Yes!"

"Now we need to find him. We'll go to my office and Olga can track down his address. Then I owe you lunch."

* * *

Olga was quick. "Is easy when you are knowing internets." She waved a sheet of paper in the air like a flag. "People are thinking they are safe in beds. Ha! No one is safe. Information is all around. Is in air. And now is on paper.

Here is Sorriso address. Is only thing you are wanting?" She slapped the paper down on my desk.

"That's what we need, Olga. Thank you. You're a peach."

"No other informations? Criminal record? Credit? Social Security? Family informations? Last time he is talking on phone? Size of shoes?"

Luke looked at her and chuckled. "I thought I was compulsive."

"Maybe, yeah… we could use his criminal record. But nix the other stuff, Olga. I'll pick it up when we get back."

* * *

After a quick lunch, we got back on the road headed for South Philly. Broad Street was smooth sailing especially when the lights were synced, which they were.

"So where exactly are we going?"

"Home. In a manner of speaking. Not far from where I grew up." I turned and smiled weakly. "You may notice me begin to shake now and then. I might also stop and stare. Or I might even babble and drool."

Luke looked at me as if I were crazy.

"It's nothing. Just a kind of post traumatic reaction to my old neighborhood and the things that happened."

"What things?" Luke asked, looking at me again, as if waiting for me to freak.

"A long story and you'll need a stiff drink to hear it all." I smiled. "I'm not crazy about my old stomping grounds. Going home is never easy."

Sorriso lived in South Philly, where my parents still lived. The farther we drove into that part of town, the edgier I got. I never liked batting around that neighborhood unless I had to. But Sorriso lived in a relatively newer section farther south, near the stadiums. Newer and bigger houses, some with a patch of ground to call their own, but just a patch. You could spit farther than the grass stretched.

Sorriso lived on Tenth in a two story townhouse set above street level like all the others lined up in a row on both sides of the wide street. All of them had some owner-added distinction setting them apart from one another. Sorriso had painted his doors, windows, and trim a surreal orange.

Nightmarish. I wondered if the neighbors had given him any trouble and I found the answer as we pulled closer with the car. The splotches of tomato stains and remnants of a serious egging let me know his neighbors didn't appreciate the color any more than I did. Maybe a lot less.

My old beaten-up Taurus didn't look out of place in the neighborhood. Luke got out and slammed the door, looking around as if he were assessing the potential of the neighborhood for expanding his housecleaning business.

"Not gonna get many jobs down here, Luke. These people do their own cleaning. It's a way of life and a point of pride with them."

"Too bad, I was thinking maybe I could spread some flyers. But you're right, it looks like they take pretty good care of these places."

"Here we go." I walked through the gate at the front of the patch of grass.

The white aluminum screen door sported a large American Eagle in the center. When I pulled open the door to ring the bell, a dog barked inside.

"Sounds like a large dog," Luke said. He told me that through his housecleaning jobs, he'd learned to cultivate a health sense of caution around strange dogs. He wasn't afraid of dogs but he maintained a wary attitude.

"I'm the first thing the dog will see," I said. "And bite."

"Yeah, but when he finishes with you, he may want dessert." Luke laughed.

A moment after I rang the bell, an older woman, a shock of unruly white hair crowning her head, opened the door. A wave of the fragrance of tomato sauce rolled over me and I was instantly transported to my childhood. I could almost taste the pasta.

"Who're you?" She said, tough and defensive. Her brown eyes looked us over warily, trust not being her strong suit.

I introduced myself and Luke.

"We're trying to locate Carl Sorriso. He's a possible witness in a case I'm investigating."

"Hmpf, he ain't home. Never comes home this early, the bum. No job. Stays out all day bummin' around. Lazy bastard. You ain't gonna find him here."

"You don't expect him back later?"

"I can sit around expectin' all day, but he never comes when I expect him. Don't waste your time. If he *was* a witness, he'll be too lazy to testify. Find another witness is my advice to you."

As she closed the door, her dark eyes widened and she poked her head out to look at something behind us. I turned and saw a car pulling up to the curb.

"Carl!" She screamed. "Carl! Get outta here. These guys are after you."

Before I could do anything, the driver revved the engine and burned rubber peeling out of the street.

"Why'd you do that?" I said staring at the old woman.

As she shut the door, she said, "He's a bum. But he's my son." With that she slammed the door and left us on the step.

Us? I thought. When I looked around I was alone. Luke had disappeared.

Someone tapped my shoulder. I turned around my fist balled, ready to strike. I stopped just before I hit Luke square in the face.

He flinched and backed off, a frightened expression on his face. Black eyes glittering, he looked at me as if he didn't know me.

"Wh-what was that all about?"

"Sorry." I clapped him on the shoulder. "You came up behind me and... this is my old turf, Luke. Someone comes up from behind, you don't turn around expecting a box of cannoli. You hit first, eat the pastry after."

"I'll remember that."

"Where'd you get to, anyway?"

"Got the license number while you were gabbing with Dillinger's mother."

"Great!"

"I wandered away to look over the front yards. Some of them are pretty cool. Flowers, gnomes, all kinds of stuff. I saw the car pull up and realized it was Carl. A split second later I heard the old bat scream. So I took down the license number."

"You're amazing!"

"Now what do we do?"

"We wait. We'll catch him again. In the meantime I've got a couple of leads to run down. Why don't I drop you back at your place?"

"You sure you don't need me?" Luke asked, a note of disappointment in his voice.

"I've gotta talk to Marty and Preston. It'd be better if I did that on my own. They won't talk freely with someone else around. You know how it is."

* * *

While we were heading back into center city, Luke's cell phone rang. I watched him react as he talked. When he was finished, he said he had a major crisis on his hands. Two of his boys had gotten into some kind of trouble and he'd have to sort things out. I dropped him off at his building and watched him for a moment before I drove off.

I got to the office just as Olga was leaving. Being part time, she left early most days.

"Messages are on desk." She pointed to my office door. "Someone is also wanting to see you. He will return but will call first. Tall man. Dramatic queen. You are knowing who this is?" She gave me no chance to respond. "I am leaving now. My sister makes dinner tonight for whole family for the birthday of a grandchild. I will help, but why is so much a fuss over birthdays children never remember? I am never knowing."

She was out the door, and I was left wondering who it was I should expect. A tall drama queen could describe a lot of people. Flipping through the pink message sheets I saw there was no note about this guy, whoever he was.

Then there was a knock on the door, and Martin waltzed in. Of course, tall drama queen. Described him perfectly.

"He called again."

"No hello?"

"This is serious, Fontana. He called again after sending me more photographs. Two sets."

"Did he give you a deadline this time?"

"Yes." Martin clenched his teeth. "A week. He wants the money in a week. He wants me gone from my job and he said the blog has to be taken down, too. If not, he brings this stuff to whoever he's got that will take care of me once and for all."

I held out my hand for the folder.

"Tell me you've made some progress. Because if you haven't, I don't know what I'll do. This guy sounds serious. He's out to get me hurt. Not just my reputation but me."

"Stay calm, Marty. Lemme have a look at the folder."

He handed me the brown folder which contained two sets of pictures clipped together.

"Just more of the same?" I asked before I looked at them.

"One set is pictures of me and some guy. Like the others. But these are clearer, more distinct. How he got them, I'll never know. And it wasn't my home system. I never took that kid to my apartment. We always went to hotels. Nice ones. I suppose someone had me followed."

"That's all? Just more sex pictures…" I let the question linger a bit.

"The others are some of that mob guy. It was funny because when I saw them they looked fam…" His jaw skidded to a stop.

"What's that, Martin?" I waited. There was no response, which was in itself a response. "You know something, Martin. Let's have it."

"Can't reveal my sources," he said weakly.

"You can't reveal to the government, maybe. But you hired me to help, damn it, so don't pull the journalistic integrity crap with me."

He stared at me half defiant, half scared.

"Marty, you print sleaze, you trade in people's reputations, and you roll in the muck. And now you're gonna hold out on the one guy who can hold his nose and try to help you?"

"Still…"

"Still, shit. That's your attitude, I can't help you. I'll give back your retainer."

"I don't think the information is relevant to your investigation." Martin sat up in his chair and stared.

"I'll tell you what's relevant, unless you think you can figure this one out for yourself." I pulled an envelope out of my desk. It didn't have cash in it but it looked like it had a wad of bills. I saw Marty's eyes glom onto the envelope.

"All right! Marco, you're a real prick."

"Thanks. Now give." I slowly placed the fat envelope back into the drawer, wondering exactly what was in it.

"Those photos," he started then stopped and reached over for the folder.

"Which?"

"These." He pulled out the group with the very familiar, thuggish looking Italian guy. "I got them while I was doing an investigation of Mafia influence in city government."

"You know who that is, then." I knew, but I wanted to make sure Marty did.

"His name is Jimmy. Jimmy Three Toes. At least that's what he's called."

"So your blackmailer pal is gonna turn these over to Jimmy."

"That's what I can't understand. Pictures of Jimmy are all over the place. For all he knows, I could've gotten them from the newspaper photo office. Stock images. I was doing an article on the mob. Just another routine piece. Nothing spectacular. So why would Jimmy care?"

"My question exactly," I said. "Maybe you hit on something in your article. Something hot. Something that even you don't know is hot. And maybe these guys want to stop you."

"I can't imagine what that might be."

"Maybe it's got something to do with this other set of pictures," I said and flipped the cover off the second, larger set. I tried not to react when I saw the first picture. It wasn't easy. It felt as if I'd been punched.

The immensity of Marty's problem became evident in a flash. It wasn't Jimmy and it wasn't Marty's other extracurricular activities that were his problem. It was the young man in these photos.

"You do realize who this is you're fooling around with? In these photos?"

"Some Italian kid. We were introduced by the same guy who told me where I could get my hands on that mob information."

"You had no idea who this kid was when you were introduced?"

"None. I'd never seen him before. He was an unknown quantity. Maybe that's why I liked the little greaser," Marty stopped and shot me a look as if he knew what kind of mistake he'd just made. For some reason I was feeling generous, so I said nothing. Maybe it was because I knew who the kid was and what this kid's "family" would do to Marty if they saw these pictures.

"You were saying…?"

"He was new. I like 'em new. You know that." Marty looked up at me. "This kid said he never gets out because his family is strict and keeps him on a short leash. But he was hot to trot and…" He stopped. Stared at me then looked down at the floor and shook his head. "Who is he? You seem to know something I don't."

"I'm not surprised you don't know him, even with all the gossip you spread and your investigative journalism. This one they keep under wraps."

"Who is he?" Martin screeched out the question.

"You know Vincenzo Chiari?"

"Vincenzo… Vin—Vincenzo Chiari? *The* Vincenzo Chiari?" The panic in Martin's eyes would've been enjoyable if this wasn't so serious. Marty was as good as dog meat if these photos got back to Chiari. "But… but… it can't be. Chiari's an old man. This was a kid. A nice kid. He didn't, I mean, he wasn't… How could I know? Is he related to Chiari?"

"Oh yeah, Marty. He's related. He's Vincenzo's son. His only son." I would've gone on and given him a list of reasons that Vincenzo had big plans for his son, had invested his whole life in his son. But I allowed Martin to figure it out for himself. All I could do was watch as the full horror of the situation began to sink in.

"Fuck. Shit. I'm a dead man. I'm as good as… But I didn't know. The kid was— wait a minute. Tell me something, Fontana."

I nodded.

"He's legal, right? I mean, the kid's over eighteen, isn't he?"

"Sure, that's not the problem, Marty. I think you understand that. The kid's legal but he's not on the open market. In fact, I'd go so far as to say he's like the rarest of rare commodities. And you've just spoiled it."

"But it's not *my* fault the kid is gay. That's just the way it is. And I didn't ask him to do anything. *He* came on to *me*."

"Vincenzo isn't gonna care who came onto who. He isn't gonna care which way the kid is wired. All he's gonna care about is who opened his rarest bottle of wine and sampled it. Ruined it, you might say."

"But, I…" Marty slumped back into his chair.

"Who could've done this? Who took these pictures?"

"I don't know. I don't know." He'd lost all his hauteur. Panic was beginning to supplant everything else. I needed to keep him from going over the edge, so we could make some progress.

"Think back. How'd you meet the kid? When did this happen? Where?"

"Questions. I need help, Fontana, not questions."

"Well, maybe you'd better leave, then. Vincenzo won't ask you any questions. He'll just do what needs doing. According to his lights. For you, that means lights out."

Martin's head snapped up and he stared at me. He was angry, but it was a toothless anger. I wanted to enjoy this but I couldn't. He was a slimy, smug, arrogant man, and he'd caused a lot of problems for a lot of people. But he was really just a helpless jerk now. A jerk on the run from himself. I didn't think he liked himself very much. He knew that nearly everyone hated him, so creating fear in others was the only way he could get anyone to even pretend to respect him. Now, the fear was his, and it was worse than anything he could ever have created for anyone with his work. Worse yet, he'd done it to himself.

"What'll it be, Marty?"

"I'm not going to let that happen," he mumbled. "I'll… I'll do whatever you want. Just don't let Vincenzo near me."

Keeping Vincenzo from getting him was the heart of the problem. There was only one thing that might work and Marty wasn't going to like it. But things he'd said piqued my interest and I needed to know more before I presented him with my solution to his problem.

"Let's start at the beginning. You said the kid was introduced to you by the same guy who led you to information on the mob and to Jimmy's pictures, right?"

"Yeah, yes. But he's a nothing. A little zero. He can't possibly—"

"If I'm gonna help you, I need to know everything you can tell me. I may need access to your files."

"Everything…?"

"Only if necessary. You'll have to trust me."

"All right. Just help me, Fontana."

"First, who was it that got you the mob information and introduced you to the kid?" I leaned forward to hear his reply.

"A guy named Carl—"

"Sorriso."

"H-how did you know?"

"Lucky guess. Tell me more."

"He was trying to worm his way back into my life."

"You dumped him, right? Big splashy breakup, right?"

"He was a conniving little shit. All he wanted was to be close to me and to the people I knew." Martin took deep breaths as if trying to calm himself. "He was too high maintenance, too full of drama. I mean, who needs that?"

Sure, who needed that, when Martin was himself the highest maintenance and most dramatically inclined queen of all?

But if I remembered anything about Carl, I knew that he was a bad seed. The type that never forgets a slight and wouldn't have been very happy being dumped. Especially by someone like Martin, a local celebrity who'd made a big deal of the breakup and never let Carl forget who dumped who and what the dumpee was losing in the deal.

"I don't suppose he was happy to be thrown over?"

"Him? That little ingrate? I guess no one likes being dumped. But Carl went nuclear. He said I'd betrayed him, just like others in his life. Carl let me know in no uncertain terms that he'd get even. An empty threat, though. He doesn't have the wherewithal. Not in any sense."

"I'd say he found the wherewithal." I fingered the file folder with the pictures.

"And I let myself get sucked in…" Martin stared glumly at the pictures. "When he came sniffing around and said he had information I could use, I stupidly listened. He gave me some sob story about being rejected by everyone else. But that he liked me and wanted to help me with information. All he wanted was to be friends again. That's what he said. Like some grammar school kid on a playground."

"Any idea who Carl hooked up with after you rejected him?" I knew he would, him being the biggest gossip monger in the city.

"Of course I know. Don't be silly. Martin Van knows everything about everyone. People expect me to know. And I do."

"So, are you going to tell me or do I have to wait for the memoirs? Believe me, neither you nor I have that long, Martin." I smirked.

"Carl, the little shit, made the rounds after me and let everyone know what he was doing, too. He hopped into lots of beds. First he went after my best friend, Leehane Deckham. You should know the name. Big society queen. No one breathes without consulting him first. Carl moved in on him like a barracuda. Leehane never knew what hit him. When he was satisfied with that, Carl moved on to other friends of mine. I guess he was pointing out just how shallow and disloyal they all could be. I'm not sure that was his intention. He isn't that subtle. But it was the result, nonetheless. I haven't been able to see those so-called friends in the same way since."

"That's it?"

"He made a play for others. Your friend Sammy included. That's how he learned that Sammy was working on some mafia assignment, too. Carl had no idea what it was, and Sammy dumped him before he could find out. But he knew something, and he told me I should ask Sammy for help on my investigative series."

"Then? What'd he do after Sammy?" I didn't remember much about Sammy being with Carl. Their "thing" must have lasted about three minutes, which wasn't unusual for Sammy but the boyfriends never liked that treatment. And some of them never forgot. Carl was one of those.

"He went back to sleeping around. Sometimes with friends of mine."

"And they all sent him packing?"

"Not all. Not right away?"

"Who did he stick with the longest?"

"That's easy. The one who tolerated him the most, the one who gave him the longest leash."

"And that would be…?"

"Preston. You know Preston."

"Preston Flaherty." Now we were getting somewhere. Except I thought Press had dumped Carl. "Didn't Press dump the kid? He got bored with Carl and gave him the heave-ho."

"Dump Carl? He tried but Carl apparently had his hooks in too deeply. If you know what I mean." Martin had regained some of his haughtiness. The self-satisfied smirk was calculated to let the observer know that Martin was in another league entirely when it came to information.

"No, I don't know what you mean. What hooks could a guy like Carl have?"

"Oh, I don't know. Could be he heard something or saw something that might make it easier for Press to keep him close at hand rather than let him wander off and blab what he knew."

"You know something, Martin, don't you?" I glared at him. "Enough games. Tell me or leave." Which I didn't really want him to do, because I knew this had something to do with Sammy, whose case I was most interested in.

"Carl had seen some incriminating evidence about Press when he was staying with Sammy. That's part of what he'd come to give me, that and the other mob material Sammy had collected. When I went to see Sammy, I found out that Press was, and is, involved, up to his too-large hips in mob connections and money. And Carl had seen some of that."

I nodded. These guys all deserved one another, you ask me.

"That's what he told me when he came sniffing around trying to get back into my good graces. I told him that I was grateful but that nothing was going to happen between us ever again."

"How'd he take that?"

"He said he just wanted to be friends. That he knew we'd never be together again but that my friendship meant more to him and he hoped we could have that back."

"That when he introduced you to Vincenzo's kid?"

"He said he wanted to show me that he was my friend and he knew someone I'd love to meet. Someone new and interesting."

"He knows your soft spot. I guess he ought to."

"I took them both to dinner, and at some point Carl left the two of us alone."

"Tell me, was Carl in your apartment some time before the three of you went to dinner?"

"When he gave me the information about Sammy's research and Press. And the night we went to dinner, they both stopped by for a drink first and…" Martin stopped, his voice trailed off.

I waited for him to connect all the dots.

"What a fool I am. He's in my place and I'm not paying attention. Didn't think I had to pay attention. That's when he must've placed the cameras."

"You're right, Marty. No doubt in my mind."

"I'm fucked. Totally and completely fucked."

"Lemme see if I have this straight. You were working on some mob investigative piece for your paper and Carl knew about this."

"Right. But that was before we split up. He was always nosing around. Liked to find out as much as he could about everything."

"So, he knows anything about the mob is information you'd love to have. Eventually he sees that Sammy is working on something about corruption and that Sammy's probably got some information you'd like."

"That's what he told me. He also said he'd found out some dirt about Preston which Press didn't want anybody to know."

"But, of course, he told *you*, right?"

"Sure. He wanted back in with me, so he said, and that's why he told me everything. Including how he was holding the information over Press and milking him for everything he could. I lapped it all up. I was a fool, even if it was all true. But getting that information… it's how I operate. It's how I fill up my column and that blog."

"And, of course, Carl was aware of your penchant for new, young, innocent guys. Guys who'd never been on the scene before."

Martin grunted inelegantly.

"So, he decided to do you a real service and introduce you to Vincenzo's kid. Without telling you who he was."

"How idiotic you make me seem. And what a fool."

"Hey, Marty. I'm not making you seem anything. You did this to yourself."

"You think I deserve it all, right? I'm just a sleazy gossipmonger, and I'm being served my just desserts. I know that's what you're thinking."

"Not entirely. And, for the record, I may think you're sleaze, but I don't think you deserve what's happening to you."

"You don't?" Martin looked at me and blinked. I thought I saw him get glassy-eyed. "So, what do we do next? How do we stop this?"

"Listen, Martin." It was time to level with the guy because this wasn't going to be easy. "I've gotta be honest with you. This isn't easy for—"

"What? You're not going to help? You said you'd help."

"That's the thing, Martin. I think we can be sure it's Carl who's blackmailing you. He's probably working with someone else. That sorta doesn't matter. We can catch them. No problem. But—"

"If we catch him and stop him, it's over, right?"

"That's what I'm tryin' to tell you, Martin. Things like this," I said picking up one of the photos, "they don't go away. These are just prints off some computer. Carl and his accomplice probably have digital copies stored who knows where. Maybe even video that they haven't shown you yet. This kind of stuff, photos and video, never goes away."

"But they said…" Marty looked haunted, gaunt.

"Carl has already shared the pictures with another person. Those photos are in a file somewhere. Carl and his friend used them once and they'll come back sooner or later to use them again. Maybe just to be cruel, they'll hand all of it to Vincenzo. My guess is that's what they intend eventually. Or, at least, that's what Carl intends for you. Carl wants to make everyone suffer for his bad deal in life. We can't stop him. Even if we blow the lid off this, go to the papers, bring everything out. It won't stop what's gonna happen."

"So, you're saying…?"

"I'm saying that no matter what we do to Carl, you'll probably have to make a new life somewhere else. As somebody else."

"Then…" Martin looked up at me as if I were his only hope. Truth is he had to be his own hope and clear out of town as soon as he could.

"Get together whatever money you have and anything else that means something to you and leave town before Carl's deadline is up. Find a place somewhere you can make a new life. Change your name, live off the grid for a while. It'll have to be your own version of witness protection but you can do it. Cut all your ties with anyone and anything here. It's the only way you have any chance of surviving this."

Martin opened his mouth but no sound came out. He stared at me, but I knew he was seeing through me to a picture of his life crumbling around him.

"That's the only way?"

"And never, ever try to contact anyone here. You do and they'll find out. Shred your credit cards. Live on cash. Until you can establish a new identity."

He placed his hands over his face and began to sob uncontrollably. I let him cry himself out.

* * *

It was a while before Marty got himself together enough to leave. I sat quietly with him until he did. By the time he walked out the door, I felt sorry for the poor bastard. He was a shit but he didn't deserve to have to start from scratch and still have to look over his shoulder wondering if and when someone would find him.

After Martin left, I called Press. I knew it was Carl that was blackmailing Martin. I also figured it was Carl who'd bludgeoned Sammy. What I couldn't accept was the idea that he did all that just to get even with them for dumping him, for making him feel small and cheap. Maybe it was one spasm of revenge that was intended to rid himself of all the feelings of worthlessness and humiliation heaped on him by all the other people in his life who'd wronged him. It made a perverted kind of sense but it was still insane. I thought Press might be able to give me another perspective or have a different insight into Carl's actions.

Press didn't answer his phone so I decided to stake out his place and pin him down once he arrived home. Home is so much more conducive to getting a person talking than cornering him in his office.

Press worked for the city so he had to live in the city but he made certain that his quarters were palatial. He was no stranger to creature comforts and he didn't intend for that to change. The building he lived in, the Dorchester, was one of the better condo properties on Rittenhouse Square, which had nothing but better properties. I'd heard he'd purchased a four bedroom extravaganza and had it redone from top to bottom. One of the bathrooms alone cost him close to one hundred fifty big ones. So I'm told. He had plenty of room and plenty of money and could certainly fit both Bart and Carl under his roof, if he wanted to.

From my seat on a wooden bench dedicated to Millie Frome in Rittenhouse Square, I had a great view of the Dorchester's front entrance. People came and went constantly. The rich and didn't-want-to-be-famous of Philadelphia lived in that building and led busy, eventful lives. Sooner or later Press would be among those returning home.

As I watched, I saw Bart and Carl stroll in together through the automatic sliding doors as if they were landed gentry. I wanted to gag, but that would've blown my cover. It appeared that they'd moved in on Press and were taking him for a great ride. Not that I felt sorry for the guy. He deserved it in so many ways. I just wished he'd get the hell home, so I could get the information I needed and leave. Before I could deliver that wish to the air, Press hopped out of a cab and sprinted into the building. So much for me getting to him in the lobby and making quick work of it. Now I'd have to corner him in his den, and that wouldn't be pleasant.

I said a quick good-bye to Millie's bench and dashed across the street to the building. The guy at the desk stopped me, of course, and asked who I wanted to see so he could announce me. That would kill the element of surprise. I had no choice but to give him my name. So I lied.

"Tell him a Mr. Martin Van is on his way up." I didn't wait for an okay.

"Hey. Wait… I've gotta…" The guy behind the desk sputtered and fumed, but there were more people waiting for his attention, and he still had to make that call to Press and inform him about me. I kept moving. The attendant was pint-sized. There were no security guards and, before they could call anybody, I'd be safely in Press's sanctuary.

In the elevator, a stern-looking older woman, tall, thin, gray hair cut short, looked at me as if I was the pig farmer's bastard brother come to cause trouble. I smiled sweetly and she looked away. The only other person in the elevator was a mousy guy who was probably worth millions but looked like a tweedy school teacher. The rich and their disguises.

Press lived on the twentieth floor. Good view of the stadiums in South Philly. Good view of my past, too. I winced at a few bad memories, as I passed the window in the hall. I rang Press's bell. There was no sound inside. He must've had the desk man's call and was playing hide and seek.

"Press. It's Marco. Open the door."

I heard a murmur or two and footsteps on hardwood floors. The door opened quickly and Press stood there, tie undone, shirt out of his pants, hair mussed. Someone was having his hair fluffed but who was doing the fluffing?

"Marco, what the hell do you mean lying like that to the desk man? Did you think I wouldn't let you up?"

"The thought crossed my mind. But there are more important things and maybe we should talk privately. Unless you want your neighbors to hear?"

"I'm not in a talking mood, Marco. Make an appointment with my secretary. I never do business at home."

"Would blackmail put you in a talking mood? Or, maybe, assault and battery?"

"Are you threatening—"

"You completely misunderstand me, Press. I wasn't threatening, I was listing the things that, say, someone under this roof is involved in. So maybe you might just want to talk about it, considering you own the roof under which this character lives and, uh, plays, shall we say." I looked him up and down.

"Bastard!" Press hissed. He tightened his belt, tucked in his shirt and while whipping off his tie, opened the door wide for me.

The apartment was elegantly furnished but understated. There wasn't too much of anything. In fact, there was almost too little. But I liked it. Showed the guy had taste as well as money, something you don't often see together among the nouveau riche. And everything was modern. There wasn't a Baroque element in the place, not even a crystal chandelier. The living room was bright. The south facing windows wouldn't allow anything else. It was like walking into a tanning booth. Press followed and indicated a seat for me, a chartreuse abstract shape that passed for a chair.

"What's all this about, Fontana? I haven't got time for your crap."

I knew I was interfering with his play time. "It's all about blackmail and assault, like I said. Carl, you remember Carl, I think he's a house guest, right? I mean, I saw him saunter into the building a little while ago."

"What makes you think he sauntered his way to my apartment?"

"Lucky guess?" I watched his face. He'd be formidable at poker. "Seems I've got some information putting Carl right in the middle of a blackmail scheme and an assault."

"The thing you told me about the other day?" He wasn't letting on he knew much.

"You remember, don't you?" I said.

"The assault on Sammy? You think Carl—"

"You got it. Now, what I'd like to know is can you fill in some missing details?"

"How can I? What could I possibly know?"

"Don't play innocent – it doesn't look sincere on you. We both know you and Carl are still involved, and you and Bart also have a thing going. Lucky you. But one of them is gonna make things a little uncomfortable in a while and maybe if you tell me what you know—"

"I don't know a thing, Fontana. Not a thing." He looked down and away. A liar often does.

I guess I should have suspected something might happen, but I was stuck in the abstract chair and couldn't turn when I heard the sound.

Someone grabbed me around the neck from behind forcing me out of the chair. I fought back but he was strong and squeezed my neck nearly cutting off my air and making it hard to struggle. The next sound was his voice and then I knew. Carl.

"What should we do? He knows. We can't let him go." Carl's voice lacked the confidence he'd had earlier.

"He's taking wild shots." Press snapped. "Don't be stupid."

I grabbed at his arm and tried wrestling him off me, but Carl had a powerful grip. The most I could do was give myself a little breathing room – literally. I stayed conscious and that was the important thing.

"He knows about me," Carl spat out the words. "I heard him say that. He was at my house yesterday. The only thing he doesn't know—"

"Shut up. Don't make this worse than it is. We'll figure it out."

"Sure, you'll figure something out. You know how many times you said that? You and your rich friends are all alike. The only thing you figure out is how to screw me for free. But I know too much, Press. Freebies are out from now on."

Carl unconsciously loosened his grip as he fumed at Press. I elbowed him in the ribs and pushed him hard. He went crashing into the glass coffee table. The sleek, silver and glass creation, now shards on the carpet. Carl was stunned and lay still as death on the floor.

Bart came screaming out of a back room when he heard the crash. "What have you done? Press? Are you all—" He stopped when he saw Carl sprawled amidst the glass. "I told you he wasn't right for you, Press. He'll bring you down."

"Shut up, Bart." Press knelt by Carl's side. The kid was really no worse for wear, just stunned. Eventually, Carl's eyes fluttered open and his mouth started working with only squeaks and moans coming out. Press brushed back the kid's dark hair and stroked his cheek. It would have been touching if it hadn't been the two of them.

"You're telling me to shut up?!" Bart stood hands on hips an expression on his face I'm not sure I ever want to see again. He turned to look at me. "You know what that low life, Carl, did, Marco? Maybe you do by now. But I'll bet you don't know why."

"Bart, please." Press hissed. Still cradling Carl, he seemed broken and tired.

"Did you hear something, Marco?" Bart looked around as if he'd heard a strange noise. "Must've been nothing. Where was I?"

"You were about to tell me—"

"I was about to tell you why Carl beat Sammy nearly to death."

"That much I had figured. And I thought you might've been in on it, Bart."

"I was there but I didn't do anything." Bart wore his best innocent face. He pointed at the other kid. "Carl was there with two thugs. They were on a mission."

"Getting even with Sammy for dumping him?" That was my best guess.

"Partly. But Carl was also there for Press. You didn't know that did you?" Bart smiled, and it wasn't pretty. "Sammy and that journalist, Martin, were gonna blow the lid off some Mafia case. Press was involved up to his fat ass, so he wanted to destroy the photos, the documents, and anything else. He was desperate to keep Sammy and Martin from telling the story. Carl was only too glad to help, since both Martin and Sammy had dumped him just like they dumped me. Carl also has connections to the Chiari family. Cousins or something, who knows? But they helped him do the job."

Press groaned and hugged Carl tighter to him. Press and everything he'd built up over the years would be destroyed by that mafia story. And this business with Carl and Bart would just be a sleazy addendum. Both Press and Carl would be paying for their actions for a long time. I couldn't say I was sorry.

"One thing still puzzles me though, Bart."

"What's that? You've got your men. Call the cops and have them arrested."

"You. You're the puzzle. Why were you there at Sammy's apartment? What did you want from Sammy?"

"Sammy had information I could use. I wanted to get even with Martin for dumping me. If you can imagine that toad dumping anyone. I wanted a way to stick it to him good. I wanted pictures or whatever I could use. But Carl was there with two goons and suddenly they wanted all the same things. Carl said they needed to deep six the stuff to save Press. There wasn't much I could do against all of them."

"But you did nothing while Carl and his men beat Sammy? Nothing at all?"

"There were three of them. All of them bigger than me. What was I supposed to do? They would'a killed me if I tried anything. Are you crazy?"

I guess I was because if I'd seen someone beating a friend to death, I'd have done something. At least now I had the opportunity to make some of it right. Besides, Bart would have to be a witness and that would probably turn his life inside out.

* * *

Detective Bynum was surprised to hear what I'd discovered but was only too happy to close the case. I made sure everyone waited for the police and, after giving Bynum a statement, I left. I'd been wanting to get out of the apartment. Big as the place was, it felt claustrophobic. Or, maybe I just didn't want to have to look at the sorry trio, who were now turning on one another like the barracudas they were.

Rittenhouse Square looked darker, even though the sun was high in the sky and there wasn't a cloud to be seen. I needed to be around people. Good people, not the Preston kind.

Every case teaches you something about people, but every one carries a price. You feel a little dirtier. You see people the way you knew they probably were but that you'd hoped they weren't. Each time, I tried convincing myself that there were good people out there. That not everyone was as bad or as cruel as the ones I'd just encountered. Sometimes I even believed what I told myself.

My cell phone rang. I didn't want to take the call but I hit the button reflexively. It was someone from the hospital and the news wasn't good. The charges Press and Carl and the others would face suddenly went from bad to worse.

Bart had said that Press was behind everything and that maybe there were other, darker, things at work. But, for me, the motive in the case was simple: Carl wanted revenge, wanted to hurt the people who'd hurt him. Playing in the circles he did, he found himself in possession of the precise tools he needed to exact the revenge he wanted. The fact that he was able to put things together into a grand plan that would ruin several lives at the same time, fascinated me. He didn't seem that smart but I suppose a lifetime of anger and hurt and rejection stirs things up in a man. He'd also obviously observed and learned while he floated in those circles. I'd never underestimate his type again.

Carl had managed everything almost perfectly. Sammy had dumped him, now Sammy was dead. Press had tried to dump Carl, had maybe even humiliated him. Now Press faced the prospect of spending the rest of his life behind bars. And Marty, poor Marty. He'd dumped Carl, too. Now Martin Van effectively no longer existed. I suppose Carl had really wanted Marty to get whacked by the mob. But, I think the actual result for Marty, with the size of his ego, the actual result was probably worse than a set of cement shoes. He'd lost his identity. Permanently. With it went everything he'd built up, everything he'd managed to accrue to himself. Wherever he'd decided to hide, Marty probably felt that he might as well be dead. Bad as he was, I hoped he'd start over and make a new life for himself.

Then there was Carl. He'd no doubt get a heavy sentence, but I feared his mob connections would see to it that something could be worked out for him. After all, he'd done them a service. Neither Sammy's research nor Marty's investigation would ever see the light of day.

I dreaded the day Carl got out of prison and felt sorry for anyone who crossed his path when he was released.

Stopping in my office, I found Olga wiping tears away and realized she'd heard the news of Sammy's death. She didn't say anything, but from the way she looked at me I knew everything she might want to say.

There was no sense of victory in this case. Justice maybe. But no cause for celebrating.

I called Luke at his office and told him what had happened. He urged me to get out, to meet him at a café and relax. He knew I needed to be around people. I knew it myself. Shutting myself away to review the details of the case would be counterproductive. There was nothing more I could do.

We met at the Village Brew. The people and the music and the noise felt good. The aroma of coffee and the taste of sweet pastry helped ease me back into a more gentle reality. Luke said there'd be no talk of the case the rest of the night. Instead, he led me home and we consoled ourselves in each other. I realized how important he was to me and how nice it felt being right where I was.

Pride is a Drag

Losing track of someone in the throngs packing the streets of New York during Pride is almost inevitable. Which is only one reason crowds are not among my favorite things. But I'd agreed to take a break from work and trek up to the Big Apple to celebrate and recharge.

I'd just cracked a strange case back in Philly and needed the change in scenery. When both Luke and Anton suggested it, celebrating Pride in New York seemed like just the right antidote to what I'd gone through. When we got there and encountered the crush of spectators and gawkers, the good idea seemed less good. It was exhilarating and rubbing up against so many hunks all packed together wasn't bad at all. The party atmosphere of the Pride festivities and the exuberant feelings all around combined to form an explosive combination. No matter what you were feeling, it gave you a boost.

Luke, Anton, and I strolled down the Avenue and with each block the crowd grew larger. Men, women, drag queens, men in leather, people in amazing costumes, and all the rest flooded the sidewalks sometimes making it difficult to move. Rainbow flags were everywhere. All the businesses got into the act, displaying "Happy Pride" signs or flags along with hastily constructed signs for "Pride Specials" hanging in windows. Street vendors, who didn't care what the occasion or whose money they collected, hawked water, energy drinks, and generic parade junk.

Once we'd taken a spot on the sidewalk near Twenty-Fifth Street, the three of us settled in and watched the floats sail by. Hunks on skates, bare-breasted lesbians on motorcycles, and just about anything else you could imagine made appearances. There were even sightings of politicians who'd come to let everyone see how accepting and noble they were.

"Gotta go," Anton said. "I promised to shoot some video of Marsha and the Dragettes." He held up his new camera, a gift from an admirer. "Hey, I can bring this along next time you take me on stakeout. Video of some slimeball you're investigating would be cool." He winked at me.

Then he gracefully slipped into the growing crowds. I watched him move and remembered how he was able to charm the crowds at Bubbles when he was the top feature for StripGuyz. He'd been with my male strip troupe the longest and was the hands down favorite among patrons. But he'd recently cut his schedule to less than half his usual so he could attend school and learn about things he could do with his clothes on. He also made time to help manage StripGuyz, and he was good at it, taking lots of work off my shoulders.

Anton and I had a working relationship that went slightly beyond the bounds of work without ever reaching anything more than a chaste friendship. There was a definite attraction on both sides, but Anton was only interested in someone who'd commit to monogamy, a white picket fence, and lots of domesticity. I wasn't ready for that but at the same time, I didn't want to cut off any hope for something more.

He still moved like the dancer he was, and he wore his clothes like a second skin on a body that was on intimate terms with a gym. People noticed and slurped him up with their eyes as he moved through the crowds. He seemed oblivious to the attention, but I knew he loved it.

"Don't get lost, Anton. We've gotta get ready for Barkley's party. You know what he's like about guests being on time."

Anton turned around, nodded at me and Luke, then plunged ahead.

I watched as he placed the camera's viewfinder to his eye, then started shooting video of everything in sight. He looked happy, and I felt an ache deep inside. But I smiled as he melted into the distance.

"Good thing he's got extra memory cards with him," Luke chuckled. "The way he shoots video, you'd think everything he passed was an historic event or a major monument." He waved his rainbow flag at a garish, bar-sponsored float which barreled down the street, speakers blaring, strippers dancing on its flatbed. "He asked me to edit it all into something we can watch later. I hope he takes some hot stuff to keep me entertained while I work." He laughed and moved closer to me, his hip touching mine.

Luke and I had developed a more earthy relationship. He had no demands about wedding rings or domesticity before hopping into bed. Luke was interested in something more with me. He'd said as much. But I wasn't the only guy he was test driving, so to speak. He was working out what he wanted the same as the rest of us and, like all of us, he'd figure it out eventually.

I placed a hand at Luke's back and he responded by huddling against me, even though the temperature hovered around ninety.

"If I see one more float with a corporate sponsor, I'm going to shoot out its tires," I said. "Corporations just like us for our disposable income."

"Could be worse, I guess," Luke said.

"Next year we're entering a float for StripGuyz. It'll be good publicity. I've been thinking about branching out to New York with our guys anyway."

"Anton will love it. He might even agree to dance on the float. I think he misses all the attention he used to get. Not that he doesn't still have fans," he said. When Luke relaxed, the accent he worked so hard to suppress eased itself back into his words. Truthfully, I liked his accent. Liked it a lot. His accent spoke of China and was a beautiful reminder of how much he'd been through. But he wanted to speak perfect English, and nothing could convince him it wasn't necessary. It didn't matter how successful he was as an entrepreneur. He wanted to be more integrated into the community and stand out less. Though with a stunning face like his, standing out was something he couldn't avoid.

"I'll ask him. It's a great idea. Hey!" I stood back and looked at Luke. "Maybe you and Anton can dance on the float together! That'd be a real sensation!"

"There's a lot I'd do for you, Marco, but don't push your luck."

I placed an arm around Luke's waist and squeezed him to me.

An acrobatic, very muscular group of male cheerleaders accompanied a gay marching band drumming its way down the street. The boys in the band weren't half bad. And their musical skills were good, too.

* * *

"She's missing," Anton announced as he ran up to us. "She was there one minute and gone the next. Nobody knows where she is." His handsome Eastern European features taut with worry, he reached up a hand to smooth his tousled blond hair, and a bead of sweat trickled down the side of his face.

"Who's missing?" I pulled him out of the way of a hunk on roller blades careening down the street.

"I was shooting video of her and the Dragettes, and all of a sudden she was gone."

"Who?"

"Marsha. She disappeared. Just like that." Anton brushed back his hair again and smoothed down his army-green tank top. "One minute she was there. The next minute she's gone."

"There are thousands of people here." I said. "Sometimes someone gets swallowed up by the crowd. Marsh probably got sidetracked and fell behind." I hoped that was all it was. I'd left my P.I. work back in Philly. I wanted to enjoy a weekend without any problems.

"How can somebody just disappear? And while you're taking pictures?" asked Luke, who hadn't missed what was going on, despite intently watching the parade.

"All I know is she was there and now she's not. Something's wrong."

"Maybe she got a call and had to tend to business. She's got a lot on her plate these days. The shows she runs, her new restaurant. That reality show on the gay network."

The crowd surged around us as a float filled with strippers in candy-red, skin-tight briefs slowly rolled down the street. Some of the guys tossed out candy and laughed as onlookers jumped after it. I pulled both Anton and Luke closer, so neither of them could get swept up in the roiling mass of people.

"Can't let you guys get swallowed up," I said. "Don't worry about Marsha. She's been around the block a few times. She can handle herself."

"No. Something's wrong." Anton insisted. "Marsha was marching with the Dragettes, like always. I took video all along the way. Then—"

"How many memory cards have you used so far?" Luke asked, and I knew he was trying to distract Anton from worrying. "How many parades have you filmed? You've probably got a ton of floats and drag queens on video."

"True. But this time is special," Anton said. "Marsha's birthday is next month. One of the big '0' birthdays. I don't know which, because she threatened to whack us if we even tried guessing." He smiled. "I wanted to put together a compilation video for her. I've got lots of material with Marsha, but I didn't have much of her strutting in a Pride Parade. But before I could get more footage, she disappeared."

"You keep saying 'disappeared' as if Marsh went up in a puff of smoke," I said. "What exactly happened? Maybe we can piece it together and figure out where she is."

"I was following Marsha and the Dragettes along the parade route. She was magnificent, as usual. You saw her go by. Didn't you think she looked especially good? Great dress, terrific make-up. And she looked happy. From the inside, you know?" Anton smiled.

"She did look like she was having a good time." Luke agreed.

"We were a few blocks from here, I stepped back for a wider shot of the Dragettes as they fanned out performing their routine." Anton said. "I got the whole act with Marsha doing her thing in the background. Then the memory card was full, and I stopped to put in a new one. When I looked up and wanted to zoom in on Marsha, she was gone. Poof! I looked around, but I couldn't see her and she's hard to miss."

"Yoo hoo! Anton!" A high-pitched, falsetto voice sliced through the noise of hundreds of onlookers. "Yoo hoo!"

Hedda waved her large hands in the air and barreled toward us. Wearing an outrageous, frilly day-glow-colored outfit, Hedda stood head and shoulders above everyone with the help of her eight inch, pink patent leather, platform shoes. I slowly took in her gaudy image from shiny shoes, to rippling ruffles, to her extravagant make-up. Thick red lipstick, like a blushing Ferrari, made her large mouth seem larger. Big arched eyebrows sat thick and dark over algae green eye-shadow, while layers of pancake make-up attempted to smooth over facial hair that refused to stop growing even for a moment. Over everything was her hair, a mountainous blond creation.

"Anton! You run so fast," Hedda gasped for breath. "Have you told them?"

"They don't believe me." Anton glared at me and Luke.

"Oh doll, Anton is right. Marsha is missing. One minute she was there—"

"and then she was gone." Luke finished Hedda's sentence.

"How did you… oh, you cute little thing, you're playing with Hedda." The towering drag queen bent at the waist and placed one hand on each side of Luke's face. He looked like a nut about to be cracked. "I haven't seen your pretty Chinese face in months. Those eyes, so dark and deep." Hedda shuddered with delight.

"W-well…" Luke began as he gently extracted himself from her grip. "My business takes up all my time, Hedda."

"I'm sure it does, doll, but now we have a problem," Hedda said and stood straight up again. "We've got to find Marsha."

"How exactly do you know she's lost?" I asked. "She could have left to attend to business."

"Always the skeptic, Marco. You never change." Hedda bent down to hug me. As her muscular arms encircled me, I thought about how her gym-built figure never quite fit the rest of her fluff and frills image. The hug came with a head-spinning cloud of a strong but unidentifiable fragrance blended with the odors of cigarettes and cosmetics.

"Not true, Hedda." I complained.

"You still feel good, too," she said as she released me from the hug. "You get hotter every time I see you. And that short hair looks good. I like a man with short hair, especially if he's you"

I was never good at taking compliments, but Hedda's effusiveness was fun.

"You still know how to throw the bull," I said.

"Well, we're not kiddin' about Marsha."

"Okay, maybe she wandered off. But she's a busy lady, and maybe she needed to leave."

"But wouldn't she tell me? *Me*, her headliner. I sing my heart out at her club every night, she wouldn't just leave me hanging at the parade."

"He's right, Marco. You're just—" Anton stopped. I could tell he was restraining himself. Marsha meant a lot to him, and he thought I wasn't taking this seriously enough.

"I believe you, I do. I'll make a few calls," I said pulling out my cell phone. "We'll find out what happened one way or another." I was about to tap in a number when a group of bare-breasted women zipped by on thundering Harleys. The crowds cheered.

"Noisy beasts. What some people will do for attention!" Hedda said, her bright red lips twisting into an expression of distaste. "Well, go on and make those calls, gorgeous. Don't just stand there looking all Italian."

I dialed Marsha's cell which went straight to voicemail. Then I tried her office at the club. No answer.

"She's not answering her phones. I'll try Barkley. He'll know," I said. Seth Barkley, or "Black Tie" Barkley, was famous for his lavish parties, most of them black tie gatherings. We were all invited to his after-Parade party, luckily not a formal affair. He'd told me that Marsha would be performing.

Anton glanced at me while I spoke on the phone, the anger in his eyes turning to worry.

When Barkley hung up, I was still in the dark. "He hasn't heard from Marsha but he doesn't think that's unusual. She's performing at his party later, and he suspects she went off to have some time to prepare."

"Sounds reasonable," Luke said.

"Maybe," Anton said. "But it doesn't sound like Marsha to me."

"Or me," Hedda chimed in. "If anyone needs to compose herself before a performance, it isn't Marsha. She's a star. She has presence. She's on all the time. If you know what I mean."

"Has Marsha been all right, lately?" I asked, wondering to myself if, maybe, she couldn't take the pressure of her newfound fame and just needed to get away for a while.

"Marsha is having a ball," Hedda screeched. "Packed houses every night. And she's helping all of us, just like what they say about a rising tide. Or is it a rising boat? Whatever. Believe me, when Marsha jumps in, the tide rises." Hedda winked at Anton. "Honestly, Marsha couldn't be happier. She's at the top. Her place is the most popular in town. Her restaurant gets rave reviews and the shows, at least the ones I'm in, are what everyone comes to see. The drinks aren't bad either. Marsha is livin' the dream."

"Well, it's gonna be tough searching for her in this mess," I said. The crowd continued to grow as we spoke and snaked its way down the sidewalk toward the Village. "Let's head back to the hotel. We can relax and get to Barkley's early. Marsha will be there. She can let you know why she disappeared."

"I haven't seen her perform in a long time," Luke said. "I'm looking forward to this."

Anton looked back over his shoulder, as if he'd lost something precious and wanted to keep searching. His distress was understandable. Anton and Marsha had been friends back in Philly. Marsha was a mentor for Anton as he came out and found his way. She'd been the only one of his friends at the time who'd supported his decision to become a stripper. She helped him work up a routine, and personally chose costumes for him. She also bought him an incredible array of g-strings and other accessories.

Marsha and I had also been friends for a long time which is how she put me in contact with Anton. Because I'd known her a long time, and understood just how big a heart she had, I knew Marsha went overboard for Anton precisely because others were being so shitty and judgmental about his desire to be a stripper. Marsha had her share of hypercritical people in her life, and she was determined not to let that happen to Anton. She'd told me as much, and I admired her for that. Whatever her reasons, she gave him courage and helped make him unique. When she brought him into audition for me, I was bowled over. He was good and not just good-looking. I hired him on the spot.

Anton never forgot Marsha's kindness and neither did I. He still looked to her for guidance.

"C'mon, Anton. Marsha will be fine. You'll see," I coaxed.

"You don't really know that, do you?" Anton's blond hair spilled across his forehead and he brushed it back. The expression on his beautiful face was grim. His jaw was tense, his blue eyes filled with an icy sadness. "Something's not right. I can't shake the feeling."

"Marsha knows how to take care of herself. You know that better than anyone, Anton. Everything's gonna be fine." Maybe Anton's intuition was contagious, or maybe I just had the same feeling that something was off. I had to admit that even I didn't believe what I'd said. I also knew, from past experience, that when Anton had a sense something was wrong, he was usually right.

"You're just trying to make me feel better. When I get a feeling—"

"Listen, doll," Hedda interrupted. "Maybe you're right, but let's stay upbeat. Know what I mean?" She fluttered her enormous hands in the air and snapped her fingers. "Marsha is not about worry and fretting. She's a diva, and divas are all about survival."

"Hedda's right. This is probably all a big misunderstanding." Luke added.

"Yeah, it's probably all nothing." Anton paused. "I'm just getti—oof!"

A short, wiry guy barreled into Anton throwing him to the ground. As he fell, the guy tried snatching his camera but Anton had a tight grip and the guy couldn't get it.

I grabbed at the would-be thief, catching a piece of his sleeve, but he slipped out of my fingers and kept moving.

Hedda swung her handbag and clipped his head which made him yelp. "Come back here!" Hedda screeched.

"Stop!" Luke yelled and started chasing after him. But the dark-haired guy slipped into the crowd. Roughly pushing people out of his way, he didn't look back.

"Come on back, Luke. It's no use," I shouted. Then I turned to help Anton who was trying to get to a sitting position.

People gathered around, gawking and murmuring.

I knelt by Anton's side and Hedda peered down at both of us. I saw that Anton still had a steel grip on the camera. He held his other hand to his head as if he had a headache.

"Is… will he be all right?" Hedda's voice was low.

"Son of a bitch!" Anton shook his head and swore. His chiseled masculine face seemed incongruously vulnerable.

"You okay, Anton?" I stroked his cheek, stubble rough under my hand.

"I-I'm… okay. Damn! What the hell happened?" As the shock drained away, anger took its place and Anton looked confused. "Did you see that guy? He tried to—"

"Looks like he wanted your camera. Main thing is you're all right. Aren't you?" I studied his face.

The anger brought the blood back to his cheeks.

"You sure you're okay?" Luke asked.

"Looks like he's good," Hedda said in a low voice.

A small knot of people still hovered around us. I heard them cluck, whisper, and whimper their dismay as they fed vicariously off the moment.

"I'm okay. Let me up." Anton wobbled to his feet. "I'm all right." Shrugging us away, he brushed off his clothing with his free hand. He hadn't let go of his camcorder for a second. "What did he want with my camera?"

"If I know my cameras, that's the most expensive model produced. I'd snatch it myself. Maybe he could have, um, I don't know, wanted it because it was expensive?" Luke said.

"All right. I get the picture."

"Let's just hope the camera still works and you can get the video off it." I said as we made our way through the onlookers. I got the impression they were disappointed that nothing more serious had happened.

"Did any of you see him? Was there anything distinctive about his face?"

"It happened too fast, Anton," Luke said.

"I did notice he had a rather nice ass," Hedda commented. "I kinda noticed that, uh, as I tried to hit him… you know, as he… ran away. You can't help noticing those details. At least I can't. Well, it was a nice rear end. You can't shoot a girl for noticing."

That got a laugh out of Anton, and I knew then he was all right.

During the long hike from the Village to our hotel in midtown, Hedda regaled us with tales of Pride parades she'd been in over the years. The walk was pleasant enough until I noticed a car tailing us. An old, gray Chrysler. I watched as the car appeared and disappeared around corners, never losing sight of us as we headed to midtown.

This cast a different light on things. Maybe Anton's instincts about Marsha were better than I thought. Something wasn't right. Me not believing in coincidences, I had to think maybe this was connected to what had happened to Anton, too. But that made no sense to me. I decided to keep my suspicions about the car to myself until I could get a better handle on things.

* * *

The Hilton's lobby was cool and quiet. Glass and brass mixed with golden oak along with plush carpets the color of melted butter and pink lemonade, gave the place an expensive appearance. It had the unmistakable smell of hotel, which is recognizable but indefinable.

The staff were obviously used to Pride Day and the characters it brought to town. No one batted an eye when gigantic Hedda marched into the lobby behind us panting and out of breath.

"That was like… torture. How can you walk so far, so fast? I could hardly keep up. I need water. I need to sit. I need—"

"To get out of those platform shoes, Hedda. You'll feel better," I said.

"It's no wonder you had trouble keeping up." Luke chuckled.

"Well, let's get up to your room, then, gorgeous. I need a lie down."

We found the right set of elevators and waited. Other hotel guests wandered up to us as the elevator arrived, but when they saw Hedda enter, they allowed us to have the car all to ourselves. Anton said nothing and no one else made a sound as we were whisked up to the twentieth floor.

"That way." Luke pointed when we left the elevator. He's got a nose for directions. Not that I'm bad at finding my way, but sometimes it's like Luke has a GPS system in his head. He led us down one hall, then turned onto another and we were there.

I swiped my key card through the lock, and the green light pulsed. Hedda rushed in behind me and, sighing noisily, flopped onto one of the beds in the main room. Anton took to the couch and sat in silence.

"Anybody want anything?" Luke asked.

Before anyone could answer, the phone rang.

"I'll get it. Could be Olga. She was researching something for me."

"Marco?" It was Barkley and he sounded exhausted.

"Hey! All through with the finishing touches?"

"There won't be any finishing touches. You haven't heard, then?"

"Heard what? Just got back to the hotel to get ready for your party."

"The party's canceled. That's why I'm calling."

"What's wrong, Barkley? You sound awful."

"Marsha is dead. Some kind of bizarre accident. I still can't believe I'm even saying this."

"Marsha! You can't be serious." I almost lost my grip on the receiver. I noticed Anton come to attention and stare at me. Hedda sat up on the bed she'd commandeered, eyes wide with alarm. Luke sat next to Hedda, his eyes on me the whole while.

"It's unreal. Every time I say it, the words don't make any sense, Marco. But it's true, Marsha is dead. There was apparently a terrible accident somewhere close to the parade route. There must have been so much confusion and noise out there. I couldn't get to the parade this year, I was too busy here." He paused and I could hear him breathing, trying to maintain control.

"It was chaotic like always," I said.

"But you must've heard something. Didn't anyone make a fuss? Didn't you hear sirens or anything? It's been on the news a while now. Everyone here is in shock."

"And you're sure it's Marsha? You're sure she's dead?" I glanced at Anton when I said that and saw a pained expression on his face. "There's no mis—"

"There's no mistake, Marco. She's dead." He cut me off. "Someone identified the remains."

"Oh," was all I could say as I watched Anton's face. I motioned him over to me but he shook his head. He balled his fists and turned to stare out the window.

Hedda moved to my side. "It's true? She's… she's…" The rest of the sentence was slurred in tears and a guttural sound of grief. I reached out a hand and squeezed her shoulder.

"I'm so sorry, Barkley. Is there anything I can do?"

"Thanks, Marco. We've got things covered. Marsha always talked about wanting to see you again, about coming down to Philly some time. But she was so busy with the restaurant and all." Barkley sounded defeated. "Now she'll…" Barkley lost it then and started crying softly into the phone."

Marsha was the funniest, most generous drag queen I'd ever met. Her stand up routine was famous and her costumes were copied by drag queens across the country. She'd had cameo roles in several major movies and on a few TV sitcoms. She'd parlayed that success into opening a swanky nightclub/ restaurant on the upper West Side – *Marsha's*. The simple name said it all. There was nothing she'd ever dreamed about so much as owning her own club. It was all she lived for and everything any drag queen could want. What a lot of people might want. Her image on a billboard in Times Square. Her picture popping up in ads everywhere. Her name appearing with regularity in the entertainment columns of newspapers, magazines, and blogs. She even had a blog of her own, "Marshapalooza," which got more hits than she could count. She'd hit her stride and found herself more popular than she'd been when she was plain old Ray Stone from New Hope. Like Hedda had said, she was living the dream.

"I'm so sorry, Barkley," I repeated. I looked around at everyone, Luke, Anton, Hedda, all of them looked to me as if they were lost and adrift.

"I'll have a memorial for Marsha in a while when all this settles and I can think again," Barkley said. "There wasn't any family, you know. All she had were her friends."

Anton looked over at me, his eyes filled with questions, an air of hopelessness about him. Hedda sat down beside him and they consoled one another.

"Does anyone know how it happened?" I asked. Especially after what Anton had said about her disappearing, I needed more information. I guess it was the P.I. side of me kicking in. I felt I should be doing something about this. I kept an eye on Anton as he placed his hands over his face. Hedda put an arm around his shoulders.

"No one seems to know exactly what happened." Barkley continued. "They said she was surrounded by friends all of them parading with the Dragettes. Somehow, despite everyone there, she wandered off and disappeared. The next thing anyone knew, she was found beneath the wheels of a tractor trailer a few blocks away. It's horrible."

"Makes no sense. Why would she leave the parade? She lived for Pride Day every year. And every detail of her routine was planned." My mind raced. "There's got to be a reason."

"What difference would it make knowing why she left the parade?"

"Could make a big difference. Like maybe it wasn't an accident? Maybe someone—"

"That's crazy! Who'd want to do anything to her? You're not making sense."

"Marsha went missing for a reason, Barkley. That might be what got her killed. We find that reason and we may be able to understand. It won't change anything but…"

"You're right, of course, Marco. Knowing might help. I just can't imagine anyone would… I'm sorry I was so brusque." He sounded tired and defeated.

"That's okay, Barkley. I understand. Let me help out. Maybe we can at least find out why she took a detour and wandered off."

"I keep seeing her as she was just this morning. I helped her dress for the parade. She wore that pure white, sequined gown she liked so much. Skin tight. Marsha might've been full-figured but she was shapely. And she was happy." His voice choked but he regained control. "I laughed with her when she chose the wig for today. That big-hair platinum blonde wig, the one she always used for special occasions. Heels, jewelry, all the rest. None of it was missing when they found her, that's what they said on the news. Not even her purse or the money she had. She was just dead, crushed by the truck. Horribly mangled." He exhaled and it sounded as if all the life had gone out of him.

"Give me a little while and let me see what I can come up with." The fact that nothing was missing, no valuables were taken could mean it was an accident. But I never took anything at face value. "One more thing."

"Sure," Barkley said.

"Do you believe it was really an accident? Was there anyone bothering Marsha lately? Was she ever depressed?"

"If you're trying to ask if Marsha was suicidal, forget it. If this wasn't an accident, then it would have to be murder. Suicide was not in Marsha's repertoire. She was one of the most stable people I know," Barkley said.

"I hadda ask. You understand."

"I know, Marco. You're not the only one who's asked about that. I guess because it's all too impossible to believe anything else."

"I'll call if I come up with anything."

Hedda stood and motioned me over to sit with Anton. I placed an arm around his shoulder and he laid his head against my chest. His muscular body felt tense. He was more vulnerable than I'd ever seen him. Usually tough and in control, Anton obviously needed to allow himself this moment of weakness. The guys in my stripper troupe looked to Anton for direction, guidance, and comfort. He never failed to solve their problems and take care of every situation that threatened to get out of hand. Anton was the definition of stability.

Now he was the one needing someone to lean on and it felt good holding him, letting him rely on me, and allowing my arms to support him.

"You don't think it was an accident, do you?" he asked without moving to look at me. His voice was tight, controlled.

"We've gotta consider every possibility." I hugged him closer but he gently pulled himself into a sitting position.

There were times Anton didn't want comfort, didn't need to be coddled. At those times he needed to be with himself, to think, and consider his options. He stood, drew a finger softly across my lips and walked into the bedroom shutting the door behind him.

Luke, who'd been watching intently from across the room, came to sit with me. He'd only known Marsha briefly but they'd gotten along well. Luke peered at me with his mournful black eyes and let out a deep sigh.

"What happens now?"

"That depends." I stroked his cheek. "According to Barkley, the police think it's an accident. My guess is they won't do much now that they've made that determination. They've got too many other cases to close. So, unless something else turns up, the case is closed for them."

"But you told Barkley you had other ideas. Like what exactly?" Luke was good in situations like this. He was able to think clearly and see patterns others might miss.

"Like maybe we can find a clue as to why Marsha left the parade."

"How? She's dead." Luke looked at me as if I'd lost my mind. "Magic? Or, have you acquired the speaking-to-the-dead thing?"

"None of the above, we have Anton and his camcorder. He videoed Marsha and the Dragettes parading down the street. It's possible he caught something on video which can give us an idea why Marsha left the parade. That would only be one piece of the puzzle. But it'd be a start."

"You're good, Marco. I wouldn't have thought of the video recordings so quickly. It's scary the way you can think so well under pressure," Luke said.

"Not as scary as some things, Luke." I hugged him closer, not wanting to let go. Times like this, when someone as solid and seemingly permanent as Marsha disappears from the scene, the fragility of life looms over everything. I wanted to hold tight to everyone and everything I love.

When I heard Anton open the bedroom door, I looked up. He seemed better now but still forlorn. He came over to the couch where we sat, a sad smile on his face.

"I could use some of that, too." He opened his arms for a group hug. Luke and I stood and moved into his embrace. Anton's muscles were still tense. It must've taken a great effort for him to hold himself together.

"Feeling any better?" I asked.

"I heard what you said, Marco, about the video, I mean." He gently pulled out of the hug and looked at us. "It's a terrific idea. I took plenty of footage of Marsha, even if she was in the background most of the time." He paused and sighed a deep, distraught sound. "I was just with her and it was like old times. She was so alive. You'll see when you look at that video."

"Let's see what you managed to get." I snatched his camcorder from the table. "Luke, you think we can hook the camera to the TV?"

"I don't have any of the cables or other stuff with me," Anton said. "I didn't think we'd be using the video to investig—" Anton stopped himself. "I didn't think we'd need any of that."

"This model has a tiny screen that flips out. We could use that," offered Luke.

"I don't think we'll be able to see enough detail that way. Besides, all three of us need to watch at the same time if we're going to catch everything. We need a bigger screen." There were lots of people I knew in New York but only one of them was likely to have what we needed. Canny Milforn, the force behind a successful series of gay guidebooks, loved high-tech equipment. "I think I know someone who can help," I said. "I'll give him a call."

"If he's gay, he'll probably be at the parade." Anton asked.

"He used to go every year, but something happened a few years back and he's refused to attend ever since. He's never revealed what happened and I know better than to ask. In any event, his OCD keeps him from getting caught in large crowds."

"He's obsessive-compulsive?" Luke said. "One of my cleaners has OCD. He's a fantastic worker. But he's a little odd, and I know he isn't a happy person."

"Well, Canny likes to think of himself as having made progress in dealing with his OCD. But he still can't handle crowds."

"You sure this guy can help?" Anton was skeptical.

"One of his obsessions is technology. He's got almost whatever technological equipment you might need. Not to mention several humongous flat screen TVs. He has the sweetest home theater set up, too. Hates movie theater crowds."

"And he'd just let us use his stuff? Just like that?" Luke asked.

"Why not? I'll call him."

* * *

True to form, Canny had avoided the parade. When I spoke to him, he said he was more than happy to help.

We gathered up Anton's memory cards and anything else we thought we'd need. Hedda agreed to hold down the fort at the hotel room. We left him behind and piled into an elevator.

Canny lived in a co-op in Chelsea, which wasn't all that far. But Anton insisted on getting there the fastest way possible and I couldn't blame him. Luke hailed a cab, and we headed to Chelsea.

Traffic on Seventh Avenue wasn't too bad which was surprising, considering that some streets were still closed for the parade. After a block or two, I spotted the same Chrysler following us as I'd seen earlier. Keeping an eye out for a tail was a habit with me. And since this joker had followed us to the hotel, I figured he'd be waiting for us to make a move. I didn't want to alarm the others but we had to evade the tail.

I asked the cabbie to make a turn.

"Turning will be taking you out of your direction," said the driver.

"Just make the turn, pal," I insisted.

"You are paying so I am going wherever you are wanting." He made the turn.

"What's going on?" Anton asked.

"We must have a tail," Luke answered, then looked at me for conformation.

"Right. Won't be easy losing him either." I leaned back and stared out the rear window. About three cars behind us now, the Chrysler made the same turn.

I directed the cabbie to turn a few more corners and he obliged without another word. We were getting farther from Chelsea but I had no choice. I didn't want this guy knowing our destination.

Despite turns and detours down side streets, the tail stayed with us. There was no way the cab would lose this guy. I had the cabbie drop us at an address on a street behind Canny's building. I thought maybe we could at least confuse the tail by going into some other building first, then somehow moving to Canny's building afterward without being seen. Once we got to Canny's place, I'd think about our next moves.

* * *

Canny opened the door and smiled broadly. Tall, paunchy, with spiky graying hair and wire-framed glasses, Canny's appearance was oddly comforting.

"Wasn't sure you were coming. You said you were coming, but then—"

"There was a tie-up on the way and we were delayed." I had to stop him before he got started or we'd never move beyond the door.

Canny waved us in and closed the door behind us. He surreptitiously rapped it softly with his knuckles several times. I was certain he knew exactly the number and the reason. He was good at disguising his little habits, but I was even better at noticing after years of knowing him.

"How's life in Philadelphia?" Canny wiggled his eyebrows, then blinked his eyes rapidly a few times. "You guys won't mind if I finish feeding my pets before we do whatever it is you need done?" Without waiting for a reply, he turned and headed down the hall to his animal salon, which is how I liked to think of the room he'd set aside for the bulk of his menagerie. Canny had countless pets and lavished tons of attention on them. I suppose they returned that affection in their own ways.

Following, we found ourselves in a very clean, cool green room. A forest of plants of all sorts, tropical and otherwise, grew in countless pots around the room. He'd also strategically hung large bare tree branches here and there for the exotic birds and anything else that might like a perch high up. There were cages for some small animals, like hamsters and mice. Tanks with frogs, lizards, a snake, and a remarkable number of other things had been placed here and there. A fruity-grainy-sawdust odor hung in the air, a pleasant reminder of pet shops I'd been in as a kid.

"Won't take long," Canny murmured as he dropped various kinds of food into the different cages.

"Shit!" Anton yelped and jumped, nearly grabbing onto one of the suspended branches. "What the hell was that?"

"What was what?" Canny, engaged in the feeding ritual, didn't turn around.

"Something small and furry just ran across my feet." Anton looked down and shook his leg.

"Could be Tiny, my Hedgehog, or maybe it was Jane."

"Jane?" I asked.

"Jane is a very small spider monkey. So small they thought she'd die when she was born. But I took her and nursed her and now she lives here." As if on cue, Jane, diminutive and wiry, hopped up onto Luke's shoulder. "She wouldn't hurt a thing."

"Y-you sure about that?" Luke glanced sideways at the little monkey.

"Monkeys can be vicious," Anton said and brushed at his pants making sure no other creatures were hanging around waiting to run up his leg.

Jane, probably sensing Luke's discomfort, hopped from Luke to Canny and chattered as if she were amused at all the attention.

"You allowed to have all these animals in the apartment?" Luke asked, looking around in amazement.

"It's my condo. They have a rule that says no dogs. Rules don't say a thing about other creatures." Canny slapped the lid down on one of the cages. "The condo board hasn't bothered me so far."

"Amazing," Anton said under his breath.

"Finished! We can get to your work now, Marco. Told you it wouldn't take long. So, what is it you need?" Jane hopped off his shoulder and, chattering loudly, leaped onto a branch, causing it to swing back and forth.

I launched into a brief explanation of the situation as Canny led us into another room. This one was a technological paradise, and Canny smiled broadly when he heard Luke and Anton ooh and aah. Computers, laptops, iPads and other tablets, flat screen monitors and more sat in orderly rows on tables. A light table, and tech gizmos I'd never seen before filled other stands.

Canny pointed out the equipment he thought would be most useful and said, "Just upload your memory cards into that device. Then you can view everything all at once on any other device individually or all of them at once. Maybe you'll like it better on one device at a time. Or, you can do it one video at a time on all devices. Or, if you—"

"This is terrific, Canny. Letting us use all this stuff. Must've cost a fortune," I said to stop him from generating an unending list of options. "Let's watch while they figure it out." I gently pulled Canny aside.

"Shame about Marsha," he said. "I was at her club recently. Classy joint and packed to the gills. She was one of our best advertisers, too. Always bought full page ads in multiple guides."

"That's Marsha. She did everything in a big way."

I watched Anton and Luke as they worked uploading the memory cards. Luke pushed a few buttons and the largest of the flat screen monitors came to life, first with grainy static then with a tight shot of a muscular man wearing only the suggestion of a bathing suit and waving a long rainbow streamer behind him as he danced down the street.

"I see I didn't miss anything again this year," Canny remarked as he stared at the screen. "Same tired old stuff. I've put in my time, I don't have to attend every parade."

Anton's video moved along, spotlighting hunky guys, gaudy floats, and even shots of the crowd. Then a frantic montage slashed across the screen: faces, bare asses, rainbow flags and banners, more faces, pecs, crotches and thighs, floats, shouting onlookers. It was a mad dramatic jumble.

"What were you thinking when you took this?" Luke asked, laughing.

"It's a montage. Get over it. There were some wild things this year." Anton snapped. "I thought it'd make a nice intro for Marsha's video."

"Look at that guy. Are those pecs or has he had hormone shots?" Luke said.

Anton concentrated on watching his video, and I thought it was good that he could laugh, forget what'd happened, even if only for a moment.

"That guy was perfect. I remember spotting him a block away. He's perfect. You couldn't ask— hey, look what that wise ass did."

"Hard not to notice that," Luke said, his eyes glued to the monitor.

"Where's the footage you guys really wanted to see," Canny asked, already bored with parade antics.

"Who knows? I took so much video I can't remember what happened when."

"You didn't mark the memory cards with time and date? You didn't keep track of what you did while you were doing it?" Genuinely shocked, Canny shook his head. "You should always keep everything in order. You'll never find anything this way." Then he tapped each tiny memory card three times.

"We can fast forward until the Dragettes appear. It's all there," Anton said. "And that's when Marsha makes an appearance."

Luke pressed a key forcing the parade and the crowds to fly by like an old silent film. People walked and gestured with fast jerky movements. I was mesmerized by the scenes playing themselves out on the screen. If you look at everything around you in high speed, you might get the urge to slow it down and change a few things. The way we interact with one another seems strange and unreal at high speed. Every gesture and facial expression looks insincere and superficial. Maybe the insincerity is what's real, and we don't notice it at the normal speed of life.

"A lotta hot bods but no drag queens," Luke smirked. "You sure you weren't secretly making a 'Guys Gone Wild' video?"

"Wait! There's one of the Dragettes," Anton said. "This is where it starts."

That brought us all to attention and we focused on the screen in eerie silence. Eventually Marsha appeared, walking with her usual regal bearing and majestic attitude. What a sight she was. Her dazzling white sequined dress reflected sunlight like shards of rainbows with Marsha floating at the center. Deftly balancing her outsized bouffant wig with the women-you-don't-want-to-know coif, she moved with a grace you wouldn't think possible for her size. But Marsha carried it off with dignity, elegance, and tasteful humor.

"Look at that smile," Anton said, his voice catching in his throat. "Marsha was a beautiful person. And never selfish or stingy. She threw money around like it was popcorn. Even when she had next to nothing. Now that she had everything, she was even more generous. And happier than I ever remember her being."

"That's what makes this so difficult," I added. "It had to be an accident. I don't believe she'd—"

"She'd never kill herself," Anton interrupted, his voice tight with anger. "Look at her. She was at the top of her game. Her club was raking in money. A while back, she told me as soon as she paid back all her investors, everything would be profit. She would never kill herself."

"He's right, you know," Canny added. "I saw her a few days ago and she was bubbling about how good things were. Went on and on about her projects and plans."

"She must've had a lot of investors. A club like that takes serious cash to get off the ground." Luke commented. Being in business himself, he knew what it took to run one. The connections he'd made gave him insight into lots of other ventures. His own housecleaning service had required a number of investors. Once he'd paid them all and was doing well, he'd begun investing in start-ups himself.

"Marsha had plenty of investors. She said there were always more who wanted in. I remember she joked about refusing to get involved with the broken-nose crowd. She was tough." Anton said.

"All clean money, then?" I asked.

"As far as I know. Why not? It's not so unbelievable. Plenty of her friends have money. Big money. Look at Barkley. He's so rich he has no idea what to do with his cash."

On the screen, Marsha paraded serenely down the street, waving to fans and friends, smiling and bowing her head. Like the drag royalty she was. Then the Dragettes started their routine and Anton focused on them. Except, you couldn't miss Marsha, a tower of sparkling white sequins, in the background. She'd begun to mug and prance and interact with the others as her part of the Dragettes act.

"Look at them. Aren't they something!" Anton laughed. It was a bitter sound. "If only they'd known. If only *I'd* known what was going to— I would've…"

"You couldn't possibly know these things. It's no use going over and over stuff, Anton," Luke said, his usual tenderness with me coming through as he spoke to Anton.

"I know but—"

"Hey! Look at that." Canny pointed to an area of the screen near the top and way at the back. "What's Marsha doing there?"

"Seems to be having an argument," I said. "With another drag queen. Can't quite see it clearly, though."

"It's too deep in the background," Canny said. "You can zoom in, Luke. Tighten in on that area. It'll be a little grainy but we'll be able to see the action a little better.

Canny showed Luke what to do and in seconds the image had shifted from the Dragettes to a tighter shot of Marsha and the guy she apparently argued with.

"Look at that guy," Luke said. "If that's a drag queen, she's the worst I've ever seen."

"Yeah, look at those clothes. Like she picked them out of the trash." Fascinated, Anton didn't turn away from the screen when he spoke to us.

Canny made an odd snorting sound. "Standards have dropped. Used to be every drag was beautiful. Every one of them."

"And what about this guy's make-up?" Luke asked. "Seems to me that—"

"Make-up? That guy doesn't have a speck of it." I said.

"That's right," Anton murmured. "No self-respecting drag queen would be seen in public like that."

"Didn't even bother to shave. Look, there's another one just like him. Equally bad." Canny pointed to the screen and shook his head. "Not beautiful at all."

"They don't move right, either," Anton commented, never breaking his stare.

"Look. The second one closed in on Marsha's other side." Luke said. "He's even worse. Didn't make an attempt to look like anything. He's wearing tattered old rags."

"Look at the crowd. They're laughing as if it's a clown show." Canny remarked.

The onlookers certainly seemed entertained by the antics. They laughed, poked each other in the ribs, and called attention to Marsha and the guys who seemed to be harassing her. Everyone apparently thought it was part of the Dragette performance.

"You sure this wasn't part of the act? Those guys are putting on a pretty believable clown show." The bad drag, odd make-up, and physical antics proved they were good at playing the buffoon which is why it appeared so funny to onlookers. The guys pulled exaggerated faces, hopped up and down at strategic times, and badgered Marsha in what could be taken as an amusing attempt to corral her for some reason. They were convincing. But Marsha didn't really seem to be part of it all.

Marsha didn't look happy. In fact, she seemed worried, even frightened. The crowd wasn't paying close enough attention to notice that she wasn't acting. I began to have doubts about this being part of the show.

"Kinda does look like an act," Canny said. "Maybe they planned this. They're guys she knows. Maybe they were supposed to look disheveled and rowdy. Maybe Marsha had them—"

"Marsha wouldn't know people like that," Anton snapped. "They don't know how to dress, how to move. They're awful. And Marsha doesn't look like she's having fun. It's not part of the act."

Marsha's tormentors kept at it for a little while, keeping the crowds entertained. All of a sudden, Marsha swayed and toddled precariously on her high heels. She appeared confused and disoriented.

"They must have done something to her." Anton said. "Look how she's acting. How could I not notice when it happened right in front of me? I should have seen this. I should have helped her."

"You were taking video," I said. "You were concentrating on the Dragettes, not on what was going on in the background. You've gotta admit it was way off at the back. You couldn't have seen it, not with all the other activity going on."

"Marsha looks confused. She's not walking in the right direction," Canny said.

"Could be some kind of chemical spray," Luke offered.

"They have that kind of thing?" Canny asked.

"You're kidding, right? They've got everything and anything. You just have to know how to get it," Luke said. "I know people in Philly who can get their hands on whatever you want. All illegal, of course." Luke watched the screen intently as he spoke. "Yep, looks like they disoriented Marsha somehow. Anybody see them spray something? Or maybe inject her with something?"

"I didn't notice anything," Anton said. "Shit! What good was I out there?"

"I've gotta watch it again," I murmured. I needed a closer look. I'd have to scrutinize it a few times to be sure what they might've done. "I didn't think they got close enough to do something like spray her or inject anything. Need to see it again to be sure."

"I missed it all. I was so intent on the Dragettes, and I thought Marsha was just having fun with them and the show," Anton said. "I missed it all."

"That's what those guys were counting on," Luke offered. "Everyone paid attention to the drag dancers and the comic routine Marsha seemed to be doing. No one noticed when they actually moved in and did something to Marsha."

"Luke's right." I squeezed Anton's shoulder. "They knew what they were doing. No one would have noticed them or what they did."

"Of course he's right," Canny said. "Look at them. Misdirection is their game."

As we watched, the two bad drag queens pretended to be concerned and attempted to help Marsha. The grainy, blown up section of the video showed them taking her by the arms, patting her back, and leading her away down a cross street. That's the last we saw of her. The camera then moved and swept the area. When the view returned to where it'd been, there was only an empty street, pixilated and gritty. Luke brought the focus back to normal and the Dragettes came back into the picture moving along down the street, continuing their antics. Then the screen went black for a second.

"That's when the card filled up and I put in a new one," Anton said sadly. Just as he finished the screen lit up again with the parade and the drag dancers, but without Marsha in the background.

"Looks like you didn't miss much when you changed cards," Canny said. "You got it all on the other card."

"I missed everything!" Anton said, voice tight. He clenched and unclenched his fists. His muscles were knotty when I laid a hand on his back. "I concentrated on shooting the damned video without paying attention to what I was really looking at."

"How could you know what to look for? Don't beat yourself up," I said, trying to sooth some of the tension by rubbing his back. "At least we've got the video. We'll give it to the police and they'll know what to do."

"They won't do anything," Anton said. "You know as well as I do, they've already put this down as an accident."

"I'll make sure they do something. I'll call Marsha's friends. We'll raise a stink all the way to City Hall. Don't worry, Anton."

"I know you will. But…" He hesitated and for a moment he seemed beaten down. I knew Anton well and I knew he was far from defeated. I could see the anger building. I saw it in his tensed fists, in the set of his jaw, and in the darkening blue of his eyes.

"Let's run the video again, Luke. I wanna make sure I didn't miss anything."

"I'm sorry but I can't watch it again." Anton stood abruptly. "I know you have to, it's what you do. I've seen what I have to and I can't watch her being harmed again." He glanced around as if he were trapped in a room with no doors. "I've gotta get out of here for a while. I'll take a walk and figure out what I should do."

"The park out front of this building is kinda nice for relaxing," Canny said. "There's a statue of a little dog there. A Scottie. He helps me think when I'm confused. Helped me through a lot of things. Just sit and look at him. I guarantee he'll talk to you."

"Thanks, Canny." Anton looked around at us. "I'm sorry. I'm a mess and I won't be much help anyway."

I walked Anton to the door and placed a hand to his cheek. "Come back up when you feel better," I said softly. "We'll all go to dinner. Someplace nice," I said. "We'll toast Marsha's memory."

He closed the door gently behind him and I went back to the video room.

"Poor guy looks lost," Luke said.

"He'll be all right," Canny said. "I can see the strength in him. Good kid."

"Let's get through this video another time or two before we call in the police," I said and Luke hit the switch.

It was only after the video began running again and we'd watched a few minutes that the thought hit me. I'd been so engrossed in trying to squeeze more information from the video, I'd forgotten everything else. But then it hit me.

The car that'd been tailing us might be waiting outside. Probably would be trolling the neighborhood for any sign of us. After everything that had happened, it wasn't hard to figure that Anton was the one they were after. More to the point, they probably wanted the video he'd taken. That's the only thing that made sense.

I jumped up. "We've got to catch him!"

"Catch who?" Luke was startled.

"What's going on?!" Canny stood dumbfounded as I moved past him.

"Anton! Tell you why after we intercept him. C'mon, Luke." I flew down the hall and out the door with Luke close behind.

The elevators in Canny's building were notoriously slow. With a lead of ten minutes or so, there was no way we'd get from the nineteenth floor to the lobby in time to intercept him. But we had to try.

I smacked the elevator button for the fifth time and the elevator doors slid open.

We jumped in and I hit the lobby button.

"What's this all about?" Luke asked sounding bewildered.

"Remember the car tailing us on the way here?" I asked.

"Yeah. Kinda forgot about it, though."

"We've been tailed ever since Anton was attacked."

"Why? What's going on?"

"Not sure, Luke. But I'll bet it's all connected to Anton and the video. Whoever it is must think Anton got them on video. And by 'them' I mean whoever it is that harmed Marsha. That's clear to me now."

"Okay, but what's that got to do with us rushing out of the building?"

"It's Anton. I was so wrapped up reviewing the video, I forgot about the car that'd tailed us. After Anton left the apartment is when I remembered."

"You think they're waiting for him? That's great, just great. We'll be lucky if we find him. The bastards better not touch Anton. Otherwise…" Luke angrily punched the button for the lobby a few times, but the elevator descended at it's own sweet speed.

* * *

"Anton wasn't anywhere in that park you mentioned," I said to Canny when we returned to his apartment after a frantic search of the grounds and the surrounding streets. "He's also nowhere in the vicinity.

Canny seemed stunned. He stood shaking his head at all the coming and going. He'd even let us back in without any of his usual OCD maneuvers, which meant that he was really shaken up.

"We looked up and down as many streets as we reasonably could. But I knew if we didn't spot him right away, it would be useless to keep looking." I repeated the information about the attack on the street and the car tailing us.

"Just because you didn't find him, doesn't mean he was kidnapped." Canny reassured us as he poured coffee for each of us.

"That's true, Marco," Luke said. "Anton is Anton. He probably wandered down some street and ducked into a café or a restaurant." Luke touched my hand. "He's tough. He can take care of himself if he needs to."

"I'm giving it an hour. If we don't hear from him, I'm getting the police involved. We've got the video. Maybe they can find something in it to go on."

"Let's review the footage again. Maybe we'll see something we missed." Luke was already at the video equipment. The giant monitor flickered back on.

We watched Anton's video again. The fake drag queens didn't look familiar in the least. Thuggish, muscular guys under the dresses, they knew what they were doing and did it efficiently. If they'd used a chemical, they probably made sure there was no way to tell afterward. The body was so mangled there'd be no marks and they'd probably used something that'd be undetectable in an ordinary tox screen. I stared at the action over and over trying to latch onto something but it wasn't happening. I needed time but we couldn't wait much longer. I wanted to get the police involved before more time was wasted.

Just as that thought occurred to me, my cell phone rang. I tensed up and could see that even Luke was alarmed. Obviously both of us had the same thought: this couldn't be good.

"Maybe it's Anton," I said without much conviction before I looked down and saw "Unknown Caller" on the screen. This was not good at all.

"It isn't him, is it?" Luke peered at me.

Canny stared at the cell phone as if it were alive. "What's going on, Marco?"

"I guess we'll see." I pressed a button. "Fontana."

A voice struggling to speak. A strangled cry. Then silence.

"Anton?" I whispered.

"Marco. You gotta—" Something interrupted his frantic cry and my stomach did a flip.

"Anton. What's going on."

"Somebody— fuck!" He sounded angrier and more sure now. "Get your hands off! I'll tell them myself. Marco? They want—" It sounded as if the receiver was ripped from his hands. Someone else was on the line.

"Fontana?" A male voice, rough and crude.

"Who is this?"

"Never mind that. We got your friend here and you have something *we* want."

"And..."

"And we're gonna make a trade. You got no alternative, Fontana. Make the trade or your friend don't get to go home."

"All right." I tried sounding calm. "What is it you want?"

"The video from the camcorder, wise ass. You bring the memory cards, we'll bring your friend. All wrapped with a nice pink bow."

"How can I be sure you'll do as you say?"

"You can't. But you don't got much choice, do you? Don't do it, your friend is ground beef. Do it and he's home free."

"When and where?"

"We'll call you with the details. No funny stuff. And no police."

The click of the phone breaking the connection was like the crack of a rifle. I was worried about Anton. He's not one to be taken down easily and that could get him hurt. I knew he could take care of himself, I'd seen him at the gym and he was formidable. That might not be enough now, though. He was obviously outnumbered, and those guys didn't sound like they were fooling around. I didn't think we had a whole lot of choice.

"Anton's in trouble?" Luke sat next to me, placed an arm around my shoulder. "Is it what you thought?"

"Yeah, the video. They've got Anton and they want the video."

Canny stared at us silently, while he opened and closed his fingers obsessively.

"Give 'em the video. This is not worth Anton's life." Luke said.

"They've killed Marsha." Canny's voice shook. "There's no guarantee—"

"We've got no choice. I'm not letting Anton hang. He knows we'll get him back," I insisted. "The kidnappers said they'd call with details."

"So, what do we do now?" Canny asked.

"This gives us time to think," I said.

"Let's keep searching the video for something. That's got to be the key. If we find anything, maybe…" Luke moved toward the video equipment.

"You're right." I took a deep breath. I had to stay focused no matter what Anton might mean to me. I had to deal with this. "Let's run it again and see what we can find."

"Shouldn't you get these memory cards to the police?" Canny said.

"They'll kill Anton if we bring in the police. I'm not taking the risk. They want the video, they'll get the video." I glared at Canny and he shrank back.

"But, the police—"

"They won't do much anyway," Luke said. "They're calling this an accident. This video won't change anything. You know that."

"I don't like cutting out the police, either. But if the kidnappers don't get the memory cards, Anton is history." Then it dawned on me. Here we were in the middle of a tech playground. "What am I thinking!? Look where we are. There's a way to give 'em what they want and let the police in on this, too."

"That's it." Luke said. He was brighter than any ten people, and he could read my mind at times. I was sure he was thinking the same thing. "Yeah, we can do this."

"Somebody gonna let Canny know what it is we can do?" Canny said from his new perch in a corner of the room.

"We've gotta play this right," I said. "We can give the kidnappers their memory cards and get Anton back. At the same time we can give the video to the police. But we've gotta do it carefully."

"We can't let the cops come in and try to run the show."

"No," Canny said, confused. "Of course — of course not."

"We can't let the police know about Anton or the memory cards. We just call them and tell 'em we've got pertinent information to the case on Marsha."

"Right, but we all know, once we give them the video, they'll start asking a lotta questions. They could screw everything up," Luke said.

"I have a friend…" Canny said hesitantly and I assumed he was going to launch into one of his inspirational speeches.

"We don't have time for a story, Canny. We've gotta study the video once more before we decide how to handle all this."

"Wasn't going to try and inspire you, Marco." Canny looked hurt.

"I'm sorry, Canny. The kidnappers might call any time and I want to be ready."

"My friend Sarge is a police Lieutenant and he has authority over different labs and such. You remember Sarge don't you?"

"I really can't— oh, yeah. Big guy, right? How can he help?"

"I'll call him, see what he thinks," he said, moving toward the phone. "And don't worry. I won't give anything away."

"Do me a favor, Canny?"

"What do you call everything I'm already doing?" He smiled.

"When you talk to Sarge, just tell him that the video on your hard drive is all there is. See? We can let Sarge view it on your monitor. I need the memory cards and I don't want him to know they exist. I'm planning something and if it works out, I'll give the cards to the police when I'm through with them."

Canny shook his head in disbelief. "I'll do it, Marco, but you're making a criminal out of me." He paused, wiggled his eyebrows, and smiled. "I kinda like it."

Then he picked up the phone while Luke and I reviewed the video. Very little that was new stood out. I could make out a smudge of a tattoo on one guy's arm but the details were impossible. Luke ran the video back and forth several times and then, on the I-don't-know-which-run, I noticed something.

"Feels like we've been going over and over the same material but something's missing. Is there a card we haven't viewed more than once?" Something felt wrong.

"We've been concentrating on the videos Anton said were the most important. The ones with Marsha and those guys."

"I have a feeling there's something else. Let's look at what we haven't gone over more than once or twice. Can you pull up those files?"

"No problem," Luke said. "Here you go." He tapped a key and the video started. It was after the incident with Marsha. Anton had obviously been recording the Dragettes as they regrouped after their routine. The usual lag between floats and groups in the parade, gave them time to take a break and get themselves together again. No one seemed to notice that Marsha was missing. No one looked alarmed or upset. Anton kept the recorder going on every little detail of their movements.

"I thought we'd missed something. Look at that. See? Let's run through it again, Luke."

"What'd you see?" Luke asked as he tapped buttons to start it again.

Canny came up behind us. "Sarge will be over in a little," he announced. "He said you've gotta turn in the video but he'll buy you a little time because of Anton. He says he can take a look though and see if he recognizes anybody. He was undercover for a lot of years—"

"Great." I interrupted what I knew would be a long story. "Now sit down and be an extra pair of eyes on this video." I ordered. As much as Canny might protest, I did know that he loved taking orders. Especially if the man giving them wore a uniform. The stories he'd told me.

We watched as Luke ran the video again. The Dragettes picked up pieces of their costumes that had fallen off during the performance and placed them in a box being carried by one of their staff. Now and then they mugged for Anton as he recorded but they kept milling around looking for whatever they might've dropped and cleaning up the area as well. As we watched, someone else came into frame.

"Look at that guy." I said.

"What guy?" Canny squinted at the screen.

"One of the thugs in bad drag. One of the ones who took Marsha. He came back." Luke pointed to a figure on the screen. "What's he doing?"

"He's looking for something on the ground. Looking and getting frustrated." I answered, wondering just what he'd lost and if he'd eventually found it.

The guy's head snapped up as if he'd heard something and his wig slid off to the side. Glancing from side to side, he then looked straight at the camera and at Anton. His eyes narrowed to slits and his face stiffened with anger. Wearing his dress as if it were a pair of overalls, he moved forward menacingly and shouted. "Stop fucking filming me or I'll bash—"

He was stopped mid-sentence by Hedda who'd entered the frame and whacked the guy across his head with her outsized handbag.

"Leave him alone. He's got a right to film. If you don't like it, shove off." Hedda hurriedly pushed the guy nearly out of frame. Several of the Dragettes ran over to surround the guy, and whopped him with whatever they held until he was on the ground. I almost felt sorry for the guy.

But, the kidnapper jumped up, snarled aggressively, and scattered the Dragettes, who ran screaming in all directions.

Looking angrily at the camera and Anton, again, he said, "This ain't finished. I want the video." The next thing I saw was Hedda moving in on him with her bag again. To his credit, Anton kept filming.

The guy glanced at Hedda, then ran off down the cross street, his dress more tattered and dirty than before. Trailing a length of torn, puce-colored material behind him, he ran to a car parked in the distance. The same Chrysler I'd seen tailing us. He was far down the block but I could see him approach the car, lift his dress, and hop into the passenger seat. The small sound of the door slamming shut was almost lost in other sounds. After a moment, the old Chrysler took off and sped away turning a corner in the distance.

"Slow it down. Maybe I can see the license plate." I knew it was hopeless without more expert equipment and some time, but it was worth a shot.

As Luke ran the video in slow motion, the doorbell rang and my cell phone started ringing at the same time.

Canny went to answer the door and brought Sarge into the video room. I nodded a hello as I flipped open my cell phone. "Fontana."

"Got a pencil, hot shot?" The same crude voice from earlier barked out the question.

"Gimmie the instructions. I'm ready."

"That fag fest still goin' on?"

"The Festival in the Village? Far as I know it's scheduled to go on for hours." I answered.

"Good. We'll meet on West End and Christopher. Don't take anybody with you. Come alone, understand? Don't try to fuck with us. Your pretty-boy friend here will be waiting for you but he won't be alone. Got that?"

"Right."

"Make any moves when you see him and he's dead. You won't see us but we'll be there. Somebody will have a gun on your boy, so don't play the hero." He paused.

"Okay, then what?"

"Put the memory cards in a plastic bag. Clear plastic. Hand them to your boy and walk away."

"What about Anton? How do—"

"Just stay put and have your cell phone with you, big shot. Somebody's gonna run the video. If it's what we want, we'll call you. Then you and your friend can go home and play hide the sausage. Play us and you can watch the pretty-boy take a bullet. Clear?"

"When do you want me there?"

"One hour. If you're late, he's dead. You try to fuck us over, he's dead. Make a wrong move, and—"

"I'll be there." I ended the call. My mind raced with possibilities. I had an idea, the beginning of a plan, but I'd need help.

Sarge looked at me, his pudgy Italian face gave him a younger appearance than the forty-some years he carried.

"It was them, right?" He asked, shifting his feet. "What do they want you to do?"

I explained as briefly as I could so I could describe my idea to Luke in private. I didn't want anyone else knowing right then. Luke would know what to do.

"That's all I get?" Sarge asked. "You're holdin' out on me, Marco. I remember how you operate."

"Sarge, if you recognize anybody on the video, you'll know a lot more than I do right now."

"You're still a bullshitter, too, Fontana. Give me a rundown and I'll get started." He wasn't happy but I didn't give him much choice.

We talked a while and I explained what he might look for on the video.

"You're the expert, Sarge. I'm depending on you."

"Gotcha," he said. "Any faces look familiar, I'll call it in and they'll pick the bastards up."

"If they can find them." I clapped him on the shoulder. "I gotta get ready for the meet."

"You gonna be all right alone? You gotta know I don't like this, Marco."

"I'll be fine and I'm not planning on being alone, Sarge. Don't worry about me. Just take a close look at that video. Canny can help you with it."

Sarge walked away shaking his head, probably assuming I'd get my tail blown off. I signaled Luke and we moved into the hall to talk. He'd placed the memory cards into a clear plastic bag as the kidnappers had ordered and handed it to me.

"What's the plan, Marco? I know you have one." Luke said.

I told him that I figured the Dragettes and others would be more than willing to help rescue Anton and uncover Marsha's murderers. So, I asked Luke to call Hedda and explain what I needed. I wanted as many drag queens as possible to pack the festival site and mill around. Who would notice a few too many drag queens on Pride Day? Then, at the appropriate time they'd get a signal to flood the kidnapper's meeting point with drag queens. They'd create the diversion I'd need to get Anton out safely. It was a plan that could work. I hoped.

* * *

What with traffic detours and crowds jamming the streets, the cabbie couldn't get me too near to the site. He dropped me as close as he could and I continued on foot. The sheer number of people made it slow going. But the slow walk gave me time to scope out the area and the people. I had no doubt that one or more of the kidnappers would be on the ground watching for me.

Knowing Luke would get my plan rolling, all I had to do was keep my eyes peeled and get to the meeting point.

The sun, low in the sky, loomed over the buildings in the Village. The kidnappers probably thought they'd have an easy time getting away, using the crush of people to mask their escape. They had no idea what was coming their way, with Hedda leading the charge.

I never underestimate the intelligence of people like the kidnappers, if they're smart enough to get this far, they're smart enough to have figured most of the angles. Including the fact that lots of people would be taking pictures. They must have judged it a small risk and one worth taking.

But Anton and his camera were a complication they obviously hadn't considered. He was no ordinary tourist with a camera. He was there with a purpose, to make a special video for Marsha. It's something they'd never imagined. Anton had focused on Marsha and the Dragettes more than anything else on the parade route. So much so that he'd caught some of the kidnappers on video. Especially the one who'd threatened Anton. He had a real close-up moment. That mistake would be potentially dangerous for them. It figured they were desperate to get the video and cover their tracks. Their desperation was something I was counting on.

I kept moving, difficult as it was to maneuver through the mobs. Hundreds of people swirled through the Pride Festival, blocking any speedy movement as they stopped at booths to eat or pick through trinkets. Ribbons of smoke filled the air from barbeque stands, while other vendors hawked kabobs, and drinks, and more. I had to slip sideways, tread on toes, and generally shove my way through knots of people gathered at stands.

Reaching the meeting point with time to spare, I studied the crowd. Every face looked sinister. The sweet young things, the twinks, the drag queens, the bears, the leather daddies and their boys. Any one of them could be in on this, any one of them could be a lookout or the bag man.

Somewhere, hidden from sight, was a sniper who would take one of us out with a bullet if he had to. That much had been implied by the thug on the telephone.

It was as if I were seeing people for the first time. I'd been to scores of similar festivals, but I'd always trusted the faces I'd seen. I'd found comfort and solidarity in those faces. Pride gatherings felt like huge family reunions where you knew everyone was a friend and no one was out to get you.

Not this time.

I surveyed everything, memorized the landscape, readied myself for anything. But I felt I needed more. When I'd scoured the location for the fifth time, it was still early for the meet. I felt edgy and all my senses were on high alert.

Waiting calmly was not an option. Instead, I plunged into the crowd and searched faces, listened for voices, read expressions.

The smoky fragrance of charred meat offered by vendors made my stomach growl with an angry hunger. I ignored the pangs and moved on. Scouring the area for faces I'd seen on the video, I came to a booth filled with rainbow items. It was as good a place as any to stop and take my bearings before I turned around and made my way back to the meeting point.

I feigned interest in items on the table and as I returned a figurine to its place, someone bumped into my back. Hard. I tried turning around but whoever it was wouldn't let me.

Instead, I felt the barrel of a gun nudge my spine. Out of the corner of my eye I saw frilly day-glo orange material and the hint of a hairy arm. A sickly sweet fragrance wound its way into my nostrils.

"Hey…" I growled, but he jabbed me sharply with the gun.

"Shut up and make like nothing's wrong." The voice was familiar.

He dug the gun into my back. I tried elbowing his ribs, figuring he wouldn't really shoot in this crowd. He didn't budge. My elbow hit the muscled wall of his stomach and didn't faze him.

"What do you want?" I said without sounding ruffled.

"Turn around. Slow. And show how much you like me, doll."

I turned around as slowly as I could, realizing why the voice was familiar. I almost smiled when I saw Hedda standing there, one hand under the folds of her dress obviously holding the gun. She grinned, big red lips, large blue eyes with that awful green eyeshadow under thick arched eyebrows.

"So, it's you, babe. This morning you danced your way down Fifth Avenue, now you're somebody's gun moll. That role doesn't fit you, Hedda. Besides, you wouldn't shoot me in this crowd now, would you?"

"Don't be too sure, doll. I'd hate to ruin that face of yours or kill you or anything. But I gotta do what I gotta do. You understand, don't you sweet pea?" She sighed dramatically, never taking her eyes off me.

"Whaddaya want me to do?" This was surreal. Hedda had been in on this all along and I'd never guessed? She was a better actress than I'd given her credit for. But why? I tried guessing what her motive for hurting Marsha might be but nothing pretty came to mind. Jealousy? Money? Love? I had no idea what deep motives raged under the surface between Marsha and Hedda. There'd never been any indication they were rivals. There could have been something pitting them against one another. But Hedda a killer? That didn't compute.

"Now we go and see somebody about something. That clear enough for you, sugar plum?"

"Clear as mud, babe. Lead on. I'll follow."

Hedda started to turn, then caught herself and did a double take. "You think you're as smart as you are cute, don't you?"

"Uh, I hadda try, right?"

"Well I'm smarter than that, doll. You're the man, *you* take the lead. Now just get in front of Mama and I'll funnel directions to you while I watch that cute ass of yours. "

"Can't blame a guy for trying." I shrugged and marched ahead of her.

Before long, a couple of other drag queens, both with baby carriages which I'd seen on the Gay Parents float, fell in on either side of us.

"About time, girls. I thought I'd have to take this walk with him alone."

"That wouldn't be such a bad thing, would it?" said the one made up like Marilyn Monroe in Andy Warhol colors, as she looked me up and down.

"Control yourself. We've got a job to do." Hedda was no nonsense, despite her clownish appearance. She walked close behind me and said, "Okay, turn right and at the next corner left."

After several more blocks and a few more turns, we were in a district I didn't recognize. Rotting warehouse walls, abandoned factories that were home to rats, mice, fleas and who knows what else. The odor floating in the air was unpleasant. One of the "girls" walking a baby carriage, screamed when a fat, fearless rat scampered across her feet. The carriage the drag queen had been holding, went flying off ahead of us as she continued to scream.

"How come you didn't blindfold me, Hedda? I mean, don't you think I'm going to report this?"

"I don't think so. I don't think you'll be able to do that, doll." She stuck the gun into my back for emphasis. "Pity. What a waste. I'm sorry." She sounded truly upset but I knew Hedda was a tough cookie.

"Ok, Hedda. But promise me one thing. Before you… you know."

"What's that, gorgeous?"

"Don't do anything kinky with me after you kill me. I'd like to think you'll treat my body with respect."

"Eww, yuk. Gaaa. You're disgusting, Fontana. I thought you were as wholesome as you look, but you're disgusting. Ewww. With a dead body? Nobody's *that* cute." Her big red lips twisted into tortured poses. Gagging sounds filled the air, her tongue darted in and out, and her eyes pressed shut against the mental images of necrophiliac activities. I almost laughed but remembered the gun under all that drama.

I tried moving off course but one of the others pushed me back in place. "Stay put or you'll learn about what we'll do with your body before it becomes just a body." This drag queen was the toughest of all of them and the prettiest. Delicate features and neatly applied make-up gave this one an innocent, sweet appearance. The soft pink dress and smooth moves spoke of elegance, but his gruff voice rumbled and his mean eyes glared with an anger that chilled me.

After a while, and after passing a lot more abandoned buildings, Hedda stopped and yanked me back.

"This is it." She nudged my back with the gun barrel.

"This?" I looked at what was probably the most decrepit of the buildings we'd seen. The door was rotting off its hinges. A brick fell out of the wall while we stared, as if the building wanted us to see just how bad things were.

It seemed more like a tomb than a building. No movement, no sound, no rats scurrying. It's bad when even the vermin abandon a place.

"Get in," Hedda pushed at the rotting door and it fell off its hinges at her touch. A cloud of foul-smelling dust and grime shot up as the door hit the ground.

I looked back at her and balked.

"Get in, doll, or I'll make you dance your way in." She pulled the gun and pointed it at my feet while cocking it at the same time.

I stepped carefully into the entryway. If the door was this rotted, could the floor be safe? Amazingly it held my weight.

"Don't worry, dollface. We wouldn't want you to fall through the floor and get eaten by whatever lives in the basement. You'll be safe enough. Just get in there."

"You're not coming?" I asked and winked.

"Right behind you, sweet cheeks. Now move!"

As I moved farther into the building, the faint outside light was swallowed by the dark. Then I heard faint voices and saw a weak glimmer of light in the distance. This once mammoth warehouse was now a rotting corpse of a building filled with scaffolding and metal stairs to nowhere. It felt dank and ominous.

I stumbled as I walked. It was too dark to see ahead without losing my footing. I slowed down and began to inch forward, Hedda still behind me. I assumed the other two were behind her. There was no escaping this.

The small voices became more distinct as we moved, and a floating dot of light appeared in the distant darkness.

"We're here!" Hedda shouted, her voice booming through the vast emptiness. She continued to encourage me forward with the barrel of the gun, and I kept moving. Up ahead, a figure walked toward us. He was backlit and just a silhouette.

When he got close I saw a face which I thought I knew but couldn't make out in the dimness. He took his place by my side and walked along with us. When we got closer to the light, I saw him clearly. He was one of the guys on the video. One of Marsha's killers.

"You're one of them," I said.

"Yeah, so, what's got your underwear in a knot? I'm one of them and if anybody doesn't like it they can take a flying—"

"Be a good girl and walk the man to the office." Hedda interrupted him. "Besides, I don't think he meant it the way you took it, Clarice. You're too defensive to be a good drag, honey. Loosen up."

"Yeah, well, everybody's always raggin' on me about this. I wanna dress the way I want. So what if I don't look so good? I feel good."

I felt as if I'd been dropped into an insane asylum. I looked from face to face trying to guess what they had in mind, but it was no use.

"It's not all about you tonight, Clarice. Take Fontana in and shut the door. He wants to be alone with this delicious hunk."

"Do I get the courtesy of a heads up? I mean, who's in there?"

"You'll see soon enough," the new guy said.

"Take a deep breath and head on in, doll."

The killer opened the door, shoved me in, and slammed it shut. The light was bright and after all the darkness it took me a minute to focus. I peered at the guy sitting at the desk across from me. Dressed in a dark suit, with a red tie, and a matching pocket handkerchief, he stared at me but I was still partly blinded by the light. He looked familiar and not familiar at the same time. There was something disconcerting about him. Then he stood up and walked with heightened dignity around to the front of the desk. Even in that suit, it was a walk I recognized. Then I knew.

"Marsha. Or, should I say, Ray? Ray Stone." Stone was Marsha's actual identity. He'd grown up in New Hope and then Philly and eventually became everyone's favorite drag queen, Marsha. His ideas grew bigger than the city he lived in, so he moved to New York to pursue the dream. Now it looked like he was just Ray Stone again.

"Surprise," he said flatly and without enthusiasm. He glanced at his long nails which were painted a glistening white, then flicked some lint off his jacket. "You were probably expecting some macho thug who wanted to tear your balls off and serve them for a snack to his boys before he even introduced himself. Or, maybe you were expecting Anton to be sitting here bleeding and vulnerable, so you could save him and be the hero."

"I wasn't expecting *you*. You're dead." I was halfway glad and halfway mad.

"Funny thing about death, Fontana. It isn't necessarily the end, is it? I didn't want to be dead so that's why I hadda die. Gabish?"

"Not much at all," I said. "You're dead, but you're not. What about Anton? Is he all—"

"The boy is fine. I'd never hurt him, never. He's too special to me. I love that boy." Ray sighed deeply. "He's changed a lot since I left Philly. Bigger, more muscles, more confidence. He knocked two of my biggest guys off their feet. I hadn't realized just how hunky he'd become since I last saw him. That boy's a terror. Hot but dangerous, if you get on his wrong side." Ray smiled in spite of himself. I think he was proud of Anton. "Once they got him tied down, literally, I mean, he couldn't do much but cooperate."

"He didn't see you? Talk to you? Didn't he wonder what this was all about?" I asked.

"He doesn't know about me and he never will. You're the only one outside my very small circle that knows. Even Barkley can't know." Ray stared at me, there was still lots of Marsha in his movements and his voice.

"Why? Why'd you have to tell *me*? Why not just trade for the video and let it go at that?"

"Because I know you. You'd never let up until you found out everything and then a lot of people might get hurt. That's the way you're built. I know that. I've seen you in action. So knew I needed to bring you in on this, Marco. I need you on my side."

"Your side? You expect me to keep quiet about this?"

"In a word: Yes."

"Why? You're perpetrating a fraud. You're hurting people."

"No. Actually I'm not hurting anyone. I'm keeping people from getting hurt. Mainly me. Wouldn't you commit fraud if it meant you'd be saving your own life?"

"I—"

"Don't give me any high-flying speeches. I don't need to know what you think is morally right. I need you to understand." He gripped my shoulder. Ray was lots stronger than he appeared. "I need you to understand and to help me." He couldn't keep the sob at bay any longer. His voice choked. A tear tumbled over his chubby cheek and splattered onto the filthy floor. "You'll be saving my life."

"Tell me how." I wasn't sure I wanted any part of this, but he seemed genuinely panicked.

"It's a long story. But the short of it is that the mob, several mobs in fact, there are so many these days, are out to kill me. All because of *Marsha's*. Stupid club." He sighed and it was a shuddering sound. "Stupid, stupid, *stupid* club. Why I ever wanted that, I'll never know." He drew in a breath and pounded his generously large fist on the old desk. The wood cracked. "Why did I let anyone talk me into it? Why? It was nothing but trouble from the start. Then *they* got involved. Those lovely Italian friends of mine. They came in full of ideas, wanting this and that for the club, urging me to do things their way because they knew better. They lavished money on me and the club, but there was a price. There's always a price. And if that wasn't enough, their Russian cousins wanted a cut. And there were others. Soon there weren't any cuts left. Not even for me."

"You could've decided to close the club. Shut it down and walk away."

"I could? You think so?" He slapped a hand on the crumbling desk. "No, I couldn't. Do you have any idea what it was like? I was walking on clouds by that time. And it wasn't just the club. You can't possibly imagine what it meant to me."

"You're right. I can't imagine."

"What was I before the club? An aging drag queen who'd had a few lucky breaks. Got on somebody's list, made a few cameo appearances here and there. And that's all. I'd never been anything else in my life. Never went to college. Never had a job anyone respected. Never did anything I was really proud of."

He paused again. Wiped the sweat from his forehead and heaved a sigh. He looked exhausted and frightened.

"When this club idea came along, I was hooked. Like the big fish I am, I sucked down hook, line, and sinker. It was too much of a draw for me."

"For anyone, I guess."

"But especially for me. The little queer everyone only ever laughed at. From when I was a kid in school and had my face pushed in the dirt more times than I can count. I ate that dirt and cried myself to sleep. But the club. The club. That piece of real estate was gonna make a difference. When the idea came up and people signed on, I knew things had changed for this silly little queen. From that point on, I'd have everything I ever wanted." His eyes shone with the memory.

I watched as he stood there lost in his thoughts, reliving what must have been the most exciting moment in his life.

"The club would be mine. Named after *me. Marsha's.* My name in huge lights over the door. My name on friggin' everything from napkins to swizzle sticks. I was a blind fool. It was all about me, and I wasn't going to let anything stand in my way," he said, his voice thick with emotion. "I never saw, no, scratch that, I never *wanted* to see what was really going on with those guys. Funny, little, no-class guys. Dressed like every day was Bad Taste Day. I wouldn't even let myself *think* the word 'mob.' I let them have what they wanted and allowed them to give me the money I needed until I was in debt up to my tits."

"That's the way they work."

"All those good feelings I'd had didn't last long. It took a while, but one thing after another eventually forced me to see those guys for what they were, and it frightened me. Really shook me up. I knew I was in deep shit. I knew then that I'd be a slave to those people for the rest of my life. My club would become my prison. *Marsha's* would be where I'd end my days and I didn't really want that. It would've been a kick for a while. I would've squeezed it for everything it was worth. But that's all I wanted, really. With those guys… well, let's just say I could never repay them. The debts just grew larger. There was no way they'd ever decrease."

He sat down, leaned his elbows on the rickety desk and placed one hand against his forehead.

"That's how they worm their way in, you know. That's how they get their glittery leash around your neck. And there's no way to remove it. Well, I didn't want that. I *don't* want it. I can't pay them back, and I refuse to be a slave. Now, they want to kill me. They know I want out. They've said they'll kill me if I don't change my mind and get back to the club."

"They didn't leave you with much of a choice, did they?" I felt sorry for Ray. He'd had stars in his eyes for so long about that club. It meant everything to him and now it had cost him nearly everything.

"It was slavery or death. I chose death. My kind of death." Ray Stone, stood and came around to the front of the desk. He looked more like Marsha again, standing erect, his regal bearing intact, his dignity restored. "I can't expect you to help me for any reason other than that you're a decent guy and you don't like what those thugs will do to me."

I said nothing. I stared at Ray.

"I know," he said. "You're thinking I should have been smarter. I should have known better. Should have kept my eyes open and should've seen them coming. But I didn't. I let them take the club. Piece by piece while I watched. But I'll be damned if I'll let them take my life."

* * *

Anton, unconsciously striking a very sexy pose, lay on his bed back at the hotel as he recuperated from his "hunk in distress" ordeal. I'd booked the suite for one more night. No one was up to struggling with Amtrak and training it back to Philly that night. Anton was exhausted but unharmed from his kidnapping and imprisonment. His captors didn't fare as well. He'd given one of them a really juicy black eye and another had a broken jaw. No one was permanently damaged. Everyone was unhappy about what had to be and all of them played their parts reluctantly but out of loyalty to Marsha. Even Hedda called me to apologize for her part in the whole thing.

I told Anton only that we did what we needed to do to get him back unharmed. He was grateful and still struggling with grief for Marsha, so that he didn't ask further questions. Anton's smart, though, and sooner or later, he'll start adding up discrepancies which will lead to questions for me. Anton was no fool. Until that happened, I'd do what I could to keep my promise to Ray. If Anton eventually guessed on his own, I wasn't sure how I'd handle it.

After a while, after he'd reconciled himself to the idea that Marsha was gone, Anton began to tell and retell the story of how he'd come close to unmasking Marsha's killers. Every time he told the tale of his capture, there were several additional muscled thugs and masculine drag queens the size of King Kong, who he'd taken down before they managed to tie him up. But each retelling held a sad undercurrent, his grief for Marsha still coloring everything he remembered.

Later that night, when Anton had recovered enough, and when things had been settled, more or less, I took Luke and Anton and Canny to dinner. We celebrated Anton's safe return and toasted Marsha's memory.

The next morning, as we taxied to the train, Anton asked about the memory cards and his video. I'd anticipated this and had a story, no matter how unlikely, prepared. Much as I hated lying, I reminded myself of my promise to Ray. So, I told Anton that we'd been instructed to trade the cards for his release. Though we'd prepared phony cards for the swap, we'd accidentally given the real cards and they were now gone. As for the copies on Canny's hard drives, they'd all mysteriously been erased, thanks to an arrangement I'd made with Luke before anyone knew what was happening.

Canny remained silent never mentioning anything. He was a lot smarter than people gave him credit for being. He knew something was going on, but he also knew enough not to ask any questions.

Sarge, the only other person to have seen the video, couldn't remember clearly what he'd seen and hadn't been able to ID any of the people on the video anyway. Whatever he thought he'd seen, and even he was foggy about that, would never have held up in court, even if that were a possibility. Which is wasn't.

Marsha's death was officially ruled an accident.

When we got back to Philadelphia, I told Luke everything. He'd never asked, he never would, that's the way he is. Discreet to a fault. But since I'd drawn him into the conspiracy by asking him to erase the hard drives, I felt obligated to tell him. Besides, I could see he knew there was more to the story than what had been made public.

Over a good bottle of Merlot at Luke's condo, we talked.

"If any of it gets out, and if they find her, Marsha's dead. Knowing these people, they'd find her," I said

"You don't have to convince me, Marco. It's sad, though. Marsha had everything and now, he's just plain Ray Stone again. Where's he going? I guess he wouldn't trust you with that information."

"I can't blame him. His life depends on that secret. I hope he'll be happy." I sipped the velvety wine, silently toasting Ray.

"There's one thing I don't understand," Luke stared off into the distance. "That whole charade with the guys on the street. Why'd he engineer that? Why not just set up the accident and let it go at that?"

"I asked Ray about that. He said that he was being watched day and night. The mobsters knew he wanted out and they weren't about to let that happen. So, dressed as Marsha, she staged the whole thing hoping the Italians would think the Russians had killed her and the Russians would think the Italians had her whacked. Or both of them might think it was one of the other crime groups who'd done it. Since they were tailing her to make sure she didn't run out on them, she decided to give them a good show. Marsha's final performance."

"Pretty smart. We can only hope she gets away with it. She will, won't she?"

"I'm guessing yes." Actually, I was really hoping Ray Stone could find a new life that'd make him happy. It wouldn't be easy.

I did my part because the only injured parties would be the mob bosses who'd lose some big bucks on Marsha's restaurant when it closed without its star attraction. I got all teary eyed over their financial losses.

Marsha was a friend and a friend deserves a chance, especially when the alternative is so bad.

I never did get the full story about who exactly it was under that truck, but one thing I know is that it pays to know people who work in hospital morgues. Marsha knew just about everyone. The body was mangled enough to make identification impossible without expensive DNA testing. No one was interested enough to go that route. There was no family that would press the case and Marsha's legal representatives knew enough to let the dead stay dead.

I figured we could do the same.

A Killing in Leather

If I could keep the contestants from killing one another before the show even began, we might just get through the night. But the tension backstage threatened to pull the whole thing down around us.

The audience already started filling up the place. Plenty of them had arrived early. I heard them before I took a look at them through the curtain. The rumble of voices and laughter crashing over the stage told me the crowd was wired. They'd expect their money's worth and then some. Based on previous Mr. Philly Gay Leather contests I'd seen, the audience would be more than happy with this year's show. If it ever got off the ground.

Backstage at Bubbles was familiar territory. It's where my male stripper troupe, StripGuyz, is based and holds shows every night. But sponsoring this contest with all the new people and rules, my turf became strange, even weird. The knottiest problem had been building for days and had me playing defense against leather-clad, muscle-bound gay contestants, all of them upset that two straight boys would be competing for the gay leather title.

Ben Tadeo, a green-eyed beauty and a leading contender for the title, having placed second the year before, approached me. He placed one large, hairy, muscular arm around my shoulder and squeezed me to him, making sure my attention was fully on him.

I refused to be intimidated and wrestled myself free. Turning to stand face to face with him, I silently berated myself for agreeing to manage the competition. I'd put myself directly on the front line for complaints and complications.

"What?" I growled.

"You can't let a straight boy win the Mr. Philly Gay Leather title. No way, Marco," Ben's clear, green eyes were riveted on me. He clenched and unclenched his hand threateningly. Ben was the kind of guy who never let good sense get in the way of his feelings. He was also, deep down, a really sweet man and a good human being. I'd known him for quite some time and I knew that though he was excitable, he wasn't at all dangerous.

"Ben" I said his name softly, as placed an arm around his shoulders. "Ben, listen to me…"

"No, *you* listen." He shook off my arm, folded his arms over his chest, and glared. Like a boulder in the middle of the road, he refused to budge.

Agreeing to manage the Mr. Philly Gay Leather competition was one of my dumber decisions. The Philadelphia Leather Coalition members said they wanted someone neutral, someone unbiased, someone who had taste and discrimination. And, they'd claimed, that I was the only one who fit the bill. I knew they were full of shit but I was intrigued by the idea of managing what amounted to a male beauty contest. Who wouldn't want to manage a male beauty contest? I like a challenge.

Anton had warned me the competition wouldn't be any fun. He'd tried to convince me that, at best, this gig would be nothing but a migraine. And most likely it'd be worse. I trusted Anton's opinion, and as my right hand man with StripGuyz, I trusted his judgment.

Of course, I didn't take Anton's advice. How bad could it be? I'd asked him.

I soon found out, and it was beyond rotten. Nothing had gone smoothly. From pulling acts together for entertainment between rounds of competition, to signing up contestants, to working out logistics, I'd had to contend with one diva after another. Contestants, staff, some judges, and even the sponsors sniped, whined, and complained every day for weeks. Even my own StripGuyz dancers complained because they weren't able to perform, since Stan, the owner of Bubbles, had "generously" given over the entire night to the Leather contest. Meaning my guys wouldn't make a cent.

The whole Circus from Hell was the worst heartburn I'd ever experienced, and having to remain neutral put me on everybody's shit list simultaneously.

Ben's complaint was the latest speed bump. Looking at him standing there, I knew this was a useless battle.

"Ben, you're better than this. Let's just agree to—"

"Don't try and sweet talk me, Marco. You can't let a straight guy win."

"I'm not letting anyone win, Ben," I snapped out the words. "I couldn't, even if I wanted to."

"Doesn't look that way to me, Marco. You're in charge, you can keep this from happening. Kick them outta the contest." Ben balled up his fists and glared. His hairy chest, bulging biceps, and leather vest gave his words a certain weight, but I refused to be intimidated.

"He's right, Marco," Liam walked over and chimed in, his silky voice carrying a gentle anger. "This is a gay contest in a gay bar in the gay neighborhood. Gay, Gay, Gay. You know what that is, don't you?" Liam's baby-smooth chest was crisscrossed by a studded leather harness which emphasized his well-worked pecs and which had a leather strap traveling from chest to crotch, where it disappeared behind the band of his posing strap. He raked one hand through his wavy brown hair and his bicep flexed nearly popping the leather band circling it.

As pleasant as staring at Liam should have been, all I could think was that I could be back in my office making some honest money investigating creeps. Being a P.I. isn't always glamorous but at least I have a little more control over what goes on. The Mr. Leather hornet's nest was nearly control proof. Not even the nice stipend they paid me was able to cut the pain much.

"I can't tell people they aren't allowed to enter this contest. Nothing in the rules says you have to be gay. If a straight guy wants to compete for a gay leather title, he's allowed to try." I frowned, then said, "Just so you know, I don't like it either."

Ben continued facing me, though his breathing slowed as he calmed down. "It's not the title those guys want, Marco. It's the cash prize, the car, and the all expenses paid trip to Orlando for the nationals." He stared intently at me, hoping, I supposed, that I'd take his point and run with it.

"Yeah," Liam chimed in. "There are some of us who aren't gonna let them have what's ours. Even if they do win, which they'd better not." He tried looking as tough and menacing as Ben, but pretty-boy Liam couldn't pull it off no matter how many muscles he developed.

I winced when Liam tossed out the threat, though. He might not be a menace, but throwing around threats in public wasn't smart. I had to think that if all the gay contestants were this angry, I'd have my hands full if the judges actually gave the title to a straight guy.

"There's not much I can do. I didn't make up the rules. I didn't recruit contestants. I can't make the judges do me any favors, and neither can you." I glared at them each in turn.

They grumbled in unison.

"Use your heads, guys. Think about this for a minute," I continued. "The rules say you have to have done some work promoting the leather community, and the ultimate winner will have to commit to doing even more work promoting gay leather causes throughout the Philly area. You can hold any winner responsible for keeping to his side of the bargain. If they don't live up to this, they forfeit the title and the prizes."

"You better believe I'll hold them to it," Ben growled. "But, first I'm gonna make sure they don't win."

"If you mean you're gonna beat them fair and square, the old fashioned way. With muscles, good looks, and fabulous routines. I'm all for it. If you mean anything else, I'm not about to let that happen."

"I'll do what I have to," Ben said. "You do what you gotta do."

Liam grunted his agreement.

I decided on another tack. "Look at you both. Getting all excited like this makes you puffy and tired-looking. Liam, your eyes have bags and Ben's face is drawn. Why not go back to the dressing room and make sure one of you wins this thing?"

Liam lifted a hand to his face and gently massaged his skin. Ben didn't move.

"And while you're prepping, keep in mind that there are only two straight contestants and eight gay ones. Odds are in our favor."

"Don't bet on it. I've seen the judges. Some of them are crazy about straight boys. Every time Wade or Michael walks through, they get all wobbly in the knees. Wade and Michael are straight. It's disgusting the way they fawn over them. Why can't queens get it right? Straight guys don't want what we've got," Liam said, then placed a hand at his waist just above his bubble butt, which was essentially bare, considering the thin posing strap he wore.

"Anyway, when this contest is over, you should both consider joining StripGuyz. You'd draw crowds and make more money than the prizes they're giving away tonight."

Liam shrugged and walked fluidly toward the dressing room.

"Who knows?" Ben gave me a look I couldn't interpret. "Let's see how this all turns out, then I *might* give you a call."

"Right." I picked up my clipboard and turned away. *He* might *give me a call,* I thought. *Like he'd be doing* me *a favor.*

I inspected the staging area and saw that the staff from Bubbles had outdone themselves. They knew this contest could be a moneymaker for Stan and the bar, so they didn't hold back. The stage, where my dancers normally work every night, was swathed in lots more lights than usual, including additional baby spotlights and a new set of black lights arcing across the whole area. A glittery upstage curtain of silver lamé shimmered in the glow of the spotlights. Black, blue, and red balloons, the leather colors, floated everywhere.

The rest of the bar, a two-floor affair, with an atrium-like area surrounding the stage, was equally decked out. Twinkle lights strung across the ceiling formed the rainbow flag and glowed gently down on everything. Signs advertising a drink called "The Sling," created especially for the occasion were placed on every available surface. I promised myself I'd try the drink once the winner was announced and I could relax. Until then I had to stay unbuzzed.

Two hours before showtime, both the leather crowd and assorted others crammed into Bubbles wanting good positioning to see the competition. The fact that the crowd was early and eager wasn't lost on me. After the competition was safely behind me, I planned to get some of my dancers to add a leather routine. Maybe we'd even have a leather night once a month.

After a last minute inspection, I headed backstage to wait for the judges to arrive. While I waited, I reviewed the judging criteria and rules, knowing I'd need to prep the judges again on scoring. I took up a spot which allowed me to watch for them and keep an eye on backstage activity at the same time.

A few of the contestants were also there, doing one last examination of the equipment they'd use for the talent segment. I watched Wade take a long, hands-on look at the tangle of ropes and chains he'd be using for his set. He checked and rechecked every piece of the rigging, which included some sort of sling in the midst of it all. I couldn't help but wonder just what talent he'd be exhibiting with all that stuff.

Wade was an incredibly attractive blond, with an enviable jawline. Though he was well built, he didn't have the hard, stringy musculature some bodybuilders strive for. Wade's was a softer, more approachable look. He appeared to have just stepped off a movie poster, and I almost felt the need to touch him to see if he was real or just a figment of my imagination.

I felt a nudge and turned to see Jamie, the barback assigned to assist me through the hours of programming. He gave me a look that said I'd been off on some other planet and should think about returning to earth. Jamie was a favorite of mine who was shy and slightly built. His glasses gave him a bookish air.

"Wade is something, isn't he?" I said.

"If you say so, boss. You realize that he's one of the two straight guys that you let into the competition," Jamie said, an accusatory tone in his voice.

That *I* let in. That's what everyone would think for a long time. Especially if one of them was chosen. I didn't make up the entrance requirements, but everyone blamed me for the straight contestants.

"Looks like he'll be fierce competition." I watched Wade arrange the ropes and chains just so, stopping now and again to redo what he'd just done.

"Looks like he can use some help," I said to Jamie.

"Don't you believe it. He knows just what he's doing, and he doesn't want help. Won't let anybody near the rigging. I asked if I could help last night and he said he didn't want anyone touching anything, because he was setting it just the way he needed it."

"Don't feel too—" I started to say, but Jamie was already off and running to tell the florist where to arrange the potted plants that had just arrived.

"What's the deal, chief?" Rosa Hidalgo, a small, perky brunette, stood in front of me. I was so preoccupied with Wade and his contraption that I hadn't even noticed her.

"Rosa!" I smiled. "When did you get back?"

"This morning. And St. Croix is wonderful. You owe yourself a vacation, Marco." She looked around approvingly. "I see you've got things under control, so what's the deal? What do we judges do?" Rosa, head of the GLBT Anti-Defamation League, had been chosen lead judge.

"I've got papers for all of you," I shuffled through the sheets on my clipboard.

"Any idea how long this is gonna take?" she asked.

"There's quite a few events. The Beefcake Parade, the Leather attire competition, then brief interviews with each contestant about their platforms, and their five-minute speeches about issues they'll handle if they win."

"I like the idea of the Beefcake Parade. About time you boys had a taste of that kind of crap." Rosa laughed. "So, after the speeches, it's over and we score them?"

"Not a chance."

Rosa groaned.

"The last segment is the talent exhibition. Then you guys get to vote. After you choose the new Mr. Leather and he takes his victory walk, then it's over." It sounded like a long night, but if I could keep it moving I might get home before dawn.

"Hey!" The deep voice belonged to Bri, another contestant, who also occasionally worked for me both in the P.I. business and as a dancer in StripGuyz.

"What's up, Bri?"

He said nothing but looked at me as if I'd know what he wanted. I'd seen the expression on his face before, and I knew he was barely containing an outburst. Tall, Bri had a shaved head and a face dominated by a nose which had been broken more than once. He also had a number of strategically placed tattoos, which only added to the fierceness of his appearance.

"We'll be starting in a second, whaddayou need, Bri?"

"Okay, boss man." His hostility ricocheted off the walls. "What I need is for you to tell me again about the straight guys you let into the competition. What right have they got bein' here? Why'd you let that happen?"

"Hold on, Bri..."

"No *you* hold on! Some of us were talkin' and this sucks big time."

"There are straight guys competing?" Rosa had a look on her face halfway between a laugh and a frown. "Since when?"

"Since Marco over here let 'em in." Bri turned back to me. "Couldn't you tell 'em this was gays only? Did you have to let 'em sign up?" Bri fumed. "If one of them wins, you're gonna hear from me, Marco. And you're not gonna like what you hear."

"How many straight men would even think about competing for a gay leather title?" Rosa laughed.

"We can't keep 'em them out of the contest. Not according to the rules. Right, Rosa?" I looked at her hoping she'd toss me some help.

"I'm sure there's a way to do anything. If you want to." Rosa smiled and left me to twist in the wind.

"The competition rules were made up by the Philadelphia Knights and The National Leather League. And the rules don't say a contestant must be gay to enter or to win. I guess they never imagined anybody straight would ever enter the contest. It's always been a gay event, always held in some gay venue. What straight guy would want to compete?"

"You have a point, Marco," Rosa said.

"And don't forget, whoever wins will be in the news as Mr. *GAY* Leather. How many straight men could handle that tag?" I said, looking into Bri's angry eyes.

"Well here are two of them," Bri spat out the words as Wade and Michael walked up to us.

"You guys got a problem with something?" Michael glared, assuming a defensive posture. "You don't like us being here? Big fuckin' shame. I'll bet you'd be the first to scream if *we* kept *you* out of something, wouldn't you? Gotta be the only victims in town, right?"

"And, we've—" Rosa began to rev her engines.

"Uh, Rosa," I said placing a hand gently on her shoulder and bending my head low to speak to her. "I don't think it's a good idea for you to be here. You being a judge."

"She's one of the judges?" Wade was wide eyed. "I've seen you on TV."

"She's just leaving," I said, directing Rosa with my hand to her back. "Right, Rosa?"

She understood without another word and walked away, not looking back.

"Guys! It's almost showtime," I said. "Don't you need to be getting into something or out of something? Competition's starting, ready or not." I pointedly looked at the three of them in turn.

"This better be a fair deal, man." Michael moved toward me, chin thrust out, dark eyes raging. "Me and Wade got as much right to be here as anybody else."

"If you win, big boy, you gonna tell your girlfriends that you're Mr. *Gay* Leather?" Bri asked. "Because if one'a you should win…" He paused and looked down on Wade and Michael like a menacing hawk. "I believe in fairness as much as the next guy, but it will definitely suck if one of you hets wins. But if you do, I'm gonna make damned sure everybody knows you're Mr. *Gay* Leather. Every chance I get. I'll be right on your back. Understand?"

Bri silently dared Wade and Michael to argue with him. A few tense moments passed filled with fuming, posturing, and a definite testosterone overflow.

"Yeah… well—well, y-you can't do… we'll see about that," Michael stammered, backing down.

"What does he mean, 'every chance he gets'?" Wade murmured, looking at me, his baby blues registering confusion and worry.

"He's just blowing off steam," I snapped. "Don't let it bother you."

They continued glaring at one another.

"Get yourselves ready. We've got people who paid to see this show. Curtain's up in fifteen. You don't show, you're out." I had just enough time to review things with the judges.

* * *

More than two hours later, after watching the audience ogle the contestants in the beefcake parade, after sweating our way through long interviews in which the candidates answered questions both from a panel and from the audience, the leather fashion portion of the competition took place. Even I had to admit the fashion show was the best thing about the evening. Each contestant modeled outfits for differing occasions and purposes. From eveningwear leather, to fetish attire, to personal favorites, each guy outdid the other. One contestant emerged dressed like a gladiator. Shaven head and oiled chest, he wore shingled leather epaulettes and a matching gladiator kilt which covered exactly nothing. But I think it was the flog and the way he wielded it which caused one of my stage hands to faint dead away.

Between each segment, I'd hired acts to entertain the audience as they waited for the next part of the competition. A contortionist who did things with his body that made me wince was the hardest act for me to watch. It was the almost naked magician who brought the audience to its feet and who even fooled me with one or two of his illusions. How he got the Great Dane to appear out of thin air is something I still wonder about.

After the magician's final curtain call, it was time for the last event, the talent exhibition. I was looking forward to this not just because it meant I'd get to go home, but because I was intrigued by what some of the guys had planned. Before the show they'd drawn lots, and Ben was up first.

I hoped his performance might give me an idea of whether or not he had stage presence and would fit into my StripGuyz troupe. I got my answer as soon as he entered.

The audience went silent when Ben took the stage. Dressed in a short leather loincloth and nothing else, he stepped onto the large gymnastic mat and paused. A soft yellow spot was trained on him, bringing every detail into focus. His broad, hairy chest heaving as he quietly prepared himself, Ben looked out over the audience. He then placed one bare foot out before the other and began moving through a graceful acrobatic performance which not only showed off his glistening oiled body but also his suppleness and dexterity as a dancer and gymnast. I followed his every balanced move, watched his muscles ripple as he turned and stretched, rolled, bounced and did summersaults. Moving quickly, he performed handsprings, which left no questions about what the loincloth covered, and ended with a dive roll that left the audience breathless. As he bowed and panted, the audience cheered its approval and tossed fives and tens onto the stage.

Liam was up next, and he'd obviously worked with the lighting tech to show himself to the best advantage. Though I don't think the kid had a bad angle. Wearing the same studded leather harness, he'd changed from the posing strap into a black fishnet thong, which, I was sure, accounted for the gasps I heard.

A sultry piece of music filled the air, and Liam at first moved languorously to its sounds. For his routine, he'd chosen an erotically charged dance which included using dumbbells, a barbell pole, paralettes, a pull-up stand and more, allowing him to show his strength and agility. As he moved, his hands caressed his body sometimes teasing with the threat of pulling off the thong as he moved. Every move displayed another set of muscles, and every move tempted the audience with erotic possibilities. His performance held the promise of nudity, but only a promise, as he writhed. A sheen of sweat glistened on his skin and helped emphasize muscle and sinew. His gyrating hips offered a hint of something more.

The studs in his leather harness reflected the colors of the spotlights and made him appear to be dancing at the center of a nebula of light. The audience, teased into submission by Liam's eroticism, tossed tens and twenties onto the stage as he ended with a handstand, then flipped back onto his feet. I applauded along with everyone else as Liam exited the stage.

As one performance followed another, I almost felt sorry for the judges. They had a near impossible task, choosing a winner from contestants who seemed equally suited for the title. Despite all the bickering and petty squabbles, each contestant had an exceptional personality. Each knew how to hold an audience captive.

With three more to go, I noticed that the straight competitors would be performing back to back. Someone had spread the word that there were straight contestants, and several of my staff reported a lot of grumbling about that in the audience. Just the reason I'd planted my staff throughout the bar to stop trouble before it had a chance to get started. All we needed was one crank throwing a bottle and everything would be chaos.

Michael, the first of the straight contestants, strutted out onto the stage, looking comfortable and ready. Unruffled, he took his place at center stage. Tall, broad-chested, and showing only the slightest bit of tension, he gracefully stepped out of his running suit to reveal his muscled frame. Clad only in black leather armbands and a black leather jockstrap, he did a slow turn to display himself to the patrons. Then he stood still for a moment and I wasn't sure if he was expecting applause or if he'd just frozen. Eventually he did a slow about-face and approached the gym equipment laid out for his routine.

He began with a free weight exhibition, stopping now and then to allow a stagehand to add weights to the bar. He lifted an ever increasing amount of weight. With each new level, he strained a bit more, huffed and puffed, but eventually got it into the air above his head. Huge muscles bulging and popping with every effort.

He eventually had the stagehand add an incredible number of plates to the bar. It appeared to be an immovable piece of equipment.

One of my staffers sidled up to me and gripped my arm. "He's gonna crush himself with that," the staffer said. "Shouldn't we stop him?"

"And let him accuse us of scuttling his act? Besides, I'm sure Michael's done this before. He's not here to make a fool of himself." I hoped I was right as I stared at what looked like a dangerous pile of weight.

Michael stooped over the impossibly large barbell, patted the plates, and ran his hands over the barbell as if to show his mastery over all that metal. His expression was serious, even grim, as he gripped the bar and drew in a breath. Then, straining for all he was worth, he lifted the massive weights. Gasps and cheers from the audience and even a few backstage staffers accompanied his movements as he hoisted the barbell over his head, powerful legs straining to hold him steady, veins popping, muscles stretching. He held the pose for a moment then, with a grunting rush of breath, dropped the weights which hit the stage noisily. And probably made a nice set of dents for Stan to moan about. Michael, still puffing and red-faced from the effort, stood enjoying the applause. But, only for a moment. Still breathing heavily, he did a small set on the balance bars, displaying surprising strength and agility.

His grim expression gave way to a smile as he moved. Then he hopped off the bars, grinned at the audience, swung his arms wide to accept their cheers, and ended his exhibition. He acknowledged the applause once more with a bow, then swept off the stage.

Wade was next and I expected a similar display of strength and masculine prowess. But, when Wade stepped through the glittering curtain and out onto the stage, there was a collective gasp. A single baby blue spot was trained on his oiled, upper body leaving the rest of his totally naked form in tempting shadow. Blond curls framed his serious face as he stood, eyes closed in contemplation.

Stan, the owner of Bubbles, rushed to my side and made a strangled sound of alarm. "Nudity!" He whispered. "The Liquor Control Board will have my ass if they've got a spy here tonight."

"Shhhh! The lighting's keeping things hidden," I said. I assured him it was unlikely there'd be an agent in the house. But he remained wide-eyed and bit his fingers waiting to see what Wade might do next.

There were no contest rules against nudity since the competition was not usually held in bars. In any event, whatever nudity there was would be only a fleeting part of a one-time performance and not a regularly scheduled act. I ignored Stan's nervous gibbering and turned my attention to the stage.

I had to give the lighting tech a lot of credit. He lit Wade's Body so everyone watching knew he was nude without actually seeing anything clearly. The tech skillfully hid parts of Wade's anatomy in deep shadow. Wade had undoubtedly worked closely with the lighting techs. It was no wonder he never wanted anyone around during rehearsals.

Wade stood gracefully still, with the blue light lending him an ethereal aura. I felt waves of tension from the audience as they waited. Wade hadn't yet done a thing and already I knew he'd moved into position to win. If his routine was at all good, he would take the crown and I'd never hear the end of having a straight man win on my watch.

Slowly, golden spotlights swept the stage, caressing Wade's body, creating the shimmering effect of gold flecks on water. At no time was he completely visible and, though nude, it was difficult to see anything through the expertly played lighting.

Curly bronze-blond hair glistening, eyes still closed, Wade gradually extended his arms out from his sides until he stood like the Renaissance figure of human perfection. There was something primal about his presence on stage. He was a sleek, intelligent animal. Yet there was also an innocence about him, which I had seen in his eyes earlier.

Having spoken to him a few times before the contest, I knew it would be difficult to be angry if he won, even if he was straight. I could only hope the others would gracefully accept the results. After staring at him a moment,

I mentally slapped myself for getting sentimental about a straight boy who'd managed to mesmerize the entire house.

My attention was seized by the lights which swirled and turned and caught Wade in a virtual hurricane of illumination. Just as suddenly the swirling lights stopped. A shaft of intense blue light cascaded down over Wade as his rope, chain, and sling contraption slipped down behind him to the sounds of a haunting Enya piece. The audience, still entranced, remained silent as they watched.

Reaching up, stretching his body, biceps flexing, Wade placed his hands on the ropes and chains. Wrapping the ropes around his arms and placing his feet into slips made of chain which gently pinged and clinked against itself as he worked, he maneuvered himself into position gracefully. He paused, the lights still strategically shadowing him, arms at his sides, legs together. His oiled torso shimmered in the pink and yellow light. Bathed in this more gentle illumination, Wade looked like a demi-god fallen to earth.

Without warning, he spread his arms, elevated his legs like a gymnast balancing on the rings, and began his program. His routine was smooth and sensual. Gradually he gained speed, and with precise, swift movements, Wade slipped in and out of the ropes and chains. Holding himself aloft with his powerful arms, he made no missteps.

As he slithered in and out of the rigging, he climbed higher into the flyspace above the stage in the web he'd devised until he was out of sight of the audience.

Those of us backstage could still see him wrapped in the rigging high above the stage. With one graceful flip, he turned head over heels, his back to the audience, and began moving down toward the leather sling. The strength in his arms was his only support. Though ropes and chains coiled themselves around his body like boa constrictors, he deftly maintained control and guided himself down inch by inch. When the audience could see him again, there was a spontaneous cheer.

My muscles tensed each time I saw Wade let go of one handhold to grasp the next, stabilizing himself with his calves smartly wrapped in the chains. Tiny bell-like sounds made by hundreds of silvery chain links clinking against each other filled the silence. Wade's oiled body, wrapped within the ropes and chains, shimmered in the spotlight as he continued his descent through the complex pattern which only he knew how to navigate.

Nearing the sling, but still well above it, he appeared to miss a handhold. Then another. His movements quickened. His hands slipped furiously over the chains and he fell fast through the now tangled contraption. His movements became erratic and panicky as he abandoned his carefully orchestrated plan.

Puzzled, I'd stepped forward without realizing it and saw one of the ropes snap.

A sudden and violent snap of the chains sent a loud, final ping through the air.

Wade's frantic movements slowed.

Another rope split off at the top and slipped lifelessly down. Wade frantically clutched at the elaborate contraption again which caused it to tangle and grow tighter the more he struggled. His hands slipped with each attempt to gain purchase. His movements became increasingly frantic.

Then, in mid-air, poised above the sling which was high above the stage, he quit struggling and his body relaxed. His head pointed down and his face was twisted away from me.

For a moment everyone stared in silence. No one could tell if this was part of the act or a terrible accident. Some might've thought Wade was showing off, teasing the audience, building the tension. I wasn't so sure. Precious seconds passed as we waited for him to continue.

I looked at Wade and then glanced at the deejay. He shrugged.

"What do we do?" Stan asked, sweaty panic overtaking him.

I shouted to the deejay, "Is this part of his act?"

Eyes wide, he shook his head.

Stan shifted his weight from one foot to the other. "If we interfere, he'll say we fucked up his performance deliberately. If we don't… think of the insurance problems."

"Screw it," I said and moved toward Wade.

Something was horribly wrong.

Someone in the audience screamed as I reached Wade. I saw one of his hands lose its grip and his arm dropped causing the chains around his neck to tighten further.

Desperately I grasped the chains and began pulling at them. They were slippery with the oil from Wade's body. As if they were a living thing, each chain and rope gripped him more tightly with any attempt to untangle him.

Frustrated, I watched as his other hand released its grip on the chain. He seemed to have given up.

"Call 911. And get a ladder. Quick!"

Someone brought a chair and placed it near me. I stepped up to see if I could reach inside the rigging from a different angle. But the chair didn't give me enough height. "A ladder. Now!" I yelled as I stepped down.

Wade's head was suspended inches from my face. His eyes were open and glassy. I hoped he could see me or at least sense my presence and know someone was there with him.

"Wade?" I half whispered.

A sudden gasp and then his breathing came in shallow, raspy gulps. His mouth moved slightly as he tried speaking. Reaching out my hand I gently cupped his face. His skin was clammy and he trembled at my touch.

A stagehand noisily dragged over a ladder and set it up beside me.

I wanted to stay with Wade, let him know he wasn't alone. I turned to the stagehand. "Climb up," I said. "See what you can do." But, I knew there was nothing anyone could do.

The skinny stagehand took each step keeping his eyes focused on Wade, not knowing what to expect.

Wade's face grew darker as the blood rushed to his head. Again, he made an effort to speak.

"Don't try to talk, Wade. The police will be here soon. They'll help." I whispered. Though I doubted it would be soon enough to save him.

I reached out again and smoothed his curly hair which was matted with sweat and oil. He struggled to draw a breath.

"Wa-was… good," his voice came in sad, ragged bursts. "Di-didn't… ha-have to worry… Michael? No one… I wouldn't… t-tell…"

"Shhhh. Hear that siren? They're here. Hold on, Wade," I said. But this kid wasn't going to wait for anything. He didn't have much time.

"Ga-gay… not… angry?"

I touched his hair again and he shuddered. "They're here, Wade. Stay with me." I stroked his face. Despite everything, his skin felt soft and delicate.

Suddenly I was angry. Angry and frustrated. I wanted to rip away the chains, get him out of the deathtrap. "Wade," I whispered as I brought my face closer to his.

"Not… an-angry?" He looked at me as if I were all that mattered in the world.

"Angry? Not a chance," I whispered, knowing he wasn't talking to me but to someone else he thought was there.

"C-couldn't help …had to…"

"Could never be angry with you, Wade." I said trying to comfort him but unable to figure out what he meant. Why was he apologizing? And who was it that he thought was with him? I looked into his eyes. They became dull and lifeless.

His body jerked spasmodically a few times. Then he was still.

* * *

Things moved around me in slow motion. The EMTs, staffers, other contestants, everyone flowed around me and Wade. For a moment, I was barely aware of what they did or said.

I felt someone gently tugging me away, pulling my hands from Wade's face. He took me by the shoulders and tried leading me away. I shrugged him off and watched the EMTs work to free Wade. That same person wrapped an arm around my shoulders and pulled me back to stand a short distance away from the knot of emergency workers.

I became aware that it was Anton who stood beside me. It was Anton who'd pulled me to him and squeezed. His warmth rushed through me, and I felt as if I was returning from somewhere far off. I placed an arm around his waist and leaned into him, comforted by his presence.

Slowly I returned to the reality of the situation. Standing on the stage, bare lights washing the area with a cold, hollow feeling, I realized there were people all around. Some rushed back and forth doing who knew what. Others huddled in small groups crying or consoling one another. The contestants stood in stunned silence, their eyes riveted on Wade's lifeless body. The judges pressed close to one another upstage, looks of shock and horror on their faces.

The EMTs worked quickly cutting ropes and untangling chains until they freed Wade. Several of them held him gently until they were sure he could be moved. Then, acting in unison, they brought his body to rest on the stage. One of the EMTs began working furiously on Wade. Eventually, he looked up at his companions and said something I could not hear from where I stood.

A cry of grief from someone nearer to the body let me know that Wade was gone.

I saw someone point at me and watched as one of the EMTs walked toward me and Anton. He looked grim, his face set in an expression I'd seen before.

"I'm sorry. He's gone. I had to call it," he said apologetically. He looked younger than Wade, who'd only been twenty-five. "There wasn't much we could do. I'm sorry for your loss."

I nodded to him, then looked over at Wade. His friend, Michael, knelt over the body. His shoulders shook as he wept. An EMT placed a hand on Michael's back and gently urged him to stand so they could place Wade in the ambulance.

As Michael stood he turned toward me, an expression of hate or rage twisting his features. He took a few steps in my direction, but stopped himself. Closing his eyes, he stood motionless then turned away, his back bent with grief.

Anton pulled me to him and we embraced. I wanted nothing more than to be alone with him, watching a movie or doing some other mundane thing. I wanted to forget the whole night had even happened. But I knew there was more coming and before I had a chance to think, the police arrived. There were so many responding, I figured there must've been several calls from people in the audience as well as the one we placed. Some officers stationed themselves at the exits while others filtered through the crowd. One plainclothes detective made his way toward the stage.

His clothes were drab but he was quick and alert. He took in the entire place as if wondering who was in charge. I realized I should take the lead, since I'd been managing the contest. Stan, as usual when there was trouble, had disappeared.

"Officer?" I said, stepping toward him.

"Detective. Detective Ransom." He didn't bother to extend a hand. "Looks like one hell of an accident." The detective's gaze swept the room again, eventually landing back on me. "But, I guess well see about that. What can you tell me?"

A tall older man, Ransom had salt and pepper hair and was built like a linebacker. His lined, unshaven face made him look as if he'd spent some time boxing in his youth. His gray suit barely contained his bulky figure. All business, he stood, chewing gum and sizing up the situation. His blue eyes were getting used to contacts and he didn't look happy.

"Things happened fast, detective. I was right here, and it all went wrong in an instant." I said. I fought a vague sense of guilt, wondering if I could have done anything to save the kid.

"And who're you?" He tried sounding threatening. It would take more than some gum-chewing police detective to make me feel threatened or fearful.

"Fontana, Marco Fontana," I said, moving closer to him.

"Fontana." He savored the name for a moment. "I've heard'a you. Some kind'a nosy P.I. What I hear, you got lucky a few times at our expense." He smirked.

I said nothing, but met his stare and didn't blink.

"What's your part in all this… what the hell *is* this anyway?" He did a half turn as he took everything in once more, as if he was having trouble grasping the meaning of his surroundings.

"It's the Mr. Philly Gay Leather competition. Happens every year. I was managing the show this time," I said.

"Managing a leather contest? What'd you do, crack a whip and make 'em jump?" He laughed at his own joke.

"Hey, whatever works for you, detective," I smirked.

"Wiseass, just like I heard," he said. "Stay put." Then he did a slow turn and in a loud voice said, "Everybody stays put where you are. Got it? On the stage, near the stage, backstage, in the audience, up in the rafters, wherever. Until we tell you to go."

Ransom tossed out a look that said he meant it, then huddled with his officers, I assumed to instruct them. Waving his hand imperiously, he dispersed his men and directed his attention to Stan, the owner of Bubbles, who'd mysteriously reappeared and approached the detective. They chatted, but Stan said something which made Ransom turn abruptly and head back in my direction looking annoyed.

"You were with the deceased when he died?" It was less a question than an order for me to tell him everything.

"I'd gone over to see if I could do anything. I couldn't."

"You should've told us."

"Told you what exactly? That I walked across the stage to help the guy? It's not like I was up in the rigging when whatever happened happened." I hated explaining myself, especially to someone who thought he could intimidate me. "By the time I moved toward him, he was already tangled in the rigging and beyond my help. Nobody could've done anything."

"Did he say anything?" He peered at me as if I were hiding something.

"He mouthed a few words but I couldn't make sense out of it."

Ransom was silent. He stared at me as if he could pull out more information using silent intimidation. When he realized I wasn't fazed, he frowned and went back to questioning other people.

After collecting names, addresses, and phone numbers, they let the audience go, though quite a few had left right after Wade's accident. Then Ransom concentrated on anybody who was closer to the action on stage. Anyone who might've had access to things backstage. The nine remaining leather contestants were herded together onstage, while the staff of Bubbles was placed near the bar. I and my competition staff were shunted off to the side and the judges were placed backstage. Ransom went about taking information from us, one by one.

He asked everyone if Wade had enemies or if anyone had witnessed arguments between Wade and others. All the standard stuff. If Ransom was thinking this was a murder, I was right there with him on that. Wade's death might've appeared to be a bizarre accident, but that didn't add up. Wade had set all the rigging himself. He'd rehearsed plenty of times without anyone present. He didn't even allow the DJ in on rehearsals, since the music was meant to work in the background and nothing more. He knew how to handle the rigging without help. Could've been an accident, but I had a feeling someone must've had a hand in it.

While I waited to be interviewed, one of the crime scene investigators called for Detective Ransom. Since I know the layout of Bubbles so well, having to spend most of my evenings there, I managed to position myself so I could make out nearly everything the detective and the CSI discussed.

"Looks like these ropes were cut and everything's oily. Chains and ropes all have some kinda oil on 'em," the investigator said.

"What do you mean, cut?" Ransom asked.

"Cut," insisted the investigator. "As in somebody took a sharp implement and sliced through the ropes just enough so they'd fail at some point. Looks intentional."

"Whaddaya know," Ransom said, glancing over his shoulder at people he now considered suspects. He sauntered over to me, a satisfied look on his face. "We got a hot one here, Fontana. You guys are in it now. Looks like somebody wanted to win this contest real bad. Or maybe there was another reason." He stared a moment, chomping his gum, and shook his head. "This contest mean so much that your boys are gonna murder each other to get ahead? Or, was there a lovers' spat?"

"You think somebody did this on purpose?" I didn't want him to know I'd overheard and probably agreed. I wanted to see how he was thinking.

"It was murder, Fontana. You're a smart guy, you probably already had it figured that way. Turns out somebody tampered with the ropes the victim was tangled in. Maybe even oiled some'a the chains so he'd be sure to lose his grip."

"Somebody cut the ropes?" I asked, even though I knew he was right.

"And oiled everything up."

"Wade was oiled up for his routine. Oil on the chains probably came from contact with his body."

"Well, the ropes were cut. No doubt about it. The kid was murdered." Ransom chewed on his gum and jiggled the change in his pocket. "Probably a lotta motives right here in this room."

"Anybody could've done it. This contest was advertised around the area for weeks. Your murderer could be some homophobic nut case."

"Aww, you people are always moaning about discrimination. Don't you guys ever commit crimes? You're telling me that gay people are more crime free than the rest of us mortals?"

"Maybe. There's a lower rate of crime among gay people, for a lot of good reasons. We don't even have sodomy laws to break anymore."

"Save it." He looked around ominously and placed a hand to his chin as if he were thinking. "We're finished with the staff of this… what's the name of this place?"

"Uh, Bub-, um, Bubbles, sir." A young officer standing nearby blushed as he blurted out the name. I recognized him as a regular, every Wednesday and most weekends like clockwork, watching the dancers and trying to melt into the crowd. He looked so different in his police uniform, I almost didn't recognize him. Obviously he hadn't told everyone about his after-hours activities and I was sure things on the force hadn't changed so much in the short time that had elapsed since I'd decided I'd had enough of their games.

"Yeah, okay, right," Ransom said. "Bubbles. Whatever." He jiggled the change in his pocket, peered around the place again. "The staff can go… for now. Stick around. No sudden vacation plans. Got it?" He frowned as he looked over the crowd, and everyone nodded.

The bartenders, shot boys, clean-up crew, and barbacks beat a hasty retreat. Once that group was gone, whoever was left must've begun feeling the imaginary heat. Ransom stood around, employing his silent 'sweat 'em out' tactic, and it was easy to see some of them react with guilt, real or imagined. Shifting their feet nervously, wiping sweat from their face, glancing around as if looking for an escape route. Nervous tics and gestures became exaggerated, as Ransom's silence stretched from minute to minute.

The detective allowed this to go on, watching how each of us reacted to the force of his accusatory silence. Obviously, most of these characters weren't used to a little pressure. Ransom was good, I'd give him that. It was a neat technique and one I'd used now and then, which gave me an advantage. I suppressed a laugh and waited him out.

Finally, Ransom cleared his throat. Everyone let out a collective sigh of relief.

"The rest of you…." Ransom paused and scanned the room looking at each person in turn. "We'll finish with the basics. Then we'll see who gets to stay and who gets to go."

"It's late, Detective. Can't we do this in the morning?" The voice came from the back of the pack of judges and I couldn't see who it was. Didn't recognize the voice either.

"Okay, then," Ransom said, and ignored the plea. "A nice officer is gonna come get information. You give him what he wants and you might get to go sooner." He flicked a finger and several officers moved to the groups people had sorted themselves into.

The contestants in their leather get-up looking like a rag tag band of post-apocalypse survivors, torture chamber masters, and Stormtroopers, occupied one corner. Though the way they huddled together as if they were about to be sold at auction, gave the lie to their appearance. I even thought I saw a stray tear tumble down the cheek of one of them.

Most of the judges stood straight-backed and silent, trying to appear important and aloof. Each of them looked anywhere but at Ransom or the officer who approached them. But Howie Sider, florist and bon vivant nuisance, looked as if he'd seen a ghost. Eyes wide, he fidgeted, coughed and generally allowed himself to stand out from the rest. The others, Rosa, Fitz, Carlton, Wayne, and Milton stood their ground showing no emotion.

I wished my staff, such as it was, would follow Anton's example. Tall and solid, he stood, arms folded, and calmly observed the police. He seemed at ease and unworried. The rest of my staff hung on me like orphans waiting for the mean warden to do something awful. I remained silent and unmoving, hoping they'd catch my confidence and calm down while Ransom finished his act and let us all leave.

One of the CSIs approached Ransom, spoke briefly to him and moved along. The detective looked up as if he'd been given a piece of key information. He turned his eyes on us and smirked. Another intimidation tactic guaranteed to have everyone wondering what he knew and what he'd do with the information.

He stared silently a second longer, then, "If you've been questioned, you can leave. And don't make plans to go anywhere, boys. You'll hear from us. That includes you, Fontana."

Everyone scattered. Even the judges lost their cool in their attempt to vacate the bar as quickly as possible.

* * *

The phone screamed me awake at seven. Which meant I'd gotten three hours of sleep. For a minute, I wasn't sure whether I was awake or still dreaming. Nothing seemed familiar. The phone kept ringing, though, and that was no dream. Groping for the receiver, I grudgingly opened my eyes, and even the gentle morning light seemed too bright.

"Hello?" My mouth was dry.

"Marco? Is that you? Marco, you've got to help him!"

"Who is this?" The voice was vaguely familiar but I wasn't awake enough yet.

"Liam. From last night? The contest?" He paused. "Remember?" There was a note of desperation in his voice.

"Liam. Studded leather harness. Fishnet thong. I remember," I said, the image of Liam standing backstage brought me fully awake. I sat up and leaned back on a pillow so my head would stop spinning. "What's the problem?"

"The police," Liam said. "They were here almost an hour ago and arrested Ben."

"The police? Arrested Ben?" I swiped a hand over my face and tried to absorb the news. "Arrested him? Why?"

"They took him out in handcuffs." Liam paused. "They asked him a few questions and then put handcuffs on him and took him. You can help him, right?"

"What'd they ask him? What's the charge? What did they say when they took him?" My mind snapped to attention.

"They asked him where he was the night before the accident. I mean the… you know. But he didn't have an alibi."

"The night before? That's all they asked? Then they cuffed him?"

"They said he'd been seen backstage. Alone. The night before the competition. After everyone else was gone for the night."

"What did Ben say?"

"He said he was meeting someone that night. I believe him. Ben's no murderer."

"Meeting someone. All right. That person can be Ben's alibi."

"But he won't." Liam sounded frustrated.

"The witness won't talk?"

"No. *Ben* won't talk. He won't say who he was meeting. The police said that wasn't good enough. Then they arrested him for the murder."

"Did the police say who it was that saw Ben backstage?"

"No. Just that somebody saw Ben. What're we gonna do?"

"Keep your shirt on and wait for my call. Don't go anywhere and don't do anything until I talk to you." I hung up, dialed police headquarters, and asked for the detective who'd been there the night before. I knew they'd probably only taken Ben in for questioning and hadn't officially charged him with the murder. But better to stop things before they went any further.

"Ransom." His voice was gruff.

"It's Marco Fontana, Detective. I was…"

"You're off the hook. At least for now. We think we've got our guy."

"So I've heard. And you're right when you say you *'think'* you got him. Because you're wrong."

"Izz'at a fact?" Ransom said.

"Facts are what's gonna prove you wrong, Ransom. So, how about you give me some information."

"Like what, Fontana? This ain't the public library."

"Like who claims he saw Ben backstage?"

"You know better than to ask for that kind of information. This investigation…"

"I'm acting on Ben's behalf."

"How? He hasn't had time to call a lawyer and you're no lawyer."

"But his friends made some calls as soon as you left his place. So, I'm working for him now."

"You people work fast. Guess I should believe what I've heard."

"So, who saw Ben?"

"One of your judges. In that contest. Who knows who else? We're just gettin' started."

"Which judge? No one was permitted in after rehearsals that night." I'd been there until rehearsals were over. The bar was closed at two in the morning, as usual. Staff hung around to clean up. Then everyone had left. So I'd been told. "Everyone cleared out by three, after they cleaned up for the night."

"Well, this guy, name of Fitzpatrick, was there after youse all left. He says your boy Ben Tadeo was hanging around backstage lookin' nervous. One of the barbacks says he heard Tadeo making threats earlier in the evening. The kid says Tadeo claimed he wouldn't let a straight guy win the contest. No matter what."

"That's pretty slim and circumstantial. You got other witnesses? Other evidence?"

"We're workin' on it, like I said. But two's a good number to hang a preliminary charge on as far as I'm concerned. I think the DA can make a case. And we're working on trace evidence. Prints, micro-fibers, epithelials, whatever we can find. There's a real mother lode on that stage."

"You think? It's a bar, Ransom. There's hundreds of customers and several shows every night. Gonna be a lotta trace to sort through. I'd say it'll all be useless, even if you find something."

"All we need is what we need, Fontana. Stay tuned."

I'd stay tuned all right, I'd stay more than tuned. I didn't know Ben well, but I remembered him. Square-jawed, muscular, green-eyed Ben. Cuffed and thrown into a cell. Poor guy had probably never been in real handcuffs. I made a list of people I'd need to see. John Fitzpatrick, Chair of the GLBT Concerns Committee, was at the top. I needed to know what he'd been doing at Bubbles after hours. I had to wonder how Fitzpatrick had gotten into Bubbles after it'd been locked up. I'm sure he thought that because he was the Mayor's token gay darling, he could do what he pleased.

I'd also definitely need to talk to Howie Sider. He'd looked too undone the night before, while waiting for the detective to let him go. That was guilty behavior and I wanted to know what Howie felt guilty about.

Aside from the judges and others who'd have to be questioned, the nine remaining contestants were at the top of my list. Liam, Bri, and Ben shared a condo in a decent building in town. From what I'd been told, Ben was Liam's closest friend, the nearest thing he had to family, and a former lover. Liam would probably need a lot of handholding until this thing was settled. Something I wouldn't mind doing.

Then there was Michael, who I guessed would not be easy to deal with, considering his attitude. I was sure he now assumed we'd decided to kill the straight contestants to keep them from winning. Crazy as that sounded, Michael might just believe it. I wasn't looking forward to talking with him.

According to Ransom, the remaining contestants were supposedly in the clear, because all of them had solid alibis. One of them had even been out of town until the day of the competition. I'd check in with them anyway. Who knows what they might have seen or heard?

A cool shower to wake me up, some strong coffee, and half a muffin I found sitting in the fridge helped propel me into the day. Once outside, I felt better. Locust Street bustled with people on their way to work, some of them springing forward, some of them sleepily dragging their feet. A bicycle cop rolled by on the street and the neighborhood dry cleaner pulled a rack full of plastic-wrapped clothes into one of the condo buildings. The fresh, cool air had me feeling almost normal. I headed east toward Washington Square. The stroll would give me the chance to plan and think.

Walking through the gayborhood never gets old, not for me. Each time I pass a bar, I wonder what kind of secrets it's keeping, what conversations it's overheard, what arguments, what clandestine meetings? There's at least one story everywhere, sometimes more than one, and everywhere you go, there are plenty of secrets. The gayborhood has more than its share. At least I liked to think so. When I walk through it, I always expect something good, something surprising, something unanticipated.

Washington Square's mix of business and residential property is like most of Philly's central district. Huge condo towers and office complexes border the historic centers. The area is littered with the remnants of a flourishing business past, now transformed and trying to make it in the new economy. Ghosts of old businesses are scattered throughout the area, like the Lippincott publishing company, which was once a gem in Philly's tussle with New York for dominance.

Liam and company rented a condo in one of the newer buildings. How they afforded it was anybody's guess. It wasn't cheap, and they weren't stockbrokers. I took out my cell phone and called ahead, just in case they'd ignored my request to stay put. Liam and Bri were both at home.

I made it through the front desk security hurdles and zipped up to the twenty-fifth floor in an elevator that gave the impression you were in a hotel rather than a residence. Liam's apartment was the last door at the end of a long, classy corridor.

Bri came to the door when I knocked. Golden-eyed, shaven-headed Bri tried looking tough when he opened the door. But the Australian rugby shorts, a skin tight see-through tee-shirt, and flip-flops, did not communicate "dangerously tough." He let me in, shut the door, and trotted off into another room.

Liam stood in the living room and waved me in, his cargo pants and a loose tank-top making him look like an ad for a high end clothing line. He'd tied a yellow bandana around his neck and it played well against the bronze skin tone he obviously kept with the help of tanning parlors. Liam's eyes were red, and it wasn't allergy season.

"They say he— he probably did it." He stared at me, and I've never yet seen a better lost-puppy look.

"I know, Liam, but…"

"You've gotta do something, Marco." Liam said as he stepped close, wrapped his arms around me, and lay his head on my shoulder. "Ben needs you."

"I'm working on it, Liam," I said and rubbed his back with my hand.

His body pressed closer. He felt warm and needy. Pleasant as Liam's embrace was, I needed to talk about the case. I gently disengaged so we could talk face to face. "You need to pull yourself together and do what you can to help."

"I will, Marco, but you're the one who really knows what to do. Besides you sort of got us all into this in the first place."

"How do you figure that?" I asked, already knowing what he meant.

"You encouraged us all to sign up," Liam said, without sounding angry. Then, his face close to mine, he looked me in the eye. His eyes were a warm brown and very seductive. "But, I forgive you. Maybe I was a little rough on you last night."

He placed his hands softly on each side of my face and pulled me into a kiss. A long deep kiss, during which he pressed his body against mine, and I couldn't resist. I didn't want to.

Finally, drawing himself away, he looked at me, smiled, and wiped at his eyes. "I'll make some coffee." He padded off on bare feet and left me standing there.

I knew manipulation when it stuck its tongue down my throat. What Liam didn't know was that I was already invested in the case, and he didn't need to try manipulating me. But I wasn't about to stop him from employing more of his brand of manipulation.

After a few moments, during which I heard Liam working around in the kitchen, Bri barreled into the room with Liam in tow looking confused. Bri was lots taller than Liam and carried more muscle.

"Liam said you're gonna take the case? Did you talk to Ben?" Bri demanded.

I could smell coffee brewing. "I've asked around. Spoke to Detective Ransom and I think I've found—"

"You found out who really did it?" Bri asked.

"I—"

"I knew he didn't do it. I know Ben. He couldn't have." Liam said.

"I didn't say I'd found the killer. But I'm trying and you guys can help." I had to slow them down before they derailed.

"How? We didn't see anything," Bri towered over me like an old-growth Redwood. "Besides who'd believe us if we did? A straight guy dies and we take the fall for it. Simple. They have a fag in prison and they'll roast him."

"Could be but… are you sure you have all the facts?" Liam said. Then he clammed up, which was a sure sign he wanted us to drag the information out of him.

I took the bait to make him happy. "And you mean by this…?"

"Well, Bri said a straight guy gets killed and we take the fall."

"You see it any different, Liam?" Bri's deep voice rumbled and his eyes widened, ready for an argument.

"Possibly," Liam answered. "I think I just remembered something."

"Okay, Liam, out with it. Ben is sitting in a cell wondering what's going to happen to him. So, if you know something, let's have it."

"It's just that we don't know for sure that Wade was straight. There's been talk and lots of rumors are true. Sometimes. Don't you think? I mean, who'd come out on that stage naked like he did? In a gay contest with all those queens standing around hooting? Who? Most straight guys I know couldn't even *think* about doing that."

"All that proves is that Wade had a little more courage than the rest. He was more competitive. He knew what it would take for a straight guy to compete and win in a gay contest."

"That doesn't change the rumors. And Wade is at the heart of them." Liam padded out of the room and quickly returned with cups and a pot of coffee.

"What rumors, Liam? I haven't heard a thing, and I get around more than you do." Bri looked miffed that he might be out of the loop. The macho muscle-man was a gossip queen at heart.

"Okay, Liam," I said. "Cough up the information."

"People say that Wade was seen with John Fitzpatrick on more than one occasion."

"Seen? What do you mean by seen?" I asked. "I need more than that, Liam. Details. Actual witnesses."

"I don't know details. All I know is they were seen together in places. Places where they thought nobody would catch them, I guess." Liam poured coffee for each of us and sat on the couch. He stared at me and then at the couch. A silent invitation.

He was a tempting sight. But I needed to concentrate on the case and Ben and finding the real killer.

"Think you can find out some of those details?" I sipped my coffee and looked at each of them in turn. "Could save Ben a lot of trouble."

"We'll find out. Whatever you need," Bri said. "You just ask."

We chatted a while longer, but neither of them added anything new. I told them to get in touch as soon as they found out anything.

* * *

I'd already decided to see John "Fitz" Fitzpatrick at some point. But after what Liam said, I pushed Fitz to the top of the list. A rich entrepreneur, he had political aspirations, which had so far netted him the chairmanship of the GLBT Concerns Committee. But he had his sights set higher, and this murder could get him headlines he didn't want or need. I figured he'd be crawling the walls by now, wondering what he could do to save his career. From what I'd seen of him, he treated every minor flap as a major crisis. Exactly the kind of personality we need in high office.

As I left the building, I flipped out my cell phone and dialed Fitz. He answered on the first ring. Like I thought, he was worried.

"Fitz, this is Marco."

"What do you want?" His voice was sharp, angry. But he paused and in an instant made a one-eighty turn around. "What can I do for you, Marco?"

"I'm trying to get to the bottom of what happened to Wade. I feel some responsibility. And maybe we can help get Ben off the hook. You remember him?"

"What did you say his name was?"

"Ben was a contestant. Cute, short, green eyes. "

"Nope, sorry. I don't think I can help anyway. I've told the police all I know. Besides, I've got no time today."

"Sure you do, Fitz. I'm a member of a sexual minority, and you're head of the GLBT Concerns Committee. How would it look if someone lodged a complaint against the head commissioner, especially if he was already involved in a murder investigation?"

"Two o'clock. My office. I can give you fifteen minutes."

I called Anton to ask if he could interview some of the other contestants. I gave him a brief rundown and a list of names. He'd helped me on cases before and was good at it. I trusted him to ask the right questions.

Howie, next on my list, was easy to track. His flower shop, Petals Boutique, was a busy place and he spent most of his time there. I wanted to get him to explain his case of nerves the night of the murder. Maybe he was just edgy that night because he was intimidated by the police. On the other hand, maybe good old Howie had something to hide. If so, I wanted to know what that was and if it was connected to the case.

I walked back to the gayborhod via Walnut Street. The city touted Walnut as one of the finest shopping streets in Center City. They were right, even if there were still a few sore spots here and there.

When I got to Thirteenth, I headed for Spruce, two blocks away, where Howie's Petal Boutique was located. It was easy to spot the gigantic sculptural flowers he'd had placed strategically around the exterior of his corner shop. They were visible for blocks in all kinds of weather.

I entered the shop, and an electric chime sounded. The cloying smell of fresh flowers wrapped itself around me. Howie was behind the counter, back toward me, pulling together an enormous, elaborate arrangement. A mix of exotic blooms, dried vines and lots of ribbons, this one would probably cost a good chunk of money. Not bad for the time it took to throw it together. He glanced at me over his shoulder, then tucked his head back down immediately as if he were too engrossed in his work to be bothered. Too bad. I'd be bothering him whether he liked it or not.

"Howie, that's beautiful. What's it for? A wedding?"

"The Wilde Inn, that new B& B over on Camac. They decided to dress up their lobby." He wasn't unfriendly exactly, but he wasn't warm and fuzzy either. "Why? You looking to get married, Fontana?"

"If I ever fall in love I'll know where to come for a seduction bouquet." I moved closer to the counter which let him know I wasn't going away.

He turned around and gave me the fisheye. He didn't want to deal with me, but he knew he had no choice. He pressed a button on an intercom.

"Timmy, come on out and finish up this arrangement. I've got some business with Mr. Fontana."

Out came an awkward, twenty-something kid with dark-dark curly hair and violet eyes. His quirky face was innocent and charming. He wasn't beautiful, but quirky is sometimes even better.

"C'mon back here, Marco. It's more private. I assume you want to talk about the… incident. I'm not sure I can help, though. I don't know much."

"You never know. Sometimes it's the silly little things we remember that mean the most." I knew Howie was as observant as a crow and was also good at keeping a secret. He knew something.

"So I've already told the police I was at the bar early the night before the contest. Even went backstage, where a couple of the guys saw me. But I left early, and there were still lots of people around. I don't know what was done or who did it, but I couldn't have done it. I had, um, a meeting all set and I hadda get going." He paused and frowned. "But the shit stood me up. Nothing I could do about it. Something else fell my way later on, and I spent the rest of the night with him."

"Who was it, Howie? Will they corroborate your story?"

"I can't say who. They'd be put into a compromising position and I really don't want to do that. For that matter, my own reputation would suffer as well."

"That's it?" He'd probably been dicking somebody's boyfriend and didn't want to open up that can of worms in public. Howie might've had a business to worry about, but a sex scandal in a flower shop wouldn't matter to anyone. He wasn't being totally honest. I could tell. "Think about it, Howie. Ben is sitting in a cell. You remember him, right? The green-eyed contestant that I caught you ogling last night. If you can help alibi Ben, now's the time. Who were you with? Come on, Howie."

"Can't say I remember the boy. No. All those muscle bunnies look alike to me." Howie fidgeted in place and shifted his feet a few times. "I don't find that type attractive, anyway. Too hard in the wrong places."

"Too bad for Ben, I guess. That's he's not your type, I mean. He's a lot like you. Won't tell anyone who his alibi is. He's sittin' down at the precinct, stuffed in a cell with who knows what for company, and he won't say a thing. I gotta wonder who he's protecting. And I also gotta think that it's one lucky bastard. To have somebody like Ben keeping secrets."

"It's not me, if that's what you're implying," Howie picked up a stem that'd been left on a table and twirled it between his fingers.

"Me, I'm not implying anything. Just letting you know about Ben. Doesn't look good for him. I won't say really bad, not yet, but he's got to start talking soon. Or somebody does, if you catch my drift."

"How can my having or not having an alibi help Ben?"

"Lemme know who your alibi is and I'll tell you." I knew it was a waste of time asking, because he wasn't ready to spill any information he didn't need to.

Howie simply stared at me.

"Be seein' you, Howie." I wasn't through with him and if things got worse for Ben, I'd be back and Howie wouldn't like it. I said my good-byes and walked out of the back room.

On the way out I exchanged glances with Timmy, who looked up from his work and winked at me. The lopsided smile that spread across his face gave him an entirely different look. Actually cute, even if he was quirky. I acknowledged the wink and the smile. He was definitely interested. I filed the information away for later.

Howie's shop wasn't far from City Hall, and it was almost time for my meeting with Fitz. I strolled back over on Thirteenth, past Woody's and some of the newly developing businesses farther down the block, until I came to Market Street.

City Hall loomed over everything. I entered through the South Portal, one of four huge vaulted entryways to a confusing labyrinth of offices and meeting rooms. My meeting with Fitzpatrick was scheduled for two, and I liked being early. I just about remembered the way to the office of the GLBT Concerns Committee, which was at the end of a lonely, drab hallway. As head of the Commission, Fitz didn't have much pull in the city, but the title gave him some small access to the halls of power and even a chance to chat with the Mayor now and again, not that he'd listen. But having the title was worth something at parties and other social functions, especially to people who didn't know better.

I knocked at the door and Fitz opened it a crack. He poked out his head. His glasses, perched on his too-large nose, made him look like an exotic bird. Edgy movements, as he looked me up and down, enhanced the illusion. When he ushered me in, I noticed him glance around to see if anybody was watching. There wasn't a soul in this part of the building so he had nothing to worry about. And nothing to brag about, either.

"What can I do for you, Fontana?" He sat in a chair behind his desk, fussed with papers, glanced up at me, then away.

"Like I told you on the phone, I'm investigating the death of Wade Hefflin."

"Horrible. It'll be a long time before I can forget that. It's all still so vivid." He paused and swiped a hand over his face. " I don't know what I can tell you, Fontana. The police questioned me last night, and I couldn't say much. I don't remember anything except that terrible sight."

"Ben Tadeo's been arrested. One of the other contestants. You remember him?"

"Maybe. There were ten contenders. Remembering them all is a little confusing. Especially after what happened."

"Ben's friends want to make sure he gets a fair deal. The police think they've got their man but I'm not so sure and I need to prove that. Which means I've gotta know where everyone was the night before the competition." I watched his face for some sign but Fitz was a cool character.

He said nothing.

"You have an alibi for the night in question?"

"No. I don't sit around every night thinking I'll need an alibi. So I don't have one. I was alone at home."

"Alone? But weren't you down at Bubbles?"

"Who said that?"

"A guy like you gets noticed. You're not just some nobody." It never hurt to flatter political types. Problem is, he didn't look like anything special. Tall and slender, light brown hair, tortoise-shell glasses perched on a large nose, and narrow shoulders. Basically nondescript.

What he looked like and who might have noticed him didn't matter. Ransom claimed that Fitzpatrick had been a witness, that he'd seen Ben backstage the night before the competition. Fitz had more or less implicated himself.

"Well…"

"What's not to admit about being at Bubbles?"

"Nothing, I suppose. It's just that I like keeping my private life private. I shouldn't have to tell the whole world my movements. Especially as I had nothing to do with this murder."

"Detective Ransom said you witnessed Ben backstage that night. You could only do that, if you were there yourself. What exactly were you doing backstage that night?" I waited for him to answer.

Fitz peered at some spot on his desk.

"Whoever killed Wade had to tamper with his rigging the night before the competition. Somebody had to have been backstage at Bubbles that night. You placed yourself there by saying you'd seen Ben. If you didn't have anything to do with Wade's death, you sure put yourself smack in the middle of opportunity."

"I'd never have done anything like that. Never." His indignation seemed real. His eyes were bright with anger. But then, he was a politician and they do indignation really well.

"Did you have a problem with Wade? Maybe because he was a straight contender for the title and you didn't like that?"

"Of course not! Wade was...Wade was a nice kid." He slipped a look at me, then stared at his papers again.

"You knew Wade?"

"Well, not exactly knew him."

"Oh?" What I meant by 'knew' and what he meant by 'knew' were probably totally different.

"I used to see him around here and there. Seemed like a nice guy."

"Saw him around? I've heard there was a bit more to it than that." I stretched what I'd heard. Truth is, I suspected there was more, because of the way Fitz was acting.

"I don't know what you're talking about." He stood up indicating that the interview was over as far as he was concerned. No smile, no frown, just an expressionless, hard-eyed stare.

"Maybe some publicity with you being connected to this murder in some way will refresh your memory. And then you'll talk." I rose from my seat and looked him in the eye. He didn't budge. He was cold and implacable like an ice sculpture. I'd have to find a way to heat things up. Whatever he knew about Wade might get me that much closer to the killer.

"You should be more careful about accusing people recklessly, Fontana. I used to like you. But you've become smarmy. I've told you what I can. I think it's time for you to leave and get back to puttering around in the gutter."

Fitz was hiding something, but it was part of the political persona to keep others in the dark on at least some things. Always keep others guessing, especially your opponents. Fitz was a wannabe politician. He had the personality down and was working on the rest.

I smiled and winked at him as I left. "See you soon, Fitz. You can count on that."

* * *

When I'd called Wade's pal Michael and asked him to meet me at the Village Brew Café, he balked at first. But his protests didn't sound real. What it sounded like was Michael needed someone to talk to and was too macho to admit that even to himself. He needed a good excuse to open up. I asked him if Wade would have helped out with an investigation, if things had been reversed. That was all the convincing he required.

Sitting at one of the café's sidewalk tables gave me the opportunity to guy watch, which, in the gayborhood, is an enlightening experience. The variety of men who pass by is almost staggering. Not just in shape and size, but in every detail that can be different. Hair, shoes, tattoos, piercings, clothing. You name it. Watching it never gets old.

I spotted Michael swaggering down the street half a block away. He frowned at every guy he caught looking at him. Which amounted to a lot of frowning. His muscleman walk and shape garnered him lots of attention of the variety he apparently didn't like. At some point, he saw me and marched over to my table, hostility radiating off his taut body.

"You got me here. Now what?" He stood, muscles bulging everywhere, and glared at me. I met his stare. That caught him off guard for just a second. Then the wall of hostility went back up. Even so, I could tell he wanted to be right where he was. He was hurting and needed to talk.

"Have a seat," I said and nudged a chair with my foot.

Michael refused.

"Okay, we'll do it your way." I sat back and looked him in the eye. "It's gotta be difficult for you. I'm guessin' you and Wade were close."

"We were friends, that's all. Just friends." He spat out the words.

"I get the picture," I said. Obviously, I'd touched a nerve. "I need some information. About the night Wade died. Maybe you can help."

Michael's stare said his help wouldn't come easy.

"It's possible you saw things that night. Or the night before the murder. Things maybe other people didn't see. You bein' backstage and in the competition." I kept my voice calm and even. Michael was the excitable type, and I wanted information, not a beat down.

Michael shifted on his feet, took a more aggressive stance. "I hear you're trying to get that guy off the hook. The one who did it."

"I'm trying to get at the truth."

"Truth is he did it. But you fags stick together, don't you?"

"I'm pulling together the facts of the case, Michael. I'm trying to find out who did this. If it's Ben, okay. I wanna make sure the evidence backs that up. If Ben did it, he'll pay. If he didn't, though, I want the person who did. And I'll bet you do, too. So, I need information."

"What makes you think it wasn't that guy? The police think he's the one."

"What did Ben have to gain?"

"Winning the contest. And even if he didn't win, he didn't want a straight guy to win. That's what."

"There'd still be you in the contest. You think he'd have killed you both?"

He seemed not to have considered that thought yet. He looked at me, then away, then back at me. "Well n-no, I guess… Maybe… who knows?" Michael's voice trailed off.

"But there must've been somebody who had a real motive for killing Wade. Somebody with something to hide, some strong passion, something to gain. That's what I want to know."

Michael wrestled with himself a few moments before he spoke. "Yeah. I saw things that night."

"Like what, Michael?"

"Mike." He pulled out a chair and sat down across from me. The table was small, and we were virtually nose to nose when he leaned in to talk. Not a bad-looking face, rough-hewn, with several days growth of beard emphasizing his strong jawline. But Michael had an edgy manner, suggesting he wasn't really comfortable in his own skin. "I saw plenty, and I guess you need to know what I saw. If that guy they're holding didn't do it, then it was another one of you."

"One of us?"

"One of you fa—gays. A gay guy killed Wade so he wouldn't win."

"Again, I ask, how come they didn't include you and eliminate *all* the straight competition?"

"I didn't have a chance at winning. I knew that, and so did everybody else. But Wade, he knew just what to do to make sure he won."

"How do you mean that?"

"He knew what turns you guys on, how to move, what to show, who to look at. He knew a lot about gay guys."

"That's strange for a straight man. I mean, Wade was straight like you, right?"

"Like me? Wade was straight, sure, but he knew about gays. I don't."

"How did that happen? Him knowing about us, I mean."

"He just knew, is all. I don't know how."

"What did you see at the bar that might make a difference?"

"I saw the guy, the one you said they're holding."

"Ben."

"I guess, yeah, Ben. He was backstage, and he was fooling around with the equipment. The night before the competition, Ben got into Wade's sling and wagged his ass at us. That's creepy, man. Waved his bare ass at *us*. Me and Wade. For all I know, he could've done something with the ropes while he was there. Wade was really pissed about him doin' that, too. He hated anyone touchin' his chains and stuff. Really hated it when that guy, um, Ben, got in the sling. Nearly punched him out."

"What time was that?"

"Early."

"And Ben?"

"He left. Wade left, too, and I hung out a little longer to make sure my weights and stuff were ready. On my way out, I saw other people messin' around backstage. I don't know names but I got a good memory for faces. One guy's been in the papers. I saw him backstage."

"In the papers?"

"Yeah, some kinda city official. He was askin' for Wade and was kinda curious about the sling and the chains. He..." Michael stopped again, appearing to weigh what he wanted to say.

When it was clear he wasn't going to continue, I went on. "Can you tell me what this guy looked like?" I didn't want to lead him by giving a description.

"Yeah, maybe. Glasses that looked like somethin' out of a comic book. Short hair. Kinda geeky."

"That would be John Fitzpatrick. Did you see him handle the rigging?"

Michael hesitated. "I didn't say that. I don't remember what he did."

"Thing is, Fitzpatrick has already admitted to being there. Got any idea why he was backstage?" I looked into Michael's eyes and saw pain, confusion.

"How should I know? He asked for Wade a coupl'a times. Even asked me. But I don't know what he wanted with him. Wade wasn't around, so he left."

"I think you do know, Michael." I hated having to force this out of him. It was obviously something he didn't want to talk much about. "Fitzpatrick and Wade were pretty close, weren't they?" Despite Fitzpatrick's denials, I knew there was something going on between him and Wade. I just needed confirmation.

"What're you tryin' to say? You're crazy, man. Wade was…"

"Wade was gay. Isn't that true?"

"No!" Michael glared at me.

"Wade never said anything that made you wonder?"

"You're crazy. Wade was confused. That's all." Michael pushed back from the table. He glanced around, worried others might've heard his outburst. "That guy, that glasses geek, was mixin' Wade up. He hung around a lot, always talking to Wade. Like he was tryin' to convince him about something." Michael kept his voice low but grew more agitated as he spoke.

"But Wade could have ignored Fitzpatrick, right? Could have stayed away or could've told Fitz to stay away. Couldn't he?"

"Wade was weak. He built up his body but he had no heart. No…" The edginess dissipated suddenly, and Michael's voice trailed off.

"Okay, Wade was weak. But he was smart. Smart enough to scope out the competition. Better than that, he knew his audience and learned everything about them. You said so yourself."

"So what? That didn't make him gay. He might'a been weak, but he liked to win and he did what he hadda do."

"If Wade knew so much about gay guys, why didn't you take some pointers from him? Why didn't he help you? Maybe you could'a won that competition."

"He wanted to help me. He told me what I could do. But I didn't wanna know, man." He shut his eyes against things only he could see and shook his head in disgust. "Wade…" He said the name with a mix of anger and deep sadness.

"What about him, Mike?" I could see he was hurting, and I hated adding to his troubles.

"He was…" He stopped mid sentence and looked down at the table, wrapping silence around him like a shield.

"How about some coffee?"

He nodded, still staring at the table, clenching and unclenching a fist.

I waved over a waiter, ordered, and turned my attention back to Michael.

"What were you gonna say about Wade?" I kept my eyes on him. Michael remained silent. The waiter placed a mug of coffee in front of him and gave me a new glass of orange juice. As soon as the waiter left, Michael looked up at me. He appeared confused, sad, filled with regret.

"Wade was cool, usually. But he had this thing…"

"What thing?"

"He had this thing about gays. I don't know. He couldn't stop talking about them. As if he…"

"As if he what?"

"Forget it, man. He wanted to win the competition. That's why he was so crazy on the subject of gays. And he kept pushing my buttons about it."

"Pushing your buttons?"

"About gay shit. Kept teasing and playing games. I hated that about him." He glanced up at me suddenly, a guilty look in his eyes.

"Did you guys fight…"

"Don't start that shit. I didn't hate him. Don't try and make it look like we were enemies, 'cause we weren't." He stared down at his coffee. "We were friends. Friends can push your buttons, too. Besides, it was that other guy who filled Wade's head with all that gay crap."

"You mean Fitzpatrick?"

"Yeah. He latched onto Wade and never let go."

That wasn't the impression Fitzpatrick tried to give me. I knew he'd been lying and hiding something. Now I had a better idea what that something was. I'd have to corner him and get him to talk.

"Maybe Fitzpatrick knows more than he's letting on."

"He's just another fag who was after Wade's ass. He don't know nothin' and that's all he knows."

"Just the same," I said. Then I noticed Michael staring off at something. I followed the direction of his gaze and caught Howie walking into the apartment building across the street from the café.

"Know that guy?"

"That one? The one who just went into the building? I saw him backstage, too."

"Sure you saw him. He was one of the judges."

"No, man. He was backstage the night before the competition."

"Yeah, he admitted that to me. Said he poked his head in, looked around and left early."

"Bullshit. He was there late the night before the competition. He was standin' around as if he was waitin' for something. Then he left with the other guy."

"What other guy? Fitzpatrick?"

"Naw, not him. But the two'a them did talk, though. That night. Except, this Howie dude was waitin' around for somebody else. It was the guy they arrested. Ben. It was them there that night. That dude, Howie, and Ben. Together. They pretended like they weren't together. But I saw 'em."

"I thought you told me Ben left early." I said.

"He did. But he must'a come back, 'cause I saw him again. Came back to meet this guy, I guess."

"They were together? You're sure?" I thought about what Howie had told me. A total pack of lies, including saying that Ben wasn't his type. The look in his eye when he'd said that put the lie to his words. Some judge he'd have been. Howie had a lot of explaining to do. For that matter, so did Ben.

"See. What'd I tell you? One of you did it. Maybe two. They must've planned it together. They talked like they didn't know each other. But they did."

"How can you tell?"

"Ben pulled that guy Howie into a corner where they thought nobody could see. I could, though. I looked down, and they were gettin' real cozy in a corner."

"Cozy?"

"Cozy – you know – they were kissing. That's somethin' I don't forget seeing."

"Kiss— they were kissing?" Suddenly I understood a few things. "Then what happened?"

"Whaddayou take me for? I didn't keep watching. I don't wanna see that shit. Makes me wanna puke."

"Did you see Howie leave the bar? The guy you saw across the street?"

"Yeah, but he didn't leave alone. Ben was with him. He followed a couple seconds after Howie, so it looked like they left separate. But they was together."

"I'll check this out, Mike. You may have helped Ben."

"What are you talkin' about?"

"Howie is probably Ben's alibi." Not probably but definitely, if Michael was telling the truth. I didn't think Michael was lying. On the other hand, Howie had been lying through his little teeth.

"They killed Wade together. Don't you see? So it figures they'll alibi each other."

"I'm not ready to say that, Mike. Something's goin' on between them, but I'm not so sure they had anything to do with Wade's death."

"You just don't wanna see."

"What I want is the truth, Mike. Isn't that what you'd like?" I felt sorry for him. He seemed adrift and without any idea how to steady himself. "I know you want to find Wade's killer. So help me out. Did you tell me everything you know?"

"I—I told you what I saw. That's what I know," Michael said and I knew that meant he'd left something out. Not a lie, just not the whole truth.

I decided it might be time stir the pot, as they say. Michael had had a strong reaction to Fitzpatrick, and when we talked about him, Michael seemed to be concealing something. If I let Michael know I'd be talking to Fitz again, I might get a rise out of him. It was worth a shot.

"I'm gonna head over to Fitzpatrick's house after he gets home from work. I wanna make sure what he says jibes with what you told me. Then I think we can get Ben out of jail and concentrate on the real killer. Assuming Fitzpatrick tells me the truth." I looked over at Michael and saw the gears turning. "What do you think, Mike?"

"Fitzpatrick's a dead end, man. You got your killers."

"I think Fitzpatrick knows more than he's admitting. But you don't have to worry about that. You've been a real help, Mike. Thanks," I said. Even if

I hadn't gotten anything further out of him, it was clearer now that Michael had information about Fitz he didn't want to share with me.

I put some cash on the table, told Mike to take his time finishing his coffee, and left. I glanced back over my shoulder when I was a block away and saw that Michael was still at the table. He looked lost, and I felt for the guy. He was lost in a lot of ways. He probably even needed to find his way back to who he really was. But that would take a lot of time.

I called Ransom on my cell phone. "Ask Ben if his alibi is Howie Sider. And can you arrange for me to talk to Ben?" Howie and Ben had both lied to me. Obviously, Howie had also been violating his promise to be impartial. And Ben seemed equally at fault, appearing to be trading sexual favors for votes in the competition. Looked like Fitzpatrick wasn't the only unethical judge. I wondered how many other judges had been seduced or had done seducing of their own. Backstage was busier than I'd imagined. If I kept digging, I'd probably find that all the contestants were playing all the judges. Well, all of them except Rosa.

Ransom told me to meet him at police headquarters where they were holding Ben. I hailed a cab, and when I got to The Roundhouse, Ben was in a conference room with his lawyer and Ransom. Things were quiet, he was still refusing to speak except to insist that he was innocent. I sat down across from him and stared at him before I spoke.

"Somebody saw you, Ben. The night before the competition. There's a witness who knows the person you were with. There's no use keeping quiet any longer. Your friends don't want to see you in jail for something you didn't do. Nobody believes you're a killer. What the hell was going on?"

I glanced at Ransom, his face a knot of curiosity. He was deeper in the dark than I was.

"Somebody says you and Howie were pretty close. Kissing close. Is that true, Ben?" I placed a hand over his hand. Out of the corner of my eye I saw Ransom wince.

"We didn't do anything wrong, and we didn't kill anybody." Ben's voice was soft and low.

"So, why not talk now that the secret's out?"

"It's not what you think. There isn't anything going on between us."

"Ben. Somebody—"

"Yeah, somebody saw me kissing him. So fucking what? I'd have kissed the Pope's ass, if it meant he'd vote for me and keep a straight guy from winning."

"You–you were--" I began.

"Trying to fix the competition. Ha!" Ransom smiled broadly and gave me a look.

"I'm not sure you should say anything else, Ben." His lawyer, a short, stout man, dressed like a million dollars, placed a hand on Ben's shoulder as if to restrain him.

"It's okay, Ross. I don't care." Ben slumped in his chair.

"Not like we're gonna prosecute him for trying to fix a gay leather contest." Ransom smirked. "Better for him if he clears the air on this."

"I approached Howie a few days before the contest. He finally agreed to meet me the night before the competition, and I just went for it. He was easy. So hungry for it. Like the others. So that's where I spent the night. When we left Bubbles there were still plenty of people hangin' around backstage. I never touched Wade's ropes and chains."

"Someone said they saw you in the sling and that Wade was furious with you about that."

"Yeah, so? I got into his sling and teased him. I didn't hurt anything and I didn't kill him. I guess I can't prove it, except for Howie. Anyway, I wasn't out to get Wade."

"But you didn't want him to win the contest," Ransom said. And you'd do whatever you had to, right?"

"No. I wouldn't have hurt anybody. I'd do whatever short of that. If I hadda sleep with a couple of the judges, so what? I wanted to get Howie to vote for me. I didn't need to hurt Wade. I had Howie and a few other judges hooked."

* * *

Just because I got Ben to talk didn't mean he was out of danger as far as Ransom was concerned. He let Ben go home but told him that he was still a suspect. And I couldn't disagree. He and Howie had a vested interest in giving each other an alibi. I needed to find something more definitive or they'd be right back to accusing Ben.

I called Fitzpatrick, told him Ben was free. I let him think that the police were hot on another trail, and might eventually take a harder look at him. Of course, the police had said no such thing, but I didn't think it'd hurt anything to get Fitz into a lather.

"Why? I didn't do anything. I wasn't there," he whined.

"I'll be over in ten and we can talk. Maybe we'll find a way out for you." I hung up as he was about to tell me not to bother.

He lived in the Old City section of Philadelphia. Classic old row houses, some of them historical, sporting plaques boasting who'd lived where during the Colonial or Federalist periods. A few new structures dotted the neighborhood and had been built by the wealthy, who wanted the advantages of city life but with some suburban trappings. Fortunately, most of the new housing respected the surroundings and echoed styles and materials of earlier periods.

Of course, Fitz lived in one of the newer homes: an architectural achievement that must have cost him a small fortune. Fitzpatrick had money and plenty of it, which was probably why he smiled so much. Never really directed the smile at you, though. It was more a result of self-satisfaction. That, or, he could have been unbalanced.

He answered the door himself. Neat, preppy-looking, a little overweight and not as stuffy as he'd appeared at City Hall, Fitzpatrick stood in the doorway and didn't budge. More calm and relaxed now than he'd been earlier, probably because he was on home turf.

"Aren't you going to invite me in?"

"Really, Fontana. I don't need the aggravation." He swiped at a fly buzzing his head. "Can't you tell me whatever it is, without coming in?"

"What have you got to hide, Fitz?" I smiled. "I'm getting closer to who killed Wade, but I need to clear up a few details first."

"Then why bother me? Why not call the—" He was interrupted by a loud crash inside his house. A muffled voice shouted expletives somewhere inside.

I stared at Fitz but said nothing.

Fitzpatrick rolled his eyes, waved me in, and shut the door behind me. He wasn't in a hurry, which meant he wasn't surprised by whatever it was going on inside. He was obviously annoyed, though, that I'd heard it and had to let me in.

We walked through a generous foyer hung with a few beautiful small landscapes. Then he marched me down a hall lined with abstract paintings and into a dining room. Carefully placed antiques littered the room and surrounding halls and gave the impression that this was a neatly organized warehouse rather than a home. Fitz was a collector, but this bordered on hoarding.

In the dining room was another antiques treasure trove. A large breakfront, weighed down with expensive-looking plates and silver objects, stood against one wall, and in front of it was a sizeable dining table. I realized that someone was getting up, with some difficulty, from the floor between the table and the breakfront.

Fitzpatrick didn't seem at all concerned. And why should he be? Standing on the other side of the table, sheepish look on his face, was Howie Sider, the florist.

"Sorry, Fitz. I was trying to move things so I could get to the silver coffee pot. A vase and two platters fell. I'm afraid they're beyond repair." Behind him, another piece clattered to the floor and shattered as he spoke. He winced and looked insincerely apologetic. "Sorry."

Fitz's face turned a dark scarlet. "Howie, you're an ass."

The broken things must've been worth a fortune. Now all he had was shards.

"Now, now, Fitz. Not another word. It's the price we pay sometimes." Howie looked at us as if he'd just dropped an inexpensive dinner plate. "I'll just take my pot and be on my way." He turned and took in the room with greedy eyes. The table, the breakfront, another tall cabinet packed with antique silver, crystal, and plenty more scattered around the room. "You have so many lovely things." He sighed and made as if to leave.

"Stick around, Howie. Since you're both here, maybe I can sew up a few loose ends." I had to wonder what was going on. The two of them had never been good friends, and Fitz was not known for parting with items from his precious collection. He'd certainly never give them away. I'd stumbled into something, and I had a feeling it had to do with the murder.

"I really don't have the ti—" Howie hissed.

"C'mon, Howie. As a favor to Ben? I'm sure he'd be grateful. I know how much he thinks of you. And even you, Fitz." I needled.

Howie's face tightened with the realization I knew something.

"All right, but don't waste time, Marco. I've got a business to run."

"Why don't we move to the living room?" Ever the gracious host, Fitz's voice was thick with anger, maybe even worry. He herded us down the hall and into a room on the right. The walls were a rich green with cream trim. The room was elegant in its simplicity. There were fewer antiques here, probably because he entertained larger groups in this room and didn't want anything broken or stolen.

He sat in a salmon-colored club chair and with a nod indicated chairs for us. Howie made himself at home on a love seat. I chose to stand.

"Ben's out of jail, I guess you both know that? But they've still got him in their sights. So, I need to make sure he's completely home free. That his alibi checks out and there's nothing I've missed."

"It's ridiculous to think I can help." Fitz said.

"And I've already told you everything." Howie was indignant.

"You two can help more than you know." I smirked. "There's something you said about the night before the competition, Fitz. I'll need more on that. And Howie, you haven't told me *everything*. Have you?"

"Well, *I* certainly told you who and what I saw that night." Fitz sounded frustrated. "I was there. I admit that, but all I did was look around. Then I left. I didn't touch anything, rig anything, or cut any ropes." His steel gray eyes were trained on me and he was resolute.

"Okay, let's assume that's the truth. The question is, why were you there? Being a judge, there'd be some ethical problems with you hanging around backstage with contestants. It's not like this is the big time, but there was lots of money involved."

"I—I wasn't thinking. I was curious about the process, and I wanted a peek behind the scenes. And at the guys. Can you blame me?"

I stared at him. He wasn't a great liar. He tried hard but I could tell.

"Behind the scenes? You were a judge, for fuck's sake. Wasn't that behind the scenes enough?"

"I know it's—it doesn't look good. Ethically, I mean. But I didn't break any laws."

"Murder-wise it doesn't look too good. You were there, you snooped around, you could have tampered with the rigging."

"You're barking up the wrong tree, Marco. Neither Fitz nor I had anything to do with this—this mess. Why would we?" Howie fussed.

"And what reason would I have to commit murder?" Fitz took off his glasses and rubbed the bridge of his nose with his long fingers.

"Well, how about your relationship with Wade? That kinda complicates things, doesn't it, Fitz?" I noticed Howie's expression stiffen when I said this to Fitz.

"We didn't have a relationship." Fitz nervously fingered a newspaper tucked into the side of his club chair. "We had dinner a few times."

"But you knew him. You dated him. You were backstage looking for him, the night before the competition." I glanced at Howie, who looked angrier by the second. "And you were seen together, Fitz. Multiple times." That was my final shot, and he took the hit with no visible reaction. I suppose that's the politician in him. Never let them see that they've gotten to you. Never appear weak. But he had to know there was more to come.

He exhaled and it was a long, weary sound. I could see him weighing every possible word he might use. He had to make sure that what came next would be controlled.

"It wasn't me. Who killed him, I mean. If you want to know the truth, I loved him. I wanted him to be free of the trap he'd made for himself by pretending to be straight." Fitz paused, placed a hand over his eyes, then took a deep breath. "And he was ready to do that. He was ready to come out. He'd have done it that night, had he won. And I would have been happy. We might even have had a chance together."

"This is your problem, Fitz: you feel too much. Too deeply." Howie spoke as if from on high causing Fitz to turn that angry scarlet shade again.

"Some people do. Lots of people have human feelings, Howie," I said, then turned to Fitz. "When did you realize Wade was gay?"

"He wandered into my office in City Hall one day, pretending to be lost. I fell for him then and there. Invited him to dinner. Invited him to a lot of dinners. We spent more and more time together, talking about his life, what he wanted, what he dreamt about, who he admired, movies, music, anything and everything. Little by little he became comfortable with himself, sure of himself, even happy with himself. He was settled with the idea that he was gay. At least I thought so. But he needed to tell people close to him, and that was going to be difficult."

"You keep falling for the same thing over and over again, Fitz. When will you learn?" Howie seemed bored with everything.

"Still neither of you has explained—" I began.

A furious pounding on a door somewhere at the back of the house interrupted me.

Howie's eyes went wide.

Fitz, startled, turned toward the sound so fast I thought he'd snap his neck.

I came to instant alert and reached for the gun in my shoulder holster.

Fitzpatrick jumped up and hurried toward the kitchen. Howie hugged the antique silver coffee pot close to his chest and stayed seated.

The pounding continued, louder, angrier.

I followed Fitz, but he turned and shot me a look.

"I'll take care of it." He straightened his back trying to reclaim some dignity.

Keeping discreetly back, I continued to follow. I hadn't gotten far when I heard glass breaking and someone shouting. It was Michael. I recognized the voice.

"If you said anything, I'll kill you!" Michael bellowed.

I arrived just as he was about to take a swing at Fitzpatrick. When Michael saw me, he pulled back and didn't connect with Fitzpatrick's face. Michael stood there, fists clenched, eyes wide with anger. His chest heaved with the effort to keep himself in check.

"What is it you want him to be quiet about, Mike?" I heard a noise behind me but didn't take my eyes off Michael. Howie crept into view, hugging the wall.

"*You're* here!" Michael yelped when he saw Howie.

"Keep him away from me!" Howie screeched and dashed back to the living room.

Michael sneered. "I knew I was right! Now you'll see, Fontana."

"See what?" I said. "Take it easy, and tell me what you're thinking."

"The police suspect *me* now," Michael shouted. "They as much as told me so. But I didn't do anything. I could never hurt Wade. It was these two. I saw them that night." Michael was a jumble of power and sadness and internal conflict.

"You also said you saw them leave, which means that you were there after they'd gone. Right?"

"I was wrong. I—I didn't see them leave. But I did see them." Michael slowly regained his composure.

"Let's sit down and sort this out. That okay with you, Mike?"

He nodded but didn't move.

"All right if we use the living room?" I asked. Fitz nodded glumly.

I stood aside, so the entrance to the hall was clear. "Shall we?"

Michael moved first, followed by Fitz.

When we got there, Howie cowered in his stuffed chair, looking terrified and clutching the silver coffee pot. Fitz resumed his chair, and Michael stood by the window. I blocked the exit.

"Tell us what you saw that night, Mike." I looked at Howie and Fitz when I said this, but there was no reaction.

"I saw them two. This one, the glasses, he was there fooling around with Wade. They left together and then—"

"Liar!" Howie came to life and pointed at Fitz. "You're a liar, Fitz. You said you hadn't seen Wade that night."

Fitz remained calm. "I didn't—"

"You were there, man. I saw you. Had your hands all over Wade. I saw that, too. You left together. You had your arm around his shoulders. Then you came back in without Wade and this creep was there, too." Michael pointed at Howie.

"You lied to me, Fitz." Howie shouted. "You lied and you asked me—"

"I never lied to anyone." He said in time to keep Howie from speaking further. "I told you the truth. You're going to believe this pumped up dimwit over me?"

"Now I understand." Howie half stood then sat back. "Wade was supposed to see me that night but he begged off. Said he had to rehearse. That's why I went back. I didn't believe him. I was right, he wasn't there rehearsing. What I didn't suspect was that he was with *you*. I thought he'd ditched me for somebody hot and young."

"He wasn't with me." Fitz insisted.

"You and Wade walked out together, man. You kissed him, you had your fucking hand down his pants. I saw it. It was disgusting. I never liked you. I told Wade not to trust you." Michael sounded frustrated.

"Apparently," Fitz regained his composure and arrogance. "Wade listened to you all too well. He didn't trust me, and he hedged his bets. He slept with all the judges, the little bastard. My vote wasn't enough. He just had to take himself around to every male judge. He guaranteed their vote, no matter what he had to do."

"You made him doubt himself. You!" Michael shouted.

"No. I tried to help him. But he never believed in himself. He was never confident that his routine would make the difference. He had to make certain the judges would vote for him, whatever way he could get them to do that. That's what he told me when he ditched me that night. At least he had confidence in his ability to fuck his way to the title."

"Wait a minute. Wait a minute. Back up. I'm not through with this point," Howie snapped. "You never told me he was with *you* that night." Still stuck on that, Howie grew angrier by the second. "You said you'd had enough of him. You said you didn't want to have anything to do with the little whore. That's what you called him, a little whore."

"Wade wasn't no whore." Michael's voice choked. "Wade was—"

"Hold it!" I said. "Let's get some facts straight." I turned to Fitzpatrick. "You were there later than you first admitted. True?"

"I..." He hesitated and Michael made a menacing move in his direction. "Yes, yes I went back. I'd left something backstage."

"Sure you did. And you saw him, Mike? Am I right?"

"Right. Then I saw this guy come in." He nodded in Howie's direction. "He finds that one," Michael pointed at Fitz, "and they start arguing. They were right near Wade's rigging. Throwin' their arms around, stabbin' their fingers at one another. Like little kids."

"So you lied about being there later on in the evening, Howie." I said.

"I? Why would I have…" He looked at Fitz, then at Michael, then his gaze came to rest on me. "All right. I was there, Fontana, you little nosy body. I was there because, Fitz, the miserable creep, called me and told me to meet him there."

"Not true." Fitz stood and looked ill.

"It's true. I saw them," Michale said, a self-satisfied smile etched on his face.

"You told me earlier that you saw them arguing, right, Mike? You told me you looked down and saw them arguing. Is that right?" I wanted to make sure he agreed to what he'd said. I remembered it word for word, because when I'd heard it, it struck me as significant.

"Yeah, I looked down and saw 'em." Michael folded his arms across his chest.

"So, you must've been up in the rigging looking down. Am I right? Where else could you be high up enough to see but not be seen?"

"Naw, that's not true. I mean, Wade would'a killed me if I went near his stuff. He didn't want nobody to go near it. I saw these two hanging around the rigging. Then they started to argue." Michael's demeanor changed. "I left and went out to tell Wade. So he could… But I—I never found him. When I came back and tried to get into the bar, it was shut tight. I banged on the door but it was shut. I went home. Tried to call Wade, but he never answered."

"Because the little whore was sleeping with some other judge." Fitz spat out the words. "How could he just hop from bed to bed? In the same night. The slut. And I was duped right from the start. I fell for his innocent act. I fell for it and I thought—"

"He *was* innocent, you fuckin' creep. Until you got your hands on him. We were friends until he started listenin' to you. Then he just used me. He didn't care about anybody anymore."

I looked at Michael, and he couldn't meet my eyes, choosing instead to stare at the floor.

"Michael, when you forced your way in here, you said you'd kill Fitz if he 'said anything.' What did you mean?" I kept my voice calm. I knew I was pushing him.

"What's it sound like I meant?"

"Sounds like you want to keep him quiet." I looked at him and he squirmed.

"So what if I do?" He squirmed when I looked at him.

"Why? Did you and Wade have something to hide?"

"Nothing. We had nothin' to hide. We were friends until Glasses here came along and started turnin' him against me."

"You told me Wade was always getting in your face about gay things, gay people," I said.

"I didn't care about that." He glowered at me.

"Maybe when Wade told you he was gay? Did that bother you? Maybe there was something between you? And you'd never wanted to put a word to it before that."

I could feel Fitz and Howie relax as Michael twisted on the skewer. How easy it was for them to watch this poor kid crumble. But I wasn't through with them yet.

"What the fuck are you sayin'? That I'm queer like Wade? Like you and these fuckin' wimps? You fags are all alike. You and these two and Wade and all the rest. You want everybody to be gay. You hope everybody is just as queer as you are. Why?"

"I accept what people tell me." I stared into his eyes. "You say you're straight and that's what I think. What you say is what you are in my book."

Michael nodded. "Once Wade started goin' out with Glasses, he was never the same. We were friends. We had a good time together. After he started seein' that piece of shit, Wade wanted to call what we did something else. And that wasn't true. We didn't do what he said. We weren't gay. This creep turned him against me. Wanted him to be public and make out like what we did was something it wasn't." Michael wavered, fading like a bad dream.

I felt for the kid, but I went on. "That was it, right, Michael? Wade knew things about the two of you that you didn't want him to tell anyone. The night he died, he said he hoped you weren't angry. Angry about what? About his being gay and you being right there with him? Am I right?"

"We were kids together. We knew each other since we were little. You know how kids are."

"Been a while since I was one," I said. Not all that long a while, but in some ways it'd been a long time. Innocence is a funny thing.

"Kids fool around. They like to fool around. Like it's an adventure, y'know?"

"You and Wade fooled around?"

"We were kids. I was horny all the time. It didn't mean anything."

"It did to Wade, though, didn't it? And it didn't stop when you got older, did it? You weren't little kids anymore, but you were still havin' an adventure."

The muscular boy-man hung his head and didn't meet my stare. "We was friends. That's all. Just friends."

"Why'd you stay with him? Especially after he decided he was gay."

His head snapped up and the look of desperation on his face was more intense than anything I'd seen in a long time. "Why do you think, smart guy? I hadda be his friend and do what he wanted or he would'a told people about us."

"Blackmail? So, this is why you got rid of him?" Fitzpatrick said.

"I never touched him. I'd never hurt him. Not like what you did. Scumbag. That's what you are. You took Wade and made him dirty. He was my friend and you made him—"

"I didn't do anything he didn't want done. And don't kid yourself about that. Wade was not the young innocent kid you liked to think he was."

Michael moved menacingly and Fitz flinched.

"You didn't know him. Not really." Michael's voice was weak with sadness.

"Who *did*?" Howie said in his most bitchy tone. "Who could know a boy like that? He hardly knew himself. He was confused. He wanted this and wanted that. He wanted to be gay but wanted to be thought of as straight. He was a mass of confusion and contradiction.

"Why did *you* want to get to know him, Howie?" I asked. "I mean, if he was such a ball of problems, why did it matter to you that he slept with Fitz instead of you that night?"

"It didn't matter. That kind of thing doesn't matter to me. But this bitch claimed Wade would be with me that night. It was my turn. Wade and Fitz had both promised he would be with me. Instead…"

"He wasn't with me, either. He was playing us both. He was playing everyone, even Michael." Fitz turned to Michael. "He played you like a guitar, and don't think otherwise."

"He..." Michael was about to defend his friend, but he obviously knew the truth when he heard it. "All I know is he was probably gonna win that goddam contest, and when he did, he was gonna come out and that woulda been the end of me. How would it have looked? Me the only straight guy in a fag competition? What would *you* think? What are you thinkin' right now?"

He had a point. Wade had backed him into a tight, uncomfortable little corner.

"But murder? Couldn't you just walk away, Mike? Couldn't you leave and forget about the whole thing once you knew what might happen?"

"I could never walk away from Wade but I could never murder him. I couldn't ever hurt him. Not in any way. Not since we were kids." His voice became low and sad, wistful. "Trouble is, I would'a let him hurt me but I couldn't hurt him. Not for anything." There were tears in his eyes and his voice was choked with emotion. Everyone was silent, not even Howie made a sound. Michael lifted his head and his eyes were gleaming. "I wanna know who did this. That's what I wanna know. He may'a been shitty to me but he was all I—"

"Touching." Howie said, there was no way he could keep quiet for long.

"I want to know, too." I started, and I saw Fitz perk up. "I want to know who did this, who murdered that kid. It wasn't Michael. Couldn't have been. I believe him when he says he couldn't hurt Wade. Love is a funny thing."

From across the room Michael looked up at me but said nothing. I nodded to him.

"Michael was telling the truth about leaving and returning to find Bubbles locked. The owner told me that he had just locked the place when he heard somebody pounding at the door, and when he looked at the security camera feed, he saw Mike. He was afraid of Mike, after the way he'd been behaving, and I can't blame him."

"So, how does that tell you he's innocent? He's the only one who could have known about Wade's routine. He's the only one who could have known what to do." Fitz said and stared at me as if he wanted me dead.

"That's not true, creep." Michael was on his feet and Fitz shrank back. "Don't worry, I'm not gonna dirty my hands on you. But don't lie to the man. You knew Wade's routine because he told me you knew. He never let me help him practice. He said you helped him enough. That hurt, man. But I took it."

"No wonder he spent so much time with you," Howie said. "And I'll bet the routine wasn't the only thing he practiced. Right, Fitz? You had him hog tied to you in a lot of ways."

"Not true. He refused to sleep with me after the first week. I tried everything to win him back. I paid for coaches, I gave him a place to practice and the freedom to do what he wanted. I opened up a whole world for him, and he refused me and spent time in bed with others, including this one." He threw a contemptuous glance at Michael.

"That's why you were so desperate? That's why you wanted me out of the way?" Howie's voice rose to a screech. "When you called me that night, you had no intention of getting Wade to spend time with me, did you? You were just interested in—"

"Murder?" I cut in. "You lingered a bit longer than Fitz thought you did, didn't you Howie?" I was guessing but it was an educated guess. "And you were there to do what?"

"Never! Never! Murder is not my style. Besides I wasn't obsessed with the little whore, like he was." Howie thrust his chin at Fitz. "I did linger and I did see something."

"That's why Fitz is parting with that silver pot, isn't it? What is it worth, Howie? Eighteenth century, if I know my silver. Gotta be several thousand. Right Fitz?"

No one spoke. Fitz swiped his sweaty hands down his pants legs. Michael glowered at Fitz. Howie just inspected his fingernails, as if he had nothing in the world to worry about.

"That pot's worth a lot, isn't it Howie." Still no answer. "But is it worth enough for you to keep your mouth shut forever about what you saw? Don't you think you'll be back for more? Lotta nice stuff here. Gotta be worth a million times more than that lousy flower joint you have."

"He won't get a thing more. I'll tell you that. He won't get another dime." The anger was like ice in Fitz's voice. "It isn't worth it. Nothing's worth anything. I loved Wade and he just laughed at me behind my back. Well, I don't care anymore. You're not getting another dime, Howie. I just don't care."

"Howie saw you do it, didn't he?" I said. "He saw you fool around with the ropes and chains. He saw you rig the set-up so that Wade would die." I waited but Fitz kept silent. The silence was loud. Howie turned his head away, as if dismissing us all. Michael wept quietly.

Fitz wouldn't get off easy just because he worked for the city. He'd be something of an antique himself when and if he got out of prison. Howie wouldn't get soft treatment either. Accessory to murder, blackmail, conspiracy all carried heavy penalties. The only flower arranging he'd be doing was maybe in the Warden's quarters.

* * *

My office was quiet. Olga had gone home for the day and I fiddled with a few papers before swinging by Knock for Happy Hour on my way home. I don't often get a chance to ignore everything and forget about work, but after the Mr. Gay Leather events, I needed a break.

They'd decided not to reschedule the competition, so there'd be no Philly Leather title and no city entrant in the nationals. Howie and Fitz had been arraigned and were looking at huge lawyer fees and a lotta time. Especially Fitz. A long prison term wasn't nearly enough for a slime ball like Fitz.

The only real victims were Wade and Michael. Beautiful, sad Wade. It would take a long time to get his face out of my mind. Who was I kidding? I'd never forget that night or that face. The poor kid had struggled with himself and when he'd finally decided to be honest, everything was taken away from him.

As I was about to turn out the light on my desk, I heard the stairs creak and squeak as someone came up to the office. I figured it was Anton coming to join me for a drink. But I was wrong.

Ben and Liam sauntered through the reception area and into my office, like two wayward students who'd been sent to the principal's office.

"Never thought I'd see the two of you again." I thought they'd disappear into the fabric of the gayborhood, going on with their parties and gym routines and whatever else they were into.

"Ben has something he wants to ask you and so do I," Liam said, placing his sleek form into the soft leather chair facing my desk. Ben stood, rock-like behind him.

"I'm all ears," I said.

"Go ahead, Ben. You said you needed me here for support, not to do your talking."

"Ye-yeah, I wanna..." Tough, fierce-looking Ben, was at a loss for words. "I just wanna say thanks. You saved my ass and I'm grateful. And—"

"And you want to take me up on my offer to join StripGuyz, right?"

"R-right. Offer still good?"

"You bet. Be there Saturday night and you'll get your shot. Not that you have anything to worry about."

"I'll be helping with his routine. He'll be great. I know a thing or two," Liam said.

"I'll bet you do." I smiled at him.

"Well, that's what I wanted to say." Ben smiled weakly and glanced around as if he didn't know the way out.

Liam looked at him, and I caught the look he gave Ben, which, if I interpreted it correctly, was a 'Get the hell out' kind of look. Ben got the message and turned toward the door.

"See you Saturday, Marco." With that he moved through the outer office door into the hall.

I looked at Liam, lounging in the chair. He was like an exotic cat, all muscle and beautiful pelt. On alert, ready to pounce.

"Did I miss something? 'Cause I was about to call it a night," I said.

"I owe you dinner." Liam stood, thrust his hands into his pockets, and stared at me expectantly.

"Not necessary, Liam. Ben was in a jam and I helped because I wanted to."

"I understand, but I was sorta looking forward to having dinner with you." Liam winked. "Got some time now?"

"I guess I'm kinda hungry, now that you mention it." I stood and moved around my desk to where Liam was. The heat radiated off his body and I moved closer to embrace him. Placing one hand behind his head, I drew him in for a long kiss.

Dinner with Liam would be even better than Happy Hour. I was sure of it.

About the Author

Joseph R.G. DeMarco lives and writes in Philadelphia and Montréal. Several of his stories have been anthologized in the *Quickies* series published by Arsenal Pulp Press, in *Men Seeking Men* (Painted Leaf Press) and in *Charmed Lives* (Lethe Press). His essays have been published in anthologies including *Gay Life, Hey Paisan!, We Are Everywhere, BlackMen WhiteMen, Men's Lives, Paws and Reflect, The International Encyclopedia of Marriage and Family, the Encyclopedia of Men and Masculinites,* and *The Gay and Lesbian Review Worldwide* among others.

He has also written extensively for the gay/lesbian press and was a correspondent for *The Advocate, In Touch, Gaysweek.* His work has been featured in *The New York Native, the Philadelphia Gay News* (PGN), *Gay Community News, The Philadelphia Inquirer, Chroma,* and a number of other publications.

In 1983, his PGN article "Gay Racism" was awarded the prize for excellence in feature writing by the Gay Press Association and was anthologized in *We Are Everywhere, Black Men, White Men,* and *Men's Lives.*

He was Editor-in-Chief of *The Weekly Gayzette*; Editor-in-Chief of *New Gay Life*, and has been an editor or contributing editor for a number of publications including *Il Don Gennaro,* and *Gaysweek.* Currently his is the Editor-in-Chief of *Mysterical-E* (www.mystericale.com) an online mystery magazine.

One of his greatest loves is mystery (all kinds) but he also has an abiding interest in alternate history, speculative fiction, young adult fiction, vampires, werewolves, science fiction, the supernatural, mythology, and more.

You can learn more at www.josephdemarco.com.

CPSIA information can be obtained at www.ICGtesting.com
Printed in the USA
BVOW011243170212

283171BV00001B/5/P

9 781590 213742